Praise for *Sleeper*

'*Sleeper* is an exciting tale with pace and surprises; David Fennell can write up a storm'

James Patterson

'A refreshingly energetic adventure'

Telegraph

Praise for *Sleeper: The Red Storm*

'David Fennell is truly the rising star of action thriller authors'

Ragnar Jonasson

'*Sleeper: The Red Storm* is thunderously good. Packed with action that leaps off the page, compelling characters and twists and turns galore, *The Red Storm* is a cracking read. David Fennell has created a gripping world of espionage, thrills and mysticism that is guaranteed to entertain. Highly recommended'

Adam Hamdy, author of the Pendulum trilogy

'A stunning action and espionage thriller set during WW2. *Sleeper: The Red Storm* seamlessly blends real events with fiction. It is unputdownable'

M. W. Craven, author of *The Puppet Show*

'A dark and entertaining spy thriller. Fennell juggles many elements including spycraft, family secrets, supervillains, even the supernatural, all whipped together at a breakneck pace'

Peter Swanson, author of *The Kind Worth Killing*

'A thrilling World War 2 espionage thriller set in a parallel history where hero Will Starling battles the mysterious VIPER organisation to save the world. Fantasy and reality mix for a high-octane adventure!'

William Ryan, author of *The Constant Soldier*

'Thoroughly enjoyable from start to finish. A fantastic thrill ride'

Chris McGeorge, author of *Guess Who*

'Thrilling and compulsive, *The Red Storm* is an all-action adventure that grips from page one and doesn't let go'

Brian McGilloway, author of *Little Girl Lost*

'WW2 thriller *Red Storm* is a splendid read by a new author that is sure to become a fixture on bookshelves. *Red Storm* sets forth a great and variable character gallery and the author takes no prisoners when setting up the tension and thrills that keep these characters on their toes. Had me reading long in to the night'

Yrsa Sigurdardottir, author of *The Legacy*

Sleeper: the definitive collected edition

David Fennell was born and raised in Belfast before leaving for London at the age of eighteen with £50 in one pocket and a dog-eared copy of Stephen King's *The Stand* in the other. He jobbed as a chef, waiter and bartender for several years before starting a career in writing for the software industry. He worked in Cyber Security for fifteen years and is a fierce advocate for information privacy. David has played rugby for Brighton and studied Creative Writing at the University of Sussex. He is married and he and his partner divide their time between London and Brighton.

To find out more, visit his website: www.davidfennell.co.uk

Follow him on social media:

Twitter: @davyfennell

TikTok: davidfennell_author

Instagram: mrdavidfennell

Facebook: DavidFennellAuthor

DAVID FENNELL

SLEEPER

THE DEFINITIVE COLLECTED EDITION

CANELO

First published in the United Kingdom in 2017 and 2018 by The Dome Press as *Sleeper* and *Sleeper: The Red Storm*

This edition published in the United Kingdom in 2022 by

Canelo
Unit 9, 5th Floor
Cargo Works, 1–2 Hatfields
London, SE1 9PG
United Kingdom

A CIP catalogue record for this book is available from the British Library.

Print ISBN 978 1 80436 150 4
Ebook ISBN 978 1 80032 863 1

Cover design by kid-ethic

Cover images © Shutterstock

Look for more great books at www.canelo.co

Printed and bound in Great Britain by Clays Ltd, Elcograf S.p.A.

1

Sleeper

For my beautiful Mum

Forever loved

Forever missed

Chapter 1

Deception

Hastings, Saturday, 3rd May 1941, 10.34 pm

Many must die for the world to change.

Will Starling bristles at Colonel Frost's parting words as he pulls his leather satchel onto his shoulder and hurries up the gloomy path through the woods. He tugs at the stiff, starched collar of his white shirt, giving passage to a bead of cold sweat that rolls from his nape and scurries down his spine. He shudders and tries not to think about Frost and his men who follow in the woods on either side. Armed, and invisible in the darkness, they watch his every move. His heart pounds like a hammer and he swallows. Despite his nerves, his excitement for this mission is at tipping point. So too is his anticipation for the twist that he is about to stir into the pot – a twist that would result in his torture and execution. If Frost catches him, that is. He would not let that happen. There was too much at stake for it all to go wrong now.

'You are one of us, Starling,' Frost had said. 'Four years I have overseen your training and I could not be prouder. Today will be your baptism of blood. Do not fail me. Do not fail our masters.'

Masters! Starling had almost baulked at that. His hands curl into fists at the thought. He had held his tongue, his expression fixed, his face a mask, a mask he had worn since this all began just over four years back. To this day it still surprises him how he has managed to hide the truth of who he is from Frost. But then again, anything is possible when the desire for retribution runs so deep.

He is twenty years old with dark hair, well built for his age, and shifts uncomfortably in the clothes Frost made him wear: a navy blazer, a stiff white shirt, a red tie and black brogues. Expensive as they are, they feel a little snug compared to the military fatigues he has worn every day for the past four years.

Four years. The time had passed so slowly yet it only seems like yesterday when he became one of *them.*

He loosens his tie, undoes the top button and breathes in.

That's better.

These civilian clothes don't sit well with him. They remind him of another time, when he was someone else.

Someone normal.

The stirring of old memories makes him tremble inside; he closes his eyes, takes three breaths and carefully pushes the thoughts from his mind.

'Another time,' he whispers, and recalls Frost's orders: 'Remember what you are, what you are capable of. The clothes are a ruse. You will fit in with the others,' he had said. Loath as Starling was to admit it, Frost was right.

He stops when he hears the approaching drone of a Spitfire patrol. The air vibrates, the trees sway and rustle as the fighters storm overhead flying south over Hastings. A squadron to intercept random raids from German fighters, he guesses.

Emerging from the trees he hears a swing band and laughter coming from a house beyond the vast wall. He sees two guards standing by a pair of tall iron gates watching the Spitfires disappear into the night. With a light tread, he approaches and coughs politely. The men jump and spin around with pistols pointing directly at him.

'Hello,' he says in a friendly tone.

'Stop right there,' says the guard on the left.

A dim light sweeps Starling's face and body.

'What do you think you're playing at?' asks the guard.

Starling smiles and steps forward. 'You must excuse me...'

'I said, stop right there!'

Starling inches closer, arms raised in a conciliatory gesture. 'Please accept my apologies. I'm so terribly late for the party. What will the Grandmaster think of me? I'm afraid my car broke down back in town and I had to walk.'

'All guests are accounted for. We weren't told of any late comers, so you can just turn back the way you came.'

'But gentlemen...'

'Them's the rules. Weren't made by us. Now you better just go back and get someone to fix your car.'

Starling cracks a sweet smile, shrugs and makes to turn. The guards look at each other, snigger in a mocking fashion and pocket their weapons. But

Starling seizes his moment and swings his fist at the guard on the left, who drops the torch and falls backward, slamming his temple on the gate pillar, slumping to the ground unconscious. Before the second guard can pull out his weapon Starling is on him, his fist slamming into his jaw in a fierce blow. The guard is out cold before his hand reaches his gun.

'Easier than I expected,' he mutters.

He crushes the torch with his foot, killing the light, and glances behind him, aware that Frost and the agents of VIPER are watching. He swallows hard, trying his best not to give himself away. Four years of hard training, all of it leading up to this moment, this sweet deception. Dragging the guards away from the path, he removes the Welrod silencer pistol from his satchel, stands where he knows Frost can see him, points the pistol toward the men and shoots.

Hurrying toward the manor house, he darts between the bushes that line the drive. He hears water trickling and stops, his foot cracking a twig. A confused face appears from behind a tree. A guard relieving himself. Their eyes lock. The guard shouts out and fumbles for his gun, but Starling slams the man's head against the rough bark and lets him fall forward into his urine.

Rapid footsteps crunch on gravel. The fourth guard. Starling dips behind the tree and pulls a small tube, the length of a pencil, from the inner sleeve of his blazer. He locates a row of small darts beneath his collar, removes two and slips one into a rest inside the tube. He hears a pistol cocking as the footsteps become slow and cautious on the grass near the tree. His assailant's breathing is fast, making his location easy to determine.

Starling slides around the trunk and shoots a dart at the guard. The man stiffens as he grabs his neck, his face contorting as the poison works fast and renders him temporarily paralysed.

He pops the second dart into the pipe and slips it back into his sleeve. No one from the party will have seen or heard what is happening outside. The music is loud and the windows are draped with heavy blackout curtains and anti-blast tape.

'Every cloud...' he whispers.

The party will be in full swing. He imagines revellers dressed in dinner suits and cocktail dresses drinking champagne and dancing as if they don't care that there is a war on and the world is in crisis. He wonders if the Grandmaster and his henchman, the Pastor, are present. He is the one person he fears the most: Gideon the Pastor, or the holy man as some people call him, an innocuous title for a monster of a man. Starling shivers at the thought of the bloody stories he has heard about him. But there is no time to think about those now.

He circles out of sight to the side entrance, removes a lock pick from his inside sleeve, picks the lock and cautiously opens the door. The reception hall is dimly lit with a scattering of candles and the smell of alcohol and smoke lingering in the air. The space is vast and ornate, but in an old style, as if it is somehow stuck in time. Crossing to the drawing room, he freezes, thinking he sees a shadow flit across the landing. Could it be that not everyone is at the party? He squints, but sees no one. A trick of the light, or a symptom of nerves, perhaps.

Reaching into his satchel, he removes three round metal balls, each the size of a fist. He presses a button on each one. They make a ticking sound, a countdown of ten seconds before the ether gas will be released. He opens the drawing-room door and rolls them along the floor towards the partygoers and the band.

The balls pop and hiss loudly as he closes the door.

And then the music stops, he hears bodies fall to the floor and glass smash on the hardwood. Someone tries to leave the room, a fist bangs weakly on the door, but Starling holds it tight. A moment later, all is quiet. The party is over.

His mission is to find the notebook and spare no lives. But Starling has other plans. The notebook is in the library on the first floor, locked in the Grandmaster's safe. He hurries up the stairs, glances around, recalling the layout from this morning's final briefing.

'Hello,' comes a flat emotionless voice.

Starling jumps, his heart thumping. Emerging from the shadows is a tall thin man with long white hair brushed back from his head. His eyes are small, like coals buried in two deep pits. A small tongue darts out and dampens his thin lips, as if he is hungry. His suit is black, like a preacher's.

Starling's spine goes cold. It's the Pastor.

'I'm afraid the Grandmaster has retired for the evening,' says the Pastor as he cocks his ear to the side. His eyes narrow as he registers that the party has gone quiet.

Something shiny opens in his hand. A razor.

Starling swallows, faltering for a moment, trying desperately not to think of the horror stories he has heard about this vile man's reputation. He feels beads of perspiration prickling like frantic ants on his forehead.

'Who are you?' asks the Pastor.

Starling has to act. Deftly, his fingers reach into his sleeve for the pipe, but the holy man's eyes flare and he runs at Starling, the razor raised in the air ready to cut. Starling is fast. He blows the dart at Gideon, whose attempt to deflect it leaves it lodged in the inside of his wrist. He grimaces and groans, his gnarly fingers stiffening as the poison seeps through his body.

Starling trembles, the razor is inches from his face. He steps back as the Pastor falls to the floor, his eyes mad with fury at this indignity. Starling edges around him, conscious that time is not on his side.

'Gideon, what is that noise?' comes a voice.

Starling looks up to see the Fellowship's Grandmaster emerge from the library. He is old and decrepit, his blue eyes watery and confused.

From the satchel, Starling removes the pistol and points it at the old man. 'Inside,' he commands.

'What have you done?' asks the Grandmaster.

'Nothing to worry about. Your henchman is incapacitated for a short period.'

The Grandmaster retreats into the library. 'What do you think you are doing? My men…'

'Quiet! They are unharmed. Your men and your guests are out of action for the moment.'

Starling glances around the room. There is a portrait on a wall. If Frost is right, the notebook is stored behind the painting. He points the pistol at it. 'Open it. Give me the book.'

The old man pales.

'I don't know what you are talking about.'

Starling glances through the curtains at the grounds and beyond the wall. It's only a matter of time before Frost figures out something is not quite right.

'We have no time. In moments the agents of VIPER will storm this house and kill all of you. There is a chance you will survive, if you do what I say.'

The old man sneers. 'Fool! What do you take me for?'

Starling's eyes blaze. He grabs the Grandmaster's wrist and drags him to the portrait with the barrel of his pistol lodged in the crook of the old man's neck. Starling twists his arm and watches as his face contorts with pain. Guilt surges through him. What has he become? What have VIPER turned him into? But he has no time for morality now. There is too much at stake.

'Open the safe.'

He presses the barrel deeper into the Grandmaster's neck. The old man struggles for breath and coughs, his face burning red. Trembling, he lifts his hands and concedes.

He opens the safe.

Starling sees a small book-size parcel inside, wrapped in an aged oilskin cloth. His mouth dries and he hesitates before slipping it into the satchel and backing out of the room.

'You can't do this,' says the Grandmaster. 'You don't know what you are dealing with.'

'Better that I have this than VIPER. I suggest you hide somewhere. They will be here any minute. With me gone they may not waste time killing you and your guests as they hunt for me. But that is something that I cannot guarantee.' He turns and hurries out of the library, skipping carefully over the twisted form of the paralysed holy man.

'You won't get far. Gideon will find you. I can promise you that.'

The Grandmaster's words send a chill over Starling. He bolts down the stairs with a grim feeling that he should have finished the Pastor off for good.

Chapter 2

Escape

The plan had unfolded as Frost had predicted, with the exception of Starling's modifications: the ether bombs and the pretence of killing the guards. Why should any more innocent people die? There's a war on and too many people across Britain and Europe were dying already. He would not add to that number just for Frost's cruelty.

Starling scurries along the shadows of the perimeter wall, with the parcel tucked safely into his satchel. He had done it! He had taken the notebook. He had handled it with tentative revulsion as if it was infected with some sort of disease. But the truth is worse than that. He knows what destruction its secrets could bring in the hands of VIPER. His only thought now is to get it far away from Frost and his ruthless pack of mercenaries.

Looking back at the house, he imagines Frost's men searching the rooms. On the ground floor the Colonel will be prowling, surveying his protégé's handiwork. He will be furious. A smirk cracks on Starling's face at the thought. He hates Frost; he hates VIPER. He despises them all for what they have done to him, to his…

His thoughts are interrupted by the two guards who are stirring as he slips through the gates and sprints towards the woods. The blast of a gunshot shatters the silence. Frost's men, his former colleagues, have spotted him. He ducks as something whizzes past his ear and splinters the bark of a tree directly in front of him. Glancing back, he sees the Fellowship's guards are up and searching for their weapons, too. Starling hears the booming voice of the Colonel barking an order. It's cut off sharply by the crack of pistols. Starling takes cover and catches his breath. More gunfire erupts. He recognises the short recoil of the pack's Johnson semi-automatic rifles. The guards do not stand a chance. He hopes they have the sense to clear out. A chase might keep some of the agents of VIPER off his tail.

With his heart racing, he hurries blindly through the woods, ignoring the twigs that lash out at his face and body. The area is unfamiliar and the terrain uneven, causing him to stumble twice. The gunfire has ceased and Starling wonders what has become of the guards. Have they been gunned down mercilessly like so many others?

Behind him, he hears howling, the signal that Frost and his pack are hunting. This time, he is their prey.

He runs.

His blood thunders in his ears and sweat cools on his face as he reaches the edge of the trees and clears the woods. The sky is an inky black canopy with a scattering of stars and a thin waxing crescent moon that provides a small measure of silvery light. He can see the narrow country road where they parked the cars earlier. They are somewhere here, but where?

The howling is getting closer.

He sees beams of torchlight scanning the woods. With the sleeve of his tuxedo he wipes the sweat from his brow and glances up and down the road. He spots a line of bushes almost twenty yards ahead. They seem out of place, as if they had just been propped there. He hurries towards them and sees a glimpse of something gleaming behind them. There!

Torch beams slice through the darkness. Frost is reckless, believing himself and VIPER above the law. They care nothing for wartime blackout rules, and he would gladly put a bullet into the heart of a local bobby or the Home Guard if they were unlucky enough to challenge him.

As Starling moves towards the cars, he wonders what his fate will be if he doesn't manage to escape. Inevitably he would die, but not quickly. Before death there would be torture, questions bellowed into his ears: Who are you? Why did you do it? Who are you working for? That is the million-dollar question. Who is he working for? Starling is no longer so sure of that himself.

For four years he had lived learning to become one of them, at someone else's request. He had his own reason for doing it, of course: revenge. Frost had called him 'the boy with the fire in his belly', and he was not wrong. Starling's desire for vengeance had made it easy for him to keep his mask up. He had fooled them all with the intention of destroying them. He had waited four long years, living with these murderers, all the while being fed secret messages from Control. He had done his best and waited for the opportunity to infiltrate VIPER and bring them down, but that opportunity had never arisen. And then, out of the blue, Colonel Frost had given him his first mission. The agents of VIPER's most important mission: acquire the notebook containing the whereabouts of a weapon so powerful it could cause destruction on a massive scale. This was no ordinary weapon. It was something ancient and otherworldly. VIPER were experts in mixing science with the occult. He had heard some strange stories and seen some weird things in his four years. If the stories about this weapon were true, he could not let VIPER have control of something so awful. Thousands would perish. *Many must die for the world to change.* That was VIPER's mantra. Starling was sick to the stomach of hearing it. He could not allow that to happen. He had set aside his own personal vendetta in order to get the notebook away and figure out what to do with it. Give it to Control or destroy it himself? The details hadn't seemed important.

The cars are lined up in a row, facing the road and hidden from view. There are three Austin 8s, a general-purpose model chosen by Frost. Anything more ostentatious might cause people to look twice and raise suspicion. From his satchel, he takes out the car keys he had nimbly stolen from the pocket of one of the more careless soldiers. The howling draws closer; torchlight spills onto the road.

Having climbed into one of the Austins, he turns over the ignition. It coughs momentarily before springing into life. He breathes a sigh of relief. Despite the war, no expense is spared with VIPER. The best of everything is provided: food, accommodation, rewards, weapons and cars. They invested a lot and expected much in return. This was one moment when he could be grateful for their largesse.

Starling steps on the accelerator and releases the handbrake. He spins the wheel and speeds up the country road as the pack emerges from the woods in one long line. They must have doubled their efforts to find him. Two are ahead of him, shining their torches at the Austin. Raising his hand to his eyes to stave off the glare, he hears the rapid crack of the Johnson rifles. The car judders at the impact of the bullets, but the Austin, like all their vehicles, is bullet proof. He glances in the rear-view mirror. His throat dries. He is not out of trouble yet. The pack are climbing into the remaining cars. He knows Frost will do everything in his power to stop him escaping. He has the notebook and he knows too much. Starling grips the steering wheel, slams the accelerator and drives for his life.

Chapter 3

The End of the Road

Starling swears under his breath. If only he'd had more time, he could have disabled the other cars. Focusing on the dark narrow road ahead he recalls the route he memorised at this morning's briefing. He knows Hastings town is nearby, and with it the possibility of finding a telephone box. All he has to do is call the operator and quote the four-digit number. He would be put through to Control and, after he gave him the code, Control would advise him what to do. He just had to find a telephone box.

Behind him the road is lit up with the beams from the headlights of the two Austins. This part of his plan makes him the most nervous. It has been three months since he passed his Driving Proficiency test. He can handle a car, but has little experience on the roads, unlike his murderous ex-colleagues who have many years driving experience behind them. It's entirely possible they will catch up with him. And when they do, they will run him off the road headfirst into the nearest tree. But the fate of humanity is inside his leather satchel. He has to think of something fast. Something they will not predict.

Up ahead, tall trees line either side of the road, their branches stretching to form a natural tunnel. With his hands gripping the wheel Starling plunges into what seems like a vacuum of darkness. He can see nothing and has no choice but to switch on the headlamps. He takes a breath and tries to get his bearings. If his memory is correct, there is a turning around the next corner, which leads to Hastings' ruins and the road down into the village. He considers his options: first find a telephone box and make contact with Control. The pack are right behind him. It will be easy to find a public telephone box but it would take a miracle for him to put through a call without getting a bullet in his back. First things first, he has to lose the agents of VIPER.

He clears a corner much too fast and almost loses control of the car. The wheel slides through his damp palms as he fights to turn it. Gasping, he manages to steady it in time. He glances in the rear-view mirror. The beams from the other cars are out of sight for the moment. Ahead he can see the right turn-off, so he eases the brakes and steers into it, the tyres crunching noisily on what is just a narrow gravel path. Switching off the headlamps he continues to drive, waiting for his eyes to adjust to the gloom, praying that he doesn't hit a tree or drive off into a ditch.

He hears the other two Austins speeding by and breathes a sigh of relief. It will only take moments for them to realise he is not ahead of them, so he must hurry.

It's too dark and he has no choice but to turn the lights back on. The gravel path is getting steeper, and the terrain clearer. He looks to the road below and sees a car speeding along it. Considering how fast it is going, it could only be the pack. It turns up the gravel path. Starling's heart sinks. He slams on the accelerator and wonders where the third car could be.

He is hot; the windows inside the car are steaming up. He winds down the driver's window and tastes the air, which is thick with salt. At the top of the gravel path there is no discernible road to follow. He can see the stone ruins of Hastings Castle and hear the surf lapping against the nearby cliffs, but he sees no one. Beyond the ruins is the village, and with it the promise of a telephone box or even a new car he can steal.

Behind him, the second Austin is gaining ground. But where was the third? No time to worry about that now. He rubs the back of his neck. Think. Think. He wonders if he has any weapons left. With one hand on the wheel he opens the satchel and searches inside. He steadies his breathing and thinks hard. After a few seconds, he decides what he must do.

Starling stops the car and gets out. Reaching back inside he releases the brake and pushes the Austin back down the gravel path, watching with satisfaction as it hurtles toward the oncoming car containing one half of the pack. As much as he would love to watch the collision he has precious little time. He turns and sprints through the ruins of the castle. Behind him, he hears a satisfying crunch and the sound of the pack's voices shouting in alarm. An explosion follows. He smiles to himself and runs in the direction of the village.

And then the blinding light of headlamps appears in the darkness, only twenty yards ahead. Starling skids to a halt, squinting in the bright light. There is a broad figure silhouetted in the glare. A figure he knows well. Frost.

'Very impressive, Will. I have taught you well.'

Starling's heart pounds angrily in his chest. 'You're not getting the notebook, Colonel.

The Colonel's eyes flick to the bag and back to Starling. He is unarmed, but Starling knows better than to feel secure about that. Behind the pack leader the agents of VIPER wait, their rifles ready to riddle the betrayer with holes.

A grim sense of loss sweeps over him and for a second it seems hopeless and that his elaborate plan has failed. But he has never been one to give up so easily. He curls his fists having already decided he would die trying, if that's what it takes.

'Give me the bag, William.'

Starling reaches slowly into his bag, takes out the Welrod pistol and points it at the Colonel. In the darkness the rifles click in unison, ready to take out their target.

The Colonel gestures to the pack. 'Lower your rifles.' He looks at Starling and raises his arms. 'I am unarmed. It doesn't have to be this way. Just give me the bag.'

'No!' Starling points the Welrod at Frost's chest.

'Why do this, William? You, of all people. I gave you a life. I gave you a purpose.'

Starling's grip on the pistol tightens. 'You murdering bastard, you destroyed my life!'

'Ah. I see. I had no idea. Many must die for the world to change, William. That is our goal. It is what you signed up for.'

There is a hint of mockery in the Colonel's voice that makes Starling's shoulders tighten, but he steadies his breathing and focuses.

'Give me the bag and we'll say nothing more of it.'

Starling's mind goes into overdrive. Nothing would give him greater satisfaction than ending the Colonel's miserable existence. But that would mean the pack would fill him with bullets. He would have to wait for that particular pleasure. Besides, there is still the remotest of chances he can win. He squeezes the trigger. His first shot hits the left headlamp. Swiftly, he points at the right headlamp and extinguishes the light, plunging them all into darkness.

The rifles fire as Starling ducks and scrambles back toward the ruins, diving behind an ancient wall as a volley of bullets speeds in his direction. Tiny specs of stone spray his clammy face. Wiping them away, he catches his breath. What now? The gravel track may be his only option. He makes a dash towards it as more of the pack hurry towards the ruins. The village road would make him an open target. He turns towards the cliffs. Fast footfalls thunder on the ground near the ruins. There is no other choice. He jumps from the ruins and sprints towards the darkness.

'There!' shouts a voice.

The rapid crack of gunfire fills the air as bullets fly past him and out to sea. He keeps running, praying one will not find his back. There is something up ahead. Eyes wide, he gasps and skids to a halt, inches from the edge of the cliff, staring down at an angry sea. If he had kept running he would have certainly fallen to his death. It is at least a 500-foot drop. Heart pounding, he inches back slowly. Then, the beam of a torchlight sweeps behind him.

Starling's heart ices over. As his eyes adjust to the torchlight, he can see the Colonel and, behind him, the pack.

'It's over William. Give me the bag.'

Starling reaches into the bag.

'Just the bag.'

Starling removes it from his shoulder and tosses it toward them. The pack leader gestures to the nearest soldier, who obediently picks it up.

'It's the end of the road. You understand I cannot let you live. My masters would not allow it, and besides, my wolves need a kill. They need blood.'

Frost's men began howling in appreciation.

The Colonel smiles.

Suddenly, the pack's howling ceases and one by one they fall to the ground. Starling watches with satisfaction as the pack leader looks about him in confusion. The Colonel sniffs the air, taking in the scent of the ether bombs Starling had set off in his bag. Fury fills his face as he covers his nose and mouth with his arm. Stumbling forward, he pulls out his Browning and levels it at him.

Starling tries to turn, but the Browning fires. Pain explodes in his chest and he stumbles backward, confusion filling his mind. His head slams against a rock and he feels himself weightless, upside down, falling, falling, falling. A bitter wind seems to cut right through him and then everything goes dark.

Chapter 4

Skipper

Starling's eyes snap open as his body crashes through the hard surface of the water. Freezing cold envelopes him, numbing the pain in his chest and head, sucking him down, and spinning him in circles, deeper and deeper into an icy hell.

How…? Who…? What…?

His limbs thrash, trying desperately to swim to the surface, but he is too tired. He sees nothing but perpetual darkness.

Breathe slowly… mustn't panic.

Exhaling through his nose, he relaxes his arms and legs in an effort to control his technique. He swims, but could be swimming downwards for all he knows. And then he feels the pull as his body begins to float up. His eyes are sore with saltwater but above him there is the slither of the moon, hazy through a veil of choppy water.

He breaks the surface and gasps, sucking in every breath greedily. Waves slap his face and ears as he fights to tread water. A hot pain sears through his temple and a fierce freezing sensation penetrates his stomach as if he's been stabbed by a hundred icicles. His strength is diminishing; he feels his mind losing focus. He knows this is no nightmare and he won't wake up in a safe warm bed. He can't keep his eyes open. His mind empties into darkness.

And then he hears a voice calling, and with it the sound of chugging, getting closer and closer. He is completely numb now; his body seems detached from his head and all he wants to do is go to sleep. He feels peaceful, stops fighting, closes his eyes and sinks once more below the surface of the water. But then something hard and sharp pokes at his back and tugs at his clothes, pulling him upwards.

-

He dreams he is sprinting through the streets of London with a pack of vicious rabid dogs on his trail. He can see his house, but strangely it is boarded up as if no one lives there. He glances behind and sees the snarling beasts closing in, their yellow teeth bloody and soiled with strips of human flesh. With a burst of energy, he springs forward and opens the front door. Inside, the house seems empty and unloved as if no one has lived there for a long time. The rooms are thick with shadows, dust and cobwebs. He thinks this is not his house, yet it is so familiar.

'I'm… I'm home,' he calls, but no one answers.

He steps inside and notices the floor is soft. He looks down and sees it is not wooden but grass, as if the house has been lifted and planted on top of a field somewhere.

There are four holes in the ground and next to each one is a mound of earth. He hesitates and then approaches them. There is a coffin at the bottom of each hole with an inscription on each one: Mum, then Dad. The third and fourth boxes are empty.

Outside the dogs are barking and clawing at the door, desperate to get inside and finish him off. The door is weak and flies open. He spins round but the dogs are upon him, tearing the flesh from his bones. He screams.

Starling wakes trembling, with tears streaming down his face and a savage pain in his head that feels like an ice pick is lodged in his brain. Shivering, he rubs the back of his head; his hair is stiff, matted with dried blood, and there is a dull ache in his chest, which makes it hard to breath. He is naked and wrapped in a rough blanket that scratches his skin. His mind whirls in confusion. He recalls being in the cold sea, swimming for his life. It had not been a dream. But how did he get here?

He pushes himself up, but his head spins and his chest feels like it has been hit by a train. He breathes slowly and lets his eyes focus. He is in a dimly lit room that feels like it is moving, creaking, shifting up, then down. He hears the lapping sound of water. There is a round window through which he can see the night sky. He is in the cabin of a boat. He looks to his right. Hanging nearby, over a small oven, is a blazer, a white shirt, trousers, socks, underwear and, on the floor, a soggy pair of black brogues.

'You're lucky to be alive,' comes a voice.

Starling jolts and looks in its direction. Sitting at a small table in a corner is an older gentleman. His hair is white and his face weathered and striking. He is smoking a pipe; the air is fragrant with its sweet, pungent tobacco.

'Who are you?'

'You can call me Skipper. Everyone does.'

'Where am I?'

'You're on board *The Outcast*.'

'*The Outcast?*'

'Part-time tugger; part-time fishin' service. Got me quite a catch tonight, I'd say.'

Starling rubs his head. 'I… I was in the sea. But how?'

The old man puffs on his pipe and considers his reply. After a moment, he speaks. 'Someone put you there.'

Starling frowns, which makes his head hurt more.

'I don't understand…'

'Neither do I,' says the old man, blowing out a ring of smoke. 'By the looks of it you associate with some dangerous folk.'

Starling does not know what the old man is talking about. His memory is foggy, his head dizzy.

The old man continues, 'Tell me, lad. Did they have an accent, a German one perhaps?'

The pain in his head intensifies, like a hammer on his brain. In his mind he can hear voices, like whispers in the wind. But they mean nothing to him.

'Why is that important?'

Skipper's eyes widen and his brow wrinkles.

'You took quite a knock on the head, it'd seem. You do know there's a war on?'

Starling stiffens. 'A war?'

'The Germans are bombin' us and we are bombin' them. Nasty business.'

Starling closes his eyes in an effort to get to grips with this strange piece of news, but the pain in his head distracts him. He gently places his hand over his temple to ease it, but it does not feel better.

The old man glances at the table and picks up a parcel the size of a book. 'I'd say this saved your life.'

Starling stares hard at it. It seems familiar but he does not know why. There is a hole in the centre with something lodged inside. He feels suddenly cold. It's a bullet.

Skipper pulls a box of matches from his pocket, lights one and places the small fire in the pipe. 'It was the queerest thing. Never saw anything like it. I saw them chase you. I saw them fall to the ground and then I saw one of them shoot you.'

Starling pales and rubs the stiff muscles of his chest.

'Why were they trying to kill you?'

Swallowing, he shakes his head and pulls the blanket over his shoulders. He has no idea what the old man is talking about.

The old man is watching him carefully, assessing him.

'I don't know what business any group of men has shooting someone like that. Don't make no sense. How old are you, lad?'

Starling furrows his brow as he tries to remember. He isn't entirely sure. The man is calling him 'lad'. He knows he is young. Is he eighteen? Twenty? He could be twenty-five or older for all he knows. 'I… I'm not sure.'

'Do you remember your name?'

'I… I really don't know. I only know I was in the water.'

'Do you remember anything at all?'

He tries hard to recall but the whispering voices have gone and there is nothing for him to latch on to. He shakes his head.

'A friend o' mine took a knock to the head once. Couldn't remember who he was. Didn't recognise his wife nor kids nor pals for that matter. He couldn't do his job neither. He knew his town and where he lived alright. He remembered places, but not people. It were like a whole layer of his memory had gone forever. It were funny at first, but eventually it drove him mad. He had to be "put away" in the end.'

'Did he get his memory back?'

Skipper shakes his head. 'He died alone as a stranger, even to himself. Sad really.'

Shivering, Starling pulls the blanket over his shoulders.

Skipper regards him thoughtfully. 'Whoever those men were, they might well be lookin' for you at Hastings. I reckon it's not safe to go back there. Tonight, I will do a spot o' fishin'. Not supposed to, mind, in these times n' all, but people got to eat and I has to make ends meet. I'll be takin' my haul to London town tomorrow morning. You can talk to the police and maybe see a doctor about that head of yours.'

Starling manages a half smile and rests his head back. His eyes feel heavy, and despite his predicament and poor physical state, he soon falls asleep.

Chapter 5

The Parcel Is Opened

Sunday, 4th May 1941

Starling sleeps fitfully and wakes the following morning to the sound of the boat's chugging engine. Bright morning light from the porthole dazzles him. His head throbs without mercy as his eyes adjust and take in the cabin. It looks different in daylight; shabbier than his first impression, yet it has an order and calmness that makes him feel at ease. On the table in the corner where Skipper sat last night is a washbowl, a small mirror and a neatly folded towel. His rescuer must have left them for him. Behind the table, built into the wall, are shelves containing a neat row of books and general bits – fishing tools, a telescope, a conch, and a collection of pipes. The only things that seem out of place are his clothes, hanging to dry, and the strange parcel, resting on top of the stove. The parcel with the bullet lodged inside – the bullet meant for him.

What happened last night?

He has no recollection, yet he thinks it odd that he doesn't feel especially frightened. Instead, he feels a peculiar emptiness as if he is somehow detached from the world and not inhabiting his own body but looking down from above. He also has a sense of determination and desire to understand the truth.

He stands up and shivers. The air is crisp and cold, the fire in the small oven having long gone out.

Questions flood his mind. Who is he? Who would want to kill him and why? His memories, and his hope of understanding who he is and why someone tried to kill him, are lost at sea, for the time being at least. Wrapped in the blanket, he shuffles to where the clothes hang. Formal clothes, he wonders. Had he attended a party? Thankfully, they are dry. He pulls on his trousers and ties up his brogues, ignoring the pain in his head and chest.

He splashes cold water from the bowl across his face and, peering at the mirror, he scrubs the dried blood from his hair before assessing his reflection in the mottled glass. Despite feeling older the person looking back at him is young, perhaps twenty, or younger? He is sturdy, broad shouldered and athletic. His wet hair is inky black, his eyes dark with a hint of sadness drawn upon them. Closing his eyes he tries to get a sense of who or what kind of person he is. His mind might be a closed book, yet his emotions trouble him. He senses despair, fear – of what? – but most of all a rage that burns like a volcano inside him. Blinking his eyes open, he looks at the stranger looking back at him.

'Who are you? What happened to you?'

He checks inside his jacket for an emblem or some identification but there is nothing. There is a hole where the bullet penetrated. It surprises him at how little it troubles him. He feels something hard in the bottom of his right sleeve. Peering inside, he sees what looks like a row of tools neatly secreted into the lining above the wrist. One by one, he takes them out and examines them. One is a narrow pipe, another a small pair of scissors that look like they are made for cutting something stronger than paper or hair – wire cutters! Why would he have these? There is also a pencil-sized piece of steel with a slight curve at one end. At first he thinks it some sort of surgeon's utensil, but that doesn't seem right. He realises it is a lock pick. How he knows this, he cannot say. He does not know what to make of these items and clumsily bundles them back into their hiding places before Skipper appears.

He glances at the parcel. Perhaps there is a clue inside it – something that could reveal his identity and why he was nearly killed last night.

It is wrapped in damp green oilskin with a Greek crucifix woven into the fabric. In the crucifix's centre the bullet remains lodged. He runs his fingers over the small cold projectile that should, by all accounts, be lodged in his dead heart and not this parcel. He rubs the pain in his chest and feels a cold anger at whoever it was that tried to kill him.

He begins to unwrap the parcel, but it is stitched together and sealed with some sort of wax. Removing the cutters from his sleeve he uses them to slice through the wax seal and open the threads.

He's surprised to see an old black leather-bound notebook inside. He lifts it out and carefully leafs through the pages, which are dry and delicate. The notebook is old. How old, he could not say. Hundreds of years, maybe more. There is a lot of handwritten text in a language he does not recognise, and strange symbols including stars, half-moons, scythes, swastikas and upturned crosses. There are etchings and fine drawings of people from long ago, including a sketch of a woman from ancient times, possibly Roman or Greek. She is standing over a stone table containing what looks like a cluster of glowing rocks. There is a second sketch of a jewelled crucifix with very short arms and much more but none of it makes any sense to him. Something falls from the pages onto the table. A small card inscribed:

Timothy Chittlock

Room 7

64 Baker Street

London

Timothy Chittlock?

He searches his fractured memory for a trace of that name but finds nothing. Still, this is surely a good lead. A clue to who he is, perhaps? Starling leaves the cabin to get some air and tell Skipper what he has found. Perhaps the old man can offer him some wisdom.

Outside, on the deck, the morning air is fresh, crisp and salty. There are a dozen modest crates of iced fish at the rear of the small boat. The sea is calmer than it was the night before, and in the distance he can see land. Skipper is smoking his pipe in the steering room at the front of the boat.

'Morning, Skipper.'

'Morning. You seem a lot jollier.' He smiles. 'Glad to see you in such good spirits.'

'I opened the parcel. It contains a notebook, and this card with the name Timothy Chittlock of 64 Baker Street, London.'

'That's a fine clue, I'd reckon,' laughs Skipper. 'Don't mean much to me, but I'm sure your neighbour, a certain Mr Sherlock Holmes, could work it out in a blink of an eye.'

Starling smiles. 'I could really do with him on my side right now.'

'Then we should go there as soon as we get to London.' Skipper's eyes narrow as he peers across the water. Lifting his binoculars he looks through them, his brow furrowing.

'What is it, Skipper?' But then he hears it. The chugging sound of another boat.

'Get inside, and stay out of sight.'

Starling hesitates.

'Go,' Skipper urges.

He hurries into the steering room and crouches down. Instinctively he scans the interior searching for a weapon: a crowbar, an ice pick, anything to defend himself. A sense of excitement and confidence overwhelms him yet at the same time his skin tingles. These are not the instincts of a normal person.

Who am I?

Outside, he can hear the other boat approaching. Minutes later, the chugging of *The Outcast* and the other boat stops.

'Mornin', Skip,' says a voice from the other boat.

'Ned,' says Skipper, in a gruff response.

'Quite a haul you got there.'

'Yup.'

'Takin' to market, are ya?'

'Where else would I take it?'

'No need to be like that, Skip. Especially as I have some news concernin' you and that rust bucket.'

'Oh yes?' replies an unconvinced Skipper. 'And just what would that be?'

'There are some men waitin' at the docks. They say they are police, but they don't look like police to me. Asking around about a boat called *The Outcast*, they are. A boat what was seen leaving Hastings last night. Appears they are looking for some cargo it might be carrying. "But he only carries fish," I tells them.'

In the steering room Starling stiffens and holds his breath. He peeks out at Skipper, who appears calm, but his fists are clenched, his knuckles white.

'Did I see someone onboard with you, Skip?'

'I'd say you were mistaken, Ned. Just me and my fish. That's all.'

'Is that right?' says Ned. 'And how about you give me those fish and we'll say nothing more of it.'

Skipper's expression is fixed; he is giving away no secrets.

'I'll give them as a goodwill gesture for you and your family,' says Skipper.

'I knew you'd see reason.'

In the steering room, Starling feels guilty and angry at this man for forcing Skipper to give up his fish, just to protect him. He hears Skipper passing the crates across to the other boat.

'That's the lot,' says Skipper.

'You don't 'alf get yourself into some scrapes, old man.'

'You've got what you wanted. Now be off with you.'

The other boat's engine starts up and Starling feels an overwhelming sense of relief.

'Watch your back, old man!' calls Ned, like some final grim warning.

Skipper returns to the steering room, his fixed expression transformed into a wide-eyed determined look like a wrinkled boy wanting adventure.

'I'm sorry,' says Starling.

Skipper starts up the engine and looks at him thoughtfully. 'He's a treacherous swine, that Ned. Don't be sorry, lad. Besides, I don't like the sound of these men, whoever they may be. We're going to change routes. I'll get you to London safely. I promise.'

'Thank you for helping me.'

'There is a reason I called this boat *The Outcast*. A damn fine reason. And that's why idiots like that Ned don't care much for me.'

Skipper lights his pipe and steers a new course. At last there is a sense of hope.

Chapter 6

Into the Hornet's Nest

It is late afternoon as Skipper steers the boat through the Thames estuary, watching for signs of any suspicious activity or unfamiliar boats. He sees nothing, but nevertheless he proceeds with caution. The closer they get to the docks, the more dangerous it will be for both him and the frightened, disoriented young man he pulled from the sea. For reasons he cannot explain, Skipper feels an affinity with him. Despite his amnesia he can see a strength and determination that might just see him through whatever trouble he is in. He fancies he is like him: an outsider, an outcast. The survivor of the guns of half a dozen men, including a direct hit aimed at his heart. He also survived a drowning. He's special, and... different. There is a reason he must live. Skipper has no idea what that reason might be, but he feels it and is prepared to risk everything to ensure it. What did it matter anyway? The life of an outcast is a life of risk. He smiles to himself and puffs on his pipe.

Leaving the estuary behind them, they pass Tilbury, then Dagenham. The river narrows as they approach the London docklands. Skipper draws the curtains on the steering cabin's side windows so that the only view in and out is through the front window.

'We're approaching the hornet's nest,' says Skipper. 'Stand behind me, in the shadows, and keep an eye on the bank on either side. Maybe you'll see a face that will jog your memory.' He hands him the binoculars. 'Seems there was an air raid last night.'

Starling peers through the binoculars and carefully watches the approach. He feels his heart quickening, not from fear, but from excitement, as if he is returning home after a long arduous trip away. There is a familiarity to the skyline that warms his heart and almost confirms that he has a connection with Baker Street. Yet there is something wrong with this version of the city. Skipper had told him more about the war and the nightly bombings the city endured. It is hard to absorb. On either side of the river, commercial offices and warehouses dealing in imports and exports would once have lined these waters. But today they are rubble and ruins, decimated by Nazi bombers. Across the city, plumes of smoke rise up into a slate grey sky where giant fishlike barrage balloons are tethered to the ground below. It is like he has stepped into a ravaged and torn city, like something from an H.G. Wells novel. It's so hard to take in. The London he thinks he remembers is not the London he sees before him. He fears for the city and its people. He fears for his family, his friends, whoever and wherever they may be.

'Just up there, to my left, are two men. They're watching us and they don't look like dockers,' says Skipper.

Through the binoculars, Starling sees two men dressed in smart suits and trilbies, watching *The Outcast* approach. Their expressions and body language suggests they are doing more than enjoying a leisurely day out.

There is a car pulling up behind them: an Austin 8.

The door opens and another man gets out. He looms over the other two and looks towards *The Outcast*. He is thickset, with dark cropped hair and a bushy black moustache that partially obscures a grim expression.

A memory flashes. Knots form in Starling's stomach, his breathing quickens.

'Skipper, I know that man. I don't know how, but I know him.'

'He's a dangerous-looking sort, alright.'

The three men get into the car and begin driving alongside the river.

'There's another to the right,' says Skipper.

Starling turns to the other side of the dock and sees a man dressed in a black suit, black shirt and gloves. Starling thinks he might be some sort of priest. He is watching the Austin 8, and occasionally glances at *The Outcast* as he strolls along. His cheeks are sunken, his eyes are like hollows, his hair is long and white and stretched across the top of his head. For a second Starling thinks he sees the glint of blue steel in his hand. But it is gone, perhaps a trick of the light. Nevertheless, his skin crawls for reasons he cannot explain.

'Can we go faster?' he asks.

Skipper smiles conspiratorially. 'I think we ought to,' he says, and pushes *The Outcast* forward.

Chapter 7

Trouble at Tower Bridge

Ahead, Starling can see the Victorian Gothic towers of Tower Bridge standing like grand sentinels over the Thames. He is relieved to see the bridge and towers undamaged and still functional as red double-decker buses, cars and people pass across it. For just a moment he allows himself to get lost in the illusion that life in London is normal and there is no war.

Skipper interrupts his thoughts. 'Those men can't drive along this side of the dock. Reckon they will take a fast road to the next stop and cut us off. We'll stop at St Katherine's Dock. It's not used any longer. The bombs have decimated it, but it will be a good springboard for us to get to Baker Street.'

'Us?'

'I'll see you through to the end. I made a promise to myself, I did. There are dangerous men following you and I won't let them have another pop at you with their guns.'

'But...'

'No buts. You ain't gettin' a choice.' Skipper smiles warmly.

Starling is grateful to the older man, and secretly relieved that he will not be alone for the journey to Baker Street.

'We'll be there shortly, so get ready to hurry.'

Starling nods and feels an odd sense of calm and purpose. He is ready, he is always ready. He steadies his breathing, all the while his eyes scan the riverbanks for unwelcome faces. His palm touches the side pocket of his blazer, where the notebook is safely tucked.

It is evening time. After tying the boat to what remains of the dock, they hurry along St Katherine's Way and up to Tower Bridge Approach, where they dodge people enjoying the weekend break.

From somewhere below the bridge the pounding drums and the melodic trumpet of a brass band fills the air. It sounds like the Salvation Army. A woman starts to sing heartily at the top of her voice.

Down at the cross where my saviour died,
Down where the cleansing of sin I cried,
There to my heart was the blood applied;
Glory to his name

Traffic is slow, the wartime lights-out rule reducing the speed of vehicles. With Skipper behind him, Starling pushes his way through the crowd, stopping when he hears three loud thumps. The crowd gasps, the bridge trembles and the dark waters of the Thames shiver as the thunder of distant explosions reverberates across the city. Starling looks east and sees the sky filled with flashes of bright white light. It is then, better late than never, that a siren wails its warning. Panic ripples through the crowd and they begin running, desperate to get across the bridge and into shelter. Starling is herded by the crowd and separated from the old fisherman.

'Skipper!' he shouts, but there is no response.

He forces his way through the crowd on the side of the bridge, clinging on to the steel girders. He swears he hears a gunshot. And then above the din he hears someone shout.

'My lad, wait!'

The crowd thins and Starling turns to see Skipper limping toward him. He falls forward, and he just manages to catch him. The old man is surprisingly light and feels more a like a sack of bones than a grown man. His chest is wheezing and he is sweating as if he had just run a marathon. He groans, but his voice is rasping, his breath short.

He steadies the old man, who seems a shadow of who he was.

'Skipper, what's happened?' he says, confused and mindful of the approaching bombers. 'We must get off the bridge.'

'Too late for me. You must go. You are in danger… grave danger.'

There's a loud bang and Starling feels the old man jerk and stiffen. His face contorts with pain, his eyes flutter and he slumps forward. Confused, Starling catches him, supporting his back, and feels something warm and sticky on Skipper's jumper. He lowers him to the ground and looks at his hand. There is blood on his fingers.

'Help, someone help,' he calls, but the bridge is empty.

They are alone. The only sound is the approaching drone of bombers and the hymn of the Salvation Army songstress who, it seems, has been abandoned by her band.

The old man's eyes flicker and close.

'Skipper, Skipper!' Starling shakes the old seaman in an effort to revive him, but there is no response. And then, from somewhere nearby, a man's voice starts to sing along with the hymn.

Down at the cross where my saviour died,
Down where the cleansing of sin I cried,
There to my heart was the blood applied;
Glory to his name

On the opposite side of the bridge, a man is approaching. He is dressed in a black suit and has long white hair. It's the priest-man he saw on the riverbank.

'Please, help me! This man is hurt.'

The man walks slowly toward them. As he draws closer, the feeling of unease that Starling felt at the dock returns. His stomach clenches. Something is not quite right.

The man crouches down beside them, cocks his head to the side and gazes over Skipper. His eyes are like dark hollows and seem devoid of emotion.

Starling's instincts tell him to run, but he cannot leave Skipper. Not after he saved his life.

And then the man falls onto his knees, looming over the old fisherman like a cobra. He removes his gloves. 'Pray with me, sinner.'

Starling feels his patience thinning. 'Please, help me get him off the bridge and to a doctor.'

'Don't you recognise me?' he says, his hands clasping together in prayer.

Starling swallows and does not respond. Other than seeing this man on the riverbank, he has no memory of him. All he has are his instincts and they are not good.

The priest-man dips his head and mutters something under his breath. Starling notices his hands are scarred with dozens of crucifixes carved into his flesh. Some of the scars are bloody and recent. Starling jolts as a memory flashes in his mind: an image of this man, his face contorted, his arm raised and, in his hand, a blade. He knows this man – but how? On the tip of his tongue is a name. Starling frowns…

The holy man… no… the Pastor. He is the Pastor.

The Pastor finishes the prayer and begins rummaging in Skipper's pockets.

'What are you doing?' Starling feels a swelling anger that this stranger should dare to search Skipper's pockets. He grabs the man's forearm. 'Leave him alone.'

The Pastor smiles; his teeth are small, like a child's.

The hairs on Starling's neck bristle. 'Maybe we should get the police.'

'That won't be necessary.'

The Pastor gets to his feet. His jacket falls open. There is something dark and metal tucked into his belt. A pistol!

'Do you have it?' he asks.

The crump, crump, crump of falling bombs is getting closer.

Starling feels his muscles coil. 'I don't know what you're talking about.'

Something slips from the Pastor's sleeve and into his hand: a long and shiny razor.

'Don't play games with me.'

And then, Skipper springs to life and grabs the man's hand, biting into his flesh. The Pastor cries out; his blade drops to the ground.

'Run, lad, run!' Skipper croaks.

Pulse racing, Starling edges back, torn between running and staying to help his friend. But the Pastor is nimble. He pulls out the gun with his free hand and shoots the old man.

Starling stumbles backward, watching Skipper jerk twice as two more bullets are pumped into his frail body.

The Pastor looks up, his previously emotionless eyes betraying a simmering rage.

With his heart rattling in his chest, Starling backs quickly away, picks up his pace and runs, hiding wherever he can behind the cover of abandoned buses and cars.

Chapter 8

The Pastor Strikes

Wailing sirens, droning bombers and falling whistlers fade to background noise as Starling sprints through the dark, empty streets, panting, his brow clammy, his heart pounding, and heavy. He tries to make sense of what has just happened. All he can think is that he is to blame. Skipper had saved his life and had died doing so. If it weren't for him, Skipper would be alive and well and steering his boat happily up the Thames. Every muscle in his body seems to twist as he thinks of Skipper's cold-blooded murder. Ducking into an alleyway he retreats into the shadows to catch his breath and think, his head throbbing, a dull pulsing ache that does not want to go away.

Despite the bombardment, he hears the clip of footsteps approaching and snatches of the same hymn, sung by the Pastor. He feels his skin crawling and hurries out of the alleyway and on into a street of Victorian terraces where he looks around for somewhere to hide, an empty house perhaps. A sudden flash in the sky lights up the street and he feels horribly exposed and alone. There is no one else around, no one to help. Everyone will be taking shelter in their cellars or the Underground. He hurries along the street and crosses into another darkened alleyway.

Stopping at a rusty gate, the entrance to a rear garden, he looks back up the alleyway. The Pastor is there, at the far end, peering in his direction. Starling backs into the shadows, holding his breath and praying for him to move on. To his relief, the Pastor does not see him and walks on.

Starling looks beyond the gate. The garden is overgrown and full of rag-and-bone booty probably looted from bomb-damaged homes. There is a three-wheeled pram, stacks of wooden crates and various forgotten toys, including dolls with missing eyes and limbs. He wonders if the house has been abandoned. It has the look of neglect about it. Pushing the gate open, he hurries toward the rear door, but it is locked. He remembers the lock pick in his sleeve and goes to work, wondering where and how he has learned to pick locks.

Am I some sort of criminal, or thief?

Footsteps crunch in the alleyway and he leans toward the lock. With a surgeon's lightness of touch, he feels for the pressure points, pushes them, and hears the clicking sound of the lock opening.

Slipping quietly inside, he closes the door behind him and in the darkness, stumbles forward and knocks over a kitchen chair. He swears under his breath at the noise. Leaving the kitchen he slides up the hallway. He freezes, thinking he hears someone at the front door. And then the back door opens. Framed inside, like an image from a nightmare, is the Pastor.

He springs forward, rushing at Starling, with one hand reaching for his throat.

Starling does not retreat. Something in him, an instinct, makes him stand still, his eyes taking in the Pastor's every move. At the right moment, he grabs the man's wrist and kicks him savagely between the legs. The Pastor grunts, but clings to him like a parasite. They fall backwards through a door and into the living room.

The Pastor is fast and reacts quickly, pinning Starling up against the wall by his neck. Their faces are inches apart, the air between them sour with what smells like rotten meat. The man's grip is tight; Starling gasps for air and tries to push him away, but the older man is too strong.

The house shakes as a bomb explodes nearby. Dust falls from the ceiling, coating Starling's shoulders and clammy face.

The Pastor's small eyes flash. 'And there fell upon men a great hail out of heaven, and men blasphemed God because of the plague of the hail; for the plague thereof was exceeding great…'

He slams his fist into Starling's stomach and releases his grip.

Whatever air was left in Starling's lungs shoots out and he crumples to the floor in pain, clutching his stomach. More bombs fall, shaking the foundations. The dusty wooden floorboards vibrate against his cheek.

'…And men were scorched with great heat, and blasphemed the name of God…'

The Pastor crouches beside him, searches his pockets and takes out the notebook.

'Well, well,' he says, leafing through it tentatively. His eyes widen, his neck turns red. 'It pains me to think you would hide this from me.'

What is so important about that notebook?

The Pastor reaches for him and hauls him to his feet by his hair.

'Who are you?'

'No one—' but then he hears a dog's whine coming from the kitchen, followed by a snarl and a growl.

A gravelly voice says, 'What the fucking hell?'

The Pastor places a razor against Starling's throat. 'Do not say a word.'

The dog barks and claws scrape on wood.

The gravel-voiced man shouts, 'Spitfire, NO!'

But the dog skids into the room. It's a squat white bull terrier with a scarred face, its eyes locked firmly on Starling. It springs forward, teeth bared in a vicious smile. The Pastor is distracted for a split second. Starling grabs his forearm and holds for the dog. Its jaws lock onto the arm and clamp shut. The Pastor cries out and tries to shake the dog off, but Spitfire bites harder. The Pastor falls back, dropping the razor and notebook on the floor.

Starling should run, but not without the notebook. It's his and he wants answers. Leaping forward, he grabs it. The Pastor swipes out at him and misses by an inch.

Starling can see his free hand searching the floor for the blade. He turns to run but a broad man is standing in the doorway with a strip of lead pipe in his hand.

'Sir, you have to get out of here.'

An angry frown forms on the man's round face. 'The is my house—' but a terrible yelp followed by a feeble whimper cuts him off. He turns to see the Pastor pushing Spitfire's limp body onto the floor. In his hand is the razor, wet with blood.

'Spitfire! Spitfire, my boy.' The animal's breathing is shallow. Starling is no expert but he could guess he was a goner.

The Pastor leaps to his feet, his expression demonic. The large man looks from his dog to the Pastor, his face burning with rage. He lifts the strip of lead and lunges at the holy man.

With the notebook tucked into his blazer, Starling runs up the hall and out the front door, his head reeling.

Outside, he bumps into a small boy who is hurrying past, carrying a crate of food. The small boy glances at the house Starling has just emerged from then back at Starling. He jumps as two gunshots are fired inside.

'Follow me,' says the boy.

Starling sees some other boys and a girl exiting various houses on the same street. They are all carrying similar small crates of food. Starling knows he must run, but he does not know where. His memory is shattered, he does not know who he is or what he is. He needs time to think. Perhaps the boy can give him shelter until he gathers his thoughts. Glancing back, he sees the Pastor emerge from the house, limping badly. He is in no position to follow them. Starling almost wants to cheer, but he follows the boy and disappears into the shadows of the street.

Chapter 9

Sam

Starling follows the boy along Fenchurch Street and up a back street. His friends are running in single file behind the girl, who seems to be in charge. There are seven in total, eight including the girl. They stop by a pair of tall wooden doors, which look like the entrance to some sort of yard. The girl glances up and down the street before entering through a small hatch in one of the doors. The others follow her through. Starling holds back, leans against the wall and rubs his throbbing head. He thinks about his fight with the Pastor. His reactions were… instinctive; his punches and kicks were aimed and timed perfectly. He evidently has skills, training and experience from a life that is lost to him right now. But why are people intent on killing him and why do they want this notebook. He needs answers but first he needs to find out who he really is.

A voice disturbs his thoughts. 'Are you alright? You don't look well.'

It is the small boy. He looks around twelve years old and has short cropped blond hair, a dirty face and a snub nose. 'I'm Sam.' he says, smiling.

He has no name to give in return. There is nothing in the folds of his memory, a first name, a surname or even a letter, as a clue to his identity. There is just the name from the notebook.

'Tim… My name is Tim.'

'Nice to meet you, Tim. Come inside. You'll be safer.'

Tim is not his name. He does not know how he knows this. He just does. He looks back to check he hasn't been followed. The street is clear, so he lets Sam lead him through the hatch.

The yard looks like an unused tradesman's work area. Dominating the space is a red double-decker bus with union flags hanging from its upstairs windows and an elaborately framed portrait of the royal family fixed to the side panel. The rear platform is draped in a plush red velvet curtain of the sort you might find in a theatre. The whole set up looks like some sort of patriotic, mobile den.

To the left of the bus is a makeshift table made from several heavy planks of wood resting on stacked-up bus tyres. The other children have put their crates on top and are standing around it. They are looking at him suspiciously and seem oblivious to the world beyond the yard where the skies flash and the bombs are still falling.

'Who the 'ell are you?' asks the girl, her brow furrowed. She seems to be the oldest, with a wiry strong frame and mousey brown hair cut just below the ears. She marches forward and stands inches from him, her arms folded, her eyes wary.

'He's with me, Kitty,' says Sam, sheepishly.

Kitty looks at Sam with an accusing expression. 'Sam Rudge, what have I told you about bringing strangers home. We ain't got the food. Besides, he looks old enough to look after himself!'

Kitty has an air of authority, a maternal protective edge to her that Starling can't help but admire.

'But he was in trouble, Kitty. You're always saying we gotta 'elp people. Not just ourselves. So I just 'elped him.'

The other boys circle around warily, watching Starling. Suddenly they don't seem like children anymore. One is holding an old tennis racquet, someone else brandishes a cracked cricket bat, another holds a length of chain and one particularly angry-looking boy with puffy eyes and large freckles sidles up with a grubby machete and pokes Starling in the chest with it.

Despite his chest muscles being tender, Starling surprises himself by not flinching. He scans the approaching boys and calculates the order in which he will disarm each one. The machete boy will be first. He has no discernible skill with the weapon he is holding. Starling will grab his wrist, break it in one hit and relieve him of the machete. He feels his heartbeat faster. But he holds back, frightened at what he is capable of.

Who am I?

'What sort of trouble are you in?' says Kitty, interrupting his thoughts.

'He was robbin' Bob Batten's house,' says Sam.

There is a collective gasp from everyone in the yard.

'You've got some nerve, robbin' Bob Batten's gaff,' says Kitty. 'He'll flay you alive if he finds you.'

Sam continues, 'I heard gunshots coming from his house. Not one but two!'

The others start murmuring amongst themselves.

Kitty's eyes widen, she leans forward. 'Is Bob Batten dead? Did you kill him?'

'No. Nor did I rob him.'

Kitty squares up to him, her nose almost touching his chin. 'Then what are you doing in our patch?'

He hesitates before answering. He does not see the value in lying. Besides, he could use some friends and perhaps if he tells the truth they might help him.

'I was hiding in that house. A man is trying to kill me.'

'He's lying!' says the machete boy.

'No 'e's not. I 'eard the gunshots, remember?' says Sam.

'Who's trying to kill you?' demands Kitty.

'I don't know.'

'Why's he want you dead, then?'

'I don't know, but I intend to find out.'

Kitty eyes him suspiciously, but he keeps his expression fixed and calm. After a moment she seems to relax.

'Alright. You can stay here for a bit, but don't you try anything. We'll be watching.'

'I'll leave in the morning. I promise.'

Kitty nods, curtly. 'Sam, stay with him at all times, you hear?'

'Yes, Kitty,' says a beaming Sam. He turns and grins. 'You hungry, Tim?'

Starling pats his stomach and remembers he hasn't eaten in quite a while. 'Maybe a little.'

Sam runs to the table and grabs two apples and a small block of cheese. 'Follow me,' he says, hurrying to the bus and through the red curtain.

Starling follows him. The downstairs of the bus has no passenger seats. In their place are sofas, cushions and rugs, plundered presumably from other people's houses. There is a musty odour, a lingering smell of unwashed boys.

'Up 'ere,' calls Sam.

Starling makes his way up the stairs and is unsurprised to see the top deck kitted out with bunks, mostly unmade. Sam is sitting at the front eating the apple and cheese.

'Come and eat, Tim.'

Starling sits beside him. 'Where are your parents, Sam?'

'Dead. All our parents are dead. Some of us are the forgotten kids who didn't get evacuated. Others, like Kitty, refused to leave London. This is 'er dad's place. He was a mechanic before 'e was killed in the war. 'Er mother died when their house was bombed. Kitty was out looking for food. She found us and took us all in.'

'But why steal food from people?'

'We don't steal everything. We just take some of it and sometimes we give some away, if it's some old dear who's 'ard up. It's what we do. We're like Robin Hood's Merry Men.'

'That's very noble, Sam.' Starling bites into the apple, which is juicy and delicious.

'Eat some cheese at the same time. It is so good!'

Starling takes a bite from the cheese and eats it alongside the apple. Sam is right. It is delicious. He smiles at the boy and garbles his approval, spitting apple as he does.

Sam finds this hugely funny and can't stop laughing. Starling laughs too and for a second forgets the horrible nightmare he has woken up to.

'What next?' says Sam. 'Are you going to find that man?'

'No. I need to get to Baker Street, I think. Then I can go to the police.'

Sam nods. 'I'll 'elp you.'

'No!' Starling replies too sharply. Sam flinches. 'I'm sorry, Sam. It's dangerous out there. I don't know if Bob Batten is dead. My guess is, he is. And he's not the first. Someone else was killed today. Someone who saved my life and wanted to help me.'

'Who?'

'It doesn't matter. It's just too dangerous. First thing tomorrow, I'll go. You stay here though. It'll be safer.'

Sam says nothing for a moment and then smiles. 'You're right, Tim. It's safer here.'

Chapter 10

64 Baker Street

Monday, 5th May 1941

The air raid is over; dawn is breaking. Starling has spent the night lying next to Sam on his bunk and has barely slept. The events of the past twenty-four hours have played heavily on his mind and he is impatient to leave for Baker Street. He rises slowly, trying his best not to wake Sam and the others, who snore quietly as he slips nimbly across the upper deck of the bus, carrying his shoes. As he descends the stairs, he looks back at the sleeping Sam and feels a pang of regret for not saying goodbye. He had warmed to the boy and felt a bond, like that of an older brother. It made him think if in his real life he had siblings or family. He hopes that Baker Street will answers those questions.

Outside, the skies are clear of bombers but thick with dust and the stench of smoke and cordite. He is unsure of his exact location and heads back towards Fenchurch Street, knowing that west is the direction he must head. Hurrying on, he sees people, wrapped in coats and blankets, trickling from the shelter of Underground stations. Their expressions are grim and he suspects they are clinging on to the hope that their homes have survived the previous night's bombardment.

Something stirs inside him and he has the sensation that he is being watched. He does not look round but carries on, increasing his pace while remaining casual, fearing that perhaps the Pastor has caught up with him. Turning a corner, he lurks in the dark recess of a doorway, his stomach clenched, his fists curled in preparation for a fight.

Moments pass before a small boy with blond hair and a dirty face appears.

'Sam!'

Sam almost jumps out of his skin and clutches his chest. 'Stone the crows, Tim. You didn't 'alf give me a fright.'

'What are you doing here?'

'You need help and I am 'ere to help you.'

'Go home, Sam.'

'Can't do that, Tim. Kitty says I have to keep an eye on you.'

'Baker Street is not your patch.'

'Well, I've decided all o' London is our patch, Tim. All of it.'

Starling curses under his breath.

Sam laughs and covers his ears. 'Blimey, Tim, my ears is not use to such language.'

Starling shakes his head and glances up and down the street. As far as he can see, no one is watching them. There is no sign of the Pastor, or those other men in the Austin 8. If anyone is watching, they would have clocked Sam by now and it would already be too late. Perhaps they had already seen him when they were running from Bob Batten's house last night. Maybe Sam will be safer if he keeps him close, for now. Starling frowns at the boy and pulls him back into the doorway. 'You stick close to me and don't do anything unless I tell you.'

Sam salutes and smiles. 'Yes, sir! Lead on.'

Starling tries to figure the quickest route.

As if reading his thoughts Sam says, 'I know the way.'

Starling snorts a laugh. 'Of course you do. Then please be my guide and lead the way.'

Sam beams back. 'With pleasure.'

Starling follows but feels a creeping sense of dread – two men have died already. He does not want Sam becoming another victim. If he has to, he will kill to prevent that happening. But for now he needs him. Once they get to Baker Street he will do whatever it takes to get him safely home.

-

They arrive at Baker Street around ninety minutes later. Number 64 is a vast stone-fronted office block and not a home after all.

The entrance has double doors with a lock that is too big for his pick. The front windows are strong, thick and impenetrable. The place is like a fortress. There is no way in from the front.

'What is this place?' asks Sam.

'I don't know.'

Starling wonders about other access points and walks further along Baker Street. At the next left, he finds a narrow lane leading to the rear of the building. There is a tradesman's entrance with a lock that is small and easy to pick. Not such a fortress after all.

The door opens into a kitchen area with rows of teapots, stacks of plates, pots and pans. With Sam in tow, he makes his way down a hallway and follows it through to the front double doors. He notices a room list on the wall. Room 7 is on the lower ground floor. They make their way down and find room 7 at the end of the corridor. They stop outside and Starling places his ear to the door. Sam does the same. Satisfied there is no one inside, Starling turns the doorknob and pushes the door open.

The room smells of lavender wood polish. The curtains are drawn. Starling fumbles for the light switch, turns it on and sees a desk with a telephone. Behind it is a bank of filing cabinets and, pinned to the walls, are maps of the United Kingdom, Ireland, France, Germany, Russia and Poland.

'It's an office of some sort,' says Sam, stating the obvious. 'Looking at those maps, I'd reckon there is a connection to the war.'

Starling had thought the same but so far what he knows about the war is only what Skipper told him on the way to London. At first it had been hard to believe, until he saw the devastation and air attacks for himself. And now it feels like he has woken inside someone else's body, into a familiar yet unfamiliar dystopian world. He needs answers and he needs them now. He turns at the filing cabinets, which are labelled alphabetically, and opens one of them. There are rows of files listed by surnames, none of which he recognises.

Under C, he finds a file labelled *Chittlock, Timothy*. He takes it out and opens it. Inside is a photograph of a bespectacled man dressed in a tweed suit, standing in front of a blackboard. His face seems familiar. Starling's mind begins to swim and he hears a voice as if it is speaking through a faulty transistor radio. The man talks in reassuring tones, but there is something else. He strains to listen.

'*You understand what I am asking you to do?*'

His stomach twists. The words don't mean anything to him. But somehow, he knows they must.

'You alright, Tim? You look pale.'

Starling shakes his head. 'I… I'm fine, thanks.'

He turns the photograph over. There is writing on the back:

Tim Chittlock, Beaulieu House, Brockenhurst, Hampshire.

'Who is he?' says Sam.

'I don't know, Sam.'

'You don't look well, Tim.'

Starling sits at the desk and places his head in his hands. 'Something happened to me, Sam. I lost my memory and all I know is there are men trying to kill me. They have killed two innocent men already and I don't know why.'

'Blimey. You are in a fix.'

'My name is not Tim, either.'

'Ooh. What is it then?'

'I don't know,' Starling says, and then his attention is drawn to the desktop where a manila folder labelled CLASSIFIED rests. The folder is entitled 'Agents of VIPER'. He feels an odd twinge of familiarity and pulls the folder towards him.

He opens it. There is a photograph on top, a mug shot of a broad-faced man with a stern expression and a thick black moustache. His shoulders stiffen and his fists curl. He is one of the men from the Austin 8 at the riverside yesterday. But there is something else. He is sure he knows this man, knows him so well that he can almost smell his stale body odour. He turns the picture over. Scrawled on the back is a name:

Colonel Victor Frost

Leader, Agents of VIPER.

The man's name rolls through the mists of his mind. He knows it. He knows him. He knows VIPER. But what is VIPER? He scrolls through the other pictures and stops at one, his heart in his mouth.

'Blimey!' says Sam. 'Is that you?'

Starling's mouth dries. It is him, a younger version of him. He is perhaps sixteen years old, his hair is shorn and he is wearing military fatigues. He turns the photograph over.

Will Starling

Agent of VIPER

That's his name. He's sure of it. Part of him is relieved to know it, but another part of him is horrified to find out he might be in league with these men. It can't be true. They are trying to kill him!

What have I done to make these men want to kill me?

'Will. Your name is Will. Are you some sort of secret agent?' asks Sam, excitedly.

Starling does not respond. His heart begins to beat faster.

What does any of this mean? How can I be an agent of this VIPER?

Somehow, although he cannot remember his family, he can still feel their warmth and love like it is imprinted on his soul.

And why does he have this notebook that so many people want? Why is he wearing a blazer with tools secreted in the lining? The desire to know the truth burns hard inside him. He has another journey to make to track down this Timothy Chittlock. He must go to Beaulieu and find him.

He removes his picture from the file and stuffs it into his pocket. He will burn it later, removing any trace of himself from the VIPER file.

A sudden noise from the corridor makes them both jump. Starling places the folder back where it was and switches off the light. Then he hurries toward the windows and opens one. Sam leaps out first followed by Starling, who gently closes the window before sprinting away after Sam.

Chapter 11

Wanted

Starling looks behind him as he hits the ground and sees the window latch move. He jumps out of view, behind a row of dustbins, pulling Sam with him. They both crouch out of sight. Moments later, heavy footsteps sprint past. Starling shudders and wonders which of his enemies it was. Had one of them caught up with him?

He waits five minutes before risking a look beyond the dustbins and up and down the back street. There is no one there.

'Who was that?' says Sam.

'I don't know and I don't think I want to know. Let's go.'

He hurries them away from Baker Street until they reach Park Lane, which is busy with morning traffic and workers beginning their day. He stops and faces Sam.

'Listen up, Sam...'

Sam is beaming. 'This is so exciting!'

Starling feels a surge of irritation. 'No, it's not. Two innocent men have been murdered and someone is trying to kill me. It is not exciting, it's terrifying!'

'I'm sorry, I meant...'

Starling sighs and places his hand on the boy's shoulder. 'I know what you meant, Sam, and I didn't mean to raise my voice. I don't want anyone else to get hurt. Least of all you. Please, just go back home, stay with Kitty and the others and keep out of sight. You're already in too deep.'

'But I can help you.'

In this strange unfamiliar world, Starling feels so desperately isolated. A lump builds in his throat. More than anything, he wants to say yes. He needs a friend right now, someone he can trust who can see him through this mess. But he cannot risk another life, least of all a twelve year old.

'No, Sam.'

Sam's eyes drop to the ground.

'When this is over, I will come back and find you. I promise. We can be mates.'

The boy looks up and smiles, his face lighting up despite its grubby streaks. 'I'd like that.'

'Me too. Goodbye, Sam.'

Sam thrusts his hands in his pockets and turns to leave. 'Bye, Will.'

With a heavy heart, Starling watches him leave, but he knows it is the right decision. Satisfied that Sam has gone, he gets his bearings for Victoria Station and spots a figure dip quickly out of view at a nearby shop entrance. For a second he thinks it might have been a shadow. But he cannot take that risk. He swallows and retreats, turning on his heels and running as fast as he can.

He arrives at Victoria where the crowds are flocking to and from the station. The clock on the concourse tells him it is 8.20. A man is loading the morning papers onto the stand. The headlines are mostly about last night's air raid but one catches his attention.

Two murders during last night's air raid

His mouth dries. He reads beneath the headline.

> Hastings fisherman Skipper Jones and local man Robert Batten were murdered in cold blood last night. A policeman spokesman said that the murders are believed to be connected and, after an anonymous tip-off, they are searching for a man believed to be around twenty years old, name unknown. He has a stocky, athletic build, is around 5ft 10 inches tall, with dark hair and is considered very dangerous. Please contact Scotland Yard with any information.

Starling's heart pounds. There's a picture next to the article: a rough sketch of him, except he looks angry and dangerous. The Pastor must have lied to the police and given them his description. He edges slowly away from the newsstand looking to the platforms. He must get out of London fast.

With his collar up and head down he hurries across to the rail map and traces the line to Hampshire and Beaulieu. Brockenhurst is his destination. He checks the timetable and station clock. The train is leaving in three minutes. He has no money for a ticket and has to think of something fast.

The train is boarding. He searches for a gap in the crowd and edges his way through the melee, allowing himself to be carried along in the mass of people.

The guard blows the whistle and Starling hurries through the first open door he sees. He slams it shut and a moment later the train is moving. He threads his way through the busy carriages and finds a compartment taken up by a woman and her three young children: one a small boy who is sucking his thumb, and two identical babies who sit crying on her lap. She seems flustered and distracted. Her cases are blocking the aisle.

'Shall I put these away?' asks Starling politely, hoping she has not seen the morning papers.

The woman looks at him, her gaze lingering suspiciously over the bullet hole in his blazer.

'Caught on a nail,' he says, smiling sweetly.

The woman sighs, 'Yes, please.'

He lifts the cases onto the rack and out of the corner of his eye sees a figure, inches away, watching him from the corridor. He turns to see a tall, broad man with a neatly trimmed greying beard and short brown hair combed in a side parting. He has green eyes and a serious expression. 'Any seat in here?' he says with an accent: Irish, perhaps Ulster.

Starling realises he is blocking his access into the compartment. The man looks at Starling for longer than is comfortable. Under the man's arm is folded copy of the newspaper with his picture. 'No,' he says, sharply.

The man narrows his eyes, then turns away and continues along the corridor in search of another compartment.

Starling watches him walk away and is relieved he does not look back. But still, there is something about him that has put him on edge.

He closes the door to the compartment, turns to the woman and gestures at the empty seats. 'May I?'

She nods agreement and he sits down.

'Have you been in a fight?' says the small boy.

'Jimmy Jones!' says his mother. 'Don't be rude.'

Starling smiles nervously. 'Why do you say that?'

'Your jacket is ripped and dirty.'

'That's enough, Jimmy,' says his mother.

Starling looks down at his blazer. The boy is right. There is dust all over him and a rip on his sleeve. What did he expect having been shot, falling into the sea, fighting and then crawling through windows and hiding behind dustbins? He glances at the woman who is tending her babies. She seems not to have noticed.

'I fought a monster,' says Starling, covering the hole in his chest.

The boy stares at him wide-eyed. 'What happened?'

'Jimmy!' cries the woman.

Young Jimmy folds his arms and screws up his face and Starling smiles.

The rhythm of the train is soothing and he wants to sleep, but his mind is too busy. He takes the notebook from his pocket, begins leafing through the pages and finds a sketch of what seems to be a disc with the planets and constellations inside it. Around its perimeter are more of the strange symbols: eyes, pyramids, scythes, swastikas, daggers and upturned crosses.

Thirty minutes pass and he is none the wiser. He glances up and sees the Irishman standing in the corridor and looking into the compartment. Starling furtively slips the notebook into his pocket.

'I need to pee,' says Jimmy. His mother ignores him as she wrestles with feeding both babies at the same time. 'Mummy, I need to pee!'

'Just wait, Jimmy!'

Starling hears the door of the next compartment slide open. 'Tickets please,' says the guard.

'I can't wait!' says Jimmy.

'I can take him,' Starling says.

'Oh, you are a dear, thank you.'

'Come on, Jimmy.' Starling extends his hand. 'Let's go and find the lav.'

The boy grins and Starling leads him out into the corridor, ignoring the Irishman, whose gaze makes him uneasy.

'Tickets please,' says the guard, emerging from the next compartment and turning his attention towards Starling.

Starling gestures at Jimmy's mum. 'My sister has the tickets, sir. I'm just taking little Jimmy to the toilet.'

The guard nods. 'It's two carriages away.'

A short time later Starling stands waiting. He hears the toilet flushing and Jimmy appears from behind the door. 'Did you kill him?' says the boy.

Starling frowns. 'Who?'

'The monster.'

'No.'

'Why?'

'Well, he was very strong…'

'I bet you were stronger.'

'Let's get you back to your mum.'

When they get back Starling stops outside the door to their compartment and peers inside. Thankfully the guard is not there, nor is the Irishman.

'Will you see the monster again?' asks Jimmy.

A chill sweeps over Starling at the thought of meeting the scripture-quoting killer again. 'I hope not, Jimmy. I really hope not.'

Chapter 12

Beaulieu

The train pulls into Brockenhurst at lunchtime in a flurry of steam. Starling says goodbye to Jimmy and his mum and stands up to leave. He notices the Irishman stepping onto the platform, so holds back for a moment and watches him walk toward the exit. A whistle blows and steam billows down the platform, obscuring the view. Starling jumps down and makes his way through the people still intent upon catching the departing train. He feels someone bump into him and turns to see the Irishman push past him. Starling thinks he has been robbed. He pats his blazer pocket and breathes easy when he feels the notebook is still there.

Outside the station it is pleasant and green, the day sunny and bright. There is no more sign of the Irishman, much to Starling's relief.

He spots a battered Post Office van parked by the roadside with an old man, wearing a dirty flat cap, leaning against it and smoking a cigarette. He tips his cap with nicotine-stained fingers and bids good day to two well-dressed ladies who hurry past without acknowledging him.

Starling glances up and down the road but can't see any signs for Beaulieu. He approaches the old man. 'Excuse me?'

'Afternoon.'

'Could you tell me how to get to Beaulieu House, please?'

The man looks Starling up and down, drops his cigarette to the ground and extinguishes it with his boot. 'Not many people ask to go to that place.'

'Why is that?'

'But it just so happens I am driving in that direction,' the old man smiles.

Starling waits for the answer to his question but it doesn't come. He hesitates, still unsure who he can trust. 'Thank you, but I am happy to walk.'

'Well, you got a choice between a long walk, or a short drive.'

A fierce rumbling engine distracts him as a gleaming silver Bentley rolls slowly by: an Embiricos, a model that is rare and beautiful, making him realise he knows a thing or two about cars. Starling's stomach clenches. The driver is the Irishman and he is looking his way. He turns to the old man. 'Yes, please take me to Beaulieu, thank you.'

'Eli Pike,' grins the old man. His smile is made up of a few crooked teeth and even those have seen better days.

Starling hears the Embiricos' engine revving and watches with relief as it speeds away and out of sight.

'Jimmy Jones,' lies Starling and extends his hand.

Eli Pike places a rough and callused bony hand in Starling's. 'And this is Babs,' he says, patting the van with his other hand. 'She's a beauty, isn't she?'

'Er... yes,' says Starling politely. 'Are you a postman?'

'Postman, hunter, safe cracker, Jack of all trades and master of none,' he says with a cackle and a cough. 'Right, let's get you inside.'

-

As they drive along country roads, narrow lanes and through a small village, Eli talks casually about the war and life in the country. Starling is a willing listener and is just thankful not to be pressed with personal questions about him.

Twenty minutes later they pull up alongside a towering wall.

Eli looks at Starling. 'Are you sure you want to go there, Jimmy? We can drive on and I can drop you somewheres else.'

Is he warning me not go to Beaulieu?

Starling hesitates, unsure what to say, but two men have died because of him and this notebook. Not only that, he is wanted for their murders. It's too late for second thoughts. Besides, he has to talk to Timothy Chittlock. Only he can help him. He must see this through, clear his name and find his parents. Beaulieu and Chittlock are his only clues to finding out what he needs. 'No thank you, Eli. Beaulieu is where I need to go.'

Eli nods once and seems disappointed with Starling's answer. He points further along the road. 'See that gate just along there.'

'That's the entrance to Beaulieu House. It is locked. There is a guard standing just inside and I can tell you now, you won't get in. But, if you're interested, I have an idea.'

A few moments later Starling is standing by the wall watching the van speed off. The horn blares, the brakes screech and the van swerves to a halt just outside the gate. An elderly man, a soldier from the Home Guard, emerges and shuffles toward Eli who gets out of the van and staggers around as if he is ill. The guard tries to help him. Starling seizes his chance, runs to the gate and through. He glances back at Eli who winks at him.

Inside the gate, the grounds of Beaulieu are well-tended. There are gardens and scattered copses. Eli told him to follow the gravel drive to the main house.

Beaulieu House is an imposing building, grey and dark with stained glass windows and a turret at each side. One turret is tall, higher than the roof, the other is shorter and looks as if it has sunk into the ground. Starling approaches the front door tentatively. It is tall and wide and made from heavy dark wood. He pushes it, but it is locked. He considers knocking but decides it's best to look around and see what he is up against.

Skirting around the house, he conceals himself behind bushes and peers through the windows. He sees a dozen or so people around his age and older. Some are chatting and drinking tea, others are reading books. From behind a different bush, he peers through another window. There are more people sitting at desks watching a teacher who is talking to them while pointing a stick at a blueprint pinned to the wall. Starling focuses. It is a diagram of a pistol. Looking back at the class, the students do not seem military or police. They look like civilians.

He makes his way to the rear of the house, where he can hear people shouting in unison from somewhere on an upper floor. There is a balcony on the first floor. Its French doors are open. Inside he can make out groups of people dressed in odd loose-fitting clothing like black karategi. They begin standing in pairs opposite each other. He hears someone call out an instruction and they start fighting in a sort of martial art style that seems strangely familiar. Their moves are mostly graceful, with the exception of a couple of students who are clunky and heavy on their feet.

Closest to the balcony is a girl with light brown hair, cut to her shoulders. Starling stands transfixed. She moves with the elegance of a ballet dancer and effortlessly floors a boy twice her size. She fixes her hair behind her ears, turns and looks outside, as if bored. She sees Starling and stares at him curiously. Starling feels his stomach flutter.

He has lost concentration. Annoyed with himself, he turns to walk away but before he can someone grabs hold of his shoulder.

'Well, what do we have here?'

A tall man with bright red hair is peering down at him with a look of recognition, which quickly turns to confusion, then to anger.

Has he seen the sketch of me in the newspaper?

He is flanked by a large red-cheeked man and a pinched-face woman with lank black hair hauled back and tied with a green scarf. Skulking behind them is a plump younger man wearing spectacles.

'Hoping to steal something, are we?' says the red-haired man.

Starling takes stock of him. He looks in his early twenties. His hair has been oiled and styled to make him seem older; his skin is pale with mountainous white-headed spots.

Starling edges back, his fists curling in preparation.

'We have a trespasser, Horne,' says the pinched-faced woman.

The large red-cheeked man grabs Starling from behind. Starling tries to shake him off but his assailant is strong.

'Get off!'

Starling is pulled to the ground. Horne and the pinched-face woman jump on him and pin him down.

'Check his pockets,' says Horne.

Starling wrestles and kicks but it'ss no good. There are too many of them and they know what they are doing.

Horne grabs Starling's hair and raises his fist. 'Kick once more pleb and I will blacken your eye.'

'I found this,' says the woman, holding up the notebook.

'Give it to me, Felicia,' says Horne.

'That's mine!' says Starling, reaching for it, but Horne just laughs and tosses the book away. The round boy with the spectacles picks it up and starts looking through it.

'Get him inside,' says Horne.

They carry Starling through a side entrance. He shouts and swears, kicking out and causing the large one to cry out. They drag him into a large room and release him. Furious, Starling leaps to his feet and raises his fists. His eyes dart left to right, quickly assessing his surroundings. He is standing in a great hall. Dominating the space is a stone fireplace with snout-nosed gargoyles glaring down. On the walls are heavy tapestries depicting ancient wars. Behind his captors is a wide stone staircase, which begins filling with more people, eager to see what the commotion is. Soon Starling is surrounded, trapped, his pulse racing.

Horne addresses the crowd. 'We found this trespasser spying in the grounds.'

The crowd laugh and Starling feels his anger rising, his face burns.

'I say, Horne,' says Felicia, 'he looks positively feral. I shouldn't get too close.'

Horne laughs and jabs Starling's still tender chest with his finger. With a mocking sneer he says, 'Apologise to the people of this school for your unwanted intrusion.'

The crowd cheer and Horne nods his appreciation, but Starling pulls back his fist and launches it fast at Horne's nose. There is a sickening but satisfying crunch and Horne stumbles backward and falls onto his rump. The crowd cheers again and Starling looks up to see the girl with the light brown hair on the staircase, watching him. For the briefest second, he thinks he sees the trace of a smile, but she looks away with a bored expression.

The sound of a woman's voice parts the crowd. 'What the devil is going on here?'

Starling turns to see a frowning woman dressed in a tweed suit.

But she is not alone.

Starling's heart sinks.

Standing on one side of her is Eli Pike and, on the other side, is the Irishman from the train.

Chapter 13

The Recruit

Starling's eyes dart around, searching for an escape route. Through his peripheral vision he spots Horne lunging toward him. Starling is ready to strike, but Horne is pulled back by the Irishman. 'Just hold yer horses there, sonny. Get you and your slippery nose down to the nurse, now!'

Horne breaks free from the Irishman's grip, glares at Starling and points his finger. 'We are not finished,' he says, and pushes his way through the crowd.

'Everyone back to class!' barks the Irishman.

The crowd shuffles away, murmuring and whispering. Starling senses their discontentment at being robbed of the chance to see the intruder get the beating he deserves.

The round boy speaks. 'He was carrying this,' he says, handing the notebook to the squat woman in the tweed suit.

Starling's eyes focus in on the notebook. It looks different.

'*A History of Bird Watching*,' says the woman. She looks at him through hooded eyes. 'Did you wander in here to do a spot of bird watching?'

Starling's eyes lock with the Irishman's. He took it and replaced it when he bumped into him at the station. To his surprise, the Irishman furtively shakes his head. Starling wants to demand the notebook back but his instincts urge him to wait it out and say nothing.

'My name is Miss Clews, but round these parts I am known as the Major. I am the head of school. And you are?'

'Jimmy Jones,' says Starling.

'Well, Mr Jones,' she says, nodding at the Irishman. 'My colleague, Eoin, tells me you've had quite the adventure breaking into our Baker Street office and making your way down to Beaulieu.'

Starling frowns at the Irishman, who stares back at him coldly.

'Come with me, please,' says the Major. She turns to Eli Pike. 'Eli, thank you.'

The old man doffs his cap and then looks at Starling. 'Sorry, mate.'

Starling says nothing and follows the Major, mindful that the Irishman is close behind.

They walk on stone flags through hallways lit with sconces and decorated with pictures of aircraft bombers, rifles and pistols. But these are not artistic paintings or photographs: they are technical drawings the purpose of which, it seems, is to educate.

'What sort of school is this?' he asks.

'I would have thought you of all people would know that,' replies the Irishman.

Starling does not know what to say to that but he thinks he might know the answer.

The Major leads them to her office, which is a large room with maps pinned to the walls. There is a mahogany leather-topped desk and two threadbare sofas on either side of a small fireplace. On the walls are photographs of the Major. In one she is driving a racing car. In another she is standing next to a bi-plane dressed in a flying outfit complete with helmet and goggles. In another, he is surprised to see her with the Prime Minister and the royal family at a garden party. In the centre of the wall, in what seems like pride of place, she is sitting closely, hand-in-hand, with a tall handsome woman. They are both smiling.

'Please sit down,' says the Major.

Starling makes his way towards one of the sofas, his eyes never leaving Eoin's.

Where is the notebook and why is he hiding it?

'Would you like some tea?' asks the Major.

Starling shakes his head and watches the Irishman walk over to the fire and pick up a poker.

His muscles tense, but the Irishman just stokes the fire.

The Major speaks. 'So, Jimmy. What is your real name?'

Starling glances suspiciously from the Major to Eoin. Eoin had been carrying a newspaper on the train. He must have seen Starling's face and must know he is lying. He is done for now.

'Starling. Will Starling… but I didn't kill those men!'

'The police are looking for you, so they are,' says Eoin, coolly.

'I didn't do anything. It was that Pastor, not me.'

Starling notices the Major and Eoin exchanging glances.

'Describe him?' says the Major.

'I don't know who he is. I thought he was some sort of priest at first. He kept quoting the scriptures, but then he killed Skipper Jones and Mr Batten.'

They look at Starling, curiously, as if sizing him up, but say nothing.

'Why would this pastor kill those men?' says Eoin.

'I don't know. He wants something. A notebook.'

'Ah… interesting. Do you have this notebook?' says the Major.

Starling glances at Eoin, whose expression is stony. 'No. Not anymore.'

'Where is it?'

'He has it.'

The Irishman's eyes flash.

'Who?' says the Major.

Starling hesitates. 'The Pastor.'

'Are you sure?'

'Yes. He killed those men and took it.'

The Major studies him for a moment, as if thinking over what Starling has just told her. Starling is not sure if she believes him.

'And what brings you to Beaulieu,' she asks.

'I'm looking for someone.'

'Who?' says the Major.

'Timothy Chittlock.'

The Major and Eoin exchange glances once again.

'Why do you wish to see him?'

Starling rubs the back of his neck, unsure what to say, or how much to reveal, but what choice does he have? He needs answers. He needs to remember.

'He can help me.'

'Help you… How?'

Starling swallows, rubs his thighs and looks from the Major to the Irishman. He has nothing to lose and, despite being unsure about the Irishman, he thinks the Major seems like a decent sort. It's time to come clean. He tells them everything, from the moment he woke up in the sea.

When he is finished the Major and Eoin stare at him, as if appraising him for any signs of lies.

'That's quite a story,' says Eoin at last.

'It's all true.'

'I have no doubt. But right now, I am unsure how Tim Chittlock is involved in this mystery. It may explain his present condition.'

'What do mean?' says Starling.

'Tim is dead. Murdered.'

Starling feels his nerves coiling. What hope is there now?

'Will you excuse us for a moment?' says Eoin. He walks with the Major to the bay window where they talk in whispers together. Moments later they return.

The Major speaks. 'Mr Starling, Eoin has made a request which I am in full agreement with. It is clear you are in danger. The men searching for you are known to us. As it happens, Eoin was on the trail of three of the men you spotted at the dockside. Do you know who they are?'

Starling shakes his head.

'They are known as the agents of VIPER.'

Starling shifts in his chair. The file implicating him as an agent of VIPER was on the desk in the Baker Street office. Does this mean that Eoin knows who he is? He can't tell and decides to keep quiet about it.

'Who or what is VIPER?' he asks.

'The Vendetta for International Power Estrangement and Repression are a criminal organisation with military links to almost every country in the war…' The Major stands and, with her hands behind her back, begins pacing up and down as if deep in thought.

Starling feels cold. He is part of this organisation. He is a criminal. And if the Major and Eoin have seen the file they keep on him, they know it too, or soon will. But if he is part of VIPER, why were the men in the Austin after him?

'…They are wealthy, powerful and dangerous puppet masters whose purpose is to acquire as much power and wealth as possible, though we do not know what their ultimate aims might be. They have weapons of advanced technology and most recently they have been investing their time in ancient mystical weapons related to the occult…'

Starling's head begins to swim; a memory is returning. In his mind he sees a man dressed in a lab coat talking to a room full of other men. Their faces seem similar but he does not know why. There are pictures on the walls: a cluster of stones glowing blue, paintings depicting fires through the ages – the great fires of Rome and London and many more. His head begins to throb. He closes his eyes and massages his temples.

A hand grips his shoulder.

'Will, are you feeling alright? You don't look well.'

He opens his eyes and Eoin hands him a glass of water. He drinks it and feels better immediately.

Troubled, Starling pushes the memory from his mind for now. He needs to find out as much as he can.

'...That sort of mumbo-jumbo does not hold any water with me, but Eoin seems to think otherwise, and quite frankly that is good enough for me. There are many lives at stake and we need as much intelligence as we can gather to put a stop to these devils.'

'Will?' says Eoin.

'I'm fine, thank you.'

'Now,' says the Major, 'Eoin has requested you stay here until we can at least find out who you are. Are you in agreement?'

Starling nods. 'Yes, thank you.'

'Good. Maybe we can locate your nearest and dearest too.'

Starling is relieved that he had the sense to remove his details from the VIPER file in Timothy Chittlock's Baker Street office. He'd be under lock and key had Eoin got wind of where he had come from.

'So, are you going to tell me what this place is?'

'We've told you it's a school. I thought you might have figured out what type of school,' says Eoin.

'A school for spies,' replies Starling.

Eoin speaks. 'Very astute. The people in this school are a rag-tag bunch. They are all carefully selected, chosen for their intelligence, or for a particular set of talents. We shape them into unique individuals who can fit into any society, in any country, and work as part of His Majesty's Secret Service. We are a branch of the Service who work alongside MI5, MI6 and the Special Operations Executive. The Prime Minister calls us the Baker Street Irregulars.'

'You will be safe here,' says the Major.

'So as not to arouse suspicion,' adds Eoin, 'we'll enrol you as a new recruit. You will join the school and become one of us, until I find your family and understand more why VIPER and the Pastor are looking for you. How does that sound?'

The Pastor. The name sends a chill through Starling's body as another piece slots into the jigsaw of his memories. It rings true to him just as his own name did when he saw it in the file. But the Pastor's name brings him no comfort at all.

Starling is not convinced this place is as safe as the Major and Eoin seemed to think it is. For now, though, he needs to trust someone and nods his head in agreement.

Chapter 14

The First Night

Starling follows Eoin from the Major's office to somewhere in the east wing of the house, where processing for his recruitment will begin. They stop at a door with the Irishman's name on it: *Eoin Heaney*.

The interior is sparse with wood-panelled walls and a small window. There is a desk with a row of filing cabinets behind it. These people like their files, thinks Starling.

'Take a seat,' says Eoin.

Starling sits patiently at the desk. Eoin takes several sheets of paper from a cabinet and sits down opposite.

'Where's my notebook?' Starling says, at last.

Eoin focuses on the paperwork without looking up. 'Safe. For now.'

'Why did you steal it?'

'Correction: I borrowed it to protect you and the people of this school.'

'But no one knows I have it.'

'The Pastor knows you have it. VIPER know you have it. It's only a matter of time before they discover you are here. You have put us all in great danger, Mr Starling.'

Eoin's words bring home the enormity of the trouble he is in. Part of him resents the Irishman for blaming him, but the other part feels guilty. He does not want to see anyone else get hurt.

'Why did you not mention you "borrowed" the notebook to the Major?'

'As safe as Beaulieu is, these walls have ears. When the time is right, I will tell her. For now, it must remain our secret. Understood?'

Starling holds his gaze but knows he has little choice in the matter. Even if he changes his mind and leaves Beaulieu with the notebook, it would only be a matter of time before the police, VIPER or the Pastor caught up with him. It would mean prison or death. Neither option would achieve anything.

Eoin passes a sheet of paper across the table. It is the Beaulieu timetable. Subjects include Espionage, Self-Defence, Physical Education, Weapons, Bombs, Radio Operations, Aircraft Today, Tanks Today, Code Breaking, French, German, Latin, English, Mathematics and Honeytraps.

'That's a lot of subjects,' he comments.

'You won't need to take them all. It's more important we get you primed and ready as quickly as possible. There is little time.'

'Primed and ready?'

'We can protect you while you are here. But there may come a time when you need to protect yourself. We can teach you. Equip you with some skills that may save your life.'

Eoin reaches into his drawer, takes out a camera and points it at him. 'Look at me,' he says. A flash of light blinds him. He blinks as Eoin concentrates on scribbling notes. Then Eoin passes across a pen and a sheet of paper with several paragraphs of printed text. 'Sign this, please.'

'What is it?'

'The Official Secrets Act. A requirement for all employees of His Majesty. It's to protect you and the state.'

Starling signs the paper and pushes it back across the desk.

-

After a brief check-up with the school doctor, Starling is pronounced fit for training. He follows Eoin through the great hall and down a narrow stone corridor leading to the west turret. They climb two flights of stairs and go down another corridor. Eventually Eoin stops outside a door, knocks, then steps inside. He speaks to someone for a moment then turns to Starling and beckons him inside.

Starling finds himself standing in a bedroom with a dresser and a wardrobe separating two bunks. Standing opposite Eoin with a terrified expression is one of Horne's friends. The round one with the spectacles. On the wall, above one of the bunks, are pages of paper with illegible handwriting.

'This is your new home, Will,' says Eoin.

'But…'

Eoin turns to the round boy. 'Edward, please make our new student welcome.'

Edward does not respond; he just stares at Eoin.

'Will, this is Edward Simms, who you may remember from this afternoon. As you may observe he's not much of a talker.'

Eoin gestures to the empty bunk. 'This is yours. I'll have some fresh clothes sent up. The bathroom is across the hall. I'll leave you to get to know one another. Supper is at six. Edward, be sure to show Will where the mess hall is. I think you two will become great friends.' Eoin snorts a laugh as he leaves.

Edward sits gingerly on his bunk and rubs his knees. Starling ignores his new roommate and lies on the other bunk. He pushes everything from his mind, closes his eyes and breathes slowly. Tiredness overcomes him. Within minutes, he is asleep.

In his dream, Starling is walking blind through a mist following the sound of a voice, a voice that is singing some sort of nursery rhyme. The mist thins and in the air before him he sees letters and numbers, some sort of code, glistening, pulsating in time to the rhyme. He tries to recognise the tune but suddenly a vast explosion melts the world around him and he hears a hundred thousand voices screaming in terror. He cries out and wakes, shivering, his face hot and clammy. Unsettled, he wonders what the significance of dream might be, but cannot for the life of him figure it is.

The room is gloomy and he is alone. Pushing the dream from his mind, he gets out of bed and crosses to the bathroom where he splashes cold water on his face. Feeling revived, he heads downstairs in search of the mess hall.

He reaches the Great Hall, then follows the chatter and the clink of cutlery on china, which hushes to a silence when he enters the room. All eyes look his way. He stiffens and scans the room. There are four long tables with people seated randomly. Large French doors open to the gardens where people are chatting and smoking.

At one long table, a cook is serving up the evening meal. Starling puts his head down and walks towards him. Thankfully, interest in him wanes and the chatting and clinking resumes.

Dinner turns out to be an unappealing watery grey stew. As the cook serves up, Starling locks eyes with Horne, who is sitting at a table in between Edward and Felicia. Horne leans across and says something to her and she laughs. Starling ignores them, grabs a spoon and napkin and sits at an empty table far away from them. As he tucks into the watery meal he feels another set of eyes watching him. He looks up to see the girl from the balcony. She turns away with a haughty expression. Sitting beside her is a girl with hair the colour of butter and lips painted pillar-box red. She glances at her friend and then back at Starling. Then she smiles and winks. Starling smiles back.

Instinctively, Starling combs his hair with his fingers and thinks he might introduce himself later.

An Irish accent interrupts Starling's thoughts. 'Not exactly the Ritz but it's the best we can do during war time,' says Eoin, pulling up a chair.

'How long do you think I have to be here?'

'That depends.'

'On what?'

'On you.'

'But…'

'Be patient, Will. There is much to be done. For now, I need you to be as fit as a soldier, never mind a spy. Training begins tomorrow.'

'What sort of training?'

'You'll see.' Eoin passes him a sheet of paper: a detailed floor plan of Beaulieu House.

'The rooms circled in red are where they teach the classes I want you to take. We are midway through the school term, and the others will be ahead of you. Do not concern yourself with that. I have briefed the teachers and allowances will be made. You will need to work hard to catch up.'

Starling looks closely at the map. There are rooms labelled: Weapons, Espionage, Radio Operations, Physical Training and Self Defence.

As if reading his mind Eoin says, 'You'll get used to it, so you will.'

Starling's thoughts turn to the dream about codes and the rhyme. 'I had a dream – there were clues. I'd like to see the notebook. I think I might be able to interpret what some of the text means.'

Eoin regards him curiously. 'Let's concentrate on your training first,' he says, standing up. 'That is your priority. See you in the morning. Goodnight.'

-

Back in his room, Starling lies back on his bunk, curiosity about the notebook clawing away at his mind.

Why is it coded? What is it concealing? Why are dangerous people prepared to kill anyone to get it?

In the dream he had heard hundreds of thousands of voices screaming in terror. It has left him feeling cold inside.

There's a movement outside. The doorknob turns once, then stops. Starling swings out of bed; his eyes flit around the room looking for something he can use as a weapon, but whoever was there has walked on by.

He peeks through the door and up the hallway. The bathroom light is on and he can hear water running. He slides across the hall and peers inside. Edward is bent over a washbasin, shaking. His broken spectacles are resting on the side of the basin. There is blood splashed over the sink's white enamel. Edward's top lip is split and his left eye is red and swollen. There are dried tears on his cheeks.

'Leave me alone,' he croaks.

'Who did this?'

Edward does not respond, but he doesn't need to. Starling is sure it was Horne.

'Let me help you,' he says, picking up a towel. He runs cold water on it, folds it over and places it against Edward's swollen eye. 'Hold this.'

Edward does not protest. He turns and sits on the edge of one of the bathtubs, his hand pressing down on the wet towel. 'I'm going to get into so much trouble,' he says.

'Why?'

Edward gazes at the floor and does not respond.

'I can take you to the medical room, if you like.'

Edward shakes his head.

'Horne did this, didn't he?'

Edward looks away without saying yes or no.

'You should tell Eoin or the Major.'

Edward shakes his head. Starling does not push it. He knows there is an unwritten rule in any environment that you do not snitch. Snitching usually results in more beatings and sometimes a lot worse.

'He can't get away with this.'

'He gets away with a lot worse. His family are wealthy and have influence.'

Edward peels the towel from his eye. Starling takes it from him and rings it through with more cold water before handing it back.

'Thank you,' says Edward.

'You should get some sleep.'

As Starling turns to leave, Edward says, 'He wants me to spy on you. He wants to know why you are here and being treated with such importance.'

Starling feels his hackles rising and snorts. *Importance?*

'He says I am to blame this on you. But I won't. I hate him.'

'Tell people you fell over, and stay as far away from Horne as you can. I can handle him and his friends.'

Edward manages a half smile.

'Let's get you back to the room.' Starling helps him up. 'You'll have a proper shiner in the morning. You wait.'

Chapter 15

Assembly

Tuesday, 6th May 1941

Starling wakes the next morning to someone calling his name. Wiping the sleep from his eyes he looks up to see Eoin standing at the foot of his bunk. In one arm he is holding clothes, in the other a battered leather satchel.

'I did knock but there was no answer.'

'What time is it?'

'7 am. There is an assembly at 8 am, in the Great Hall. Make sure you are there.'

Eoin drops the clothes onto the bed. 'Extra clothes, and a training kit. There are textbooks and everything else you need for lessons in the bag. Bring it and your training kit with you.' And with that, Eoin leaves the room.

Starling heaves himself out of bed and hears Edward just beginning to stir beneath the covers.

-

The Great Hall is alive with the laughter and voices of students.

'Morning,' says a voice.

Starling turns to see the girl with the butter hair and painted red lips.

'Good morning to you.'

She smiles and extends her hand. 'I'm Violet.'

Her hand is soft and warm. 'Will.'

'I know. Everyone knows who you are.'

Starling is a little surprised to hear that. 'They do?'

'Oh yes. We're all speculating like mad on why you're here. I know we shouldn't. Top secret and all that, but who doesn't like a bit of gossip.'

Starling opens his mouth to speak but does not know what to say.

Violet continues, 'You must meet my friend. She's dying to get to know you.'

'Violet!' says a voice.

Violet turns and pulls someone from behind her. It is the girl from the balcony.

'Will, meet Anna Wilder,' says Violet, shoving Anna forward.

Anna Wilder pushes back, her cheeks flush with indignation. Then she turns and storms off into the crowd. Starling does not know what to make of her. Snooty seems like a good description.

Violet shrugs. 'Don't mind her. She'll come around.'

Starling has no idea what she will come around to and changes the subject. 'What's the deal with Horne?'

Violet makes a vomiting gesture and leans toward Starling conspiratorially. 'A rich chump with family connections, which means he gets special treatment here. Stay clear of him. He's trouble.'

Starling is distracted when Eoin and the Major appear at the foot of the staircase accompanied by several other people. The Major is talking to a slender man with a wide serious face and a long hook-like nose.

'That's Nicholas Morrow. MI6,' says Violet. 'Slippery fellow, if you ask me.'

Next to him is a taller lady with a dreamy expression and a whistle round her neck. It's the handsome woman from the picture in the Major's office. Standing next to her is an Indian gentleman wearing a vivid green turban.

'And that's Miss Davenport, who teaches games and physical training. Mr Singh is Communications and Code Breaking.'

The Major stands on the stairs and faces the crowd. 'Good morning,' she says loudly.

The crowd continue to chatter, seemingly oblivious. She raises her arms and drops them slowly in a hushing motion, but no one seems to notice. She rolls her eyes and nods politely to the tall lady with the whistle. Eoin, Morrow, the Major and Singh cover their ears as she blows hard.

The chatter dwindles and fades to a whisper and then complete silence.

The Major nods her thanks and turns to the students. 'Good morning all.'

'Good morning,' the students mumble in unison.

The Major smiles, and then her expression turns grave. 'In the last few days the Germans have walloped London and Coventry. There are many casualties and far too many deaths.' She pauses for a moment, in thought, before continuing. 'There are occupying forces in the Netherlands and we also know that, in the next few days, Paris will be taken. The Third Reich is spreading across Europe like a tumour.'

There is a grumbling from the students. Starling senses a feeling of unease and reflects that in just over twenty-four hours he has strangely come to terms with the world at war and this cold and dangerous existence he has woken up to. Is this because that is what his real life is all about? Was he, as the file in Baker Street stated, an Agent of Viper?

I can't be. I would never betray my country.

Or would he? Did he have reason to? The thought makes him go cold. He has no memories, nothing concrete to cling to. All he knows is the Agents of VIPER and some mad pastor are trying to kill him, and he has something they both want.

'…Never has the work of this school been more vital to the war effort. Your commitment and bravery will go down in history, which is why we must continue to learn and become the best at what we do.'

A rumble of agreement ripples through the crowd.

The Major gestures at Nicolas Morrow. 'Some of you will know Mr Morrow. He is here to assess certain students for a posting at MI6. So please, do your best to impress.'

There is a murmur of excitement from the crowd.

The Major continues, 'The war is not abating, it is building. The Army, the Navy, the Air Force all need new recruits and so do we. I am always on the lookout for new talent and today I would like to introduce you to a new addition to the school.'

Starling stiffens.

'I would ask you – no, I will tell you – to forget what you saw yesterday and welcome our new student, Will Starling.'

Starling does not react to the gaze of the many curious eyes, but he can feel one pair in particular boring into him from the foot of the staircase. He turns to see Nicholas Morrow, frowning at him.

'Will is going to undertake a fast-track training program with Mr Heaney as his mentor,' says the Major. 'So please, make him feel welcome.'

Everyone claps, with the exception of Horne and his friends.

'Righto, everyone. It's almost 8.15 am and another school day begins,' says the Major, rubbing her hands together.

-

The men's changing room is narrow, bare and cold, with a single row of grubby wooden benches dividing the limited floor space. Dropping his kit on a bench, he removes his blazer and feels a shove from behind. He turns to see Horne's humourless face looking back at him. Beside him is his mate, the weirdly angry looking giant with the red face.

Starling keeps his cool. He knows he could take both of them out easily, in less than seven seconds by his calculation. Horne has made a mistake already by being too close. A knee in the groin would disable him and before his knees hit the ground, Starling's fist would be gracing the giant's nose. Seven seconds. No more. Easy. His heart begins to beat faster, a primal urge for violence surging through him and the desire to teach these amateurs a lesson. But he won't. Not now, anyway.

Horne snorts and then walks to the other end of the changing room. The giant lingers to glare at Starling through button-like eyes.

'Sneddon!' barks Horne.

Sneddon flinches and backs away, jabbing a thick digit in the air.

Starling is relieved they have gone. His self-control was about to be tested but, lucky for those two, it wasn't. He considers what he was prepared to do. His desire to hurt those two idiots makes him shudder.

Who the hell… what the hell am I?

In time he'll find the answers to those questions, but for now he must keep a low profile and not draw attention to himself by being rash and stupid. He looks across at Horne and Sneddon.

That does not mean, however, that I cannot have some fun.

Chapter 16

The Race

Starling makes his way to the front of Beaulieu House, where the cross-country runners are gathering. It begins to spot with rain and goosebumps prickle his skin. Violet, Anna and Horne's friend Felicia are waiting. Despite the morning being cold and dull, there is an excited hum in the air.

Eoin stands at the front of the crowd. 'Start warming up,' he calls and begins jogging on the spot. 'I want you to put everything you have into today's race. Forget your aching muscles. Forget the stitch in your side. Forget your gasping lungs. Run like your life depends on it. Because one day, it will.'

A grim silence hangs over the crowd.

More rain begins to fall. Starling looks upwards. Thick grey clouds are rolling across the sky like giant sheep. A feeling of déjà vu unsteadies him, a memory flashing into his mind: a rainy day in a remote and treacherous landscape. He is wearing dark green fatigues. There are others like him but bigger, older, with shaven heads. He knows them, but not their names. A voice is booming at them – a stern, angry voice. They are running across fields, up hills and mountainsides, their heavy boots thudding on the coarse, uneven terrain.

'Will!'

Starling snaps out of his fugue and sees the others running into the distance. Eoin is looking back at him, beckoning him to hurry. Starling swears under his breath and springs after them, troubled by the memory.

He catches up with Eoin, who points to a wooded area in the distance. 'We're running through those woods, then along the river and across to the assault course. We'll meet back here. It's your first time, so do your best and try not to get lost.'

Eoin runs off in pursuit of the others.

Still spooked by the memory, Starling lags behind, his performance hindered by a blurred sense of reality. *Who am I?* He rubs his head and feels the gash on his temple under this thick hair. It is still tender. The pain jolts him and he looks ahead trying to see where everyone is, but the landscape is misty and the view is obscured. He increases his pace, breathing slowly through his nose and mouth, exhaling in time to the rhythm of his running.

He hears the crunching of twigs and turns to see a man he doesn't recognise leaping over a wire fence and disappearing into the woods. Starling runs at the fence, leaps over it and sprints after him. The ground is uneven and slippery. Thick clustered trees slow him down. He runs for twenty minutes with no sighting of the man or anyone else. He stops to get his bearings and catch his breath. He has a stitch in his side and his muscles burn with the exertion.

'No resting!' shouts Eoin from somewhere beyond the trees. Starling focuses on the direction of his voice and runs toward it. Although he cannot see him, he can hear the Irishman's fast and heavy footfalls and follows in their wake.

He estimates fifteen minutes has passed before he clears the woods and catches sight of Eoin and the others. They are running uphill, alongside a river. He sees Anna and Violet amongst the melee following Horne, who is way ahead of everyone.

He steadies his breathing and takes measured runs toward the crowd. Trailing behind them is the burly Sneddon, who glances back at him. His gait is awkward as he struggles to get up the hill. Starling sprints past him, narrowly missing a podgy pink fist swiping close to his face. He almost laughs but races on, passing three more runners including Felicia.

He runs for twenty minutes along the bank against the current and stops at what seems the most dangerous part. The water is swirling furiously, drowning out any other sound. Starling watches as the others wade through the waist-high treacherous rapids. Beside him are Anna and Violet. They work as a team and hold on to each other as they step down. Starling follows, but someone shoves him and he falls against Anna. They both topple over. Starling swallows a mouthful of grey, gritty water as the undertow drags him downstream. He swims to the top and grabs hold of an old uprooted tree jutting overhead. Anna surfaces beside him, gasping for breath, her hair sodden and plastered to her face.

'Grab my hand!' calls Starling.

Anna grips his arm and Starling guides them out of the water and onto the muddy bank.

'What the hell do you think you are doing?' she shouts.

'I just saved you!'

'You've just cost me this race!'

Starling opens his mouth to explain but Anna has is already making her way back down to the river. She wades across to the other side where Violet waits. Starling can almost feel the steam coming out of his ears and turns his attention to whoever pushed him. Felicia is the only one nearby. She smiles slyly, before hurrying up the bank and back into the race.

Starling wades carefully through the water and hauls himself up the riverbank, plodding through the thick mud. He picks up his pace as the ground grows firmer and assesses what lies ahead. The runners are sprinting towards a wall that looks like a great brick slab plonked in the middle of the countryside. It is approximately fifteen foot wide and twenty foot tall and less than quarter of a mile ahead, perhaps one thousand feet. If he runs uninterrupted, he could make it in three minutes, maybe less. He inhales and exhales, filling his lungs with oxygen, and springs forward.

The runners are spread out. Felicia glances back at him, but Starling ignores her. He can see Violet and Anna following in the tracks of Horne, who is still leading and almost halfway to the wall. Starling hurries forward and breaks into a sprint. Like a hound pursuing a fox, he focuses on Horne and pounds across the field.

Now is my time to have fun.

Felicia turns to face him, raising her arms like some sort of goalkeeper trying to prevent him from getting to the back of the net, but Starling runs wide and skims past her. He overtakes several more runners and sees five ropes hanging down from the wall. Horne, Violet and Anna are almost there and leap across a pool of water at the foot of the wall. They begin climbing the ropes.

Starling leaps across the small pool like a long-jump athlete and reaches for the thick rope, but he slams against the wall, his hands gripping desperately, his knuckles grazed and bleeding against the rough bricks. The rope is slippery and difficult to maintain purchase. Tightening his grip, he pulls with all his strength, but he keeps inching further down. He grits his teeth and holds on, but the rain crashes down, hampering his efforts. Blinking through the rain he tries to look above but the water stings his eyes. He wipes them with his forearm and sees Horne almost at the top. Anna and Violet are close behind but are struggling against the downpour. Their technique is poor, with limbs wrapped around the rope, they haul their weight slowly up. In this weather, there is a better way to climb a slippery rope. Using one foot, Starling catches the rope and with the other he creates a loop. He is then able to stand on the rope with ease and haul himself upwards.

He is close to the top when he sees a shadow looming directly above him. Horne is crouched, watching him like a hyena stalking its prey. Starling hesitates, suspicious. He glances down and swallows, his throat dry. If he slips, or there is an *accident*, he could be done for. He steadies his breathing and carries on climbing, his eyes never leaving Horne's. He reaches forward, his fingers gripping the ledge. Horne stands up and raises his foot. He presses it down on Starling's fingers. The pain is unbearable. He hears Violet shouting at Horne to stop, but his strength is sapping, he can't keep his grip and then he falls. Scrambling for purchase, Starling clings to the slippery rope, his hands and legs burning with the friction. Eventually, he stops his slide and looks up to see Felicia hopping over the edge. Violet and Anna are looking down from the top. Violet is waving her arms, shouting for him to climb up.

Starling is sodden, his muscles ache, the skin on his hands and legs feels like it is on fire. He wants to cry out, but he won't let himself. He must not give up. Ignoring the pain, he climbs back to the top.

Violet and Anna have already taken off. He can see Eoin in the distance beside a row of monkey bars, gesturing at everyone to hurry. Horne is ahead; Felicia, Violet and Anna are following close behind. He looks quickly at his hands. The skin is hanging off. He removes his vest, tears it in two and wraps the material around his palms and fingers. He slides quickly down the rope. His feet hit the ground lightly and he springs forward. Breathing through his mouth and nose, he increases his pace and soon flies past Felicia, who shouts an unladylike obscenity at him.

Horne is crossing the monkey bars with Anna and Violet inches behind him. Starling leaps onto them, wincing at the pain in his hands, but thankful they are protected with his ripped vest.

Horne, Anna and Violet are neck and neck, heading toward what look like shallow underground tunnels. Horne crawls into one; Violet and Anna dip into the other.

Starling drops off the bars and hurries toward the tunnels. He dives into the tunnel behind Horne. It is dark, cold and wet with an earthy smell, like a long empty grave. He can hear Horne squelching through the mud ahead. Starling tries to catch him up but his hands and knees sink in the quagmire, slowing his progress. He pulls them out and lies down on his front with his arms and legs flat, crawling across the surface of the mud, ignoring the stones and wood that scrape his bare chest. He should be spent, but a fire burns in him and he carries on.

But then something tugs at his foot. It is a hand. Felicia! Starling pulls his foot away, freeing from the grip but losing a plimsole at the same time. Felicia grabs him again. She is strong, but he pulls his foot free and crawls fast toward the opening where the back of Horne's head is framed.

Horne is out of the tunnel. Seconds later Starling emerges and sees him disappear into a copse of trees. The rain lashes down, washing the mud from his tired body.

Eoin is ahead, calling to Starling. 'Well done, Will. Faster. You are almost there!'

Starling pelts through the copse, zigzagging around trees and jumping over rocks. Through the woods, he sees Horne and beyond him, Beaulieu House. He dashes forward and clears the copse and onto open land all the way to Beaulieu. Sprinting downhill, in seconds he is level with Horne. He sees a stream ahead and launches himself at it. The water is deeper than expected. Horne is beside him now, his expression grim and determined. Starling pulls himself to the other side, ignoring the pain in his bare foot from the scraps of wood and gravel.

He can see some of pupils outside the school watching and cheering them on. The Major and Morrow are there too, looking on with interest.

Starling pushes on. Horne is beside him again, inching his body forward to get ahead but he calls on his last reserves of energy and forces himself in front. Starling skids to a stop close to Morrow and drops to his knees on the grass, gasping for breath. There is an almighty cheer.

'Bravo, Starling,' says the Major.

'Good work, Will!' says Eoin.

Horne manages to look both furious and confused.

'Impressive, Starling,' says a tinny voice.

Morrow is watching him through narrowed eyes. 'I will be keeping a watchful eye on you.'

There is something about Morrow that sets Starling on edge. He cannot quite put his finger on it.

Violet and Anna arrive. They congratulate him and Violet gives him a warm hug, much to Anna's apparent surprise. She keeps her distance, although twice he catches her looking furtively at his mud-streaked bare torso.

Chapter 17

Spy School

Starling showers and instantly feels like a different person. To his satisfaction, Horne and Sneddon leave the changing room without any fuss. They can see he is clearly not the soft target they had anticipated.

Using Eoin's map of Beaulieu house, Starling navigates the corridors, looking for his first class: Radio Operations. According to the map it should be on the first floor. He crosses the Great Hall, hurries up the staircase, turns right and stops outside the second door on the left. He places his ear to it and hears Mr Singh talking.

He knocks twice and steps inside.

'Ah, William. I've been expecting you. Please join us,' says Mr Singh.

Starling closes the door and glances around the room. There are six tables in rows of two. Each table has a suitcase on top. Seated around each one are three students. Starling can see familiar faces including Violet, Anna and Horne with his two idiot friends. There is one table with a single student, sporting a large back shiner on his left eye.

'Please, sit with Edward,' says Mr Singh.

Starling hesitates, but heads toward the table. He can see Edward go rigid.

'Relax, Edward,' he says, glancing at Horne, whose eyes dart from Edward to Starling. Something in Horne's frown tells Starling that the plan to get him into trouble has backfired.

'Open up your communications devices, please,' says an enthusiastic Mr Singh.

Edward unfastens the clasps and opens the lid of the case. The smell of fresh wood polish fills Starling's nostrils. Inside is a gleaming new radio communications set built neatly into the suitcase. There is a compartment containing the headphones, a large rectangular power pack and a panel with dials and buttons that operates the transmitter and the receiver.

'It's a Whaddon Mark VII,' says Starling.

'Yes, it is,' says Edward.

He can feel Edward looking at him.

'How do you know that?'

Starling shifts uneasily. 'Erm… a lucky guess.'

The radio has an unsettling familiarity to it, as if he has seen or used one before. Starling listens attentively to Mr Singh, ignoring Edward's curious gaze.

By the end of the class, Edward has warmed up and they have even managed to exchange a few more words. He feels the beginnings of a bond, although it is still somewhat fragile.

-

The following morning, Starling attends the Deadly Gadgets class taught by Eoin. The Irishman demonstrates a range of weird devices such as Time Pencils for detonating explosives, nitrate paper that explodes on contact with flames and bombs disguised as clockwork rats.

'Wind them up and watch them scurry toward their target,' says Eoin.

Starling cannot resist winding up a fake rat bomb and sending it toward Horne and his henchmen. He has never seen anyone move so fast. The class roars with laughter.

Later, Starling attends Self-Defence, which is taught by the tall, athletic Miss Davenport. Her class is held in the gymnasium, a vast ornate room on the first floor that looks like it had once been a ballroom, the place where he first saw Anna. Across the room he sees her standing comfortably in her loose-fitting black karategi. He watches her for a moment, transfixed, before Miss Davenport speaks.

'Righto, everyone. Today is Starling's first self-defence lesson. As you know, self-defence is key to survival. Therefore, no kid gloves in this class.' She gives a guffawing laugh.

Starling notices some students rolling their eyes.

Miss Davenport continues, 'Starling, pretend I am a ruthless Nazi killer stalking her prey. You are an undercover agent in possession of secret information that is key to saving hundreds of lives. We will fight to the death,' she says. 'I will be gentle,' she adds, but Starling swears her eyes have taken on a canine quality.

Out of the corner of his eye, Starling sees Eoin entering the room. He stands out of the way and watches on with interest.

Miss Davenport turns to face Starling, her fists raised in attacking mode. '*Schweinhund!*' she bellows in a mock German accent. Starling ignores the giggles from the class and watches as Miss Davenport's fist flies toward him. He leans to the left, the fist narrowly missing his ear. Miss Davenport throws several more punches, swipes and kicks but he dodges every single one.

Starling watches her, determining what she will do next. It isn't that she is a terrible fighter; she is fast and skilled, but he seems to be able to anticipate her every move by reading her body language. How on earth can he know this? The answer makes him feel cold. But deep down he has known since he saw the file in Baker Street.

I'm one of them. I'm an agent of VIPER.

Miss Davenport tries her best but cannot quite hit her target. Minutes later, puffed out and red-faced, Miss Davenport relents. 'Very good, Starling. Clearly you have done this before.'

'No, Miss, this is my first time.' What else could he say?

The class giggle again.

He glances at Eoin, who is still watching him.

Miss Davenport looks despondent. 'Oh… Maybe I'm losing my touch,' she says.

'No… you were very good,' says Starling.

'Really?' she says, smiling.

'Really.'

Miss Davenport turns and looks across the gym, her expression clouding over. 'Good Lord, what is that?' she says.

Starling tenses and looks, but before he can see what it is his legs are kicked from under him. He falls to the mat, his arm in a vice-like grip and Miss Davenport's knees pinning down his chest.

'Ha!' she cries. 'Never let your guard down in front a murderous Nazi, Starling.'

The class erupts in laughter and, despite his shock, Starling laughs too, which injects in him a sudden surge of hope.

Perhaps I'm not one of them. Perhaps I'm a good person.

Miss Davenport addresses the class. 'Break into twos and press on!' She stands up, takes Starling's arm and helps him up. 'Sorry, old boy,' she says.

Starling shakes his head. He can't help liking Miss Davenport and her passion. 'I let my guard down. You win.'

'I'm impressed, Starling. Your non-contact avoidance of my attack was highly skilled. I find it hard to believe you have not had lessons before this.'

Starling looks away and says nothing more, relieved that she doesn't press him further. He looks to Eoin and sees him leave quietly, shutting the door behind him.

Chapter 18

Shooting Class

Thursday, 8th May 1941

Starling wakes with a sense of urgency. His muscles are tight and the throb in his temple has returned like a visceral warning for him to get moving. More than twenty-four hours have passed since he saw Eoin leave Miss Davenport's Self-Defence class. He senses that the Irishman has left Beaulieu and wonders if this could be an opportunity to explore and search for the notebook? It must be somewhere in the school. That said, Beaulieu is vast and it could take him weeks, if not months, to find it.

He feels that he has very little time, though where this thought has come from he can't say. What he does know is that he must find the notebook.

He makes his way to the Major's office to find out if she knows where Eoin is.

'You'll find him at the shooting range, where I believe you have your next lesson, Mr Starling,' she says, quickly peering up at him through half-moon spectacles.

The distraction of the notebook had made him forget his lessons. 'Erm… I apologise for disturbing you, Major. I'll go there immediately.'

'Righto. Hurry along then. You are already late.'

Starling hurries through the grounds and hears the sound of a gunshot. The class has already begun. He runs through a copse and sees a row of six faceless scarecrows stuffed with straw and dressed in patched-up suits and hats. Nearby is Eoin standing next to a table with a holdall on top of it. In his hand is a pistol. He is talking to a group of students. Among them he sees Anna, Violet, Horne and his crew. Eoin looks up as Starling approaches.

'You're late, Starling.'

'Sorry, sir.'

'For the benefit of Starling, a quick recap,' says Eoin. He holds up a pistol. 'This is the Webley Mark IV, British made and standard issue. It is a revolver. Can anyone tell me what makes it a revolver?'

Starling opens his mouth to answer, but Horne speaks up first.

'It's…' starts Horne but is interrupted by Eoin.

'Hand please, Horne.'

Horne's neck reddens and he slowly raises his hand. 'Sir?'

'Yes, Horne.'

'A revolver is a repeating firearm that has a revolving cylinder containing multiple chambers and one barrel for firing. The term "revolver" refers to a handgun, but other weapons may also have a revolving chamber. These include some models of…'

Eoin cuts Horne short. 'Thank you, Horne, we get the idea.' He opens the holdall. Inside are several more Webley revolvers. 'Partner up and take one pistol between two of you.'

Starling looks around. There are several boys including Horne hovering around Violet and Anna, hoping to partner and show off with them. He notices Violet looking his way. She glances wickedly at Anna. 'Anna and Will are shooting together!' she calls to Eoin.

'Very good,' says Eoin. 'Anna, please help Will.'

Starling sees Anna's face burning red. Violet winks at Starling and he frowns.

Anna makes her way through the crowd and stands next to Starling without looking at him.

'Have you used a gun before,' she asks, haughtily.

Starling glances at the bag of guns and says nothing. Part of him is repelled, but part of him is also excited about the opportunity to know what it is like to hold and shoot a gun. But there is something else. Something at the edge of his memory.

Anna puffs and shakes her head.

Starling suspects she thinks he is nervous. His patience with this stuck-up girl is fading fast. He wants to say something clever when he notices Horne. He is gripping his Webley and glaring in his direction. Starling wouldn't be surprised if he tried to put a bullet in him and claim it as an accident.

Eoin walks through the crowd, handing out boxes the size of a small fist. They contain bullets.

'Load the bullets and take aim at your target,' demands Eoin. 'Point your gun at the scarecrows and get ready for my signal.'

'Watch what I do,' says Anna. 'Point the barrel away from you toward the ground.'

Starling watches as Anna flicks a switch at the side the gun. 'It's a top-break revolver. This switch unlocks the gun.' She pushes the barrel down, revealing the chamber.

Starling takes six bullets from the box and hands them across. Although still irritated by her, he watches with admiration as Anna's slender hands skilfully load the bullets and lock the gun back into place.

Six students including Anna, Violet and Horne stand at the frontline.

'Aim!' bellows Eoin. He walks behind each one of them, checking their positions. He stops beside Violet. 'Steady your aim, Violet.'

'It's too heavy,' she says.

'Then support your gun hand with your other arm.' Eoin takes he gun from her and points it toward the targets. He cups his free hand under his gun hand and looks back at her. 'Like so.'

He walks to the top of the line, gives one final check and shouts, 'Fire!'

Starling covers his ears. The air is filled with deafening blasts.

Anna's and Horne's scarecrows shudder; their straw filled arms flap lifelessly in a sinister dance as their bullets hit their marks.

'Good work, Miss Wilder and Horne. The rest of you need more practice. Pass the guns to your partner.'

Anna hands the Webley to Starling, which is warm to the touch. His fingers curl around it and hold it with an unsettling confidence. He trembles and feels a wave of dizziness pass over him.

'Look at Starling's face!' laughs Horne. 'Try not to shoot yourself in the foot!'

A surge of anger rushes through Starling.

'Don't listen to him,' says Anna. 'Concentrate.'

Starling takes three deep breaths and focuses. He recalls Anna's instruction but there is something else. He knows what he is doing. Pointing the barrel at the ground, he opens it and slowly inserts the bullets into the chamber. He takes up his position at the frontline.

'Aim!' says Eoin.

Starling's gun is stiff and difficult to lock. He fiddles with it clumsily until it gives way and closes. He pushes the barrel up, locking it in place. He aims. The gun is heavy and wobbles for a moment before he steadies it.

'Fire!'

Starling flinches as the gunshots ring out. He squeezes the trigger but nothing happens.

'Starling?' says Eoin.

He hears murmuring from the other students but ignores them. The trigger is jammed. He slams the gun with the palm of his hand without really knowing why. Something clicks. Supporting the gun hand with his free hand, he aims the Webley at the scarecrow, one eye staring down the top of the barrel and over the sight. His stomach is in knots, but he breathes slowly.

His arm is steady; the sight is aimed directly at the scarecrow's heart.

He squeezes the trigger firing off six rounds without flinching. Dust flies from the scarecrow, its arms flailing in a vain protest as the bullets thud one by one into its straw chest.

Starling swallows. He has hit the target with each bullet.

There is silence; no one speaks.

He hears a creaking sound and watches as the scarecrow flops forward and falls to the ground, a twisted and lifeless straw corpse.

His mouth dries. For a moment he thinks he has been lucky, but he knows this is not the case. Moments back there was something he could not quite fathom. He understands now what that was: he knows how to fire a gun. Confused, he wonders who he really is as he lowers the Webley.

There is a cheer from the other students.

He looks around to see them closing in around him, slapping his back and congratulating him. All except Horne and his crew.

Starling's mood lifts instantly as he laps up the sudden praise. He glances at Eoin, who is regarding him with an unreadable expression.

'That's all for today,' says Eoin. 'Place the guns in the bag on the table. I will be counting them.'

'Nice work,' says Violet.

'Thanks,' replies Starling and looks at Anna.

'You are full of surprises, aren't you?' she says, folding her arms.

He looks away. She is right to be curious.

The class begins to disperse.

'Starling,' says Eoin. 'Come to my office. I need to talk to you.'

'Yes, of course.'

Eoin nods, hands him the bag containing the guns, and together they walk back to the school.

Chapter 19

Languages

Starling is standing in Eoin's office watching him lock the bag of pistols into a steel cabinet. The Irishman has said nothing since they left the firing range.

'How many languages can you speak?' he says at last.

Confused by the question, Starling frowns. 'Just English.'

Eoin nods. 'You did well today,' he says, changing the subject.

'It was just luck,' says Starling, folding his arms.

Eoin snorts. 'Is that what it was?'

'Yes!'

'And you also got lucky during Self-Defence?'

Starling swallows and fails to answer.

The Irishman looks at him with an inquisitive stare. 'You've never fired a gun before? Not once?'

'I was lucky, that's all.' But Starling feels a nervous tingling in his stomach and knows Eoin is not convinced by his answers.

'Perhaps you're right,' says Eoin.

But Starling sees the doubt in his eyes. He frowns at the Irishman. 'Why don't you believe me?' he snaps.

'I didn't say that I don't believe you.'

'But you don't, do you? You think I'm a liar!'

'I think you're confused.'

'What does that mean?'

'It means I think there's more to you than we think.'

'So you do think I'm lying?'

'I didn't say that.'

'But it's what you meant.'

'Not exactly.'

'Then why don't you just say what you mean?' Starling's anger is at tipping point. Suddenly, the events of the last few days hit him hard and he cannot contain his patience any longer. He wants to let rip and get everything off his chest, but Eoin turns casually away and looks out the window. 'Thank you, Will.'

Starling's hands curl into fists. 'Is that it? Is that all you have to say?' He desperately wants to kick something but turns and heads for the door.

'*Ich habe nicht gesagt dass Sie gehen können!*' says Eoin.

Starling stops, his heart pounding, his hand gripping the doorknob hard. *I did not say you could leave.*

'*Tout n'est pas fini entre nous*,' says Eoin.

Starling trembles. *I'm not finished with you.* Eoin had just spoken in German and French, and he had understood every word.

'Sit down, Will.'

For a moment he feels paralysed and unable to move from the door. But then a warm hand rests on his shoulder and Eoin guides him to a chair. Starling does not protest. He sits down, his mind a flurry of confusion. He hears the sound of liquid pouring and suddenly there is a glass of water in front of him.

'Drink this.'

Starling drinks slowly, one sip, then two, before downing the lot. It makes him feel a little better. 'I... I don't understand what is happening to me.'

'Don't try to, yet.'

'But I have to know. I feel like I'm a stranger in my own body.'

'You're not. Trust me.'

Starling looks at Eoin with a sense of hope. 'What happened to me? How did I get to this point?'

'I have a theory. If I am right, then we are all in terrible danger.'

'What do you mean?'

'We'll talk about that later. For the moment, come with me. I have something to show you.'

Eoin locks his office door from the inside then shifts one of the filing cabinets away from the wall and pushes his hand against one of the wooden panels. There is a clicking sound and the panel shifts slightly, revealing the faint outline of a door. He pushes it open and a rush of cold, musty air sweeps into the office. Starling can see a dark and narrow stairwell with a lantern on the top step.

'Beaulieu is a honeycomb full of secret passages and tunnels,' says Eoin, lighting the candle in the lantern.

'In days gone by they provided an easy escape from the enemy. Nowadays they are useful for getting to class ahead of the students. Only certain teachers know of these passages. Let's keep it that way.'

'Yes, of course.'

Starling follows Eoin down and across a series of linked stairs and passages, all of which are narrow and tall. Straggly cobwebs hang everywhere like deadman's bunting, wafting against his face and hair. Here and there he hears the sound of muffled voices and laughter as they pass dormitories and classrooms. The deeper they go, the colder it becomes. The air is damp all around them and the walls are dripping with moisture.

When it seems they can go down no further, Eoin stops and points to the end of the passage. 'There,' he says.

As they draw near, Starling can make out a heavy, wooden cell door reinforced with steel bands. There is a small barred window. Stepping closer he peers inside and sees an empty cell containing only an old table.

Eoin reaches into his pocket, takes out a large key and unlocks the door. He hesitates and stares into the cell, his face gaunt and troubled. He steps inside and places the lantern on the table. Starling follows him.

In a far corner, Eoin pulls a flagstone up from the floor. Underneath is a shallow hole. From it he lifts an old wooden box and sets it on the table. It looks like something a cobbler might house his tools in.

But then the box begins to tremble and the table begins to shake. Starling hears a humming sound and notices flickering movements as insects begin crawling out from the cell walls seeking a way out.

'What's going on?' asks Starling, the hairs on his neck standing on end.

Eoin cautiously opens the lid.

An unearthly blue light erupts from inside and floods the cell and the corridor beyond. Starling raises his hand to shield the glare. When his eyes adjust he sees a glowing shard of blue stone, about two inches long, inside the box.

'It knows we're here. It can feel our presence, our energy, our emotions.'

'What is it?'

Eoin lifts the stone from the box and holds it up, between his thumb and index finger. 'It's a fragment.'

Tiny lights like miniature fireworks begin sparkling around Eoin's fingers and hand. Starling notices his face is beginning to shine with a layer of sweat.

'A fragment of what?'

'A fragment of the Stones of Fire.'

A memory stirs in Starling's mind; the muscles around his spine tighten in a snag of knots. The notebook and the Stones of Fire. They are related. But how? And then he remembers something. Something he has known. The notebook is the key to finding the Stones.

'Please take these and go and stand the other side of the doorway,' says Eoin, passing the box and the lantern from the table. Starling does as he is told.

Eoin sets the fragment on the table and takes out a pistol from a shoulder holster under his jacket. He holds the gun by the barrel and slams the butt of the pistol down onto the fragment.

A booming sound envelops them, so loud that the walls shake. The fragment sparks furiously and streaks of blue lightning snake up and across the cell.

Eoin hurries outside and closes the door. They both peer through the small window. Starling watches the fragment shake angrily, lightning sparks and surrounds the table and dry smoke fills his nostrils as the blue flames begin to consume it. In seconds the table is reduced to ash. The fragment lies among the remains, its unearthly blue light dulling to a low throb until it stops and goes out.

Starling swallows. He thinks about the dream he had with a thousands voices calling out in terror. His mind swims. *Many must die for the world to change.* Where had he heard this?

'If that is what can happen with a fragment, then what are the Stones capable of?' asks Starling.

'The Stones are a weapon capable of causing mass destruction. If VIPER find them, the world will be in a lot of trouble.'

'They won't find them.'

'What makes you so sure?'

'The notebook is the key to finding them. They don't not have it. We do.'

'You're correct.' Eoin re-enters the cell and places the fragment back in the box, which he places back in the hole. He slides the flagstone on top, then covers the area with dust and ash. Locking the cell, he takes the lantern and leads Starling back via a different route.

'The fragment belonged to Tim Chittlock. Tim was a good friend of mine, a clever man, considered a crackpot by many in the service. He was a scientist, but he also believed in mysticism and magic. The Stones of Fire was a pet project of his. He was certain they were hidden somewhere in this country. Tim became convinced he was being watched and followed. In our job, paranoia comes with the territory, but Tim believed he was on to something. Something bigger than all of us. Something more dangerous.'

'The Stones of Fire?'

'Yes. I didn't believe him at first – until he showed me what the fragment could do. I was shocked, but still I did not believe that the Stones would present any danger if they could be found. He told me about the Fellowship of Fire, a secret society who guard the Stones. I thought it was more nonsense, but when the agents of VIPER started snooping around, I knew something was wrong.'

They stop at the end of a passageway, blocked by a bricked-up wall, where the acrid smell of soot claws at Starling's nostrils and throat.

Eoin continues, 'Tim hid the fragment in the cell and disappeared for days. We were used to him doing this because he was often hidden away researching and experimenting. Then one day he called me. He sounded erratic and hysterical and I did not know what to make of it. He said they had found him and he was in terrible danger. He was frantic. I had never heard him talk like that. I rushed to his home and found him. He had been tortured and was barely alive. I knew it was VIPER – I recognised their handiwork. He held on to me and told me he had given his notebook to the Fellowship for protection. VIPER had forced this information out of him. And then he said, "Help him…" "Who?" I asked. "Among them is a sleeper… Help him." He died moments later without saying any more.'

'I'm sorry your friend died.'

'I'm sorry too,' says Eoin. 'Tim had a man working within VIPER. He is our only hope and I believe only he can crack the codes in the notebook and find the Stones.'

Starling's mouth dries. 'Do you know who he is?'

Eoin ignores the question and takes something from his pocket. It is wrapped in pale linen. He unfolds the material and reveals the notebook. 'I'm leaving for London immediately. I'd like you to take this and look after it.'

Starling takes the notebook and stares at it, relieved to have it in his hands again yet overwhelmed at the secrets it contains. The thought of the Stones and the damage they can cause terrifies him. He wonders about the Fellowship and how they fit in this expanding spider's web. Timothy Chittlock clearly trusted them. But why?

How could anyone trust an organisation with someone like the Pastor as a member?

Eoin turns towards the wall, pulls out a loose brick and peers through to the other side. He pulls a metal catch above his shoulder and the wall turns inwards. Starling is surprised to see the Great Hall on the other side. They are in the fireplace.

'Whoever killed Tim did not get what they wanted. I told you Tim was clever. He was always one step ahead of us, and them. Somehow he managed to plant a spy in the Agents of VIPER camp: a double agent training to be one of them and learning all their secrets. This person patiently and calmly waited to carry out his mission. People like this are known as sleepers. Tim's double agent would be an unknown, someone outside the norm. Someone whom no one would suspect. Who better than a young man such as yourself?'

Starling feels his muscles coil. 'What do you mean?'

'I think that person is you, Starling. I think that you are Tim's sleeper.'

Chapter 20

The Siege

That evening Starling is lying on top of his bunk, basking in the warm yellow glow from his bedside lamp. His mind is racing. Eoin's theory that he is a sleeper agent turns over and over in his mind. It seems preposterous, but it would explain his fighting and shooting abilities. He wonders about his family – if he even has one – and if they know who he is, or where he is for that matter.

Edward stirs in his bunk. He could do with someone to talk to right now, even if it is Edward, but seconds later his roommate snores quietly.

Starling sighs and thinks about the fragment, the Stones of Fire and their disturbing ethereal power. He is still not entirely sure what to make of it all. But seeing what the fragment is capable of has made him think there is more in this world than he thought possible, which is both exciting and terrifying. Because of the notebook there have been three deaths already and, if Eoin is right, and VIPER get the notebook and Stones, there will be many more deaths to come. He looks at the notebook resting on the bedside table. The location of the Stones is hidden somewhere in the coded text. For a moment he thinks he should destroy the book, burn it to ash so that no one will ever find the Stones. But what if someone already knows where they are? What if they find the Stones and sell them to VIPER? His gut twists at the thought and then something clicks inside him and he realises what he must do.

For the next few hours he pores over the text, trying to decipher the codes. He scrawls on sheets of paper and places them on the floor, rearranging them into some sort of order.

Wrapped up in the job at hand, he does not hear Edward rising, nor does he realise his roommate is standing behind him studying the sheets of paper and trying to unravel the mystery code.

'Move the top sheet two to the right and then move sheet four to the bottom and then—' says Edward.

Starling jumps and spins round. 'What are you doing?' he snaps.

Edward jolts. 'I… I was just trying to help.'

Starling stares at him for a moment and then looks back at the papers. This was taking him a long time and he didn't seem to be getting very far. What harm would it do to have a second pair of eyes?

'I'm sorry, Edward. I didn't mean to shout. I could really do with some help.'

Edward shrugs, crouches down and begins rearranging the sheets.

'Look at the code. It has a rhythm. Do you see it?'

Starling studies the lines and begins to see a repetition of some symbols. But that is all he can see.

'It could be a prayer,' says Edward, tapping his head. 'Or a poem.'

Edward smiles.

'What is it?'

'It's a song.'

'A what?'

'A song.'

Starling frowns, not quite believing him. Edward begins writing on one of the sheets while humming a tune. Starling recognises it immediately.

Oranges and lemons,
Say the bells of St Clement's.
You owe me five farthings,
Say the bells of St Martin's.
When will you pay me?
Say the bells of Old Bailey.
When I grow rich,
Say the bells of Shoreditch.
When will that be?
Say the bells of Stepney.
I do not know,
Says the great bell of Bow.

Starling stares at the words on the sheet. It's the tune from his dream only two nights back. Of course. That's it! He rubs the back of his neck, trying to imagine what its relevance could be.

There is a knock on the door. Starling opens it. Violet is standing in the doorway. 'Hello handsome,' she says.

'Erm… hello.'

'There's a telephone call for you in the Major's office.'

Starling's eyes flash. It could be Eoin. He glances back at Edward. 'Keep at it. I'll be back soon.'

At the Major's office he stops outside and knocks twice.

'Come,' she calls.

The Major is sitting at her desk and talking into the phone. 'Yes… yes… of course,' she says, her face grey and solemn. She looks up at Starling. 'He's here now, Eoin. Would you like to speak to him?' She hands the phone across.

'Hello…' says Starling.

But there is no answer.

'Eoin… It's me.' Silence. And then Starling can hear voices shouting, followed by gunfire. His grip on the phone tightens. 'Eoin! Eoin! Can you hear me?' he shouts.

Eoin does not respond. There is more gunfire and, in the distance, a great bell chimes. Starling has heard it many times before. It's Big Ben.

Starling looks at the Major. Her face has clouded over.

'What did he say?' asks Starling, his stomach a storm of knots.

'He has discovered more about your past and believes the school, and you especially, are in great danger. He says we have to get *it* out of here immediately. They are coming. They might even be here already.'

'Who are *they*?'

'That remains to be seen. Eoin requested I take you away from here immediately.' The Major opens one of the drawers in her desk, takes out a revolver and starts filling it with bullets. 'Do not worry about Eoin, Mr Starling. He is a remarkable man. Now, would you like to explain to me what this is all about?'

But Starling is only half listening. Through the window he can see shadows moving quickly across the school grounds. He feels the hairs on his neck rising. Something is not right. And then he hears the sound of glass breaking from the direction of the Great Hall. It is followed by several gunshots. Someone screams.

The Major's eyes widen. 'Good Lord, he was right. They're here!'

Starling feels himself go cold. He has left the notebook unprotected with Edward. He runs to the door and pulls it open.

'Starling, wait!' calls the Major, but he is already out of the office and sprinting towards the Great Hall.

Smoke is beginning to fill the area. Several gunshots ring out and he hears more screaming and shouting. He can see several canisters strewn across the floor with smoke billowing furiously from them. Pulling a handkerchief from his pocket, he covers his mouth and nose, hears voices and looks in their direction. Through the haze he sees Anna and Violet fighting a man with a gas mask covering his face. In one hand he holds a torch; in the other, a pistol. The smoke is getting the better of Anna and Violet. Starling can see they are weakening. A shot rings out. Violet stumbles into the smoke and Anna falls to her knees coughing. The man in the mask looms over her, his pistol pointing at her head.

A surge of anger grips Starling. He charges forward, stiffening his muscles in preparation for maximum impact. The man does not see him coming. Starling hits him full pelt in the ribs. The gunman grunts as the air expels from his lungs as if from a burst tyre. He topples back, dropping the torch as Starling falls to his knees and gasps. Violet is lying on the floor with a bloody chest; her lifeless eyes stare blankly into the smoke. He scrambles back and collides with someone.

'Violet. Is that you?' says Anna.

Starling's heart pounds in his chest.

The gunfire starts again from all sides of the Great Hall. Picking up the discarded torch, and stuffing it in his pocket, Starling ducks and grabs Anna's hand. 'Come with me!' he says, pulling her across the smoke-filled room. She resists.

'Anna, it's me, Starling!'

'Violet!' she calls, ignoring him.

Starling has lost the handkerchief in the charge and covers his mouth and nose with his arm, his eyes stinging and streaming.

'We have to go!' shouts Starling, and hauls her to a halt beside the fireplace. He hears the voices of other students arriving in the hall and hopes they are armed. Groping the wall above the chimney breast, he searches for the unlocking mechanism. He pushes and fumbles blindly for what seems like an age until eventually something clicks. The wall inside the fireplace opens.

They stumble through. Starling presses the closing mechanism. The wall starts to close agonisingly slowly. As it does, Starling sees emerging through the smoke a figure carrying a sniper's rifle. It is not a masked attacker; it's one of resident students.

Horne.

'Get out of here, Horne!' cries Starling, coughing.

Horne looks around him, searching to pinpoint the location of Starling's voice.

'Run, Horne!'

Horne raises the rifle and swings it across the room.

The wall slides shut. Starling hears the sound of rapid gunfire and wonders if Horne has killed someone or has been killed himself. But something niggles at him. Why was Horne not shooting at the masked men?

Starling and Anna stand for a moment coughing and wiping their eyes, listening to the gunfire on the other side of the wall.

'What's happening?' asks Anna.

'The school is under attack.'

'By whom?'

'I don't know yet.'

'How did you know about this place?'

'It's a long story.'

'I have to go back out. Violet is still out there.'

'Anna, we have to leave.'

'Not without Violet!'

'We can't go back out there.'

'Open the door!'

'It's too late!'

'What are you talking about?'

'We should just go.'

'Not without Violet!'

'She's dead, Anna!'

There is a stillness in the air between them; the only sounds are the muffled blasts from the other side of the fireplace.

'She… she can't be. We were just… You're lying!'

'I'm sorry, Anna. I wish I was. But you must trust me. If you want to live, then come with me.'

Anna says nothing for a moment.

'Who did this?'

'I think it's VIPER… Please, come with me.'

Anna says nothing.

'Fine! Stay here then.' Starling points the torchlight down the passage and glances at Anna. In the briefest of seconds he sees the grief on Anna's face transform to a cold determination.

'We should hurry,' he says.

Thankfully, Anna allows him to lead her away through the underground tunnel. He tries to get his bearings and takes them up a stairwell that he hopes runs up the west turret. Through the walls, he can hear more gunfire and explosions and feels sick with guilt that he is not helping.

He stops at the top of the stairs, places his ear against the wall and listens. There is nothing. He shines the beam on the unlocking mechanism and pushes it. There is a creaking sound and a portion of the wall opens. He peers cautiously up and down. They are in the men's bathroom. The light is bright and it smells of stale, damp towels.

They climb through the opening and run down to Starling and Edward's room. He stops at the bedroom door and listens. There is silence. He peeks inside. Edward is huddled in the corner, trembling, his face pale. Starling looks around him. There is no one else there. Breathing a sigh of relief he grabs the papers, stuffing them into the fireplace and lighting them with a match. He takes off the Beaulieu blazer, puts on his old one and slips the notebook into his side pocket. Looking at Edward he says. 'We have to get out of here.'

But Edward shakes his head. Starling walks toward him and speaks calmly. 'If you stay here, you will almost certainly die.'

The sound of gunfire is drawing closer but still Edward does not budge.

'Edward, come with me. I will keep you safe, I promise,' says Starling, even though he knows it is a promise he may not be able to keep.

Anna takes Edward's hand. 'It'll be fine, Eddie. Just come with us.'

Edward trembles and then nods his head slowly.

Starling glances out of the bedroom door. Smoke is rising from the west turret stairs. Their only choice is to run in the opposite direction. They hurry up the corridor. He hears a shot and a bullet embeds itself in the stone inches from his head. He turns to see a man, broad and well-built with dark hair, emerging from the smoke, his face obscured with a gas mask. Starling has seen him before. He feels his mouth drying. It is Colonel Victor Frost.

Chapter 21

Exploding Rats

Frost points his gun at Starling but the billowing smoke obscures his aim. Starling wastes no time. This is their only chance.

'Run!' he shouts.

Bullets fly in their wake. Turning a corner, a window looks out over the grounds where the moon shimmers on bodies lying near the garage. He is unsure if they are students, teachers or the enemy. He catches sight of the vivid green turban of Mr Singh. He is brandishing a pistol in each hand, shooting without conscience at two masked men. Starling feels a glimmer of hope as he sprints up the corridor.

They turn a second corner and his heart sinks. It's a dead end. Spinning round he sees Frost and two other men in masks. Frost removes his mask and stares cold and hard at him.

'Give me the notebook, Starling,' he says.

'Sing for it,' replies Starling, his hackles rising.

Frost smiles calmly. 'Kill them,' he says to his companions. The two men raise their guns. Starling steps in front of Anna and Edward, shielding them. He has to think fast. 'Wait. I'll give you what you want. You don't need to hurt them.'

'How good of you to give me that option.'

Starling feels a draught and hears a ticking sound from the floor. Two small clockwork rats scuttle from either side of his legs towards the three men. They are the low-impact explosives type. Enough for a diversion. He throws himself back as they explode, narrowly missing a volley of gunfire.

'Will, this way,' says a voice to his left. He turns to see a narrow opening in the wall that Anna and Edward have already entered. Eli is standing just inside. Starling leaps into the passageway and slams the door shut behind him.

He hears Frost's guttural voice. 'You cannot escape me, Will. Not now. Not ever.'

Starling feels his blood run cold.

Eli is holding a lantern. It lights the dark space with a dim, shadowy light.

'You need to get far away from here,' he says. 'Take Miss Wilder and Edward, too. Go to the garage – a driver is waiting for you in Eoin's Embiricos. There is a radio in the boot. It is charged and ready. Once you're safe, send out the distress call, "*The birds have flown the nest*". Let us know where you are and we will find you. Got that?'

'Yes. But what about you?'

'Never mind me. I can look after meself.'

Eli pulls some coins from his pocket and hands them across.

Starling frowns.

'Just in case. There should be enough here to tide you over for a day or two.'

Frost and his men are battering at the entrance to the escape route.

'I'll hold off our friends. Follow the stairs all the way down. Mr Singh will cover you.'

Starling removes the torch from his pocket and switches it on. 'Good luck, Eli.'

The old poacher smiles. 'You might find something useful in the back of my old van, if you have time to look.'

'Thank you,' he replies, although he's not sure what he means by that.

'Mind how you go, now.'

As the pounding increases, Starling hurries down the stairs with Edward and Anna behind him. Around them, on the other side of the walls, he can hear the sound of shouting and gunfire. He hears the Major barking orders and then a rally of gunshots. He hopes they all come out of this alive. Then, suddenly, they reach a stone wall at the bottom of the passageway stairs – it seems they can go no further. He shines the torchlight over the wall, searching for the unlocking mechanism. But it is just stones and nothing else. He starts pushing them randomly and is joined by Anna and Edward who follow his lead. At last something clicks. The wall opens under their collective weight and they fall out into the path of an armed man wearing a mask. Edward stands up and backs away. The man raises his gun.

'No!' cries Edward, and then a shot drowns out his voice.

Starling's heart pounds.

'Edward!' he calls, but Edward is still standing. The masked man falls to his knees and crumples forward on to the ground. Behind him, Starling sees Mr Singh approaching with his guns pointing at the man. Mr Singh kicks the body, confirming he is dead and then looks towards to the garage where the Embiricos and the old Post Office van are parked.

'The driver is dead,' he says.

Starling sees the bloodied body of the driver at the entrance to the garage. In his hand are the car keys. Starling glances at the Embiricos and back at the keys.

'I can drive,' he says.

'Go. I will cover you.'

Starling turns to Edward and Anna. 'Wait here, both of you!'

'Ready?' says Mr Singh.

'Ready,' replies Starling, running furiously toward the garage. Bullets pelt the gravel in his wake as he snatches the keys from the dead man's hand, dives inside and rolls across the floor between the Embiricos and Eli's van. Panting, he lies low for a second. He crawls to the rear of Eli's van, curious about what he meant by *something useful*. Inside are a stack of rat bombs. He grabs four of them and tosses them into the Embiricos.

He jumps into the driver's seat and starts up the engine. It rumbles into life like a growling lion. Slipping it into gear, he accelerates and speeds out of the garage, swerving in the gravel to stop beside Anna and Edward. Bullets prang off the bodywork, much to his relief. They might just get out of here alive. He leans across and pushes open the passenger door. 'Get in!' he shouts.

They clamber inside. Edward squeezes himself into the back and lies down for cover. 'There's rats in here!' he cries.

'Go now, quickly!' Mr Singh shouts. Starling glances in the side mirror and sees him face off three gunmen who are running towards them.

Anna pulls the door closed and Starling slams the accelerator and speeds away from the house and on into the night.

He throttles the Embiricos through the dark country lanes, his hands gripping the steering wheel, his concentration firmly on the road ahead. He's not sure where they are going but he knows he has to get far away from Beaulieu. His pulse is racing; blood pounds in his ears, drowning out the barrage of questions from Anna and Edward.

He knows Frost's cars will follow them soon enough. They must keep going, but to where? Think. Think. Of course! There is only one place. He glances at the petrol gauge, sees it is almost empty and swears under his breath.

'What's the time?'

'Starling, tell me what is going on?' demands Anna.

'Who were those people?' Edward stutters.

'The time… what time is it? Now!' asks Starling, raising his voice, his patience thinning fast.

There is a pause, and Edward speaks. 'Forty minutes past nine.'

Starling nods. 'We have time.'

'For what?' says Anna.

The road widens, clear in the light of the half moon. Starling spins the wheel, tossing his passengers to the side as the Embiricos skids and faces the direction they have just come. In the distance, he can see the outline of Beaulieu. The west turret is on fire and smoke is billowing from other parts of the house.

They say nothing for a moment. Then Edward breaks the silence. 'Do you think they are all dead?'

'I hope not,' replies Starling. 'But we can't worry about that now.' Part of him regrets not staying to fight but he knows it is too dangerous. The notebook would be in the hands of the enemy, and he, Anna and Edward would also be dead.

He sees the beams of three cars leaving Beaulieu and driving quickly in the direction he had driven. Taking three deep breaths, he rolls the car forward into the shadows of a small copse and switches off the growling engine.

'Get down, you two,' he says, and slides down the seat himself.

With hooded eyes, peeking over the dashboard, Starling watches three Austin 8s fly past. He breathes a sigh of relief but freezes as he hears the screech of brakes. From the side mirror he sees the rear lights of the last car as it stops dead in the middle of the road. He holds his breath and waits. The door opens and a man gets out and peers in their direction through a pair of binoculars.

They have been spotted.

Starling closes his eyes in an effort to think. What can he do? And then he remembers. 'Edward, pass me two rats.'

Edward hands them across and Starling turns the clockwork keys just as the man jumps back into his car.

He starts up the Embiricos and drives out of the copse. Opening the driver's door, he places the rats on the ground, their wheels carrying them obediently toward the car that is now reversing towards them.

Starling pushes his foot down on the accelerator and, through the rear-view mirror, watches with a measure of satisfaction as the rats explode under the car, causing it to swerve off the road. The three men escape, shaken, and stumble onto the road, coughing.

'Where are we going?' asks Anna.

'We're going to catch a train.'

Chapter 22

The 9.59 to London

'It doesn't look like we're being followed,' says Anna, as they approach Brockenhurst.

Starling glances in the wing mirror and sees darkness behind him.

'Let's not get ahead of ourselves. There may be other VIPER agents in town,' he replies.

'Oh God!' says Edward.

'We need to get out of sight,' says Will, worried that the Embiricos' roaring engine and sleek styling is making them stand out when they should be out of sight. Driving cautiously towards the train station, he parks off the road in a concealed spot, a short distance away. There are a handful of people, none of whom are looking suspiciously their way – yet he knows that could all change in a moment if VIPER emerge from the shadows.

'Hurry,' he urges, opening the driver's door. 'Edward, grab the other two rats. Just in case.'

Edward's face pales as he lifts them tentatively, as if they might suddenly explode.

Starling opens the boot. Inside is a small suitcase containing the radio, which is much heavier than it looks. There is also a shoulder bag made from battered brown leather. He fishes it out, pulls the strap across his shoulder and puts the rats gently into the bag. He closes the boot, locks the car doors and rests his hand on its warm bonnet, caressing it. He does not want to leave it, but they have no choice. He reaches for the radio, but Anna beats him to it.

'It's heavy,' says Starling.

Anna's right eyebrow arches. 'You think because I am female, I can't carry a radio?'

'Erm... no,' says Starling, 'that's not what I meant... Sorry.'

'Good,' she replies, tartly.

Starling shrugs and leads Anna and Edward towards Brockenhurst Station.

'What's the plan?' asks Anna.

'We go to London.'

'Why London?'

'Eoin is there for a start. And the churches mentioned in "Oranges and Lemons" are there.'

'"Oranges and Lemons"?' asks Anna.

'I'll explain later,' he replies, stepping into the station office. Anna follows.

Edward remains rooted, his hands wringing. 'We should stay here and wait for a rescue party.'

'Edward, we had a lucky escape,' says Starling. 'Those men are looking for us and will be here very soon. By the time a rescue party arrives, we will be dead.'

'You don't know that!' snaps Edward.

'I'm not prepared to risk it!'

Edward trembles in silence.

Starling takes a breath and tries to remain calm. 'We are going to London, Edward. You are not staying behind.'

Anna speaks up. 'Will's right, Eddie. We have to get out of here.'

Edward fidgets with his blazer. 'I can't... I... I'm not going to London and that's that.'

'They will kill you like they did the others,' says Anna.

A whistle blows. 'Last train to London,' calls the guard.

Starling glances at the station clock. It is 9.59. In the near distance, he hears the sound of speeding cars approaching. 'They're coming!' He tries to grab Edward's arm but Edward pulls away and bolts toward the station exit.

Anna drops the radio and runs after him, but he is gone.

'There is nothing we can do, Anna. We have to go, now!'

She rounds on him, her eyes wild and furious as if this is all his fault. He turns away and looks toward the platform. 'Stay if you want to!' he says, picking up the case, but Anna takes it from him and together they run towards the train.

'You're too late, you're too late,' the guard shouts, his arms out blocking their path, but they push past and sprint to the door of the last carriage. Starling is first and pulls it open. Anna climbs up, heaving the radio with her.

Starling watches as Frost and his men run onto the platform. The train rolls forward gaining speed. Steam billows down the platform and through it he can see a furious Frost, baring his teeth and running ahead of the others;

but he is not fast enough, and skids to a stop as the train hurries away from Brockenhurst. Starling can just make out Frost's angry face melding into the swirling steam and breathes a sigh of relief. Sitting down he wonders where Edward is and hopes he has the sense to hide long enough to survive this.

The train rumbles into the night. The carriage is quiet, with only a handful of occupants huddled together and whispering, who glance suspiciously at Starling and Anna. Starling is mindful and keeps an eye on them as he explains as much as he can about the notebook, the Stones of Fire, his memory loss and what has happened to him.

For a while, Anna does not say anything. She ponders what Starling has just told her. Eventually, she breaks the silence. 'Do you believe the Stones can create fire?'

Starling wants to tell her about the fragment, but the less everyone knows the better for now.

'No,' he says, avoiding her eyes. 'But some people do and are prepared to kill for them.'

'It's clearly some sort of silly myth,' she says. 'Essentially stone is composed of grains of minerals arranged in an orderly manner. The aggregate minerals forming the rock are held together by chemical bonds, none of which, to my knowledge, are combustible or can create fire. Unless…' She pauses.

'Unless what?'

'Unless the stone is flint. Even then, you would need a piece of steel and all that could be achieved is a spark.'

Starling understands the supernatural mythology of the Stones is hard to swallow. He tries to smile at Anna's logical explanation, although he is impressed with her scientific knowledge.

They sit in silence for a moment before Anna breaks it. 'At Beaulieu you could shoot and fight better than any of the other students. Where did you learn to do that?'

He shifts uneasily in his chair. 'I told you I lost my memory. I… I don't know.'

Anna watches him through narrowed eyes.

Does she think he is an enemy spy?

After a moment she shrugs. 'If the Major and Eoin trust you, then I suppose I do too.'

'Forget that for now. We need a plan for London. We're not out of the woods yet.'

'Agreed. We could just make our way to Baker Street,' she says.

'No. That is what they will expect us to do.'

'Then what do you propose?'

Starling sits forward and Anna leans closer to hear what he has to say.

-

It is almost midnight when the train approaches Victoria. In line with blackout restrictions, all carriage lights are switched off. In the bright moonlight, the London skyline fills Starling with a mixture of emotions just like it did on *The Outcast*. He feels excited, as if he is somehow returning home, even though he has no memories of the city beyond waking up on *The Outcast* four days ago. But like then, he has other things to think about now – other concerns lie ahead. All that matters now is finding the Stones before VIPER do.

The other passengers begin to gather their belongings and make their way to the aisle outside the carriage as they prepare for the train to stop.

Starling and Anna stand by the doors that face away from the platform. As the train slows Starling pushes open the door. 'Good luck,' he says to Anna.

'Thanks.'

She steps to the open door and jumps, landing with the grace of a cat on the walkway between the tracks. She springs up immediately and runs alongside the train, her arms open. Starling tosses the suitcase in her direction. She catches it, but it slides from her grip and falls on to the track opposite. Starling's heart sinks.

'Please don't be broken,' he whispers in a quiet prayer.

The train comes to a stop and Starling follows the other passengers onto the platform, mingling among them as if he was a member of one of the families. He scans the platform for anyone suspicious, but it is dark, which is in his favour.

He spots four male silhouettes at the entrance to the concourse. One of them greets a passenger with a handshake and another opens his arms to a woman who runs enthusiastically toward him.

The other two men remain watchful. With his head down, Starling walks with the other passengers, quickening his pace as he sees one of the men pointing in his direction. Both men turn and start navigating the crowd as if tailing him.

Starling dashes ahead and, with relief, sees Anna hurry out of sight and onto Victoria Street. Cheered by the knowledge that their plan to split up is so far successful, he turns and runs across the main concourse.

He steers a course away from Anna through a corridor, which is thankfully empty. Starling sprints down it, winding up a rat bomb at the same time. He hears the echoing footfalls of the men behind him, stops and turns to face them, his heart pounding in his chest.

'Do you know what this is?' he shouts, waving the rat. The men slow and do not respond, but he knows they are wary. 'Don't think I won't use it.'

One of them laughs and reaches into his pocket, but Starling tosses the rat and runs. There is a gunshot and he ducks as a bullet chips the wall to his left. The rat explodes and a cloud of dust and masonry follows him out of the tunnel and onto the street outside. Wilton Street. He coughs and runs towards Victoria Street where he hears Anna's voice. She is sitting in the back of a black cab. He jumps inside.

The driver, a bulldog of a man, stares at the smoky corridor. 'Was that a bomb?' he says.

'I think so,' says Starling, coughing, his mouth dry with the smoke and dust.

'You was lucky, mate. Blimey, we get no peace here. Where to?'

Starling has not thought about that. Where could they go? They need somewhere that is close and remote enough to use the radio without attracting attention. He thinks hard, and recalls a place hidden deep in the folds of his memory. 'Primrose Hill, please.'

'Primrose Hill it is,' says the driver.

Starling glances back at the corridor. There is no sign of the men. He is relieved, but also terrified. Had he just killed them?

Chapter 23

Primrose Hill

The cab driver takes them up Regent's Park Road and pulls over. Starling pays the man, gets out and waits until the cab is out of sight.

'How do you know this place?' asks Anna.

Starling rubs his neck. 'I don't remember how – I just do.' He recalls Skipper's story about his friend who had lost his memory. The poor man had not recognised family or friends, yet he knew the town where he had lived all his life. It was as if a layer in his mind containing all the people he knew and loved had been taken from him forever. He had gone mad in the end. The thought of suffering a similar fate terrifies him.

'Why here?' asks Anna.

'The hill will provide us a clear, open space where we can operate the radio without interruption. We should be safe here for the time being. Once we get a signal out, we should know what to do next.'

They trek across the darkness and settle on a secluded spot at the top of the hill under the protection of some bushes. Sitting on the damp grass, he takes out the torch and shines its beam at the suitcase. The radio is neatly built inside. Just like the one at Beaulieu, it has a large rectangular power pack and a panel with dials and buttons, which operate the transmitter and the receiver. There is a compartment that holds the headphones, and strapped inside the suitcase lid is the user manual. Switching on the radio, he turns the dial and listens for a signal, but there is nothing.

After a few minutes of turning the dial he says, 'I think it's broken,'

'I'm sorry I dropped it.'

'It was my stupid idea to throw it off the train. I should have taken it with me.'

'It wasn't stupid. You would never have got away from those men if you were carrying it.'

She edges closer and Starling can feel the heat from her body. It feels strange having her so close, the same person who was so dismissive of him, but he likes it.

Focusing on the radio, he removes the headphones, reaches for the manual and starts paging through it for clues. There is a diagram of the chassis, which he recognises from Radio Operations class. Unclipping the transceiver panel, he places it on the grass and shines the beam into the chassis. The power connector is in place and the fuses are all seated. The scale lamps are intact and the earthing leads are in place. So what is the problem? He leans forward for a closer look and peers in through the gap that houses the power connections.

'There's a loose wire,' says Anna, her head almost touching his.

'Got it,' he smiles, his fingers reaching through the gap. The solder holding the power supply wires to the chassis is broken.

'Give me the torch,' says Anna, taking it from him and pointing the beam inside the chassis.

Reaching into his sleeve, Starling removes the wire cutters from his blazer, cuts the wire and wraps it round the broken solder, reconnecting the power supply.

'Fingers crossed, that will do it,' he says.

He switches the radio on but there is still no response. He turns dials and knobs and pushes the 'On/Off' button several times. Anna regards him quizzically.

'Maybe the power supply is flat,' she offers.

'Perhaps, although Eli had told me it was charged.'

'I have an idea,' says Anna.

Before he can respond, she lifts her hand and slaps the side of the radio. To their surprise and relief, it trembles and sparks into life.

Starling and Anna smile at each other as he turns the tuning dial. The sound of white noise and static crackles through the headphones. Relief sweeps over him.

'Well done, Starling.'

'How is your Morse code?'

'As good as anyone's,' she says, and confidently reaches for the radio. She looks at Starling. 'The birds have flown the nest?'

'That's what Eli said.'

Starling watches transfixed as Anna puts on the headphones and starts pressing the telegraph key. After a moment he closes his eyes and takes three deep breaths. At last, they might get out of this mess.

Almost two hours pass with no luck. They huddle together to keep warm as Anna continues tapping the distress call at intervals, her free hand poised with a pencil and paper, ready to write down instructions.

Starling is concerned the battery may not last much longer and is about to think of a back-up plan when Anna looks up.

'They've heard us.'

'At last! What do they say?'

There is a pause and then Anna begins scribbling on the paper.

.... . / ... .- ..-. . /.... — ..- ... . / .—- ... – / .- – ... – ... . .-.
.-.... -. . / ... – .- ... – / .–.... .. – . -.-..... .- .– ... -..

None of it means anything to Starling. 'What does it say?'

'The safe house 13 Abberline Street Whitechapel. Do you know Whitechapel?'

Starling shakes his head. 'No, but I will get us there somehow. We should wait until morning. Those men, if they are still alive, may be looking for us. There may be others too. At least during the day we can blend in with the crowds.'

–

Anna lies down to try and get some rest. Starling does not intend to sleep, and he does not want to worry Anna. As the hours pass, his fertile imagination makes him think VIPER had seen him get into the taxi and tracked down the driver, who told them Starling and Anna were sitting all alone on top of Primrose Hill. They could be on their way here right now. He shakes his head and pushes the thought from his head.

He looks at the text in the notebook under the torchlight, hoping to unravel some clues.

'Do you really think the Stones are in London?' says Anna.

'I think so.'

'You don't seem very sure.'

'I could be wrong, but it just seems the right place to start, considering Edward's translation of "Oranges and Lemons".' Starling pockets the notebook and switches off the torch. He can feel Anna appraising him. Perhaps she thinks he is mad.

'We should get some rest. It will be dawn soon. I'll keep watch,' he says, rubbing his hands to keep them warm.

As he sits in the silence before dawn, the gravity of their situation plays on his mind. The siege of Beaulieu was horrific. His stomach clenches at the image of Violet lying dead in the Great Hall. And what of Edward, Eli, the Major, Mr Singh and the others? Were they dead? He does not want to contemplate that. This was all because of the notebook and the Stones. The responsibility for finding them is now down to him. Wasn't it always, he thinks, hugging his knees tight to his chest. And what has happened to Eoin? He might be the only person to have uncovered information about Starling's past. Was he dead too? Was he gone forever and, with him, the keys to Starling's memories that he so wanted back?

'Are you alright?' whispers Anna, interrupting his thoughts.

Starling looks in her direction. She is sitting up and looking back at him with a concerned expression.

'I'm fine,' he lies, but the truth is he is terrified. He is a stranger in his own body, caught up in a quest to find a terrible weapon in the middle of a world at war. How did this ever happen? He wants to pour it all out to her, but the sound of bird song shows that dawn has snuck on up them. The first rays of the sun dapple through the gaps in the bushes and lifts his spirit. They still have a chance to get through this, but first they have to find the safe house. Starling does not know Whitechapel, and finding Abberline Street might be tricky.

'We should go,' he says.

Anna nods in agreement.

Starling heaves up his cold and stiff limbs, straightens his tie, and combs his hair into a side parting with his fingers.

'Best we don't look as if we have been sleeping in the bushes all night.'

Anna begins to brush off the grass and twigs from his clothes. She takes a comb from her pocket and sweeps it through Starling's hair. She fixes his tie properly.

'That's better,' she says, stepping back and combing her own shiny brown hair.

Starling feels a little flush inside and smiles.

Anna smiles back and pockets her comb.

Together they walk out of the bushes and into the open space of Primrose Hill where, through the whitebeam trees, they can see the city of London waking up and beginning a new day.

Starling looks east, in the direction of Whitechapel, which is a long walk from where they are standing. 'We should go. We can take turns carrying the radio,' he says.

They leave Primrose Hill and walk onto Regent's Park Road. It is still very early and the only signs of life are the blackout blinds being drawn from the windows of early risers.

They walk to Camden Town and into the tube station, where early commuters are beginning their journeys to work. With the last of their money they buy two single tickets to Whitechapel.

The train pulls into the platform and Starling sees their reflection in the carriage windows. His picture has been in the newspapers and the Beaulieu crest on Anna's breast pocket is an unusual feature. They both stand out.

'We need a change of clothes,' he says.

The train stops; the guard alights and cranks open the doors.

'They keep all sorts of supplies, including clothes, in safe houses,' says Anna.

'Good,' says Starling, relieved there will be one less thing to worry about.

The guard blows his whistle and hops quickly onto the train, cranking the doors shut as Starling and Anna huddle among the throng.

'We have no clue where Abberline Street is. If only we had a map.'

'Leave that to me,' says Anna, who turns and threads her way through the commuters.

Starling watches as she talks to the guard, her face warm and smiling, a different person from the one she usually reveals.

'What did you say to him?'

'I asked him where the nearest library was. We can get a map there.'

Chapter 24

The Safe House

Friday, 9th May 1941

The guard has directed them to Bishopsgate Library. Starling thinks the library an odd building, resembling a narrow castle, sandwiched in between two equally narrow but much less grand blocks of flats.

A thin balding librarian nods curtly to them as they enter. His eyes linger on the crest of Anna's blazer. Does he recognise the criss-crossed pistols and dagger? Starling feels a fluttering sensation in his stomach and considers leaving, but the librarian looks away casually and starts putting books onto the shelves. Starling relaxes and decides that he is just being paranoid.

No one else gives them a second glance as they make their way to the shelves of maps. They could be students visiting the library for a day of study, or so Starling hopes.

The reference area is quiet and warm with the familiar and welcoming smell of dry and dusty books. Starling wastes no time and quickly finds the *London A-to-Z*. Anna keeps a lookout, ensuring no one is watching, and shields him as he shoves it into the bag.

'Got it?' she says.

'Yes.'

Starling sees a sign for Ancient History books and has an idea.

'Let's go,' says Anna.

'Not yet.'

A man's voice interrupts their exchange. 'May I help you young people.'

The librarian is standing beside them. Up close, Starling takes stock of him. He is dressed in a brown tweed suit and wears a garish yellow bow tie.

'We're looking for Greek mythology.'

The librarian narrows his gaze at Starling and points to their left.

'Thank you,' says Starling, looking away, hoping the man's prolonged look was not down to recognising him from the newspapers.

He starts to scan the bookshelf labelled Mythology, unsure what he is hoping to find. He hears someone approach and feels his muscles tensing.

'Have you travelled far?' asks the librarian.

'Yes. We're from St Luke's,' says Anna, quick off the mark.

'St Luke's? I can't say I've heard of it.'

'It's in Wimbledon,' she says.

'Yes, Wimbledon,' says Starling.

'Oh, well, I don't know that area very well.'

'Where can I find books on the Restoration?' says Anna, changing the subject.

The librarian hesitates before answering. 'This way, if you please. The subject is a speciality of mine, actually.'

'Oh, that's nice.'

Starling listens to their voices fade and then starts pulling books on Greek mythology from the shelves. He leafs through them, scanning their contents for clues. Ten minutes pass, then twenty, but he finds nothing of value. From the other side of the library, he feels Anna staring at him and he looks up.

'We should go,' she mouths.

She is right, of course. They are wasting valuable time and besides, he is unsettled by the librarian, who is still hovering around. Starling nods and starts putting the books back. He sees one shelf labelled Greek Gods. Suddenly he feels dizzy; something begins to unravel in his head, and he tries to push through the folds of his mind.

Think… think… come on! Something dating back years – something from biblical times and something long before that.

Confusion clouds his thoughts and he steadies himself against the shelf. His fingers brush against a book called *Greeks Gods and the Thracians*. Something sparks inside of him. That's it! He makes sure no one is watching and slips the book inside the bag next to the *A to Z*.

He finds Anna pretending to browse the shelves. He catches her eye and nods. They leave quickly and hurry up Bishopsgate Road, with their heads down.

'Something came to me in the library. A memory of something I once knew, but it was patchy with little to hook onto. I think it is something to do with the Stones being inlaid in Moses' Breastplate of Judgement. And there was also suggestion the Stones could be of Greek origin. I found a book that might hold some answers.'

-

Using the *A to Z*, Starling and Anna find their way to Abberline Street, a dingy little road tucked away in the dark recesses of Whitechapel, where it seems the sun rarely shines, if ever. Damp and slippery cobbles make for slow and difficult progress. The houses are rundown Victorian tenements from which come the sound of mothers at the end of their tether, and babies crying for attention and food. A skinny boy with a dirty face and grave expression watches them approach. He reminds Starling of Sam. Starling smiles to himself and wonders where Sam is.

'Number thirteen,' says Anna, pointing.

It is dark inside, but Starling could swear he caught sight of movement.

'Someone is inside.'

'Yes, I saw.'

'We should let them know we are here,' he says, stepping forward and knocking the door. From the other side, he hears the sound of footsteps on a wooden floor, the clicking turn of the lock and the sliding of a heavy bolt. The door swings open and a stout woman in a headscarf and housecoat stands in the doorway. ''Allo dears,' she says. 'I've been expecting you.'

She glances quickly up and down the street and then beckons them inside. 'In you pop.'

Starling follows Anna into a dimly lit hallway, their feet echoing on the bare floorboards. He notices there is no ornamentation or decoration inside that might reveal it as the entrance hall to someone's home. If anything it feels empty and cold.

The woman locks and bolts the door. 'You took your time,' she says.

'Who are you?' asks Starling.

'You can call me Aunty. Everyone does.' She smiles at them with crooked and chipped teeth.

The smell of something savoury drifts down from the kitchen at the rear of the house and Starling realises how very hungry he is.

'I've just made some tea and cooked a spot of lunch,' says Aunty. 'I expect you're hungry.'

'Yes, thank you,' says Anna.

'Let's get you sorted, then.'

There is a steaming pot of something bubbling away on the cooker. A transistor radio broadcasts Gracie Fields singing 'Wish me luck', which Aunty starts to sing tunelessly along to. In contrast to what they have seen of the house so far, the kitchen is warm and cosy. Starling sees a pistol and a box of bullets lying on a small table and exchanges nervous glances with Anna.

'Sorry, dears, force of habit leaving that lying around,' says Aunty, noticing. She puts the pistol and bullets into a drawer. 'You just never know who might pop by,' she quips. 'Now, sit down and I'll serve up lunch.'

Starling notices an unpleasant underlying odour that is only just masked by whatever is cooking in the pot. He looks at Anna, who glances at Aunty, and back to Starling with a questioning expression. Starling shrugs; he is as confused as she is. He turns to Aunty. 'How did you know we were coming?'

'I heard about the attack at Beaulieu and then caught your distress call. I responded and sent you this address.'

'Do you work for the Secret Service?' asks Anna.

'That's right, dear.'

'What happens now?' asks Starling.

'We sit tight and wait for someone to come and pick you up.'

'How long will that take?'

'I couldn't say. We are in a spot of bother as you know.'

'Have you heard from Eoin, or the Major?'

'Nothing yet. Best we just sit tight and wait.'

Aunty serves up greasy corned beef fritters with bread and dripping and three mugs of strong tea. Starling's growing anxiety about Eoin dampens his appetite, but nevertheless he eats, knowing he needs to keep his strength up. Despite its appearance, the meal is delicious.

Chapter 25

The Trapdoor

Starling sits next to Anna at the kitchen table, reading the book on Greek mythology.

'Listen to this,' he says. 'The Greek god of war, Ares, was given a stone of great power by his lover, Aphrodite. It was known as the Firestone and was a jewel of the finest blue sapphire. It was embedded into his shield – when struck in battle, the jewel would emit a fierce lightning and strike down his foes. Many died horrible deaths. Eventually, Ares was slain in battle by the spear of Diomedes. The same spear was used to destroy the Firestone. Only it didn't destroy the Firestone, it merely shattered it into twelve different-coloured rocks.'

Starling opens the notebook and turns to a page depicting a map of the Mediterranean. There is thick grey line charting the journey from Greece to Egypt. 'If the notebook is correct, these same rocks might somehow have shown up in Egypt many years later.'

He flicks through the pages of the notebook and stops at the sketch of the high priest, Aaron. 'There are twelve rocks on Aaron's breastplate of judgement, which some believe had a *divine* power. Seems a strange coincidence.'

'It all seems to be so far-fetched,' says Anna.

'I thought so too, but I have seen a fragment of these rocks and felt its power.'

'But you said you didn't believe they could cause fire.'

Guilt swarms through Starling. 'I'm sorry. I just thought the less people know the better.'

'People! Don't you trust me, Starling?'

'Yes, of course I do!'

Starling is unsure if Anna is angry or hurt that he held this information back.

'We are in this together now, Starling. It's my life on the line too. No more secrets, no more lies. Promise me?'

'I promise.'

He meets her gaze and holds it, and for the first time feels affection for her.

She smiles. 'Tell me more.'

Starling feels excitement building. 'Perhaps the Firestone was destroyed, but the rocks together can still wield their power.'

'So whoever unites the Stones will have divine God-like power,' says Anna.

'That's correct.'

'And if someone strikes them, that unfortunate person will be destroyed?'

'That's the theory.'

'What if… what if they are in London and a bomb falls on the Stones?'

Anna's question shifts something from the hidden recesses of Starling's mind. A memory opens in the blink of an eye. He feels a tightness in his throat, as if it is being squeezed. He swallows, but he knows – he understands now. 'The city will be destroyed. The war will end. All will be lost and VIPER will control the Stones.'

Anna pales. 'This is all so difficult to… swallow.' She stands up and folds her arms. 'I might get some rest, if you don't mind.'

'Of course.'

Anna leaves. He hears her quiet footsteps making their way upstairs to the bedrooms.

It is dark outside and he estimates it must be around eight in the evening. He closes the books and wonders about VIPER. Was it their intention to see London destroyed before they claim the Stones? He wonders what the odds might be of a direct hit, but prefers not to do the maths.

A spider scuttles across the surface of the table and comes to a halt at the candlestick. The candlelight flickers, casting an amber glow around the kitchen.

There is still no word from the Service or Eoin; Starling feels his nerves tense again and drums his fingers on the tabletop. His instincts rattle him, and he wonders if Eoin is still alive or if he has been captured and killed.

The spider begins to form a web below the rim of the candlestick. Starling's thoughts whirl as he watches its unwavering determination. He sighs, stands up and begins pacing the kitchen, his concerns turning to the safe house and just how safe it is. Bored with his own company, he walks to the living room to speak with Aunty. Perhaps she knows more than she is saying.

She is sitting on an armchair looking through the grey-netted curtains at the empty street outside. Starling crosses the room, stands in the recess and watches the cobbled street too.

'How long have you known Eoin?' asks Starling.

'I've known him many years. He's a good man, considering his history.'

'What do you mean?'

'He's a rogue and a law unto himself. An ex-Fenian with a shady past, if you know what I mean.'

Starling frowns, but says nothing, unsure he even wants to know.

'The Prime Minister likes him and recruited him personally.'

'The Prime Minister?'

'Yes. Eoin has many years' experience behind him. He has skills that many people don't, and he is more useful in the fight against VIPER and the Nazis than against us.'

Starling's attention is drawn to a man in an overcoat, who is walking down Abberline Street and glancing at each house he passes. He slows as he approaches number thirteen but, much to Starling's relief, he walks on without looking up.

'Do you think he is dead?'

'I doubt that. He has the luck of the Irish, that one,' Aunty snorts.

The living-room door opens and Anna appears. She has changed into black brogues, a man's sweater and trousers, and she is holding a cloth cap.

'There are two men outside,' she says.

'Step away from the window, Starling!' demands Aunty, her voice grave.

Starling looks out and sees the man with the overcoat standing across the street. But he is not alone. There is another man with him, tall and broad with a thick black moustache: Colonel Frost.

'Time for you to go,' whispers Aunty.

His muscles tightening, Starling eases quietly away from the window and stands by Aunty, who is on her feet and ready.

'Into the kitchen. Quickly!' She ushers them both out of the living room.

The candle has melted and the last of the light is flickering to its end. Starling blows it out as Aunty pushes the kitchen table across the floor. As Starling's eyes adjust to the gloom, he can see a trapdoor where the table had been.

'Gather your things and climb down here,' says Aunty.

Starling grabs his shoulder bag and takes out the last remaining rat bomb.

'I'll have that,' says Aunty.

Starling does not argue and hands it across.

Stuffing the notebook into his blazer pocket, he hears the clicking sound of a lock being tampered with. He glances towards the front of the house, his heart racing, then quickly pulls up the trap door. A waft of something putrid almost makes him gag. That would account for the smell that hung around the kitchen. There is a small ladder leading into a pit of darkness.

'What's that smell?'

'Never mind,' says Aunty. 'The tunnel will take you to Plumbers Row. Find a place to hide and watch for me. I will meet you there later.'

'Aunty—' Starling protests but his words are cut off by the crack of a gunshot, once, then twice. The door is being kicked and forced open.

'Quickly!' says Aunty.

Anna pulls on her cap and tucks her hair inside before climbing down.

The crashing on the front door increases.

'Go!' hisses Aunty.

Starling starts to climb down the ladder. Its rungs are damp under his fingers and rough with rust and time. He stops for a moment, looking back at Aunty, whose brow is shiny with perspiration.

'If I don't make it call Baker Street on this number.' She hands him a small piece of paper and a purse full of coins.

Starling's brow furrows.

'Tell them the safe house has been compromised. They will get you to safety.'

'But…'

'Don't look back. Just keep going,' she says and closes the trapdoor. Starling can feel the vibration as the table and chairs slide back into place. He hears the ticking of the rat bomb, followed by Aunty swearing at her opponents at the top of her voice. There is an explosion followed by a rally of gunfire, and Aunty's voice is no longer shouting.

Chapter 26

The Tunnel

The ladder wobbles and dust sprinkles from the trapdoor, coating Starling's fringe, eyelashes and lips. He lowers himself down, takes the torch from his pocket and switches it on. The tunnel is narrow, damp and earthy and makes him think of an unfilled grave. He wipes his mouth and eyes with the sleeve of his blazer, coughing and almost gagging. The smell is horrible – as if they are standing in a pit of rotten eggs.

'Aunty?' asks Anna, clearly alarmed about the explosion.

Starling shakes his head. 'I don't know.'

For a moment they say nothing, neither wanting to acknowledge what might have happened.

'She'll be fine,' says Anna.

'Of course she will.'

'What is that smell?'

'I don't know. Let's just get out of here.'

They follow the light of the torch through the tunnel. There seems to be no end to it.

Out of the corners of his eyes, Starling sees movement on the walls. It makes the hairs on the back of his neck stand on end. He hears a scuttling sound and in the torchlight sees the glint of hundreds of small black eyes staring back at them.

Rats!

Not clockwork ones, but real rats. Starling can't breathe, an inexplicable fear grips him, and he stops. He feels Anna bump into him.

'Starling, what's the matter?'

His head begins to swim and a memory stirs: he is cold and locked in a cell. Rats rain from a hole in the ceiling. He is being tested.

'Starling?' Anna's voice shakes him from his fugue.

He swallows, edges away from the walls and tries to focus on the route ahead. Something brushes against his feet and then tiny sharp claws began climbing his trousers, pulling at the fabric. He grimaces and bats his trousers with the back of his hand. The rat squeaks in protest.

'What was that?' asks Anna.

'Nothing. We're nearly there.'

'The walls are moving!' says Anna. 'Oh my God, it's rats!'

'They won't harm you. Just keep moving,' says Starling – a little unconvincingly, he thinks.

The smell is getting worse. He steps on something soft, which crunches and squeals under his feet. His stomach lurches. There are rats on the ground, crowding and shuffling around their ankles. The smell is stronger; he gags and then retches. The passage walls begin moving with increasing intensity; the squeaking grows louder as every rodent warns about the intruders.

Starling arches forward and throws up. At his feet several vomit-covered rats feast off what had been his lunch. He shakes, unable to move. On each of his shoulders is a rodent scratching his face, reaching for his mouth and whatever sustenance it might bring them. There are others climbing his legs. He must not let this beat him. With three deep breaths, he pulls the rodents from him, tossing them aside. Anna brushes them off her sweater and seems more in control.

'We have to run,' says Starling. 'Just run as fast as you can.'

Starling points the torch into the distance and runs up the tunnel, ignoring the crunching and squealing underneath his feet.

Ahead he sees a ladder similar to the one under the Abberline Street trapdoor. They hurry toward it with the rats in their wake. Starling hands Anna the torch. 'I'll check it's clear first,' he says. She points the narrow beam at the ladder and he climbs up to the top, where he discovers a manhole cover.

'Switch off the light.'

The tunnel is plunged into darkness. Starling pushes against the heavy steel. The ladder wobbles precariously with the effort but, after a moment, the cover gives and Starling peeks outside.

The night air is cool and fresh compared to the horrible stench of the tunnel.

Plumbers Row is a cobbled street full of bombed and burned-out buildings. Rubble is scattered everywhere. Much to Starling's relief, it seems to be deserted. Pushing the manhole cover aside, he climbs out and peers down into darkness.

'It's clear,' he whispers.

His eyes sweep the area as he pulls Anna up. At one end of Plumbers Row is a solitary building, still standing amidst the dereliction. A large sign outside reads 'Whitechapel Bell Foundry'. It has survived the bombs, and perhaps its luck will rub off on them if they hide there and wait for Aunty.

The side entrance to the foundry has a wooden gate bolted and secured with an oversized padlock that takes Starling a few moments to pick open. Behind the gate is the foundry yard, where a huge unfinished bell hangs from scaffolding. On each level of the scaffolding is a platform leading to a balcony with access to the main building. They hurry up the steps to the top platform and a doorway leading to the third floor. The door is unlocked and he steps cautiously into a large room, which is some sort of workshop that smells of ashes and metal. On one side is an oven full of tables covered with various tools and screws. One squat, arched window with dirty glass has a cricket ball-sized hole in it. Through the hole, he can see along the length of Plumbers Row back towards the tunnel. It is the perfect spot to sit, watch and wait.

Moments pass slowly until finally the manhole cover shifts. Huddled together, cheek to cheek, Starling and Anna peer through the small hole in the glass. A broad figure emerges from the ground.

But something is not quite right.

'No...' whispers Anna.

It is not Aunty.

It is Frost.

Chapter 27

The Bell Foundry

Anna backs away and Starling too retreats from the window, allowing himself enough distance to watch Frost without being seen. Aunty must be dead. Frost is scanning the area. He looks in the direction of the bell foundry, first at the gate and then up to the window where Starling stands rooted to the spot.

Starling swallows, but does not move.

Despite the darkness, Starling swears he can see Frost smile as he walks towards the entrance to the yard.

Starling looks around for an escape route, but there is none. The only way out is the way they came in. He has to think. He goes out onto the platform and, over the top of the bell, he sees the gate opening. They are done for. Hurrying back inside he scans the tables for a weapon. Anna has picked up a hammer. But using tools as weapons against guns won't help them for long. Starling has an idea. It seems stupid and dangerous but what choice do they have? He picks up some of the heaviest screws.

'Do you have a handkerchief?' he asks.

Anna produces one from her sleeve. Starling takes it and begins tearing it up. He whispers the plan and, to his surprise, she agrees. She looks at him and smiles, almost fearlessly.

'Easy.'

Her confidence spurs him on and they slip cautiously out onto the scaffolding platform. He can see Frost below with a pistol in his hand, searching the yard. Starling tosses the screws into the air and they scatter across the ground. Frost spins on his feet pointing his pistol first in one direction then another.

Starling signals to Anna and she moves across to the other side of platform behind the bell. The platform boards creak and Starling sees Frost looking up in their direction. Frost begins climbing the steps, his pistol pointing towards them. Starling dips back into the shadows and waits.

It is only moments, but it seems like forever before Starling hears Frost approach, his large frame moving cautiously across the platform.

Hiding in the darkness of the workshop, Starling holds his breath. Frost stops at the platform entrance, his gun, a Browning automatic, raised and pointing inside.

Starling readies himself but Frost glances to his right. For a moment Starling thinks Anna has blown their cover, but then it comes: the thunderous clang of the bell slammed by the hammer. The air vibrates and the platform trembles as Frost covers his ears. Starling springs from the shadows, charging towards him. The bell rings again and Frost, searching for the bell ringer, does not anticipate the force of Starling as he slams hard into him, driving him to the edge of the platform. The Browning slips from his grasp and clatters against surface of the bell as it falls.

Starling tries to pull back but he is too far forward, his upper body hovering dangerously over the precipice. Frost starts to fall but quickly grabs Starling's arm and pulls him onto the rough metal of the bell. Together they tumble down, Frost squeezing Starling's neck and snarling like an animal.

They hit the lip of the bell, topple over and crash to the ground. Choking and winded, Starling lands on top of Frost whose grip has loosened. Starling acts fast, lifting his fist ready to slam into Frost's face, but the Colonel's head is turned sideways, his eyes closed. For a moment Starling thinks he is dead, but he can see his chest moving.

Starling sees the Browning across the yard. Scrambling off Frost he races toward the gun and swings around, pointing the pistol back at his slumped form. Frost remains unconscious, eyes closed. Starling hears Anna running down the steps.

'Are you hurt?'

He is bruised and sore, but otherwise alright. 'I'm fine,' he says, and allows himself to be helped by Anna out of the bell foundry. They both remove the small pieces of torn handkerchief they had used to protect their ears.

-

As they make their way down Whitechapel Road, Starling checks that they are not being followed, his hand firmly on the gun in his trouser pocket, his eyes wary of passers-by who, thankfully, do not give them a second look. His head is muddled with the events of the evening. They have been lucky again, he thinks. He wonders just how much longer their luck will hold out.

A red double-decker bus pulls up at a nearby stop. Starling has no idea where it is going, but it will take them away from the Bell Foundry and Frost, who could wake at any moment. They board the bus and sit together upstairs.

'How are you feeling?' asks Anna.

Starling does not want to admit he is terrified, confused, and that all he wants is for this nightmare to end. He takes three deep breaths and lets the warmth of the bus calm him. 'Better,' he says.

Anna squeezes his hand and Starling is grateful – so grateful – not to be alone.

They sit in silence as the bus makes its way into central London. They are on Oxford Street.

'Let's get out here,' says Starling. 'Soho will be busy so we can lose ourselves in the crowd.'

They walk down Dean Street and stop at a café selling Italian coffee. He checks the coins Aunty gave him. There's enough to get some sustenance and later make a call to Baker Street.

Inside the café, American jazz, laughter and cigarette smoke greet them. The people – who seem artistic types, 'the bohemian set' he has somewhere heard about – are relaxed and having fun. The contrast to Starling's life over the past few days makes his head spin. It is like a different world.

No one bats an eye at the two young people who have just walked in or seems to notice the curious bulge of the Browning in Starling's blazer pocket. Anna finds an empty table in the corner away from the door. An enthusiastic waiter with a shock of dark curly hair and a thick moustache wipes down their table.

'What can I get you?'

'Coffee,' says Anna.

'*Si.*'

'Coffee, please,' says Starling.

'*Si, si.* Very easy,' he laughs. 'Two coffees coming up.'

'Let me see the notebook, please.'

Starling takes it from his pocket and hands it across.

Anna flicks through the pages and opens at a sketch of a robed man holding a disc high above his head. He is standing on a mountaintop. A beam of light shines from the moon straight to the disc. She points at the disc.

'What this chap is holding is…' She flicks through the notebook and opens on a grainy photograph of a circular piece of metal with the constellations engraved upon it. '…is one of these.'

Starling studies the photograph of the disc. Like so many other things recently, it seems frustratingly familiar.

'I think it's an astrolabe,' explains Anna. 'It's a sort of tool used for determining the location of the sun and the planets and stars. My guess is the chap in the sketch is using his to find the Stones and I think this photograph is the one that will help us.'

Starling feels a surge of excitement. 'Anna, you are a genius! I know I have heard or read about astrolabes, but I can't think where.' He notices a poster on the wall opposite. It is in vivid colours and shows London's pre-war tourist sites. He narrows in on one particular building, an idea dawning. 'That's it,' he says.

'What?'

At that moment, the waiter arrives and places their coffees and some water on the table. '*Grazie*,' he says and leaves them again.

'I know where we can find one,' says Starling.

Chapter 28

The British Museum

Starling and Anna stand in the shadows of the British Museum's forecourt, looking around. He has been here before, but when? His mind swirls; he steadies himself as images flicker in his head like random scenes from a movie. Among the images are astrolabes. Focusing, he pushes through the storm that is his memory, further, deeper, until he eventually remembers: it was years ago, perhaps four, he was looking at them curiously, his hands and face pressed up against the glass of the display cabinet, wide like a glass coffin on legs. And there was a man watching him. A man he knows but cannot place. He concentrates on the memory.

'Do you know what these are?' the man says.

Starling shakes his head.

'They're astrolabes.'

Starling looks at them. There are several, some made from brass, some silver and some gold. On their faces are maps of the night sky and lots of symbols.

'What are they for?' he asks.

The man smiles conspiratorially. 'One day one of them will help you find a great treasure. One of them will set you free and give you what you most desire.'

Starling focuses on his memory of the man and tries to make out his features through the storm. He can see him now. He knows the face. The spectacles. It was…

Starling feels something squeeze his arm.

'Starling, you're miles away,' says Anna. 'What's wrong?'

He takes a breath and runs his fingers through his hair. 'It's nothing.'

But Starling had remembered. Four years ago that man had been little more than a stranger. He looked different then, too. Younger compared to the photo.

It was Timothy Chittlock.

Starling's mind reels with questions. Was Eoin right about him being Chittlock's sleeper? It had seemed a ludicrous suggestion, but Starling has come to understand that he was no ordinary sixteen-year-old. Chittlock had been laying a path for him. But why? And what did Chittlock mean when he said the Stones would give Starling what he most desired? And what of these feelings of grief and anger, which constantly haunt his darkest moments? Where do they stem from? Could they be why he became a sleeper? Finding the Stones seems the only way for him to get any answers. First things first, they must find the astrolabe.

'Starling?'

'I'm fine.'

He takes three deep breaths and looks at the front of the museum. It has been mercifully spared by the bombs, for the time being anyway. The rows of columns remain sturdy, though some are charred from blasts that had not quite hit the mark.

There is no one around. It is late and the museum is locked up for the night. They make their way to the front entrance where Starling examines the lock but finds it is too big and complex for his picks. They look for another entry point and skirt around to the east wing, darting behind the columns one at a time. He spots a tall sash window, its individual panes protected with anti-blast tape, almost six feet from the ground.

'This should do,' he says, wondering how they can get up there. But Anna already has the answer.

'Lift me onto your shoulders.'

Starling crouches underneath the window and Anna straddles his shoulders.

'I'm ready,' she says.

Starling pushes up. Anna is surprisingly light and within seconds she is off his shoulders and onto the windowsill.

He hears the crack of breaking glass and is grateful the anti-blast tape has prevented it shattering onto the floor inside. Moments later something falls on his head. It is a thick golden rope of the kind that might hold back a large curtain. He tests it; it seems secure. He looks up to see Anna beckoning him. He hauls himself up beside Anna.

The museum is vast, dark and empty as if… as if… everything is gone.

'This place looks like it's been cleared of exhibits,' says Anna.

A twinge of anxiety grips him. He hopes they are not wasting their time.

It makes sense, obviously. With London being bombed almost every night, why keep all that precious history on display, waiting for the next attack.

'Hopefully not everything,' says Starling.

'Do you remember where the astrolabes are?' says Anna.

'Unless they have been moved, they should be upstairs.'

Starling shines the torch down the main foyer. The narrow beam of light picks out the emptiness. It is spooky – more like a mausoleum than a museum. He leads them across the marble floor, their footsteps echoing in the cavernous hall.

Up the staircase and onto the first floor, he shines the beam into every corner. They run from room to room, opening and closing doors, but all they find is dust. Desperate, Starling hurries down to the ground floor, searching everywhere, opening gates and entering every possible room, but there is nothing. Absolutely nothing. He wants to cry out in frustration but instead kicks an old tin bucket that has been left behind by a cleaner. It clangs noisily across the room and Starling swears angrily under his breath.

They stand in silence for a moment thinking what to do next. Starling hears a creaking sound and then a door closing.

'Who's there?' calls a voice.

Starling flicks off the torch.

It is a man, old probably, judging by the gravelly tone. 'I have a weapon and I'll use it,' the man says.

Starling and Anna slip deeper into the shadows, crouching down out of sight. As his eyes adjust to the gloom, Starling watches a small, trembling figure of a man appear, looking all around him. Starling wonders who he is: a cleaner, a night watchman? No, he seems well dressed and has the look of an academic. Could he be the curator? If he is, what is he doing in a museum at this time of night with nothing to curate?

The old man is carrying an overcoat, which he clumsily pulls on before shuffling towards the main foyer, occasionally glancing back in their direction. Starling hears a heavy door opening. The sound of distant traffic floats into the museum from outside. Then the door is pulled shut, the heavy lock turns and all is silent.

'That was close,' says Anna.

Starling looks in the direction the curator had just come and makes his way cautiously toward it. Underneath a stairwell there is a doorway. He pulls the door open and discovers another wider stairwell leading down to a dark and windowless basement.

'What is this place?' says Anna.

'We'll soon find out.'

Satisfied there is no indication of anyone else being down here, Starling switches on the torch. The basement is, in fact, a large office with a bank of filing cabinets along one wall and, in front of them, a mahogany desk covered by a stack of papers. It is cool down here and Starling can feel a breeze. He points the beam towards it and sees another doorway on the opposite side of the room. He opens it.

Warm air blasts into his face and with it an age-old smell of dust, oil and iron. It is a familiar smell. He shines his torch into the darkness and sees another stairwell, this one leading down into the ground. He hears a familiar rumbling noise in the distance: a tube train. This doorway is the entrance to the Underground. But why have an entrance here of all places? And then he remembers. The British Museum had an underground station, closed for use in 1933, but still very much here. But what was it used for now? Starling's heartbeat quickens. He looks at Anna and smiles.

'I think we might have hit the jackpot.'

Chapter 29

The Astrolabe

Starling and Anna make their way down the stairwell and into the deserted Underground station. The stone steps are well-worn and lead to a circular tunnel lined with pale green tiles, that are grubby with age and neglect. The station's name is barely visible underneath the grime.

The passageway down to the platform is narrowed by hardwood boxes, filing cabinets and framed pictures draped in blankets. Starling hears the rumble of another train and a blast of air cools his face. At the end of the tunnel, fixed to the wall, is a grey metal box with a lever switch labelled Lights. He pulls the lever and for a moment it seems nothing will happen, but then there is a fizzing and crackling noise and, one by one, the lights along the platform come on.

'Wow,' says Starling, rubbing the back of his neck.

'Look at all this stuff,' says Anna.

It is like any other Underground station, except laid out on the platform and track is what seems like all the British Museum's exhibits. There are bookshelves, paintings, Egyptian statues, rows of sarcophagi and mummies. There are Greek statues, Roman busts, Japanese swords and armour, Viking helmets, swords and shields. Hundreds and thousands of years of world history all stored out of harm's way in a disused London Underground station.

This is the jackpot, thinks Starling, but not exactly the one he was hoping for. In here, somewhere, amongst all of this history, is a single astrolabe that he needs to find. A needle in a haystack. The thought of searching through all this stuff is daunting and he has no idea where to start. Lucky for them they have the whole night ahead, but he has the feeling that might not be long enough.

'This might be more difficult, than we think,' says Anna, rather stating the obvious.

Starling tries to get his bearings. He glances up and down the tunnel. 'I think this is the eastbound route,' he says.

'I can start here,' says Anna.

'I'll take the westbound and search the adjoining corridors and see what I can find.'

Anna smiles. 'Good luck.'

'Thanks. You too.'

'If I find anything I'll call you,' she says as he makes his way to the other platform.

After almost two hours of searching boxes, Starling's task is interrupted by a thudding sound from up above. The walls vibrate and the dust ripples like shifting sand. It is late, and he knows above them, in the skies, the Nazis are dropping bombs. He takes small comfort that they are safe underground and turns his attention to the rows of boxes ahead of him.

He spends another few hours rifling through crates stuffed with straw protecting jewellery, vases, pots, wooden tools, but there are no signs of the astrolabes.

And then he hears Anna's voice echoing through the tunnel. 'Starling, come quick!'

He runs to the eastbound platform. Anna is pulling a blanket from a display cabinet concealed behind four tall blue and white vases. Easing his way through, he sees the cabinet Chittlock had shown him four years earlier.

It contains the same astrolabes: two golden, one silver and three bronze, all the size of plates. But there is a smaller one, made from a dark metal. It is chipped, scorched and worn with age. It looks familiar. Starling opens the notebook and compares the photograph with the small dark astrolabe.

Engraved upon it are the planets and the constellations and, around its perimeter, are symbols: eyes, pyramids, scythes, swastikas, daggers and upturned crosses.

'It's the same one, isn't it?' says Anna.

Starling smiles. 'Yes. It's the one we are looking for.'

Chapter 30

Memories

The cabinet lock takes seconds to open. Starling lifts up the heavy glass lid and takes out the astrolabe. It is cool to the touch and heavier than he expected. He runs his fingers over the battered surface, feeling out the symbols as if they might provide some clue to what he should do with it.

'How old do you think it is?' says Anna.

'I don't know. As old as the Stones, I suppose.'

They say nothing for a moment, staring at it in awe. It is ancient and, judging by its scars, it has been through many wars.

The walls and ceiling tremble with the distant thudding of the night-time bombs.

'We should stay here until morning,' says Anna.

Starling nods and pulls two blankets from the exhibits.

They sit together on the platform, wrapped in the dusty blankets to keep themselves warm. At last the bombing stops. They pore over the notebook trying to figure out how the astrolabe works, but the etchings reveal nothing. Judging from the sketch of the man holding aloft the astrolabe, they both agree that for the astrolabe to work they must be high up a mountain, when the moon is full.

'London is a little short on mountains,' quips Anna.

Starling manages a smile, sighs and continues to flick through the notebook, stopping at a sketch of what looks like an elaborate Greek crucifix, inlaid with jewels. At its centre is a large eye. Starling wonders what relevance the crucifix has.

Anna yawns.

'Why don't you get some sleep? I can keep watch,' says Starling.

'I'll never sleep down here. It's a little creepy. Besides, we're doing this together, remember?'

Anna's words make him feel warm inside and he is so grateful she is with him. 'Together,' he says, and for a moment he wants to tell her how remarkable she is, how much he admires and likes her, but he can't quite muddle the words together. Instead, he manages, 'I'm sorry you got dragged into this.'

'It's what I signed up for.'

She removes the cap from her head and begins combing her fingers through her thick hair. 'I can keep watch if you want to get some sleep.'

'I'm with you. It's not the easiest of places to sleep.'

They say nothing for a moment and then Starling speaks. 'Tell me about you. How did you end up at Beaulieu?'

Anna looks away, staring into the middle distance. 'I was born in Paris. My father was British, and a writer; my mother was German, and an artist. They were Socialists, political activists who travelled across Europe waving the flag for Socialism. In 1934 we moved from Poland to live in Berlin. My parents were appalled at the rise of the Nazi Party in Germany. They thought they could help stop it but…' Anna stops talking for a moment, looks away and hugs her knees. '…During the Night of the Long Knives, they were taken from our home and marched outside to a dirty back street. I watched from my bedroom window. Mother, father and other members of the party were lined up and executed by the Secret Police.'

Starling swallows, unable to comprehend what it must have been like for young Anna to witness her parents' cold-blooded murder.

'I was put into care in a horrible place and treated no better than a stray dog. And then I was visited by a man. He was a friend of my father. He brought me back to England and put me into a boarding school and later he recruited me. Revenge for my parents. It was my duty, he told me. Who was I to argue? He had saved me, after all, and I had a lot to thank him for.'

'What was his name?'

'Chittlock. He was a teacher at the school, until recently.'

Starling feels a chill to the core. Revenge for her parents' death. His stomach is in knots, his head and heart mixed with emotions that he cannot make sense of. Something in what Anna says seems to ring true for him. Too deep and true for comfort. He doesn't want to search down this memory. It feels too painful.

'Do you hear that?' whispers Anna.

Starling can hear a light clattering of footsteps echoing from the passage leading to the eastbound platform. He looks in its direction and freezes.

Emerging from the tunnel is a man, dressed in a suit and trilby. The man comes to an abrupt halt and stands perfectly still, staring in shock at the two young people wrapped in blankets and sitting amongst hundreds of unboxed rare and valuable exhibits. 'They're here!' he shouts.

Chapter 31

The Chase

Saturday, 10th May 1941

Starling jumps up, stuffs the notebook and astrolabe into his blazer pocket and picks up Frost's Browning. He looks around for an escape route. There is only one.

'We'll have to go through the tunnel,' he says.

Anna nods, grabs the torch and hops onto a sarcophagus resting on the rail track. Starling follows and together they slide down to the track below. He glances back at the man who is navigating his way through the scattered exhibits. Anna puts on her cap and tucks her hair inside.

'That's my cover blown,' she says with a wry smile.

'Let's get out of here,' says Starling.

They hurry up the uneven, oily surface of the track into the tunnel where the darkness is absolute. Anna turns on the torch, its beam providing a small amount of light, enough to make their way up the track without tripping over.

Starling turns to see the man lowering himself onto the sarcophagus. A second man has joined him. They are both now carrying pistols.

'Run!'

A gunshot echoes through the tunnel, the bullet whistles past them.

'Get down!' says Starling.

Another bullet flies dangerously just over their heads. Anna turns off the torch. 'We're sitting targets with this light.'

Their eyes adjust to the gloom, and they stumble forward as quickly as they can. Starling crouches down as Anna runs ahead and points the Browning at the silhouetted figures hurrying up the track. The gun is heavy and he trembles, his stomach churning at the thought of what he is about to do. But what choice does he have? It is him and Anna against these men. There is only one choice. He aims the gun, squeezes the trigger and fires. The noise is deafening and the men throw themselves to the ground. Starling fires again and again, crying out in anger as he does so. The men do not move but, as far as he can tell, they are unharmed.

He hears them whispering, fires again three times, and then runs blindly after Anna. His foot slips on the oily surface and he falls, dropping the Browning, his face slamming against a rusty track. Winded and sore, he stands up, head spinning and hurries on.

'Are you all right?' says Anna.

'Yes,' he says, although his left cheekbone is throbbing.

The tunnel begins to vibrate and Starling sees lights flash by in the distance. There's a train coming. It is later in the morning than he'd thought.

Anna reaches out and holds his hand for support. It is warm and he squeezes it, but not too tightly.

Working together, they navigate the uneven slippery track.

He can hear the men behind them, but they don't seem to be gaining ground.

Starling can see they are approaching the end of the tunnel, which is blocked with a wire fence. His heart sinks, but suddenly he sees that there is a gap at the top, which they can squeeze through.

Starling hears a thud and then one of the men swears. He wonders if he has fallen.

He looks beyond the wire fence. There are lights shining in the adjoining tunnel that provide a small of amount of visibility. The track could be live. They will have to be mindful. He stands with his back to the fence and cups his hands into a footrest.

'Stay clear of the rails. This is probably a working track.'

Anna climbs up and over effortlessly, slipping through the gap in the wire. Starling pulls himself up and then looks up the lighted tunnel. He can see the platform ahead, like a porthole in the darkness, with commuters waiting for the next train.

'It's a live track,' says Anna, confirming his suspicions.

By his calculations, it has been a few minutes since the last train. That should give them enough time.

He exchanges looks with Anna, who seems to know exactly what he has in mind.

'Ready?' she says.

'Ready.'

They dash up the track as fast as they can, staying clear of the live rails. Starling glances behind, hoping the two men are nowhere near the fence yet.

They keep running but something is not quite right. It doesn't seem to be getting closer. A horrible thought occurs to him. He has made a terrible error. He swallows. In the depths of the underground, in the narrow dark tunnels, determining the distance of an endpoint accurately is more difficult than above ground. How could he be so stupid?

There is still no sign of a train. How long has it been since the last one? He estimates minutes, perhaps three, but that was wishful thinking. It was six minutes, maybe even more. That would mean… and then he hears it. The air trembles and the track vibrates. Starling's heart begins to pound.

Anna has heard the train and increases her pace. She is almost six feet ahead of him.

The train rumbles in the distance and spurs Starling on faster.

The weight of the astrolabe slams against his side; his arms are wide, pumping the air and providing the balance needed for the uneven surface.

The rumbling is now a rapid rattling of steel on steel, wheels racing over tracks. Starling glances behind him and sees the light of the train, small but growing. Its distance is impossible to determine. *Run. Just run.*

He can see Anna near the entrance to the platform. 'Hurry,' she shouts.

Starling can feel the train speeding toward them. He turns to see the driver's face. He is yawning and oblivious to the young people on the track ahead. Starling sprints forward toward the light, no longer a porthole but the entrance to Holborn station. He hears shouts from the commuters but ignores them. Anna has swung up to the platform, helped by some of the travellers. Starling can feel the wind of the oncoming train. He reaches for the edge of the platform but he is weak and tired and loses his grip.

'What the bloody hell are you two playin' at?' says a voice.

With his very last ounce of strength, he pulls himself onto the platform and lies on his back, gasping for breath as the train speeds into the station.

Chapter 32

The Lovebirds

As soon as Starling is able to stand, they run to the exit, ignoring the glares of disapproval from the people on the platform. Starling's heart thuds against his chest as if it is trying to beat its way out of the confines of his tired and sore body. With their heads down, and not enough money, they race through the turnstiles, passing a guard who shouts for their tickets.

Outside, the street is bustling. The morning air cools Starling's face as they hurry away from the station. Keep moving – they have to keep moving, but where should they go? Baker Street is the obvious choice, however, the agents of VIPER, or the Pastor, might be watching out for them. He looks west down High Holborn. He thinks they should just keep going until they come up with a place to in which to base themselves and then make the call to Baker Street.

Anna loops her arm in his as they cut across to Newton Street, which has seen the worst of the previous night's air raid. Dust and smoke choke the air. Firemen are hosing down the last of the flames.

A policeman, wearing a protective tin hat, is standing close by watching them work. Starling and Anna keep a low profile and pick their way over the rubble holding hands to keep each other steady. Anna's flat cap is pulled over her head with her hair tucked inside. Dressed like a boy and walking with a swagger, Starling has to check twice it is actually her and not some strange bloke.

''Ere! You two. Wot you doin' there?'

Starling's heart sinks. The policeman is beckoning them over.

'Come 'ere,' he says, frowning.

Starling and Anna exchange nervous glances and realise they are still holding hands while Anna is dressed as a young man. Anna's grip on Starling's hand loosens.

'Wot's keepin' ya?' says the copper.

They make their way toward him; Starling steadies his breathing and smiles warmly. 'Sorry constable, we were a little distracted.'

'Wot do you mean distracted? Wot you doing hanging about 'ere, holding hands like that? It ain't right!'

'I'm sorry, officer, we were—'

'Where's your gas masks?' he says, interrupting him.

'We lost them,' says Starling.

'You lost 'em!' said the policeman, his voice rising in pitch.

'No, we didn't, Tommy,' says Anna. 'We left them at home, remember?'

Starling glances at Anna; her eyebrows arch as she looks at him.

'Oh yes,' he says realising the ruse. 'We left them at home and we are just going back to get them now just in case a gas bomb explodes and—'

The officer points at Starling's blazer pocket. 'You forgot your gas masks but not those. Wot's in your pockets, then?'

'Just a book and… erm… nothing important.'

'I'll be the judge of that,' says the policeman, holding out his hand.

For a moment Starling thinks to run but they would never make it across the rubble, not the two of them. He hands across the notebook and astrolabe and considers how to knock the policeman out without attracting attention.

The policeman leafs through the notebook and glances suspiciously at Starling and Anna. He then examines the astrolabe. 'Wot's this then?' he says, holding it up.

'Erm… It's for a project I'm working on,' says Starling.

'What sort of project?' says the policeman, studying the astrolabe with interest. 'It looks old, as if it should be in a museum.'

'I don't know about that,' says Starling, with a nervous laugh. His hand curls into a fist and at that same time he hears sniffing. He turns to see Anna holding her cap in her hands, head bowed, shoulders shaking.

'Blimey,' says the policeman, 'he's a girl!'

The policeman looks at Starling, his eyes wide.

Starling shrugs.

'Wot's the matter?'

'We're on our way to hospital to visit my grandfather,' says Anna. 'His street was all but destroyed in the air raid. He was one of the few survivors, but they don't reckon he has all that long… to go.' Anna starts sobbing, takes out a handkerchief and wipes real tears from her eyes. Starling puts his arms around her shoulders and wonders how she can do that.

'Oh my word,' says the policeman, handing the astrolabe and notebook back. 'You should have said sooner.'

The policeman's gaze lingers on Starling for a little longer than is comfortable. 'Do I know you?' he asks, with a frown.

'No, sir, I don't believe we have met.' Starling looks away and tries to sound as polite as he can. 'We should really get going.'

'Yes, you two lovebirds get off to the hospital and see the old fella.'

Lovebirds?

Starling smiles and notices Anna blushing. Starling pretends he did not hear what the policeman said.

They thank him and then hurry off across the rubble, but Starling can still feel him watching them. His face is obviously still familiar from the newspapers. Could the police still be looking for him? He doesn't want to think about it. They were lucky to get past this copper, who has clearly not been paying attention to the papers. They may not be so lucky next time.

'We need to find a telephone box. Aunty gave me the Baker Street code.'

Anna seems quiet and he wonders if the lovebirds comment has bothered her. Without saying much they search the streets and eventually find a phone box on Charing Cross Road.

Starling drops the remaining pennies into the slot and dials the operator.

'Operator, how may I help you?'

'Baker Street 0764.'

'Putting you through.'

The phone rings for a few moments and is answered by a man's voice. 'Hello.'

Starling hesitates before answering. The voice seems familiar, but he cannot be certain. He glances at Anna, who is scanning the area, checking they are not being watched.

'The safe house has been compromised. Aunty is dead.'

There is silence for a moment.

'Who is this?'

'My name is Will Starling. I'm with Anna Wilder. We are agents from Beaulieu. We need to come in.'

'Where are you, Starling?'

'Charing Cross Road.'

'Find somewhere quiet and out of the way. I will come and find you.'

'What's your name?'

'Dalton.'

The name echoes at the back of his mind and niggles.

'Where can I find you, Starling?'

Starling sweeps his hand through his hair, thinking, and then remembers the perfect place. 'Fenchurch Street. There is a disused bus repair yard. You can find us there.'

'Good. Stay out sight and I will find you.'

Starling places the receiver down and frowns. *Dalton. Why does that name sound familiar?*

Chapter 33

Fire and Brimstone

They make their way to Fenchurch Street, then up the alley, and stand at the tall wooden doors, the entrance to the yard. There is no one around, and it is strangely quiet. The hatch is ajar, which seems odd.

Starling pushes it open.

The place looks just the same as when he left it, with the old bus, home for Kitty and her gang, and the makeshift table covered in the previous night's haul of food. It is deathly quiet. Starling feels a fluttering in his stomach. There is no one here.

'Hello!' he calls, his voice echoes unanswered.

Anna walks ahead of him. 'Hello!'

But there is no response.

And then Starling hears a yelp from inside the bus. He holds his breath and looks at Anna, who returns his gaze. Something is wrong. They both know it.

They walk towards the bus and Starling pulls the red velvet curtain across. Inside, the cushions are torn and strewn across the floor. He sees a lone shoe amongst them, then the person it belongs to lying flat out on the floor, eyes closed and nose bloody. It is the freckled boy with the machete, which he still grips firmly in his hand. His chest is moving – he is still alive.

He sees Kitty sitting nearby him. She is hugging her knees and trembling, her eyes red raw with tears.

Then he sees Sam.

He is shaking, his eyes wide with fear, a golf ball-sized bruise on his jaw. A black-gloved hand holds his forehead back and a long thin blade lies against his exposed throat.

'Hello. I knew you'd come back,' says the Pastor, in clipped tones.

Starling feels his spine icing over. 'Let him go.'

'Come, come. First things first. You know what I want.'

Starling levels his gaze with the Pastor's dark, soulless eyes. They flash for a moment and Starling could swear they turn red as the blade of his white knife presses into Sam's flesh. A droplet of blood rolls down the boy's neck.

Starling feels a rising rage but fights to keep calm. 'Let him go.'

'The notebook.' says the Pastor, firmly.

'The notebook is nothing. It has served its purpose. I have the Stones. I can give them to you,' he lies.

The Pastor appraises him. 'Show them to me.'

'They're not here.'

The Pastor sighs.

'Why do you want them?' asks Starling, trying to buy some time before Dalton arrives.

'Show them to me,' replies the Pastor.

Starling's skin prickles. How long can he delay him? 'Why do you want something that is clearly an instrument of the devil? Is he your god now? Is it Satan you worship?'

The Pastor's eyes flare and bore into Starling's. He has rattled him.

'There is no shame, Pastor. Satan holds all the power, after all.'

The Pastor chuckles darkly. 'Young man, you have quite the tongue. I shall enjoy cutting it from your mouth.'

'You will never have that opportunity.'

The Pastor shakes Sam. 'Show me the Stones.'

'I told you, I don't have them with me.'

The Pastor tugs roughly at Sam's head and presses the blade further into his flesh. Sam whimpers as more blood gathers beneath it and flows like a red tear down his neck.

Starling steps forward, his hands raised. 'No... wait... I can take you to them.'

'You're lying,' growls the Pastor.

'If you kill him, you will not see me or the Stones.'

'You will not escape me, boy.'

'Do not underestimate me, Pastor.'

'Do not underestimate *me*, boy.'

Starling stands firm and feels Anna close by. Then, out of the corner of his eye, he sees the freckled boy move. Is he awake? Starling's gaze remains on the Pastor's cold eyes.

And then he hears a hard thud. The Pastor's face contorts in pain as the freckled boy slams the machete into his shin. Starling lunges for the Pastor's knife hand, grabbing his wrist until it bends backward to breaking point. Anna surges forward and launches her fist hard at his temple. The Pastor stumbles back, the knife slipping from his grasp. Anna kicks it across the floor and out of the bus.

Sam crawls toward Kitty, who has not moved.

Starling turns to Kitty, Sam and the freckled boy. 'Get out of here!' he shouts.

They scuttle from the bus without hesitation.

Adrenalin pumps through Starling's body. His rage surges forward, and with Skipper's murder and the threat to Sam at the forefront of his mind, he slams his fists without conscience. The Pastor falls back to the floor with Starling on top of him thrashing him repeatedly. A black cloud darkens Starling's mind; he cannot stop.

The Pastor lies still, but Starling rages on.

Anna touches Starling's shoulder. 'That's enough, Starling. He's finished.'

The Pastor's eyes are closed, his lips and nose bloody.

Starling is panting, his heart pumping like an out-of-control steam train. A primal urge sweeps through him – old, savage and unrecognisable. Kill him, finish him, his instincts tell him. Looking down, he sees the Pastor's bloodied lips part in a smile, his teeth tinged red, his hollow black eyes giving him the appearance of a sinister and mad clown. Some fragment of humanity makes Starling pause. And as he does, the Pastor's hands reach for Starling's throat and squeeze tightly.

'He will be tormented with fire and brimstone in the presence of the holy angels and in the presence of the Lamb…'

Starling tries to pull the hands away, but the grip is firm.

'…And the smoke of their torment goes up forever and ever; and they have no rest day and night, those who worship the beast and his image, and whoever receives the mark of his name.'

The Pastor gets to his feet, holding Starling by the throat as if he is a lifeless dummy.

Anna runs at the Pastor but he pushes Starling forward, using him like a battering ram. Starling can feel Anna behind him, her hands reaching in vain for the Pastor as he pushes them both hard against the side of the bus. Anna cries out in pain and slides to the floor.

Starling claws at the Pastor's face, kicking hard at his legs, but it seems to have no effect. It is as if he is immune to pain. The Pastor carries him across the room and slams him into the bus windows. Starling's body crunches painfully against the glass, which cracks on impact. He can't focus, his head begins to spin and darkness beckons. The Pastor laughs and tosses him across the inside of the bus. A window shatters, Starling falls to the ground; fragments of glass fall on top of him, cutting his hands and face. Pain sears through his body; he groans, powerless and weak as the Pastor straddles him and grips his throat, squeezing the breath from him.

Parts of Starling's life, a life lost in the mists of his memory flash before him: a terrible loss – the murder of his family. He cannot remember their faces but he feels the gaping loss. Something in his soul has died and at the core of his heart is the need for vengeance. Tears prick the back of his eyes.

The Pastor squeezes tighter. Starling chokes and gasps for breath, his face burning and rushing with blood. It is all about to end. When he dies, the Pastor will kill Anna, Sam, Kitty and the other lost children.

He cannot let that happen.

Starling's arms thrash on the floor, his hands searching for something, anything. The Pastor stares down at him, waiting for that final second when Starling's life will leave his eyes.

The darkness is getting closer. *No. No. Not like this.* Starling's fingers brush the edge of something sharp, a thick shard of glass. He shuffles it into his palm, squeezing hard on the edges and slicing open his skin.

His vision is blurring. With a final ounce of strength he plunges the shard blindly at the Pastor. The Pastor screams and his grip on Starling's neck loosens. He gasps for breath, coughing uncontrollably, his lungs filling gloriously with air. Scrambling back, he pushes himself quickly into a standing position, but his head is light and he is unsteady on his feet.

The Pastor is on his knees crying and trembling, his hands hovering over the shard that is lodged in his right eye. Starling grimaces and skirts around him leaning on the side of the bus for support.

Anna is clutching her side, her face ashen. Dizzy and in pain, Starling helps her up and they stumble out of the bus. Starlings sucks in the cool refreshing air. The Pastor screams once more. Starling shudders and follows Anna through the hatch in the gates. Together they run down the alleyway towards Fenchurch Street.

Chapter 34

The Greek Cross

Running down Fenchurch Street, Starling catches sight of a green Humber parked at the side of the road. Resting against it is a red faced and panting Sam. He is talking to a man with slicked back blond hair, dressed in a dark blue suit. Kitty and the freckled face boy are nowhere to be seen.

The man watches Starling and Anna approach.

'Sam?' says Starling, narrowing his gaze at the man in the suit.

The man interjects, 'Will Starling?'

'Dalton?'

The man nods and smiles thinly.

'We have to get out of here quickly,' says Starling, glancing back in the direction of the yard. There is no sign of the Pastor – yet. He opens the rear doors of the car. 'Get in Sam. You're coming with us.'

'Bleedin' hell. Who was he?' says Sam, rubbing his neck.

'A bad man. Are you hurt?' says Starling.

'I'm chipper,' says Sam, but Starling can hear a tremor in his voice. Sam jumps into the passenger seat and looks back at Starling with a worried expression.

Dalton gets into the driver seat and looks distastefully at Starling's bloody hand. 'Try not to bleed all over my car,' he says.

Starling furrows his brow and studies Dalton's face. 'Have we met?'

'No,' says Dalton, easing off the brakes and shifting gears. The Humber moves forward and picks up speed. They pass the yard. Starling glances at the doors. There is no sign of the Pastor. He turns to Anna, who is gently dabbing Sam's neck with a handkerchief.

'Anna, meet Sam,' he says.

'Hello Sam.'

'Enchanté, Miss, enchanté,' he says, bowing his head slightly.

Anna smiles and looks at Starling.

'Are you hurt, Anna?' he says.

'Bruised jaw and ribs. All in a day's work. Not as bad as you. We need to stem the flow of blood.' She removes her jumper and tears off the sleeve from her shirt, wrapping the cloth tightly around Starling's palm. He winces as the binding tightens.

'Sorry,' says Anna.

Sam sits quietly, hugging his arms. 'Lucky you came along when you did, Starling. I thought he was going to kill us.'

'I'm glad you're safe, Sam, but this is not over yet.'

Dalton seems to be taking them towards the river and the north Thames Embankment, or so Starling thinks, but instead he turns down Tanner Lane and along the road between the warehouses and the waterside. They drive slowly over rubble, passing several bomb-damaged warehouses that are beyond repair. The car stops beside a postbox, opposite an old shipping warehouse called Butler's Wharf. Dalton gets out of the car and Starling and the others follow. Holding his bloody hand close to his side, Starling looks around him. To the west, busy on either side with queuing traffic, is Tower Bridge. It was there, almost a week ago, that he witnessed Skipper's murder at the hands of the Pastor.

Across the water is the north of the city with its crumbling war-torn cityscape. He can see some of the churches mentioned in the 'Oranges and Lemons' rhyme, and towering over them is St Paul's Cathedral flanked by two enormous barrage balloons. Somewhere out there, he thinks, are the Stones of Fire. They are close. He knows it.

Dalton escorts them inside the unused warehouse. They are led up a flight of stairs to a room with tall windows overlooking the river. There is a long metal table near the window with a bench on either side.

'Get some rest. Help will be here soon,' says Dalton, turning to leave.

'Are you leaving us?' says Starling.

'I'll be outside if you need anything,' he says, closing the door behind him.

Starling has an uneasy feeling and opens the door to look outside. There is a bitter smell of tobacco in the air. Dalton is sitting on an old office chair, leaning against the wall, puffing on a cigarette. He looks back at Starling, curiously. Starling says nothing, dips back inside and closes the door. After all that has happened, it is hard to know when he might be overreacting.

'What's going on Starling? What's this all about?' asks Sam.

Starling smiles at Sam. What harm could it do to tell him? He deserves the truth after what he has been through, Starling thinks. He starts to give Sam a potted summary of the last few days.

'I knew you was someone important, Starling. I told Kitty, but she didn't believe me.'

'I'm not important, Sam. I'm just trying to do the right thing.'

Sam looks at Anna and then back at Starling. Folding his arms, he says, 'You is too humble, Starling. You are more important than you think.'

Starling shrugs and tries to smile. He takes out the astrolabe and the notebook and places them on the table. 'Let's try and figure out some more of this puzzle.'

Leafing through the pages, he begins tearing them out. First, the picture of the cross, followed by the sketch of the man holding up the astrolabe on the mountain. He lays them out on the table and runs his fingers through his hair. 'Ouch,' he says, his finger grazing a piece of glass.

He eases it out and drops it on the floor. Anna stands behind him. 'Let me,' she says and tips his head gently to the side. 'It's a mess. I'll see if I can get some water.'

She stands in the doorway, speaks with Dalton briefly and then looks back inside. 'Be back shortly.'

Starling and Sam sit at the table and look down at the pictures.

'Somewhere in here,' says Starling, 'is the final piece of the puzzle. The Stones of Fire are somewhere in London.'

Starling recalls the churches from 'Oranges and Lemons' and glances through the window and beyond the river. 'Could they be in one of those churches?' he wonders aloud.

'Which one?' says Sam.

'That's what we need to figure out.' Starling looks down at the etching of the cross. The design is elaborate, thick and broad with short, rounded arms and a rectangular base. Within its frame are rows of neatly arranged rectangles and circles. Encrusted jewels, he suspects, and in its centre is what looks like the pupil of an eye. Starling does not know what to make of it. He hands the etching to Sam. 'What do you think this is?'

Sam studies it. 'It looks familiar,' he says.

'Really? Keep looking and think hard, Sam. You could save all our lives.'

The door opens and Anna walks in cradling a basin, with water sploshing from it. Draped over her arm is the remains of her shirt, torn into rags. She sets the basin on the table and slides along the bench, sitting next to Starling. She dips one of the rags in the water. 'This might hurt a little,' she says.

–

Evening comes, and the moon is full and low and casts a mercurial sheen across the city rooftops. Starling winces as Anna removes yet another piece of glass from his head, a task that has taken almost two hours. With the aid of his torch and a lock pick, she removes the more stubborn pieces and wipes the small wounds with a rag dipped in the bloodied water.

'That's the last of them,' she says.

Starling's head throbs; it has been like torture and he is relieved it is over.

'Sorry, it was a little horrible for you,' she says, fixing his hair.

'It wasn't too bad,' he lies. 'Thank you.'

Starling feels Sam watching him. Sam winks and silently mouths, 'Aye, aye.'

Starling glowers and turns back to the pictures spread out in front of him. He focuses hard – the Greek cross, the mountain, the astrolabe, the moon. What does it all mean?

He looks at Anna and Sam. 'If the Stones are in London, what mountains are there to climb and hold the astrolabe high up?'

'None,' says Anna.

'Correct. So what is the next best thing?'

'Somewhere very high up,' offers Sam.

'Yes, but where?' Starling stands up and paces for a moment before walking to the window. He glances nervously at the moon, now swathed in charred clouds. Tonight is their only hope. They cannot afford to wait for the next cycle.

'We have to find them and get them out of London. Tonight, if we can,' says Starling.

The wail of a siren shatters the silence. An air raid! The hairs on Starling's neck stand on end. He looks out the window and across the river. Small dark figures are hurrying to the safety of the shelters as the crump, crump, crump of bombs explode further east.

Searchlights slice through the sky looking for enemy aircraft. One beam swipes across St Paul's and lights up the golden ball and cross that rise up above the dome.

Starling runs his fingers through his hair. Something tugs at his memory. He turns to the table, grabs the picture of the cross and looks at it, then back at the cathedral. He searches the recesses of his mind. He knows this cross. He looks across the water and laughs to himself.

'Of course,' he says. 'That's it.'

'What's it?' says Anna.

'This is not a Greek cross. It's a floor plan.'

'For where?' says Anna.

'St Paul's Cathedral,' says Sam. 'I knew I'd seen it before.'

'Exactly,' says Starling, turning and looking across the water at the great cathedral. 'That's where we have to go next.'

As if on cue the clouds part, revealing the moon. The city seems to shimmer dangerously in preparation for the destruction that is only minutes away.

'Look!' says Sam, pointing at the table.

Starling follows his gaze and sees small blue lights like miniature fireworks spiral across the astrolabe. It is the strangest thing.

'What's happening?' says Anna.

'Blimey!' says Sam.

'The Stones really are close,' says Starling.

'But how can you be sure?' said Anna.

'The astrolabe is a device for finding them. It defies all logic, but the full moon has activated it.'

His heart starts racing. 'We should get out of here,' he says, tentatively reaching for the astrolabe, his fingers brushing the lights. There is no heat and it seems safe. He takes a breath and then picks it up. The lights are cool to the touch and spread across his hands and wrists. It is almost hypnotic. With precious little time, he shoves it into his pocket, grabs the notebook and the torn-out pages.

Anna and Sam are already at the door. Sam is pulling at the handle.

'The door's locked,' he says.

Anna tries to open it, but it is no good.

Starling hears the sound of a car engine and hurries to the window. A car has pulled up beside the Humber. Dalton is standing close by as if waiting to greet whoever is inside. The doors open and two broad men wearing suits get out from the rear. They look to Starling like heavies. A third man, who is thin and balding with spectacles, gets out. It is the librarian from Bishopsgate

Library. *What is he doing here?* And then a fourth man follows and looks up at Starling with a grim smile. Starling feels his muscles coil.

It is Colonel Frost.

Chapter 35

Flight from Butler's Wharf

'Starling!' cries Anna. 'Help us open the door.'

Starling's eyes dart around the room searching for another exit, an escape route that he may have missed, but there is nothing. They are trapped.

'Come away from the door,' he says.

Anna and Sam look at him with questioning expressions.

'What is it, Starling?' demands Anna.

'Dalton has tricked us. He's a double agent.'

Anna's face pales.

Sam presses his ear to the door. 'Someone's coming up the stairs.'

Anna and Sam stand beside Starling.

The lock turns and the door is pushed open. The two heavies enter with pistols pointing firmly at Starling.

Starling takes three deep breaths.

Frost steps in, walks between his men and crosses the room, his face grim and his fists clenching in and out as if he is preparing for a fight. He is a beast of a man, remarkably unharmed after his fall at the bell foundry. It will obviously take a lot more than a fall to down this monster.

Starling can feel Sam shrink behind him.

Frost stands before Starling and stares deeply into his eyes.

'Well, if it isn't the prodigal son.'

Starling can feel his heartbeat quickening.

'You've had quite the adventure, my boy.'

Starling bristles. 'I'm not your boy.'

'Not any more…' Frost runs his eyes greedily up and down Anna. Looking back at Starling, he says, 'You have good taste.'

Starling eyes flare in anger.

Outside the siren continues to wail, lights flash in the sky and the falling bombs draw closer. Frost turns his head and calls to the librarian, who stands sheepishly in the doorway.

'Mr Stringer, join us, please.'

The librarian hesitates and then steps cautiously into the room. 'I really ought to be going now,' he mumbles. 'It is rather late and mother will be worried.'

'A moment of your time. That is all.'

Stringer clasps his hands together and turns to leave, but Dalton steps in his path. He reluctantly approaches, eyes down.

'Look at them,' says Frost. 'Do you recognise them?'

Stringer nods and then points to Sam. 'Not that one.'

Frost looks warily at Sam.

Starling shifts uneasily and Frost catches his discomfort in the blink of an eye.

'And what were they doing at the library, Mr Stringer?'

'Researching history. Greek history and the Renaissance period, a speciality subject of mine, actually. I—'

'Researching history,' interrupts Frost. 'Quite.' He looks at the notebook in Starling's hand. 'Starling, I presume you have made some headway on finding the location of the Stones?'

Starling swallows but does not respond.

'As I thought.'

'May I go now?' Stringer says with a tremble in his voice.

Frost continues to stare at Starling and ignores Stringer. 'I don't blame you for what you did. Considering your circumstances, I would have done the same.'

Starling swallows. He does not know why, but somewhere in his fractured memory is a dark truth that he does not want to face. He breathes slowly through his nose and retains his composure.

'Colonel, may I go?' says Stringer.

'This is a free country, is it not?' says Frost.

Stringer nods, backs away and then stops. He coughs politely. 'There was a small matter of remuneration.'

'About that…' says Frost, reaching into his coat pocket and pulling out a pistol.

Instinctively, Starling and Anna duck, pulling Sam with them. The shot is explosive; the bullet hits Stringer in the centre of his forehead. A spray of blood splashes across Dalton's face as Stringer crumples to the ground.

Sam cries out and Anna puts her arm around him and pulls him to her.

'Where are the Stones, Starling?'

Starling is breathing deeply, trying to hide his terror. 'I should have finished you off at the bell foundry.'

'Your mistake. Didn't you learn anything from me? Now, tell me where the Stones are. If you do not, I will kill your friends one by one until you do.'

Starling's mind is racing. He and Anna cannot take them all on.

'You,' Frost gestures at Sam. 'Come here.'

Trembling, Sam looks down at the floor.

Frost sighs impatiently. 'Wykes, fetch the boy.'

One of the heavies grabs Sam by the arm and hauls him from Anna's clutches.

'Hey!' cries Starling. He rushes forward and pulls Sam back, but a firm grip takes hold off his hair and he can feel Dalton's gun barrel against his temple.

'On your knees, little one,' says Frost.

Sam is too frightened to move. Wykes kicks his legs from underneath him and Sam falls at Frost's feet. He raises the pistol.

'One by one, Starling.'

'Tell them, Starling,' cries Anna.

Starling feels a crushing panic as Frost squeezes the trigger.

'St Paul's Cathedral!' he says. 'They are in St Paul's Cathedral.'

Frost looks through the window and across the river at the great cathedral.

'You will have to do better than that, Starling.'

'I don't know where precisely but I can find them, I swear. Please don't hurt him.'

Frost smiles, clearly enjoying Starling's fear and pleading.

'He's telling the truth!' says Anna. 'Please...'

After a moment, Frost puts the pistol back in his coat pocket.

'Very well. I will give you the benefit of the doubt. We shall make the journey to St Paul's together.'

Frost walks to the window and takes out a torch and binoculars from his coat pocket. He begins to flick the torch on and off, signalling to someone. Starling watches as Frost peers through binoculars at two tiny blinking lights on Tower Bridge.

Anna has a better view and is trying to interpret the message. After a moment she frowns, looks at Starling and shakes her head.

Wykes leads the way downstairs followed by Anna, Sam and Starling. Dalton, the other heavy and Frost follow behind with their guns ready.

At the bottom of the stairs Wykes stops and raises his arm. Starling can hear the sound of a clattering and creaking vehicle approaching. It sounds familiar. Wykes approaches the door and opens it.

Dalton pulls Anna and Sam into the shadows. Frost squeezes Starling's shoulder and jabs his ribs with the barrel of his gun. 'Do not open your mouth, or try any of your tricks.'

Through the gap in the door Starling sees the vehicle drive past. Its wobbling and trembling are unmistakable. It is Eli's old Post Office van. The van stops at the nearby postbox. Starling hears the van door opening. Someone is whistling, and then, 'Nice evening for an air raid,' says a voice. It is Eoin, but he is speaking in a cockney accent. Starling holds his breath and exchanges glances with Anna in the gloom.

'Late to be picking up the mail,' says Wykes.

'People still send letters, even in wartime, mate,' says Eoin, in a jovial tone.

'Those people are working you into the ground.'

'We all have to do our bit.'

Starling hears the creaking sound of a door opening. The postbox. There is a shuffling noise and then it slams shut.

'I'll be off then.'

'Goodnight,' says Wykes.

Starling tenses and Frost tightens his grip.

The van starts up and drives off. Why is he leaving? Eoin must know they are here.

Moments later the sound of the van disappears into the night swallowed by the drone of approaching bombers.

'Start walking,' says Frost.

Outside the searchlights swing through the skies like swords in battle. Whistlers fall from the bombers and hit the ground without exploding. Time bombs, thinks Starling. Tonight, London would become a minefield.

'Colonel,' says Wykes, pointing back in the direction where they had entered the wharf, 'there is another message.'

Frost frowns and eases his grip on Starling's shoulder. 'It can't be,' he says, looking through the binoculars. 'I don't recognise the code.'

Starling looks at Anna. She has understood it.

'Agents of Beaulieu. Duck!' she whispers.

Is the message from Eoin? It must be. Wisps of smoke are escaping from the slot in the postbox.

Anna pulls Sam to the ground. Starling drops too, covering his ears as an explosion rocks the ground and fills the air with masonry, smoke and dust.

There is a moment of quiet calm before the groaning and swearing starts.

Starling coughs and looks up. Clouds of black smoke swirl from the decimated pillar-box. At ground level, the smoke is thin and he can just about make out Anna and Sam. They seem unhurt.

'Hold hands. We're getting out of here,' says Starling. The smoke is thickening. There is no sign of Frost or his men, but he can hear them shifting close by.

The bomb was small, more diversion than destruction. Starling covers his mouth to stave off the thick, black choking air and leads his friends away from the warehouse groping the walls for support and searching for a way out.

A gunshot rings out, piercing the smoke above their heads. It is followed by the sound of heavy footfalls close behind.

Someone is following them.

Chapter 36

The Light That Had Seemed So Bright

Starling blinks the smoke from his streaming eyes and covers his mouth with the sleeve of his jacket. He can feel Anna's soft hand holding on tightly to his. An image from the past flashes in his mind. He stops, tightens his grip and recalls a small hand holding tightly on to his. But the image dissipates as quickly as it arrived.

Whose hand was that?

He pulls Anna forward and she in turns pulls a coughing and choking Sam.

'Cover your nose and mouth with something,' Starling rasps, his voice almost inaudible. He presses on, pulling them all behind him. Reaching forward, his fingers graze the rough bricks of a warehouse building. Using it as a guide he leads them through the black fog away from Frost and his men.

The smoke begins to thin and he pulls them clear. There is precious little time but they need a moment to recuperate, so they sag against the building, gasping in the glorious clean air.

Mindful that someone is close behind them, Starling scans the area for an exit. He hears the Thames lapping against the walls of the quay and sees the moon glinting off the water. Ahead is Tower Bridge. They need to cross it to get to St Paul's. There is a pathway along the river leading to the bridge, but it is too open, too exposed. They would be easy targets for whoever was following them.

He glances around. At the corner of the wharf building is a slit-like alley leading to the rear of Butler's Wharf. It might be a route to Tower Bridge Road. It is a risk and could take longer, but it would have the benefit of cover. It seems to be the best option.

'This way,' he commands.

They turn a corner into a street lined with walls and mounds of rubble, the bomb-ravaged remains of warehouses and offices for the once thriving docks.

'Keep going,' says Starling. 'I will catch you up.'

'I'm staying with you,' says Sam.

Anna grabs Sam's hand. 'Come with me, Sam. Starling won't be far behind.'

Sam looks up at both of them, unsure what he should do.

'Please, Sam,' says Starling.

Sam nods his head. 'You better be quick,' he says.

'As quick as the wind,' says Starling and watches them run off, hiding for cover among the scattered mounds of rubble.

He thinks again about the small soft hand from his memory, but his attention is diverted when he hears coughing and sees Wykes stumble into the alley. He is carrying a Browning pistol. He leans against the wall, clutching his chest and spitting onto the ground. Starling keeps out of sight. He had hoped Wykes would follow the path up the river, but that would be too much luck to expect.

Wykes opens the Browning's magazine and looks inside. Then he searches his pockets once, twice, three times. He must be short of bullets. The Browning can hold thirteen rounds of ammunition. Wykes had fired a shot minutes back. That would mean he has twelve bullets, at most, remaining.

Wykes pushes the magazine back into place and looks up the alleyway.

Starling darts out of view, but he knows he's been seen. He curses his stupidity.

'Is the bloke coming?' whispers Sam.

'Sam! What the hell are you doing here?'

'I couldn't leave you. This is my city, Starling. We have to save it.'

Starling sees Anna in the distance behind the cover of a burned-out car, looking back. Sam had obviously let her run on and doubled back.

Starling peeks round and sees Wykes making his way toward the corner where they are hiding, but the smoke has slowed him for the time being. Starling darts back as a bullet flies from the Browning.

Eleven bullets remaining.

Starling gathers up rocks and rubble. 'Get ready to run, Sam,' he says, stepping out from the corner and tossing the rocks hard at Wykes. Pain sears through his injured hand and up his arm. He shudders and steadies himself. Two of the rocks miss by inches but one connects with Wykes' knee. Starling ducks behind the corner as Wykes fires again. Two bullets chip the brickwork above his head, spraying fragments of masonry into his face.

Nine bullets remaining.

Blinking the dust from his eyes, Starling wipes his face and turns to Sam.

'Go!' he says, and watches Sam run toward Anna, hopping dangerously over the rubble in the gloomy street. Starling follows him and hears the crack of a third shot. A bullet whizzes past his ear and he tumbles to the ground, pulling Sam with him and rolling behind a pile of rocks.

Eight bullets remaining.

'Listen up, Sam. He's short of bullets. I'm sure of it. In a minute we're going to make a run for it, but I'm going to try and make him use them up. After three I want you to run as fast as you have ever run in your life. Do you hear me?'

Sam nods. 'What about you?'

'I will try and distract him.'

Sam pales and clenches his fists.

Starling peeks over the rubble and sees Wykes struggling across the uneven terrain. At least the destruction provided them some advantage.

He looks at Sam. 'After three. Remember, just keep running.'

Sam nods. 'Just keep running… just keep running,' he repeats.

'One… two… three!' Sam scurries off as Starling stands up and tosses several more rocks at Wykes. To his relief, one strikes his shoulder with a satisfying thud.

Warm blood seeps through the bandage on Starling's aching hand, but he ignores the pain and hurls two more rocks. Wykes stumbles back, raising his arm to stave them off, his face furious. He points the pistol at Starling and squeezes the trigger. Starling gasps and freezes.

But there is no crack and no bullet. Only a click.

Starling and Wykes' eyes meet with a shared disbelief.

Wykes was down more bullets than Starling could have hoped for. He wants to laugh, but he watches as Wykes begins to search his pockets frantically. He removes something from his pocket and smiles grimly. It is a bullet. Wykes' gaze fixes on Starling as he puts the bullet slowly into the gun.

Starling swears under his breath and runs, darting in between the shadows and rock piles.

The moon is high and the skies flash with the guns of war.

Sam is a short distance ahead, his little legs powering over the stones.

Tower Bridge comes into view through a gap in two half-demolished buildings. 'Keep running,' he calls to Sam and flies past the smaller boy. 'Faster Sam! Faster!'

Starling's attention turns to rapid thuds and small clouds of dust that rise in quick succession at his feet.

Someone else is shooting at him.

He glances up at the bridge and swears the shots are coming from the top of it. Is it a sniper? He dives and rolls towards the burnt-out car and out of sight of the gunman's range. He turns, his stomach tightening at the sight of Sam, who has not caught up.

Starling beckons to him with both arms. 'Keep running, Sam,' he shouts. 'You're almost here!' And then, above the din, he hears an odd thudding noise like a tennis ball slamming hard against a wall. Sam stumbles backward.

'No!' cries Anna.

Confusion sweeps through Starling like a grey cloud. Sam has stopped and sways on his feet, his arms limp. He looks so small amongst the decimated dock buildings. His eyes lock on to Starling's and he smiles his lopsided smile. A small patch appears on his chest and begins to grow larger and larger.

Horror shakes Starling from his confusion. He feels a choking worse than the black smoke. Trembling, he raises his hands to his temples and tries to scream, to cry out, but no sound comes from his mouth. Grief swells through his body.

Sam falls to his knees, his eyes never leaving Starling's, and then the light, that had seemed so bright, leaves them forever.

Starling can hear nothing but the blood pumping in his ears.

A figure looms over Sam's body. It is Wykes, smiling.

Starling's grief crumbles like ash as rage sweeps through his every fibre.

'I'll kill you… I'll kill you all!' he cries and makes to run at Wykes, but Anna hauls him back, pulling him with all her strength.

'Not now, Starling. Later,' she says, in hushed tones. Starling resists and cries out as her hand grips his softly.

In the distance, he hears the cries of the Londoners who had not quite made it to shelter. London would fall if he did not find the Stones. He has to do this for Sam and take his revenge later. A cold rationality grips him. Wykes is advancing toward them. Starling turns and flees with Anna.

Chapter 37

Across Tower Bridge

Starling's grief builds to a simmering fury that fuels his desire for revenge. He desperately wants to make the sniper – whoever he is – pay for what he has done to Sam. But that would have to wait. Right now, Wykes has one more bullet and Starling is under no illusion whose name is on it.

They run from the ruins and out onto a main road. Starling glances quickly around him. They are on Tower Bridge Road, he is sure of it. There is no one about. Cars and buses sit abandoned, parked haphazardly in the panic as people have scarpered, seeking shelter from the air raid.

Starling has an idea. 'Look for a car with keys. Perhaps someone will have left them during the rush.'

Anna wastes no time and searches a row of nearby cars. Starling takes another row, darting from car to car pulling open doors, peering inside and cursing his luck at finding nothing. Across the road is a bus with the driver door lying wide open.

Starling glances behind him and sees Wykes' shadow appear from the ruins.

'Hide,' he hisses.

Anna rushes to the side of the road and out of sight.

Starling runs to the bus, climbs up into the driver's seat and closes the door. He crouches down on the floor by the pedals and listens.

He can hear Wykes stepping cautiously up Tower Bridge Road, stopping every now and then. Starling does not move and tries to work out where he is. He is close, at the rear of bus, Starling thinks. And then he feels the bus shift slightly as Wykes steps onto the rear platform.

Starling holds his breath as Wykes walks up the aisle.

Starling glances up at the small window separating the passenger and driver areas. He swallows. If Wykes takes one look through it, he is done for.

Wykes approaches. Starling turns his head slowly and looks at the cabin door. He will spring at it and make his escape if he has to.

Something clatters on the roof of the bus, and Wykes stops. Anna must have thrown something to divert his attention.

Wykes starts up the stairs. Starling can hear his muffled tread upstairs and then a second clatter outside.

Another diversion.

Starling feels the weight of the bus lean slightly to the right. He hears Wykes walk back down the aisle, down the stairs and onto the road.

His steps move away from the bus. Starling's brow is damp with sweat. He thinks about Sam and fresh tears well in his eyes. He wipes them away with curled fists as a rage roars inside him like a furnace.

I will finish Wykes and Frost. All of them. I swear, Sam, I will do it.

Over the dashboard he sees Wykes hurrying towards the bridge. He must think he and Anna are on their way to St Paul's. Starling waits a few more moments until Wykes is out of sight and pushes himself up. Something jabs against his shoulder. The key for the bus is still in the ignition. Sitting in the driver's seat, he places his hands on the immense steering wheel and thinks.

Can I drive something this size?

Outside, German bombers swarm the skies. What choice does he have? He looks back to where they have left Sam's body and, with a heaviness in his heart, he turns the key. The engine shudders and then shuts down. He tries again. This time the engine coughs and chokes three times before giving up. Starling hears Anna climb on board.

'It might just be cold,' she says. 'Keep trying.'

Starling tries again and the engine rumbles reluctantly. Behind him, in the distance, he hears gunfire and the screech of car brakes. He looks back and sees the old Post Office van valiantly pursuing Dalton's Humber. He has no doubt Frost is in that car. They are heading towards the bridge. Starling's pulse begins to race.

The bus engine rumbles, flattens and dies. Starling grits his teeth and turns the key again. The engine coughs and trembles, stronger this time. 'Come on!' he shouts and, as if obeying his plea, the engine makes a clucking sound and the entire bus shakes into life.

'Well done, Starling!' says Anna.

Starling focuses on the controls, gripping the brake lever to his left and easing it down. He presses the accelerator with his foot and the bus rolls forward. The steering wheel is huge compared to the Embiricos and much harder to manoeuvre, especially with his sore and bloody hand. He slips the gear up to second, then third and picks up speed. Keep it steady, he tells himself over and over. Ignoring the blackout rule, Starling switches on the lights. He cannot afford to lose time now by crashing into something he does not see. He presses the accelerator to the floor.

'Hold on!' he shouts.

Then straight ahead, Starling catches sight of Wykes. He is signalling with a torch to the sniper at the top of the bridge. Wykes is standing on the middle of the bridge road, his pistol pointing at the bus. Starling hears a creaking noise as if the bridge beneath them is moving. Behind Wykes, the bascules have started to rise. Starling swallows. They are done for. He can see a smile forming on Wyke's face. He obviously signalled to the sniper to raise the bridge.

A surge of anger races through Starling. This is not over yet.

'Anna, get down and hang on as tight as you can!' Starling shouts.

'What are you doing?' she calls, but there is no time to explain.

He can't quite believe what he is about to do. But what option does he have? Wykes is aiming the revolver. Starling can see his finger squeezing the trigger and ducks behind the wheel as the gunshot rings out. The windscreen shatters. Cool air fills the driver's cabin. The bus swerves but Starling holds it firm and steers toward Wykes. There is a sudden look of dismay on the man's face. Starling smiles. But then Wykes runs at the bus, his stride long and strong, and leaps onto the bonnet.

With grim determination, Starling mounts the rising bascule and speeds up.

Wykes clings on to the bonnet with one hand; the other claws at Starling's face through the broken windscreen. With his heart pounding, Starling leans away from Wykes as the bus hurtles toward the edge of the bascule and flies into the air.

There is calm; the bus makes no sound. A gentle wind fills the cabin, blowing through Starling's hair and cooling his hot face. Wykes scrambles forward, but Starling raises his fist and with all his strength launches it at the man's broad nose. He hears a satisfying crunch as Wykes' head rocks back. His grip loosens. He fights for purchase but it is too little, too late. He slides across the bonnet with nothing to grab hold of.

Starling watches without regret, or remorse, as Wykes slips from the bonnet and falls, screaming. He sees Wykes' body slam against the edge of the bascule, silencing him as he plummets towards the dark waters of the Thames below.

With his heart in his mouth, Starling grips the steering wheel firmly. The bus tilts forward to meet the other bascule that is now at a forty-five-degree angle.

'Hang on, Anna!'

The bus slams into the bascule front wheels first. He hears a cry from the rear as metal scrapes against the road surface, sparks arching up the sides of the bus like fiery wings. The steering wheel spins to the right, sliding through Starling's sore and bloody hand. The bus swerves. Starling pushes the brake pedal to the floor, but it feels like it is not working. He spins the wheel to the left as the bus mounts the pavement and crashes sideways against the steel barrier.

On his right, he sees the side of the bus peeling away. Ignoring the pain in his wounded hand, he hauls the steering wheel to the left while pumping the brakes. The bus swerves again, tilting left then right, the brakes screeching in protest. Starling's strength is spent, his wounded palm is sweaty and bloody and losing traction against the steering wheel. The end of the bascule is ahead; the bridge flattens out, the bus jolting at the sudden change in angle. He pulls the handbrake lever with his good hand and the bus skids to the left, spinning three hundred and sixty degrees, the side panel flapping dangerously before finally coming loose and clattering behind them on the roadside.

With all his remaining strength, Starling steadies the wheel, but the bus tips to the left, driving forward on two wheels.

Starling throws his weight to the right in the desperate hope he can provide balance, but it is futile. The bus tilts further, he falls to the side of the cabin, banging his temple on the overhead control panel as the bus topples and crashes to the ground, glass shattering and sparks flying as it slides and scrapes to a stop near the bridge exit.

Starling lies in a heap on the cabin's side, his head spinning. The bus is creaking, protesting. For a moment he stares vacantly at the torrid flashing skies above. He is still alive, but what about Anna?

He almost doesn't want to look, but he hears her voice and peers into the rear of the bus.

Anna is gripping firmly on to a passenger seat, safe though understandably pale.

Still dizzy, Starling massages his temples and looks at the bascule. It is up as high as it can go and shows no sign of lowering. He can hear gunfire from the top of the bridge. The sniper must be firing at Eoin. Fury grips Starling and tears flood the back of his eyes. He will make that sniper pay. And then the bitter smell of diesel swamps the cabin, bringing him to his senses. A fire has started in the engine. Time to get out of here!

Chapter 38

London Crumbles

Starling jumps over the driver's seat and pushes up the cabin door, which opens like a hatch. The sky is fraught with searchlights and droning bombers and rapid gunfire. He pulls himself up and stands on the side of the fallen bus. The left panel is missing and the passenger area is exposed. He clambers over the edge of the seats toward Anna.

'The engine is burning. We have to be quick,' he says.

He reaches down and pulls her up. They drop clumsily down the undercarriage to the ground below and give the engine a wide berth before running along the barriers and off the bridge.

An explosion rocks the ground.

Instinctively Starling and Anna grab each other and turn to see the front of the bus in flames. They watch without saying anything, Starling edging closer to Anna without realising. He feels her breath close. She is looking at him and he feels a warmth inside.

Something trembles in his blazer pocket. The astrolabe. He takes it out. It is glittering rapidly. 'We're getting closer,' he says.

'We should hurry,' says Anna, stepping back.

They sprint down to the waterside path towards the Tower of London, running breathlessly, their shoes clipping rapidly on the black cobbles. Starling glances nervously back at the bridge. The bascules are still up and there is no sign of Eoin, or Dalton, on the other side. He looks behind and no one is following.

The flashing skies cast long flickering shadows of their tired bodies against the walls of the Tower of London. They are horribly exposed. One shot from the sniper could take either of them out.

Anna hides from view as Starling turns up Water Lane and then glances up and down the wide expanse of Lower Thames Street to ensure there is no one suspicious approaching. When he is sure it is safe, he hurries across and hides in the shadows of a narrow exit road opposite. He glances around, waiting a moment, and then beckons Anna to follow.

They run through dark streets. The tall buildings obscure the moonlight and the glare of the searchlights, but not the terrifying rumble and boom of destruction that can be heard from every corner of the city. The ground quakes and the buildings shake as if they would collapse at any moment. Starling wonders if this is what the end of the world would be like. Masonry dust and smoke fill the air, shrapnel falls from the skies, bouncing off roofs and walls and landing perilously close on three occasions.

Despite his determination and resolve, London is crumbling around him and he is frightened. Starling begins to recognise the area and knows they are getting closer. The street ahead leads to a wider expanse, where looming tall in the sky is St Paul's dome, its great ball and cross silhouetted in the moonlight.

'What do we do when we get inside?' asks Anna.

'We find the eye. The eye will show us where to go.'

Chapter 39

The St Paul's Watch

Starling and Anna crouch in the cemetery garden at the rear of St Paul's scanning the building for a side door. For a moment it seems there is nothing, until a sliver of light shines from a gully at the side of the cathedral. It extinguishes as quickly as it appears. They hear the sound of slow footsteps, boots on stone, and the tune of someone whistling 'Wish me luck as you wave me goodbye'. It makes Starling think of Aunty and the safe house, the last time he heard it. He steadies his breathing and slinks into the shadows beside Anna.

The whistler turns out to be an older man with a slight build who walks with a stoop and the stiff pace of someone who suffers from arthritis. He is dressed in an out-dated military uniform with a tin hat and a pair of binoculars around his neck. He is also carrying what seems to be a long spear, which is very odd. He does not appear to be a warden. Starling wonders who he might be. The old man crosses through the courtyard and checks the cemetery garden, looking all the while in their direction. *Has he seen or heard them?* Starling and Anna hold their breath and do not move an inch.

The sound of a bomber distracts the man. He fumbles around his neck and peers through the binoculars. He mumbles quietly under his breath then turns towards the front of the cathedral. Starling and Anna exchange glances. They are both thinking the same thing. Starling goes first, hurrying towards the gully and quickly down the steps. The door is unlocked and they both slip inside, closing it shut behind them.

It is dark and warm with a faint trace of incense in the air. Starling takes out the torch and switches it on. The battery power is running low, the beam is fading but there is enough light to see they are in a wide and tall vaulted corridor made of stone. There are sconces on the walls and statues guarding numerous tombs. They are in the crypt. Starling quickly gets a sense of his bearings and looks at Anna. He points west toward the front of the cathedral.

Anna shakes her head and points north. Starling shakes his head, defiantly, even though he has no idea how to get upstairs.

Maybe she is right. He relents and follows Anna through the unlit corridor, passing several more tombs along the way. It leads to a wide set of stone steps and a large gate. Anna runs up the steps and leaps gracefully onto the gate and over. Starling joins her on the other side and they walk out on to the cathedral floor.

Starling had forgotten how immense the cathedral is, more so now that they are the only people inside. It seems more an ancient stronghold than a place of worship and he has a sense the structure could magically protect them from the falling bombs. But he knows this is a fantasy. It is stone and mortar like any other building and would crumble in minutes if a bomb hit it.

He takes out the drawing of the cross, unfolds it and walks backwards toward the altar. Anna appears at his side and studies it with him. He looks across the vast space and turns the drawing of the cross over in his hands.

'I was right. It is definitely the cathedral floor plan.'

Anna points to the shaft. 'These are not jewels. They are benches and alcoves. But where is the eye?'

Starling looks across at the rows of benches. In the centre of the cross should be something representing an eye. He walks to where the eye should be, looking down at the marble floor in front of the altar. It is then that he sees it.

'Anna, look!'

Anna stands beside him and looks down.

'Do you see it?'

'Yes!'

The marble design in the centre of the floor is almost like a giant's pupil. There is a brass grate like a dull golden iris forever peering upwards. Starling and Anna follow its gaze and look up at the dome.

'Somewhere high up,' says Starling.

'St Paul's has the highest point in London.'

Starling swallows and rubs the back of his neck.

'What the devil are you two doing?' says a voice.

Starling turns to see a stout man appear from behind the altar. He is wearing a monocle, a military cap and some sort of chain mail underneath his officer's jacket.

'Taking shelter from the air raid, sir,' says Starling, saying the first thing that pops into his head.

The man walks toward them, frowning. 'How did you get in here?'

'There was a door...' says Anna.

'To the crypt,' adds Starling.

The man regards them suspiciously and glances at the floor plan in Starling's hand. His eyes narrow.

Time is running out.

'If you please, sir, I need to get up there,' says Starling, pointing at the dome.

'Out of the question.'

Starling and Anna glance at each other.

'Sir, please. I have very little time. I must get to the top of the dome.'

The man snorts, reaches into his pocket and takes out a notepad and pencil. 'What are your names?'

Starling hears footsteps and turns to see the old soldier with the spear appear from the west doors at the front of the cathedral.

The man with the monocle looks up. 'What's going on Private Warby? These two...'

But there is someone else in the shadows, pointing a rifle at the old man's back. Starling can see it is no ordinary rifle. It is an M1 Garand, semi-automatic. The kind of rifle used by a sniper.

Starling freezes; his hands curl into fists. Who else could it be but the sniper from the bridge?

'Excuse me, Captain Snelling, sir,' says Private Warby.

'Private Warby, what in the blazes is going on here?'

Starling interrupts. 'Captain Snelling, sir. That man behind Private Warby is a traitor and a murderer. He killed our friend.'

Captain Snelling looks at Starling as if he is mad.

'I'm sorry, Captain. I didn't 'ave much of a choice,' says Warby. As they get nearer, Starling sees the face of the sniper.

'You!' he says.

'Rupert?' says Anna.

Rupert Van Horne shoves Private Warby forward, his eyes darting nervously from Anna to Captain Snelling and back to Starling. He is trembling, but his hands remain steady on the gun. His expression flickers unnaturally between psychotic and remorseful.

Starling shakes with rage. 'You killed Sam, you bastard!'

'I should have killed you, too, and I will. Give me the notebook and whatever else you have in your pocket.'

'No!'

Horne turns the rifle towards Anna. 'Don't play games with me.'

Starling steps in front of Anna and faces the barrel of the rifle, his eyes fixing on Horne's.

'You killed a boy, an innocent.'

'Shut up!'

'Why are you doing this, Horne? Why betray us all?'

Horne starts to laugh. 'Don't you recognise me, Starling? We know each other from years back. Four years to be precise. But, of course, apparently you have lost your memory. I don't believe that for one moment.'

'You're wrong. We have never met. I don't know you…'

'Liar!'

'Young man, please put down that gun,' says Snelling.

But Horne ignores him. 'Four years ago we were narrowed down to two candidates. We fought, you and I, with bare fists in front of them all.'

Horne's words are a trigger awakening a distant memory. The mists of Starling's mind part. He is in an underground room, putrid with stale sweat and cigarette smoke. Men are jeering and placing bets. Among them is a tall broad figure. Frost. Four bare-chested boys lie bloody on the ground. Two are unconscious, two are nursing their wounds. Starling's knuckles are grazed and running toward him with a fast-flying bloodied fist is a younger Horne. Starling snaps out of the memory, unsteady on his feet. He feels Anna's hand on his shoulder.

'Are you alright?'

Starling nods.

'Frost chose you. Not me! You who came from nowhere!'

'Poor Horne. You really don't know what you are dealing with. You kill children and betray your country.'

'We are not betraying our country. We will be making it great again.'

Captain Snelling interrupts. 'I have heard enough. Put that gun away, sir. This is a house of worship not a battleground.'

'Captain Snelling, he is a traitorous swine,' says Starling.

The captain steps toward Horne. 'As head of the St Paul's Watch I command you—' but he does not finish his sentence. Horne's cold eyes stay on Starling as he points the rifle at the captain and fires. The blast echoes through the cathedral.

Starling turns to see the captain fall back onto the marble floor.

There is silence. Horne smiles.

Anna hurries to the captain and crouches beside him. Private Warby stands still and calm, his old eyes, watery and blue, flitting between the captain, Starling and Horne.

'The girl is next,' says Horne.

Starling feels his blood boil like oil.

'Warby…' says Snelling. He sounds weak, but he is alive.

'Yes, Captain.'

'Boer manoeuvre number seventeen, I think.'

'Good choice, Captain.'

Horne frowns and points the rifle at Warby, but the old man is surprisingly fast for his age and arthritic bones. He swings the spear down so that the head smashes the knuckles of Horne's trigger hand. There is a crunching sound followed by a cry of pain as Horne drops the rifle. Warby swings the spear sideways against Horne's temple with a frightening force. Horne's eyes roll in his head as he falls to the ground. Starling grabs the rifle and points it at him.

'Now, that takes me back,' says Warby, who stands over Horne with the tip of the spear nestling into the crook of his neck. 'Shall I finish him off, sir.'

'Good Lord, no,' says Snelling. 'Remember where you are. Is he conscious?'

'No, sir.'

'Then tie him up, Private.'

'Very good, sir.'

Anna helps the captain into a sitting position. His face is pale. There is a small hole in the chain mail by his left rib.

'We should get a doctor,' says Starling.

'It's a graze. I'll live. Now, are you going to tell me what this is about?'

Starling and Anna exchange glances. They both know they have to be honest, at least to some degree, one that would not make them sound like delusional fantasists.

'My name is Will Starling and this is Anna Wilder. Anna is an agent of the Secret Service and I am…' Starling stops.

What am I. Who am I?

'You see, there's this…'

'Bomb,' says Anna, getting in quick. Explaining mystical stones with the power to destroy them all might just be too much for him to swallow.

'Yes, a bomb, somewhere in London,' says Starling.

'There are many bombs in London right now,' says the captain.

'Not like this one. It's big, enormous, with the power to wipe out the city. That's why the Nazi's are bombing us. They know it is here. If they strike it, then it is all over. The war is lost.'

'Please, Captain Snelling. Starling is telling the truth,' says Anna.

The captain pauses momentarily. 'But why are you here?'

'Please, there is no time to explain. We must hurry.'

Another pause, Starling feels his heart racing.

'The rifle, please,' says the captain.

Starling hesitates, but hands it across.

'Warby?'

'Sir,' replies Warby.

'Take these young people where they need to go. Access all areas.'

'Yes sir.'

'Thank you,' says Starling.

'Go. I will keep an eye on the prisoner.'

Chapter 40

On Top of the World

'This way,' says Private Warby, gesturing to the staircase beyond the altar, but Starling and Anna waste no time and rush ahead, taking the broad circular steps two, sometimes three at a time.

At the second floor, the entrance to the Whispering Gallery, Starling slows. It is dark and cavernous with occasional flashes of light from the warring skies above. He grips the smooth stone of the balcony wall, his eyes sweeping the gallery's wide circular expanse. A memory awakens, a voice from the past makes him falter.

'*You must find your way to the top, and once you do, the Stones will find you.*'

The voice belongs to Timothy Chittlock.

Private Warby arrives at top of the stairs. 'Blimey, this don't get any easier,' says the old soldier.

'Starling?' says Anna, with a hint of concern in her voice.

'It's nothing,' says Starling, and crosses the gallery, exiting through to a narrow steep staircase leading up to the Stone Gallery. They climb on quickly, reaching a doorway that leads to an iron staircase. The surrounding walls are tall and constructed from a solid white stone. They are at the base of the dome. Starling pushes on climbing all the way to the top where he sees another door, the entrance to the balcony of the Golden Gallery. He pushes the door, but it is stiff. Anna joins him and together they give it one hard shove. The door flies open.

Cold air, smoke, droning bombers and the rapid ack ack ack of anti-aircraft gunfire flood his senses. Bombers and fighter planes seem almost within reaching distance. Across the capital, pockets of fire are raging. Clouds of black smoke hang over the city, which seems on the verge of collapse.

Starling knows this is nothing compared to what could happen if a bomb struck the Stones. He looks up at the ball and cross, grandly silhouetted in the mercurial light of the full moon. Clouds are closing in, threatening to shroud its luminescence. He must move quickly – a clear night is needed for the astrolabe to show him where the Stones are.

'Help me find a way to the top,' he says.

They circle the balcony looking for somewhere to climb up. There is nothing.

Scaling the wall seems like the only option, but Starling glances over the edge of the narrow balcony and down past the roof of the dome. It is a long way to the bottom and he does not fancy his chances.

Private Warby arrives, puffing and panting and holding his spear with both hands for support.

'Private Warby,' says Starling, 'I need to get to the cross.'

If Warby is surprised at Starling's request, he does not show it. 'Right ya be,' he says.

The old soldier looks to the top of gallery and focuses in on a spot between the pillars. He lifts his spear, pokes it around in the gloom and then smiles. 'Got it.'

Lowering the spear to one side, he pulls down a narrow wooden ladder. 'That's all I use the ol' spear for these days. That and clearing off the debris from those bleedin' Nazi buggers,' he says, pointing to the skies. 'Now, the ladder will take you up to the ball where you will see a hole about the size of my thumb.' Private Warby shows Starling his thumb to illustrate the point. He reaches into the side pocket of his old army jacket and takes out a large ring containing a dozen or more heavy-looking iron keys. He removes one and hands it to Starling. 'Insert this key into the hole and push up. A hatch will open. Climb through and use the same key to open the second hatch on top. The cross has its own rungs on the north side.'

'Thank you, Private Warby,' says Starling, taking the key and placing it in his pocket.

'Pleasure. Thank you for letting me apprehend the enemy once again. I never lost it, you know,' he says with a wink.

Starling climbs the ladder and Anna follows. He gazes beyond the balcony at the city below and feels his head spinning. It is so far down and, without the security of the balcony wall, his stomach lurches. Through the chaos in the skies he hears Anna's voice.

'Don't look down, Starling! Keep going.'

He closes his eyes for a moment and takes three deep breaths. Tightening his grip on the ladder, he pulls himself up, ignoring the pain in his injured hand. At the top of the gallery, he sees a fixed, curved iron ladder that runs over the domed roof and connects with a third ladder, which is painted gold and leads up to the great ball. Simple but ingenious camouflage, he thinks.

Buoyed by the great ball's close proximity, he clambers across the dome, ahead of Anna, and up the golden ladder, wincing at the cold wind that numbs his face and fingers. He sees the keyhole and the faint square outline of the hatch door, and inserts the key, relieved to feel the faint tremor of the mechanism unlocking. The hatch door is stiff and heavy; it takes all his strength to push it up. Inside, it is pitch dark with the dry, dusty smell of age. There are layers of cobwebs, which drape his face, head and shoulders like a bridal veil.

He clambers up and brushes away the cobwebs. Something with too many legs crawls over his ear and across his face. In a moment of disgust and panic, he swipes it from his face. His grip on the ladder loosens and he slips down two rungs. He grabs the ladder, but the key slips from his grasp and falls into the gloom below.

Chapter 41

Oranges and Lemons

Horrified at his carelessness, Starling listens as the key clatters against the ladder and then falls and slides down the side of the wall of the ball. He sees Anna just below the hatch door.

'Anna, watch out!' he shouts, hoping the heavy key does not hurt her.

Anna's hold on the ladder tightens and she looks up. 'What happened?'

'I stupidly dropped the key. Do you see it?'

'No. I heard it, though. It might still be inside.'

Holding the ladder with his good hand, he pulls the torch from his pocket with the other, flicks on the light and points the fading beam below. Anna is right. The key is still inside, but teetering on the edge of the hatch.

And then, a nearby explosion rocks the ground like an earthquake, the cathedral shakes and the ball trembles. Starling gasps as the key wobbles, shifting closer to the opening, hanging half-on and half-off the edge. With his heart pounding, he inserts the torch into his mouth and scrambles down the ladder, the beam fixed securely on the key as if its light might magically stop it from falling.

He stretches his arm and reaches for it. It is a hair's breadth from his fingers. Leaning further in, his grip on the ladder is held by just two middle fingers to give him that extra bit of length. The key begins to tip over the edge. Wide-eyed and desperate, he lurches forward, but it tips over and falls.

'No!' he cries as the key falls, but Anna is fast and nimbly plucks it from the air. Their eyes meet for a moment.

His fingers ache from gripping the ladder but now he throws his weight back toward it, closing his eyes, relief sweeping over him. He climbs up to the top and is joined by Anna. They are so close; it is as if they are embracing. He watches her as she inserts the key and then together they push open the second hatch.

A fierce gust of wind sweeps through the opening. He climbs through and helps Anna up.

They are standing on top of the ball at the base of the golden cross, which is almost as tall as a tree. Two enormous barrage balloons, like tethered leviathans of the skies, are floating above the cathedral. Around them they can see squadrons of Nazi bombers and Messerschmitts cramming London's skies. And putting up a valiant fight are the battling Hurricanes and Spitfires.

It is as if they have emerged into another world: one where they are small and insignificant; one that is perpetually dark and cold and filled with droning engines, rapid gunfire, whistling bombs and crackling flames.

He turns his focus to the cross and circles its base in search of the ladder leading to the top. He finds it on the north side, as Private Warby had said. Anna is first up; Starling follows, climbing the golden rungs, and for a moment he is reminded of a story told to him when he was young: the story of Jack climbing the beanstalk into the clouds. Someone read it to him once. Someone in another life, before all of this. Someone he can no longer remember. He swallows and pushes the distraction from his mind.

Ignoring the chaos in the skies around him, he reaches the top of the cross, which oddly resembles a giant flower made up of large golden petals.

Sticking close together they crawl across the top and then stand up in the centre. Starling takes out the astrolabe, his pulse racing. It is not glowing as before.

'Why is it not working?' says Anna.

'I'm not sure.' He glances nervously up at the full moon, which is temporarily hidden by cloud, and hears the thunderous roar of an engine. He turns to see a Messerschmitt flying past. He can see the pilot looking directly at him. Starling meets his gaze as the plane flies wide and out of sight.

'Starling, we have to hurry. I don't like the look of him,' says Anna.

Starling focuses back on the astrolabe, waiting for something to happen. But nothing does. He frowns. Doubt begins to creep through him and he looks back at the moon, wishing he could shout and swear at the clouds, if only that would help shift them. But he doesn't need to. They part as if sensing his need.

And then the astrolabe's dull grey metal begins to glow and spark with miniature fireworks.

'At last!' says Anna.

Starling's heart pounds as the lights grow in intensity. They spiral up and across his body and high into the sky. A cooling sensation flushes through him, causing him to forget everything and laugh.

He hears Anna's voice calling him. It sounds so far away, yet she is standing right in front of him. 'Starling… Starling… are you alright?'

'Yes!'. he cries, his eyes wide with wonder. He holds the astrolabe high above his head, like the man on the mountain. The glowing becomes a rapid and bright flashing. And then there is a muffled boom that tremors the air and for a few moments the torrid skies are gloriously lit with streaks of blue light that stretch across the entire city.

And then they are gone, as quickly as they came, and the sky is dark and full of danger. Starling looks about, desperate for a sign or some sort of signal. But there is nothing, just darkness and flames.

And then he hears the mournful ringing of church bells. He isn't clear where it is coming from and scans the city, speaking out loud the old rhyme. Anna joins him.

'Oranges and lemons,
Say the bells of St Clement's…'

He looks in the direction of St Clement's but sees nothing. He is not sure what he is even looking for.

'…You owe me five farthings,
Say the bells of St Martin's'
'When will you pay me?
Say the bells of Old Bailey.'
'When I grow rich,
Say the bells of Shoreditch.'
'When will that be?
Say the bells of Stepney…'

Starling follows the order of churches but there does not seem to be any clue. And then he sees it.

'…I do not know,
Says the great bell of Bow.'

The great Bow bells of St Mary le Bow are ringing. He can see the church and its spire at Cheapside, just east of St Paul's. But there is something strange about the little church. Surrounding it, like something otherworldly, a blue light is forming like blue bees round a honeypot. It begins to extend upwards, shining like a beacon all the way to the sky.

'That's it!' he cries. 'That is where the Stones are hidden.'

'Watch out, Starling,' shouts Anna, pulling him down.

He hears the rapid fire of a machine gun. Heading straight toward them is the Messerschmitt, its guns pointing and firing at the ball and cross. The bullets miss them this time, but the Messerschmitt turns and circles back, stalking them like a shark.

Anna is running back to the ladder and gracefully swings over out of harm's way.

A dozen bullets chip at the cross and one hits the astrolabe, shattering it into several pieces. One piece flies at Starling's left cheekbone, slicing through the skin to the bone. He cries out in pain and falls back against the giant petals, dropping the remains of the ancient device. Warm sticky blood rolls down his cheek.

The Messerschmitt flies past and Starling sees the pilot look at him with a grim smile. Once again the fighter plane turns sharply, its guns pointing directly at Starling. This time the pilot would not miss.

But Starling is not yet finished. He sprints over the top of the cross, bullets pranging inches from his feet, and dives at the top rung, gripping it tightly with his good hand and swinging over the edge. He grunts as his body slams hard against the side of the cross, his ribs and left knee taking the biggest impact. His feet dangle in the air, his heart pounding; he dares not look down.

His body aches as the Messerschmitt roars furiously overhead. He scrabbles for purchase, hampered by the pain in his ribs and knee and his injured hand. He lowers himself quickly and carefully, trying his best to beat the next onslaught of bullets. They come quickly, crashing angrily over his head and hands as he reaches the top of ball. It is a miracle he has not been hit.

He climbs down into the cover of the ball and waits for the Messerschmitt to pass. It flies by and he scrambles recklessly down and across the gallery roof.

'Hurry, Starling!' It is Anna's voice. 'He's coming back!'

He climbs down to the balcony where Anna wraps her arms around him and squeezes so hard he winces. 'I thought… I thought… you were dead,' she says, her face buried in the crook of his neck.

'Ow… ow… I'm still here,' he says.

'Quickly, get inside!' says Private Warby, who is now holding a very old and long rifle and is aiming it at the oncoming fighter. Bullets rain on the gallery. Private Warby fires.

The bullets cease.

'Blimey, I think I hit him,' says Warby.

Starling looks at the Messerschmitt. The pilot's window is cracked and the plane seems out of control. It is hurtling toward the gallery.

'Hurry!' shouts Starling, as he and Anna run to the doorway. Private Warby drops the rifle and follows Starling and Anna. Out of his peripheral vision Starling sees the looming fighter plane. It is on its side, the wings slicing the air vertically. It passes feet from the Golden Gallery, its tail grazing the stone structure beneath their feet. The gallery trembles and they steady themselves on the balcony wall. The Messerschmitt tilts and glides across the rooftops below before crashing into a ball of fire somewhere near Blackfriars.

'Ha-ha!' shouts a jubilant Warby. 'I've still got it!'

'Mr Warby, thank you for everything,' says Starling.

'For King and country,' shouts Warby, with a dramatic salute.

Chapter 42

St Mary le Bow

In spite of his aching ribs and sore knee, Starling runs down the iron stairs. He can feel the skin around the wound on his cheek tighten as the blood congeals. He would have a scar there, for sure. He presses the drying wound with his fingers; the pain is hot and causes his eyes to water.

They hurry through the Whispering Gallery and down to the cathedral floor. Starling's eyes lock onto Horne's, who has regained consciousness. He is lying on his side, his bonds secured tightly around his wrists and ankles. On seeing Starling he scowls and says, 'You will never be free of them. They will hunt you down until they find you.'

Starling says nothing for a moment. He thinks about Skipper, Violet, Aunty and, most of all, he thinks about Sam, the boy who had given him shelter when he needed it most, the boy who smiled and laughed at the oddest things, the boy who had formed a devotion to Starling that had resulted in him losing his life. Cruelly murdered by the servants of VIPER. The fire in his belly twists and burns inside him.

'Let them come. I will be waiting,' he says.

Horne's face is red with fury. 'I will not go to prison, you know. My family have connections.'

'Then it will be easier for me to find you. Wait for me, Horne. One day we will meet again and I will not be so merciful.' Starling surprises himself at the coldness of his warning.

Horne tries to wrestle himself free, but Captain Snelling jabs him with the rifle.

'Try any more of that I will put a bullet between your eyes,' he says.

Horne glares at him and settles down.

The captain turns to Starling. 'Get everything you need?'

'Yes, sir. Thank you.'

'Very good,' says the captain. 'You look like you've been through the wars,' he adds.

'It's not over yet, sir,' says Starling.

'Good luck to you.'

Starling nods his thanks and turns to Anna. 'Ready?'

'Ready.'

-

Starling looks up at the strange blue light stretching up into the sky like a column. There are bombers circling it like carrion birds. His heart sinks.

'The bombers know where the Stones are,' says Anna.

'One direct hit and it's all over.'

They run toward the church.

'Where is the light coming from?' says Anna.

'The astrolabe is like some sort of mystical key that locates and activates the Stones. The Stones shine a light that can penetrate matter, like earth and stone. The light is like a signal, I suppose.'

'How do you know that?'

'I don't know. I just do.'

At the bottom of the church steps, Starling stops and turns to Anna. 'There's still a chance for you to live, Anna. If you go now, you might just make it.'

Anna frowns. 'Do you really think you could have come this far without me? Sorry, Starling, you might be some great super spy, but you are nothing on your own. Let's move on, shall we?'

Starling is stuck for words and knows what Anna has said is true. With no time to argue, he hurries up the church steps and stretches his hand out to the blue haze. It feels cool, just like the astrolabe lights. He steps inside it and gasps. It feels like he is slipping through a shower of fire and ice, yet it neither burns him nor freezes him. He shudders and stumbles through to the other side. Anna follows, trembling.

'Are you alright?' says Starling.

'That was just weird.'

The interior of St Mary le Bow is small and unremarkable after the immense opulence of St Paul's. There is a stone font and rows of wooden benches lead to an altar draped in a white cloth. The walls tremble and the water in the font ripples under a slow throb that seems to be coming from underneath the floor. Starling looks down and sees a blue glow emanating from the gaps in the flagstones.

'There must be a crypt,' he says, glancing around for a doorway. 'See if you can find the entrance.'

They search every wall and corner of the church, running back and forth checking the same places over and over, but find nothing.

Starling runs up the steps to the altar and looks around. 'There must be a way,' he says, hot and frustrated.

A faint waft of cool air brushes his face.

He frowns and looks in the direction it came from and sees the bottom of the altar cloth shifting slightly. He hurries toward it and pulls it up. Underneath the altar table is a flagstone with wider gaps than the others. 'I've found it!' he says.

Starling takes out the screwdriver from his sleeve and uses it to leverage the flagstone up. Anna slides her fingers underneath and together they heave the stone up and push it across.

The blue light shines brightly below, lighting up what looks like a narrow stone corridor covered in cobwebs. Starling lowers himself down feet first and hangs mid-air. There is almost a two-foot drop between his feet and the ground. He lets go, hoping to drop on his uninjured leg, but that is easier in his mind than in practice. He lands gracelessly, grunting at the shooting pains in his ribs and knee. He takes a deep breath and shuffles aside to allow Anna to follow him down.

'The floor's moving!' says Anna.

Starling looks down and sees the surface of the ground shifting. Looking closer he can see spiders, bugs and mice hurrying around them. They are crawling up the walls and through the hole and into the church above.

'They're running from the light,' says Starling.

'This is all getting too strange,' says Anna.

Starling leads the way towards the source of the light, turning around one corner then a second and third. They seem to be doubling back on themselves all the time, as if they are in a maze. He stops at the end of a corridor. Ahead is a cavernous square space. In its centre is a small building – a crypt within a crypt – that has seen better days. Its exterior walls are cracked and adorned with fierce stone gargoyles. Hazy blue light shines from their eyes and mouths, making them appear as if they are alive. There is a door made from heavy but rotten wood. It slides open with little effort.

Inside the crypt, the light is blinding. When Starling's eyes adjust, he sees a round stone table on top of which are twelve magnificent jewels of different colours, all of which combine to form the brilliant blue beacon. He takes a deep breath.

It is the Stones of Fire.

Chapter 43

In the Midst of the Stones of Fire

'I was expecting something… bigger,' says Anna.

'Me too,' says Starling, although the truth is he was not sure what he was expecting. Each of the Stones is the size of a large pebble. Combined in their original form, they would be the size of an ostrich egg, which on reflection might be big enough for a god of war, he thinks.

Suddenly, there is a thunderous clanging above them that causes Starling and Anna to inch closer together. The walls start to shake and dust falls from the ceiling. It is as if the great bells have fallen on the church floor above.

'The bells have stopped ringing,' says Anna.

'Let's gather the Stones and get out of here.' Starling removes his blazer and lays it out flat on the stone table. Tentatively, he reaches for the Stones. They spark, crackle and spit as his hand draws close. He lifts the red one and holds his breath waiting for something to happen, but it just shimmers and throbs in his hands.

'It doesn't hurt.'

Slowly the light begins to fade, as if his touch has somehow calmed it down. They scoop the remaining Stones into the blazer and Starling ties it up like a package. The brilliant beacon is no more. Instead, the blazer looks like a glowing bundle of blue fire.

They hurry toward the crypt door, but Starling spots movement in the shadows. He stops and grips Anna's forearm. He sees a sharp glint of blue reflect from a blade. He knows that blade. The knife bearer emerges from the dark, with a grubby, bloody bandage on one side of his face. His expression is grim, his one remaining eye fixed hard on Starling.

The Pastor.

'It's over, Pastor. Get out of our way.' says Starling.

'The Stones will not leave this holy place,' says the Pastor, stepping into the crypt.

As if knowing what the other is thinking, Starling and Anna separate, their eyes never leaving the Pastor.

Another booming explosion rocks the crypt. Cracks appear on the walls; dust and masonry fall around them.

'We will all die if we don't get out of here,' says Starling, but the Pastor seems not to care. Is his plan for all of them to die here?

Starling and Anna exchange glances as Starling sets the Stones on the table. She knows they will have to deal with the Pastor together.

The Pastor speaks as if conducting a sermon. 'Ezekiel 28:14: You were an anointed guardian cherub. I placed you; you were on the holy mountain of God; in the midst of the Stones of Fire you walked…'

The Pastor's eye is opened wide, his expression grim and deranged.

'…I destroyed you, O guardian cherub, from amidst the Stones of Fire.' He rushes forward swiping his knife at Starling, but Starling falls back just in time. He can hear the Stones throbbing with intensity, powered by the tension that fills the small crypt. He feels the room vibrating as a storm erupts around the Stones.

The ground and walls begin to shake with the combined force of the bombs and the power of the Stones. Starling steadies himself against the crypt wall. But the Pastor looms forward, his glittering blade once again raised in the air.

'…I destroyed you, O guardian cherub, from amidst the Stones of Fire.'

Out of the corner of his eye Starling sees Anna swing her leg upward with all the grace of a ballerina. Her foot connects with the Pastor's wrist, causing it to bend backwards with a horrible crunch of bone. He cries out, drops the knife and cradles his broken wrist. Fury lights up his face and he lunges at Anna's throat with his good hand. She punches and kicks him, but his grip is firm. Starling runs at him, smashing his fist into the Pastor's damaged eye. The Pastor screams and lets go of Anna.

Starling pulls her away and tucks the wrapped-up Stones under his arm like a rugby ball. The walls of the crypt shake violently; the ceiling cracks and begins to fall down in clumps. Starling swallows, hoping for one last piece of luck and, hand-in-hand with Anna, hurries out of the crypt.

He hears the Pastor cry out once more and looks back, but the crypt is crumbling and falling to pieces. He feels a cooling breeze and looks up to see the rim of the Bow bells peeking through a crack in the church floor. Beyond the Bow bells he can see the light of the moon shining radiantly in the sky. The ceiling creaks under the strain and the Bow bells crash through and hurtle toward the crypt, but Starling and Anna are already running back through the crumbling walls of the maze.

Chapter 44

Return to the Wharf

Starling and Anna sprint through the maze, leaping over rubble and dodging the collapsing walls. Dust and smoke fill the air in a dense, blinding fog making Starling unsure if Anna is in front or behind him. He gropes his way forward, tripping over the uneven surface.

'Anna?' he calls.

'I'm here!'

She is somewhere ahead of him and he hurries forward. He hears other voices, and then a firm hand grips his arm. He gasps and pulls away, thinking the Pastor has survived and followed him.

'Starling?' says a voice through the din.

'Eoin!'

Eoin pulls him forward and shoves him gently ahead. 'Climb!'

Starling cannot not see anything, but leans forward and feels what he assumes is a large mound of rubble. He coughs, rubbing his stinging eyes and looks up. There are two torch lights pointing down and the sound of voices above him. He can hear Anna.

'There he is!' she says.

There are others encouraging him on. He recognises their voices. It is Mr Singh and Eli Pike. Starling climbs forward scrabbling for purchase and shifting his tired, sore body upward. He can feel Eoin close behind him. The dust thins the higher he climbs. A pair of hands grabs his arm and hauls him up.

'There ya go, Starling my lad,' says Eli Pike.

Starling steadies himself against Eli.

'Thank you.'

'Lift your head up and I'll pour some water into those eyes,' says Eli.

Eli pours cold water over Starling's face. He blinks and, through his blurred vision, he begins to see the bright full moon hanging over St Paul's. The skies are clear of bombers. They have left having failed to strike the Stones. London is saved.

Eoin is on his feet.

'Let's get everyone out of here quickly. There's an unexploded timer bomb down there and it's about to blow.'

Starling looks back down at the pile of rubble he and Eoin have just climbed. What had been St Mary le Bow is now a smoking crater.

'It's lodged in the floor of the nave,' says Eoin. 'Everyone out, now!'

They turn and run from the disintegrating church back towards St Paul's where Starling can see the old Post Office van.

Eoin opens the rear doors.

Starling hesitates. In the gloom he sees someone crouching in the corner, bound and gagged. He swallows. It is Colonel Frost.

'You caught him.'

'Aye lad. That I did.'

Eoin beckons them inside as Eli starts up the engine.

And then the timer bomb explodes, rocking the ground beneath them. Starling looks back in its direction. Clouds of dark smoke fill the streets like a heaving black monster. He shivers and feels a peculiar emptiness that he cannot quite explain.

They sit in grim silence as the old van trundles through the war-torn streets. Starling can feel all eyes – except Frost's – looking at the bundle on his lap, which is no longer glowing and seems like nothing more than some rocks wrapped up in his blazer.

He hands it across to Eoin.

For a moment, it seems the Irishman does not want them, but then he takes the bundle and Starling feels an overwhelming weight lifting from his shoulders.

Frost is trying to speak through his gag. Starling pulls it roughly from his mouth, curious to hear what he has to say.

Frost licks his lips and glares at Starling with eyes full of hate.

'You think this is over?' he spits. 'You have crossed them and you will pay the price. You will all die, I can promise you—' But before he can finish Eoin's fist flies at Frost's face. Frost's eyes roll in his head and his body goes limp.

'I'm so bored with you,' says Eoin.

No one says anything.

Starling hugs his knees and closes his eyes. He feels Anna's hand cover his and is grateful for her warmth.

The events of the past few days flash by him and tears threaten.

'I want to go to Tower Bridge Road,' he says at last.

'Starling, we need to get you to a doctor,' says Eoin.

Starling shakes his head.

He can feel Eoin's probing gaze, but the Irishman does not object. 'Eli, take us back to Tower Bridge Road.'

-

Starling walks passed the burnt-out car, his stomach a pit of raw nerves. He can see the small form of Sam lying alone in the rubble where he had fallen earlier. He trembles inside and hesitates. He wants to call out his name but that would be pointless. Sam is gone. Dead, just like Skipper, Violet, Aunty and the others who got in the way.

He kneels by Sam's body, gently picks up his head and rests it on his knees, and carefully wipes the dust from his friend's eyes and face. Grief swells inside him. If he had tried better to protect him he would be alive today.

'I'm sorry Sam. I'm so sorry.'

Moments pass and a cold rage begins to grow inside him. Although he does not remember his parents he knows they are dead. He can feel it. That is why he has become the person he is. His muscles twist at the thought of all the other innocents who have died at the hands of VIPER or the Pastor. They are all monsters.

'This is all VIPER's doing, Sam. I'll make them pay for it, I swear I will. I promise I will hunt them down and when I find them, I will make them pay. I promise you Sam, I will make them pay!'

Starling dips his head and fights back tears. He has battled through all of this without truly understanding who or what he is. He trembles and thinks of Skipper's friend who had gone mad after losing his memory, and makes a promise to himself to never let that happen. At least not until he had his revenge. He looks up at Eoin, who is watching him close by. He stares hard at the Irishman.

'Who am I?' he demands.

Chapter 45

Sleeper

Eoin instructed Eli to take them to St Ermin's, a Victorian redbrick mansion-block hotel in Westminster where the Secret Intelligence Service had annexed a number of floors and secretly went about the business of spying, code breaking and communication in the comfort of one of London's finest hotels. No one noticed the Service personnel. They moved amongst staff and clientele like ghosts.

Starling had been looked over by a doctor and had his wounds treated, cleaned and dressed. Before his meeting with Eoin, he had requested some time to himself. He desperately wanted to know what Eoin had found out, but part of him was afraid of what he might hear. Was he alone in the world? Were his parents dead? He needed solitude right now to help prepare for whatever the Irishman had discovered.

Eoin had checked him into a room that was luxurious and grand, yet Starling barely notices. He takes a long hot bath and washes away the dirt and dried blood from his skin. Most of it is his own but some of it the blood of his friends.

Someone had been into the room while he had bathed. Waiting for him on the bed are a new set of clothes: a red collarless shirt, blue tweed trousers with braces and a brand-new navy blazer embossed with the golden Beaulieu crest. He is one of the Beaulieu elite now. A few days back he might have been pleased, but now he is numb inside and feels nothing.

He dresses and hears a knock at the door.

He almost doesn't recognise her. Dressed in a flattering pale blue dress is Anna. Her hair is shiny, her lips are red and her eyelashes seem longer and darker.

'You look beautiful,' he says without even thinking.

She laughs and it lifts his mood.

They say nothing for a moment, and then she steps forward and wraps her arms around him. He seems to float and pulls her close until he can smell the fine scented soap drifting on the surface of her smooth pale neck. He kisses it, feels her shiver and then finds her lips, where he becomes lost and, for a few glorious moments, forgets everything.

-

Later that evening Starling is sitting at a desk opposite Eoin in one of the hotel rooms the Secret Service has taken over and converted into an office. Despite the events of the past few days and his reluctance to hear bad news, he cannot stop thinking about Anna. He wants to hold her and kiss her again, but that would have to wait.

'What will happen to the Stones?' he asks.

'They will be shipped abroad, possibly to the colonies, and buried in a very deep hole somewhere.'

'Someone will find them again.'

'Aye, I have no doubt. God willing that will not happen in our lifetime.'

'What about the Fellowship? They have a lot to answer for.'

'Yes, they do, and we will deal with them in due course.'

'Why was Tim in league with them? The Pastor was an evil man.'

'Yes, he was. Although one could argue that we are on the same side of the Fellowship. They are a society sworn to protect mystical and religious objects. However, their methods for doing that leave a lot to be desired. The Grandmaster and his cronies turn a blind eye to the Pastor's practices, believing what they do is for the greater good. As I say, we will deal with them.'

Against the odds, Starling and Anna had escaped the collapse of St Mary Le Bow. Had the Pastor also managed to break free? Starling felt a quiver in his stomach. No, he was dead. He had to be.

Sitting on top of the desk is a manila folder stamped CLASSIFIED. It is slim, yet it sits there like the elephant in the room. Is this really the record of his life before he lost his memory?

'Are you ready?' asks Eoin.

Starling nods.

'I went back to Tim Chittlock's house and found some files locked away in his basement. The news is not good, Starling. I'm sorry.'

'Are my parents dead?'

'I'm afraid so. They were killed by VIPER, and you would have been too had Tim not intervened and prevented you from going home that day.'

He rubs his arms and swallows. 'Why were they killed?'

'VIPER wanted something.'

'What could they possibly want that would require them to kill innocent people?'

'I'll come to that in a moment. Tim was a friend and colleague of your father's. They had much in common.'

'Was my father a spy?'

'Not quite. He was a scientist who worked for a research organisation called Teleken. They led the world in telekinetic research and believed certain people had the power to move objects with their minds. Unknown to your father, mother and Tim, Teleken was funded by VIPER. They had developed a drug, which they claimed could make a person telekinetic. It was a sensational claim at the time and people were queuing up to become part of the trial. Your mother was one of them.'

'Did it work… was my mother…?'

'No, the drug did not make anyone telekinetic. The research was dropped, as was the funding. However, it was not a total disaster as your father discovered some years later. When your mother took the drug, she was not aware that she was pregnant.'

'Pregnant?'

Eoin picks up the file, removes a photograph and hands it across.

It is a shot of Starling, smiling and happy, when he is perhaps eleven or twelve years old. But he is not the only person in the picture. He is holding someone's hand. He can almost feel it now, small, warm, with a firm grip as if it does not want to let go. He blinks and remembers the flashback when he held Anna's hand at Butler's Wharf only hours back. He stares at the picture. Smiling up at him is a little girl. Like him, she has thick dark hair. Starling's stomach lurches. He recalls the dream he had on *The Outcast*: the one with him running away from the wolves to the safety of home where he found four graves. Two with coffins for his mum and dad; the other two were empty. He had thought nothing of it. It was just another confusing dream.

'In my dream, I saw four graves.'

'To the outside world the Starling family are dead, killed in a terrible accident. Tim saw to this to ensure you were not exposed.'

His mind swims and for the briefest of seconds a memory flashes through. He hears her laughing and calling his name and then he remembers.

'Rose...' he whispers, unable to take his eyes from the picture.

'Yes, you remember. She is your sister.'

From the recesses of his mind sparks of emotions ignite every fibre of his body – happiness long past, grief, and the one that feels so familiar to him now: rage. Rage at what he has lost. Rage at the murder of his parents. Rage at the kidnapping of his sister – his blood and the heart of the family. He trembles and feels nauseous.

'Through some quirk of nature, VIPER's telekinetic drug trial worked on your mother's new-born child, although they did not become aware of it until she was older.

He searches the folds of his memory to find even a scrap of something that will help him recall any of his sister's telekinetic behaviour, but he finds nothing.

'Tim recruited you and primed you as a sleeper agent so that you could train, listen and learn about VIPER. He promised you your heart's desire if you helped bring them down. Do you remember what that was?'

He nods his head slowly. 'To find my sister.'

'That's right, but when Tim told you about the Stones and the danger they presented you diverted your attention to preventing VIPER from finding them. You did a most honourable and brave thing, Starling. We cannot thank you enough.'

He is only half listening. 'Where is she?'

'First things first...'

'Where is she?' demands Starling.

'Rose is being held in a VIPER stronghold known as the Red Tower.'

'I have to go there and bring her home.'

'Before we make any decisions you must understand you are still in danger. VIPER will not allow the indignity of losing the Stones of Fire to pass by without consequence. Also, in that head of yours lies VIPER intelligence that makes you valuable to us and a threat to them.'

'But I don't remember any of it.'

'But you are starting to. You've had flashbacks and you just remembered Rose's name.'

Starling folds his arms. 'What do you want from me?'

'Let's do this my way. We will find your sister and we will tear down VIPER forever. But trust me, Starling. Trust me and I promise I will make this happen.'

He can't stop thinking about what he has lost and the void it has left in his soul. His heart feels twisted and out of shape; its only desire is to rescue his sister and seek retribution for VIPER's crimes. If he has to he will bring them death and destruction. But Eoin is right, they cannot rush into this and Starling knows he cannot do it alone. And Eoin cannot do it without him. For four years he was undercover, learning and waiting for his moment. He knows what he must do now. He will go back behind enemy lines, break them and destroy them.

Sleeper. Liberator. Executioner.

That's what he was. That is what they have all made him. He smiles, his destiny clear to him at long last.

Acknowledgements

I'd like to thank my partner, family and friends for their support, patience, love and humour. Without these pillars, *Sleeper* would not be published today.

Thank you, Rebecca Lloyd for your expert editorial advice. Every author needs writing buddies. Thank you Jean Levy and Olivia Kiernan for your encouragement, critiques and partnership on our many literary networking events.

The Red Storm

For my dad

Chapter 1

Murder in Mornington Crescent

London, 13th July 1943

Ilia Koslov's right hand nestles firmly against the comforting warm steel of the Nagant pistol concealed in the pocket of his green trench coat. Drawing on the end of a Woodbine, he exhales a bitter grey cloud of smoke and crosses Hampstead Road, hurrying towards the glossy red-tiled fortress that is Mornington Crescent tube station. Under the rim of his fedora, tilted forward to obscure his face, he scans the area. The streets are empty. It is morning, still dark; traffic is thin and most Londoners, he imagines, will be slumbering in their beds or sitting down to eat their paltry breakfast rations.

He ignores the wizened old guard who bids him good morning and presses the button to call the lift. He hears it creaking and cranking as the steel chamber is hauled to ground level. Pulling apart the lift gates, he hesitates. The London underground is nothing more than a glorified tomb. Full of ghosts and hidden corpses, many taken by his own hand. He shudders and tries not to think about it. Once again he has a job to do and he must be swift.

As the lift lowers deep into the earth, his hand grips the pistol, pointing it forward. The steel box arrives and he slides open the gates, his eyes alert, his gun ready. The tiled corridor beyond is full of shadows, but he is confident there is no one there yet. Edging forward, he glances left then right before making his way to the agreed meeting spot on platform one.

The platform seems unusually clean. The rectangular cream tiles that line the walls, and the blue and red tube symbol, have a sheen to them. Perhaps Agent Sedova has cleaned the place to impress him. He chuckles darkly at his little joke as he walks the length of the platform, his eyes assessing every corner and every shadow.

He steps back from the platform at the rattle of an approaching train. The whoosh of cold air reeks of stale oil. He wrinkles his nose and studies his faint reflection in the windows of the train as it flies by. It feels like he is watching a live movie reel of himself. He straightens up, pushes out his chest and affects a pose like Clark Gable. Something hard presses into his back. He freezes and grips the Nagant, his pulse racing. In the windows he sees the outline of the agent behind him. He swallows and curses himself for letting his guard down, and, even more, curses Clark Gable.

'Remove your hands from your pockets and put them in the air,' says Agent Sedova.

Koslov feels his spine ice over and does as he is told.

Sedova's hands search his pockets. The agent finds the Nagant and tosses it to the rail track. 'Why are you here?'

'I… I have news,' Koslov replies.

'I'm listening.'

'There has been a change of direction…' He leaves the sentence hanging, in an effort to assert some control over his predicament.

Agent Sedova pokes his back harder with the pistol.

'The British spy is dead.'

Sedova lets out a heavy sigh. 'Do not try my patience. Which spy?'

'Starling.'

He thinks it odd that Sedova says nothing, and, for a moment, he thinks the agent has disappeared. He turns to look but the pistol is thrust into his back again.

'This is not news, Koslov. Is that it? Is that all you have?'

'No. We are to find the sister. Our leaders are very interested in what she is capable of doing.'

'We?'

'You and me. We work together like an alliance.'

'But you were sent here to kill me.'

Koslov feels his stomach twisting. How did Sedova know this?

'No, no, no.'

'Liar.'

He hears a second train approaching. A distraction. 'Agent Sedova, let me explain.' He whirls around, his arms raised in a conciliatory gesture.

'I did not say you could move.' Sedova is holding a British silencer pistol, aimed at his chest. 'Move towards the edge of the platform.'

Koslov feels the blood drain from his face. 'Please, Agent Sedova. I have a family.' The rattle of the train drowns out the phut of the silencer as a sharp pain explodes in his chest.

'So do I,' says Sedova.

Confusion fills Koslov's mind as he falls backwards, thudding hard onto the track below. He hears the train approaching and thinks he might catch it and go home to see his beloved Misha and their daughter Sasha. His eyes blink and he looks up to see Agent Sedova looking down on him with cold, hard eyes. Angry or sad, he cannot tell. He opens his mouth to speak but something screeches nearby and then everything goes black.

Chapter 2

A Sniff of Betrayal

Chartres, France, 14th July 1943, the following evening

Will Starling lies on his belly, concealed under bushes and weighed down by a backpack crammed with twenty-five pounds of Nobel 808 explosive. It is a warm summer evening; his clammy face mists up the lenses of his compact, Canadian 6x30 binoculars. He blows on them before wiping the glass with the cuff of his shirt. Adjusting the focus, he watches the blurred shades of green and grey form into lush green meadows and the sturdy steel legs of a towering pylon, an immense obelisk transmitting power from Paris through to Chartres and beyond – power the Nazis were using to their advantage. Starling takes stock of the tower, sweeping the binoculars up the ugly lattice structure. It would take a lot of explosive to bring it down.

'Is it clear?' asks Emile.

Starling nods. 'It's clear.'

'We should hurry, no?' whispers Claudette.

'Not just yet,' says Starling. His eyes follow the sun as it sinks and disappears behind a distant forest. The sky is brushed with an amber glow and provides enough light for them to carry out the operation without attracting unwanted attention with torches.

Emile and Claudette huddle on either side of him. Despite being the leader of this mission, he can't help feeling like a spare wheel to his newlywed companions. Emile is athletic and handsome in a typical Gallic way and Claudette is pretty with dark hair and a wicked sense of humour that has Starling laughing out loud sometimes. They are hopelessly in love, living each day as if it were their last. It is the perfect disguise for being amongst the occupying German forces, who find them innocuous and therefore ignore them.

Behind the smiles and sunny expressions, however, Emile and Claudette detest the Nazis, their feelings buried deep, emerging in the hidden meeting rooms of back-street bars and cafés where Starling and other members of the Special Operations Executive and French Resistance meet to discuss the latest orders from London.

'Before we go, I have something to ask you, *mon cher*,' says Claudette.

Starling hands the binoculars to Emile.

'*Oui, ma cherie?*' says Emile, scouring the landscape.

Claudette snorts. 'I was talking to Will.'

She has become like a sister to him, and, despite remembering almost nothing about his real sister, he has, on occasion, had to stop himself from calling Claudette by Rose's name. He knows he should have kept his distance, but Claudette's personality, her humour and passion are just too seductive.

He often thinks about Rose and wonders if she is like Claudette. In his dreams she appears in snapshots. She seems innocent, fragile, but also stubborn – nothing unusual in any of those traits. However, Rose was not like other girls. Starling had acquired secret research papers authored by his father, which revealed a little more about his past. His father had worked for Teleken – a VIPER-funded, scientific organisation that had developed a wonder drug that allegedly gave the user kinetic powers. Starling's father had championed it and his mother had agreed to be one of the guinea pigs. However, the drug had been a failure. None of the guinea pigs had developed anything other than the need to vomit for three hours after taking it. All except Starling's mother, that is. She had vomited the morning before taking the drug, unaware that she was pregnant with Rose.

Neither Starling's father nor his mother could have anticipated what fate had in store for them. The drug had fed the foetus and seemingly modified Rose's genetic make-up. Starling's father had no explanation as to how this could have happened. A miracle of modern science, he had concluded.

In the paper, Starling's father described how, at the age of five, Rose had lost her temper and her scream had caused all the windows in the house to shatter. Reading this had stirred an uncomfortable and frightening memory for Starling. He remembered his parents being confused, scared even, and recalled a terrified Rose sobbing and apologising for something she knew she had caused but had not been able to control.

In another episode they had been in a local park on a sunny afternoon. Their mother had been unpacking a picnic and an eight-year-old Rose watched on as Starling and his father tried out a new cricket bat. His father had bowled a googly, catching Starling off-guard. He had whacked the ball with fervour and accidentally sent it spinning towards his mother. As he panicked and cried out, the ball suddenly stopped in mid-air and spun slowly before flying obediently into a smiling Rose's waiting hands. To his parents' horror, other people had witnessed this event. This had been the beginning of the end. Soon after that, the agents of VIPER had come for Rose and his family.

The knowledge of what followed stirs the dormant rage in him. Closing his eyes, he feels it bubbling like lava. His parents had been murdered by the corrupt and criminal VIPER organisation. His kidnapped sister was reportedly locked up in a hidden fortress known only as the Red Tower. But two years had passed since he had learned this. Rose could be dead now for all he knew. And what did he know? In his fractured, unreliable mind his family appear as if they are bit-part players in snippets of a motion picture he is unsure he ever saw. He takes a breath and tries to focus on the job at hand.

Claudette ruffles his hair, taking him away from his sombre thoughts.

'You are miles away,' she says.

Despite himself, he smiles. 'I'm fine.'

She eyes him suspiciously for a brief moment and shrugs. 'If you say so. Anyway, I 'ave a surprise for you.'

'I love surprises!' he replies cheerily.

'Do we 'ave to do this now?' asks Emile.

Claudette ignores him. 'Will, we would love you to do us the honour of becoming godfather to our firstborn.'

Starling's heart sinks. He looks incredulously from a beaming Claudette to Emile, who shrugs off his wife's eccentric, easy-going attitude. Not to mention terrible timing.

'Please say yes,' says Claudette.

Suddenly the weight of responsibility has doubled and Starling feels a shadow cross his soul. He shuts his eyes and breathes slowly. Of course, he is happy for them, but he is angry, too – angry that this news has been dropped on him now.

'Will?' she says.

'Yes, you know I will, but you should not be here. It's too dangerous... Why did you not tell me this earlier?'

'Because you would not 'ave allowed me to come! That is why. And you need my 'elp.'

'We could have managed without you!' he replies, a little too forcefully.

Claudette's face falls, and he feels a twist of guilt as she looks to Emile for support.

'Will is right,' Emile says.

Starling rests his hand on Claudette's arm. 'Emile and I will fix the explosives. You are to stay here.'

Claudette opens her mouth to speak but Starling anticipates it. 'No arguments!'

Emile removes a torch from his pocket and hands it and the binoculars to Claudette. 'Stay here, *cherie*. We need a lookout. Signal to us if you see anything unusual.'

Claudette gives a sulky nod as Starling heaves himself into a crouch, his shirt wet with perspiration under his backpack. Emile kisses Claudette goodbye and turns to Starling.

'Ready?' asks Starling.

'*Oui.*'

Starling and Emile dart from their hiding spot and sprint across the open field. The only sound is the rustle of grass in the breeze and the thud of their feet on the soft ground. The backpack bounces on Starling's back like an overweight, angry baby. For a fleeting second he worries it might explode, sending him and Emile in bits towards the pylon before they have a chance to reach it, but he pushes the thought from his mind.

The base of the pylon is immense, bigger than he expected, and he worries if they have enough explosive to bring it down.

Emile helps Starling off with the backpack and carefully unbuckles the flap. A chemical, almond smell fills the air as he removes six sticks of gelignite. Starling takes them from him and begins fixing them to the legs of the obelisk. When all the legs are packed, Starling removes a slim, green tin cartridge from his jacket pocket. He opens it, hands four brass Time Pencils to Emile and keeps four for himself.

'Thirty-minute detonation time,' instructs Starling.

Emile nods.

'Use two per leg, in case one pencil fails.'

Using pliers, Starling breaks the copper end of the four pencils, cracking the glass vial inside and releasing the acid. He hands the pliers to Emile, holds the detonators up to the light of the red sky and checks the vials are empty. They seem almost the same size as the cathedral spires, which stand tall on the hill where Chartres was built. He wrinkles his nose at the sulphuric smell, like rotten eggs, and is relieved to see the acid is starting to do its work, eroding the wire so that it would, in thirty minutes' time, blow the detonator and ignite the gelignite. Countdown has begun. He inserts two pencils in each explosive, conceals them with foliage and checks his wristwatch, a waterproof Timor with a brown leather strap – a gift from his secret service mentor, a brusque Belfast man called Eoin Heaney.

It is 9.05 pm but there is still enough light.

'Claudette?' says Emile, suddenly.

Starling looks up, follows Emile's gaze and sees their companion sprinting across the field towards them. Something is not right. He swallows and scans the horizon behind her, but sees nothing.

Claudette arrives, panting and out of breath. 'Soldiers. I had to come. The stupid torch would not work.'

'How far away?'

'At least a mile. They are walking in a line with their rifles out, heading in this direction.'

'They know we're here. We've been betrayed!' says Emile.

'They are not alone.'

'What do you mean?' asks Starling.

'I don't know what to make of it. There are monks with the Nazis. Four of them.'

'Monks? But there are no monasteries here,' says Emile.

Starling feels his shoulders tighten. Hidden in his fractured memory is something about monks. Something he cannot reach. He tries to remember, but nothing surfaces.

'Will, do you know who they are?' asks Claudette.

He glances from Claudette to Emile and back to Claudette. 'It's probably nothing,' he says, rubbing the back of his head. 'Let's move. We have a job to do.'

His orders are to blow the pylon and head immediately to Chartres Cathedral to meet his contact, an agent with the codename Marie-Antoinette. The entire operation will be scuppered if he can't find a way to draw the soldiers away from the pylon. He glances at the backpack. There is one solitary stick of explosive remaining and one Time Pencil. A plan begins to formulate in his head. It is risky, probably crazy, but he is not going to let anything stop this mission from succeeding.

'Emile, Claudette, if we have been betrayed then it is too dangerous for us to stay here. I need you to head south, then circle round and meet me at the cathedral, as quickly as you can. Keep out of sight and stay safe.'

Emile and Claudette nod their agreement.

Claudette hugs Starling warmly and kisses him on both cheeks. 'Be careful, my friend. Make sure we see you. Godfather, remember?' She pats her belly.

'I remember.' Starling smiles encouragingly but has a grim sense that the outcome might not be what they hope for.

Emile grabs Claudette by the hand and they run, disappearing through the bushes and crossing a road to the fields and meadows beyond. With his friends safely out of the way, Starling can concentrate. He slips his backpack on and begins sprinting north, dipping under shrubs and hiding behind trees on the outskirts of the woods.

He hears the sound of a vehicle, the unmistakable grumble of a German Kübelwagen coming from an easterly direction in the woods. There must be a track there. He hurries towards the noise, which stops suddenly. Starling peeks from behind a tree and sees the dark green Kübelwagen with the black and white Balkanskreuz – the Nazi cross – painted on the side. A machine gun, a Maschinengewehr 34, is mounted at the rear. There is just one occupant, a solitary German soldier, who hops out of the vehicle and lights up a cigarette. He removes his helmet, places it on the bonnet and sweeps his fingers through his pale hair.

Starling circles round the rear of the vehicle without making a sound. He picks up a stone and tosses it over the soldier's head and into the bushes on the other side of the road. The soldier jumps and takes his Luger from its belt holster.

'*Wer ist da?*' he demands, pointing the pistol at the bushes and flicking his cigarette to the ground.

Starling inches behind him, picks the helmet from the bonnet. '*Guten Abend…*'

The soldier spins round as Starling raises the helmet, slams it against the man's temple and watches in satisfaction as his legs give way and he falls unconscious to the ground.

'…and good night.' Dragging him out of sight, Starling removes his uniform and puts it on. It reeks of stale sweat and cigarette smoke. Slipping on the helmet, he drops his backpack onto the passenger seat and starts up the Kübelwagen's engine.

The car is designed to drive on rough terrain and Starling steers it easily off the track and through the woods until he reaches the perimeter. He can see the other German soldiers and the monks standing around the bushes where he, Claudette and Emile had lain only twenty minutes earlier. He gets out and checks the boot, finding rope and various tools including a large spanner. Suddenly, his plan has upgraded to a new level.

Starling removes the machine gun from the vehicle and places it on the ground. With the pliers he snaps the glass vial of the Time Pencil, sets it to detonate in two minutes and inserts it inside the last stick of gelignite, which he places by the driver's pedals on the floor of the car. With the engine still running, he ties the rope around the steering wheel and the brake, securing it tightly so that the wheel cannot turn. Then he wedges the spanner against the gas pedal so that it is temporarily pushed to the floor.

He releases the brake and watches the Kübelwagen drive itself out of the woods and into the field where the soldiers and monks are on the move, approximately 200 feet away. The officer in charge sees Starling and shouts something Starling cannot hear. All eyes are looking towards him and the Kübelwagen as it drives drunkenly towards them. Starling picks up the MG 34 and fires mercilessly at the soldiers and monks. He shoots to kill and they hit the ground, most dead, some only injured.

Starling ducks down just as the Kübelwagen explodes in a satisfying ball of flame. He hears cries and then gunfire.

There is little more he can do here now. He starts to run, praying that this was enough of a diversion to lead them away from the pylon.

Chapter 3

Rise of the Cerastes

Starling sprints through the woods, his body drenched in sweat from the heavy German uniform and warm evening. He emerges into a clearing where the light from the dusking sky casts a hazy pearl sheen across the open fields and the nearby ruin of an old church. Stopping to get his bearings, he hears a ringing in the west. It's the bells of Chartres Cathedral.

He picks up his pace along the outskirts of the trees. The stillness is eerie. Something's not quite right. The hair on his neck stands up, as if he knows he is being watched. He is not alone. Glancing towards the ruin, he thinks he sees a tall, dark figure disappear into the shadows. For a moment, he thinks of his old foe, the Pastor, and shudders. But it could not be him. He had died in the crypt of St Mary le Bow two years before.

He hears a twig crack to his right and swings round. He feels something whoosh past his ear. As he crouches down, a knife shudders into the bark of the tree behind him. It seems strangely familiar. He pulls it out, turns it over in his hand and his heart begins to pound.

In the distance he glimpses the pale face of a hooded monk looking his way. Starling stares, his stomach clenching. He has seen monks like him before. He knows the order.

The monk disappears into the gloom. Starling holds up the knife. The shape of the grip is unmistakable: a snake. But not any snake – it is a viper. This monk is from the Cerastes, the order of VIPER.

Starling needs to find out why he's here and moves cautiously towards the run-down old church. He sees the monk looming in what was once the entrance, his face hidden in the shadow of his hood, his arms tucked into his sleeves. Starling moves closer. The man is dressed in drab grey robes, tied at the waist with a thick, red, snake-like rope. A symbol of the order to which he belongs.

Starling knows he is here for him and him only. But how could he have known Starling was here? Where could the intelligence have come from? Was there a mole in the Secret Service?

The monk retreats into the gloom of the ruins. He is trying to draw Starling closer, but Starling is not going to fall for that today. Logic tells him to get the hell of there, stick with the plan. But the monk might be useful; with some persuasion, he may tell him where the Red Tower is. Clenching the snake dagger firmly in his palm, Starling follows the monk.

Inside the ruined church, he stops, his eyes scanning around. He can see no one. He hears a man cry out above him and sees the monk's robed form leap from the wall. Suddenly he lands on Starling's shoulders and a flash of red flies past as the monk pulls a rope towards his neck. Starling blocks it with the dagger and, as the monk pulls the rope tight, Starling slices through it, hurls the man off his shoulders and turns to face him.

Dropping the rope to the ground, the monk pulls two long knives from his sleeves. He raises his arms with the knife tips pointing downward like the teeth of a viper. Starling has only the single dagger with which to defend himself. He does not stand a chance. As the monk runs at him, Starling tears the German helmet from his head, holding it in one hand with the dagger in the other. The two men connect with a screech of metal on metal, Starling thrashing the helmet against one knife and twisting the dagger against the other. The monk's strength pushes him backwards. It all seems futile and Starling kicks out in despair. The kick hits the monk's stomach, winding him. He shudders but remains poised, his focus weakened just for the moment. Starling wastes no time, flicking his wrist and bringing the dagger down on the man's hand.

The monk drops one of his knives and steps back.

Starling glances at the knife lying on the dusty ground. With it are droplets of blood and two of the man's fingers. The monk retreats, disappearing further into the ruins. Starling follows and arrives at what looks like the remains of the altar, where he sees the monk with his hood pulled back. He has torn some material from it to bind his bloody hand.

'Who are you?' asks Starling, taking stock of the man. His hair is shorn, his face is lean and his expression unsettlingly calm. Starling notices a tattoo of a viper above his ear. The symbol of the Cerastes.

The monk does not respond. Instead, he walks towards Starling, the remaining knife balanced in his good hand. Considering he has lost two fingers, he does not seem to be in much pain. Starling lifts the dagger to fight but the monk is fast and slides along the ground, toppling Starling over onto his back with his feet. Starling hits the ground with a thud and both the dagger and helmet slip from his grip. He scrambles to his feet as the monk swipes his knife, but Starling pulls back and the blade merely slices through the German jacket. The monk pushes forward, his lean face glaring at Starling, his mouth twisting into a sneer, a low noise like a growl emerging. He is strong, but Starling holds his nerve and lashes his boot out at the monk's injured hand. The monk stumbles back, nursing his wounded and bloody hand. Starling scoops up the dagger and runs at him, their weapons caught in a lock once more. The monk's face is inches from Starling's. He whispers in his ear.

'*Tempestas rubra advenit,*' he says.

Starling freezes, his mouth dries. He feels he has heard these words before.

The monk seizes the moment, pulls back and lashes his foot hard at Starling's chest, knocking the wind from him and sending him spiralling back towards the altar. Down and dazed, Starling is straddled by the monk, his knife arm pinned down by the man's knee. Smiling grimly, the monk raises the knife one more time. Eyes wide and mouth dry, Starling thinks this is the end. His free hand searches the ground and finds only grit and debris. He scoops some in his palm and flings it at the monk's eyes. The knife plunges, but Starling grabs the monk's wrist and, holding it firm, slams the knife down into the man's thigh.

The monk screams and falls to the side.

Starling scrambles forward pulling the knife out of the monk's flesh, and holds the knife to the man's throat. 'Why are you here?'

The monk's eyes meet directly with Starling's. '*Tempestas rubra advenit,*' he says again. And again, Starling's stomach clenches. There is something in the words, something from his past, that he can't quite recall.

'What does that mean?'

The monk's jaw starts to move, his tongue darts between his teeth, but he says nothing.

'Tell me what it means,' demands Starling, pushing the knife against the man's flesh, but the monk pulls away and slams the side of his face on the floor. Blood seeps from his mouth and he spits out what looks like a hollow tooth. His mouth is open, his tongue turning something over. It is a red pill. A poison capsule.

Starling swears and steps back. The monk's body begins to shake violently. He seems to be choking; the whites of his eyes turn scarlet and a gruesome red froth gathers in his mouth. He is taking a long time to die but there is nothing Starling can do.

What on earth could cause that reaction?

As the monk finally stills, Starling tries to piece together what's going on. The Cerastes were here looking for him but it doesn't seem right that they'd be working with the Germans. Had VIPER and the Nazis joined forces? VIPER's influence spread far and wide – it was well known they had senior people in positions of power in all governments across the globe, including Germany's – but their goal of creating a new world order would be in direct competition with the Third Reich's ideology. There had to be a simpler explanation. The German soldiers accompanying the monks could not be Nazis – they had to be soldiers of VIPER in disguise.

Starling hears voices from the woods. Picking up the helmet, he runs to the back of the ruins, hops over the remains of an old wall and runs in the opposite direction. He must get to Chartres Cathedral as quickly as possible. He cuts back into the shadows of the trees. Twigs lash at his face and hands as he sprints through the gloomy woods, but he barely notices them. He can think of nothing but the monk's words. They were a warning, but not just that – they were a threat.

Tempestas rubra advenit. The Red Storm is coming.

Chapter 4

Codename: Marie-Antoinette

The ancient town of Chartres is built on a hill on the left bank of the Eure river. With the enforcement of the curfew the streets are quiet and full of shadows. All the shutters are closed. There are no street lights; the blackout is as well observed here as it is in London.

Starling's boots echo loudly on the cobbles as he runs up a narrow street. Wiping the sweat from his brow, he stops and checks his watch. It is 9.40 pm. Five minutes past the detonation time. 'Shit!' he whispers. How could that happen? Were the Time Pencils faulty?

He turns a corner and almost collides with two armed German patrol soldiers, who reach for their weapons but stop when they see Starling's uniform. Their green collar patches and shoulder straps indicate they are privates. However, on the upper left arm of the taller of the two is an embroidered pip, a pyramidal star marking him out as a Oberschütze, a senior private.

They seem as surprised to see him as he is them. They say nothing for a moment as they look him up and down.

'*Guten Abend*.' Starling breaks the silence with a tense smile. He fixes his helmet and buttons up his jacket.

'*Guten Abend*,' they reply, their suspicion obvious. The senior private frowns at the cuts in Starling's uniform and the patches of dirt and asks, '*Wie heißen Sie?*'

Time is tight. Starling glances at the cathedral spires at the top of the town. Marie-Antoinette will not hang around forever and he has Emile and Claudette to think about. He fakes a coughing fit, raising his hand to his mouth to buy time as he thinks of a name. He says the first thing that comes into his head – 'Hitler!' – and regrets it immediately.

The men look at each other in disbelief, before turning back to Starling.

'Hitler?' says the senior private.

Starling laughs. '*Nein… nein…* Himmler! *Ich heiße* Himmler.'

They seem even more confused. 'Himmler…?' one says with a slow drawl.

Starling sighs. He has had enough. His eyes dart between the two men, sizing them up and calculating that it will take no more than ten seconds to bring the two fools down. His fists curl. The senior private's eyes narrow as if he has detected a shift in Starling's demeanour. Their eyes meet but, at that very second, a mighty explosion shakes the ground beneath their feet and lights the sky beyond the town where the pylon is located.

'*Schieße!*' say the soldiers, in unison.

At last.

Fearing the Allies are bombing them, the townspeople start emerging from their homes into the narrow streets. They jostle past Starling and the soldiers, making it easy for Starling to move away.

A second explosion fills the air and people begin running for shelter. Through the melee, the senior private calls to Starling and points in the direction out of town, 'Himmler! *Kommen Sie mit!*'

Starling nods, but allows the swelling crowd to grow between them. When the two soldiers are herded out of sight, he makes his way to the cathedral at the top of the town.

Starling stands in the shadows in the forecourt at the west entrance to Chartres Cathedral. When he'd arrived a year before, Claudette had given him a tour of the town and told him the history of its magnificent Gothic cathedral.

'Typically Catholic and oppressive,' she had described it, with a wry smile.

He hadn't been sure what she had meant until now. Looking up at the façade with its vast, round, stained-glass window, he remembers her telling him that the west window represented the apocalypse, the Last Judgement. He thinks of VIPER. Isn't that what they want? An apocalypse of their own making? *Many must die for the world to change.* In their own twisted way they wanted to restart the world by wiping out most of its population and oppressing the rest. The thought of it sparks at his rage. He would never let that happen.

He hurries across the forecourt and up the stone steps, stopping at the three tall, heavy wooden doors. The stone eyes of Jesus and every biblical saint and sinner seem to follow him, judging and suspicious.

A third explosion blasts the night and lights up the sky.

The pylon must have fallen by now.

Starling pushes the door open and steps inside, closing it behind him and breathing in the faint traces of incense. The light from the fourth blast flashes behind the stained-glass windows, throwing a blue hue across the vast interior. Chartres Cathedral is breathtaking as he walks under its immense flying buttresses towards the centre and the famous stone labyrinth carved into the floor.

Emile and Claudette are sitting together facing towards the altar. They see him and he nods, but they turn away looking worried. He remembers he is still wearing the German uniform. He takes off the helmet and jacket. His hair is thick and long on top and he sweeps it back with his fingers. When they recognise him, they are relieved. Claudette stands, but Starling gestures for her to sit.

He sees the labyrinth, in the nave, and a woman kneeling at a bench, her head bowed as if in prayer. The labyrinth is faintly lit by four candles at the north, south, east and west points of the nave. There is no one else around. It must be Marie-Antoinette. Who else would risk coming here when they think they are being bombed?

He walks quickly up the aisle, stopping at the bench where she is kneeling. Glancing respectfully towards the altar, he genuflects and slides in beside her. He smells a sweet scent in the air, like a blend of exotic flowers, swathing her with an invisible cloud. Kneeling, he blesses himself and glances sideways. Her hair is brown, shaped in the pompadour style and she is wearing a pillbox hat with a black, netted veil covering a chiselled face, heavily made up. She seems older than him, perhaps by ten years or more.

Speaking the secret code words, he says, as if to himself, 'Death is nothing.'

The woman touches her forehead with a gloved hand, makes the sign of the cross and sits up. 'But to live defeated and inglorious is to die daily.' Her accent is unmistakably Parisian, as is her sense of style. She seems oddly out of place in a rustic town like Chartres. This is his contact. This woman is codename Marie-Antoinette.

'You're late,' she says.

'We ran into some trouble.'

She turns to look at him and he meets her gaze. Through the veil he sees full lips painted a deep red and large, dark, questioning eyes.

'We were betrayed.'

'By whom?'

Starling has really no clue who betrayed them. He doesn't believe it was any of the local Resistance he works so closely with – they are all so passionate and determined – but he wonders if one of them has got drunk one night and let something slip. 'I don't know that yet. Besides, we have other problems now. There are monks from VIPER here.'

'The Cerastes are here?'

'Yes.'

'*Merde!*' she says.

'Do you know why?'

She bends down to pick up her purse and opens it. She takes out a slim, silver cigarette case and hands it to him. 'They are looking for this.'

'What is it?'

The case is cool to the touch. The edges are sealed with a red wax and on it is an embossed insignia of an owl.

'Inside are the plans for a powerful weapon VIPER are developing. You must take it to London, at once, without letting it fall into their hands.'

Starling slips it into his trouser pocket.

'Can you swim?' she asks.

Starling frowns. 'Yes…'

'Good, we must leave immediately.'

With no time to question her, Starling turns and beckons to Emile and Claudette at the rear of the cathedral.

'Who are they?'

'They are my friends. The betrayal has put them in danger. They cannot stay here any longer.'

'No,' says Marie-Antoinette. 'That was not part of the deal.'

'Deal? What are you talking about?'

'We are not taking them,' she hisses.

'Yes, we are! Their association with me puts them at risk. If they are caught, VIPER will execute them.'

'It isn't my problem.'

'No, it is not. It's *our* problem.'

'No, it is not possible.'

'Claudette is with child!' says Starling, through gritted teeth.

Through the veil, he sees the agent's firm expression soften. After a moment she nods. 'Very well.'

Starling shakes his head, furious that he had to argue. As he turns away from the agent he notices something on the floor at the centre of the labyrinth. Pieces of a chess set have been carefully placed, but not for a game. The pieces are positioned alongside each other as if in alliance.

What on earth?

In the middle is a tight circle of pawns surrounding something red and blue and shiny. It is a solitary toy fusilier, a tin soldier brandishing a sabre as if he is running into battle. A memory slices through Starling's mind. He has seen this tin soldier before. He feels dizzy and rubs the back of his head.

'Will?' says Claudette, who is now standing by his side, her hand holding his arm softly.

'I'm fine.' He crouches down and picks up the soldier. It is two inches tall, hollow, and with a split up its spine. Starling's heart beats faster. He turns the soldier upside down and sees two letters scratched into the faded green paint of the toy's base.

WS

'What is that?' says Claudette.

He feels cold inside. He remembers sitting at a desk in a bedroom, a room that was new to him. Standing in the doorway was Timothy Chittlock. His face was solemn. It was several years ago when Starling first went to live at Chittlock's house after the death of his parents. He had sat at that desk all night, barely able to move. His hand sore from gripping the tin fusilier. The same one he held now.

There are voices outside the cathedral. Emile hurries to the west entrance and peeks outside. 'Soldiers!'

'We must hurry,' says Marie-Antoinette.

'Who gave you the order to meet me here?' asks Starling.

Marie-Antoinette turns for the north exit. 'We don't have time for this.'

'Someone knew I would be here. Who was it?'

The agent does not meet his gaze. She ignores his question and walks away. Starling follows and grabs her arm. 'You know more than you are letting on. Tell me!'

The soldiers' voices are getting closer.

Marie-Antoinette pulls away from his grip and glares at him. 'I only know him as the Owl. I don't know who he is or what he looks like. That is all!'

Starling searches his shrouded memory for a clue as to who this Owl could be but finds nothing. Whoever he is, he has sent a clear message: VIPER are back and they are everywhere. They are closing in and Starling is at the centre of it all. Buried in his head are all of VIPER's secrets. They want him dead.

'Please, we must leave,' says Marie-Antoinette.

Starling nods his agreement and the four of them hurry to the north exit.

Outside, in the shadows beyond the grounds, is a dark Citroën Traction Avant. Starling hears the shrill barking of a small dog and sees a shadowy, rat-faced creature glaring at them from the driver's seat.

'Quiet, *cherie*. Mummy is here,' says Marie-Antoinette, in hushed tones.

The dog's barking is relentless. Starling shoots a worried glance back at the cathedral, sure that the noise will attract attention.

The Parisian agent opens the boot and pulls out two blank artist's canvases.

'The girl can ride up front with me. You two in here,' she says, hiding the canvases under a bush.

Starling has a bad feeling about this, but there is no alternative. There is just not time to think of another plan.

'Claudette, please try and calm that beast down,' he says.

She smiles and kisses him on the cheek.

Starling climbs into the boot as Emile and Claudette embrace. Moments later, he and Emile are squeezed together in an awkward, foetal spooning position. Starling would laugh if their lives were not in terrible danger.

Marie-Antoinette slams the boot closed, plunging them into darkness. Above the din of the yapping creature, he hears her footsteps and then the car's doors creaking open. The vehicle shifts as the two women get inside. The engine starts and they move off steadily. Starling breathes a sigh of relief that the dog has finally calmed down.

'Will,' whispers Emile.

'Yes?'

'If anything 'appens to me, promise me you will look after 'er.'

'Everything will be fine.' Starling realises his tone is not convincing.

'Promise me.'

'I promise.'

The Citroën slows. Starling hears French voices. People are returning to their homes now that they know the Allies are not bombing the occupied town. Marie-Antoinette honks the car's horn three times. Starling rolls his eyes. That sound would surely attract the Germans.

The vehicle rolls slowly for another ten minutes before picking up pace. He swears he hears a German voice shout behind them, but it is lost as the car picks up speed.

'We are out of the town,' calls Claudette.

They drive for a further ten minutes, then Starling hears the dog growling as the Citroën slows.

'What's going on?' he asks.

'There is a checkpoint ahead,' says Claudette. 'There are monks also.'

'Those are not German soldiers,' says Starling. His heart pounds as the vehicle stops. He hears Marie-Antoinette roll down her window. 'Ah, *bonsoir, Capitaine.* Nice to see you.'

'Madame,' he replies, in a curt manner.

'How can I help you?'

'Please switch off your engine.'

The dog growls and barks and Starling hears two sets of heavy boots walk around the car. He feels Emile's body tighten in the small dark space of the boot and places a reassuring hand on his arm.

'Madame, it is forbidden to be out at this time of night. You must know this.'

'Ah, *oui, oui.* You see, I must take my cousin...'

The captain interrupts her. 'The engine, Madame, and your papers, please.'

'Of course. I will just get my bag.'

Starling hears a shuffling sound and jumps at the blast of two gunshots.

'*Merde!*' says Emile.

The Citroën's engine roars, the wheels spin violently and the car takes off. The dog is barking frantically.

Gunshots clang at the back of the car. Emile jolts against him. They are so tightly squeezed together in that small space.

'Let me make some more room,' Starling says, shoving his elbow hard against the back of the rear seats. After three attempts, the back falls inwards and cool air spills into the boot. The small dog growls in his ear.

'Emile, let's get into the back seat. Quickly.'

Emile does not respond.

Starling hears more bullets prang the car and smash the rear windscreen above them.

'Emile?'

But still he does not respond.

Starling shakes his friend. 'Emile!'

He wants to shout out Emile's name, but he does not want to alarm Claudette. Reaching over Emile's chest, he feels warm and sticky blood. Grabbing his wrist, he feels for a pulse. There is none. His stomach lurches and he hugs his friend, pressing his face into his lifeless back.

'I need your help!' shouts Marie-Antoinette. 'Under the rear seats are pistols. Use them. Our enemies are closing in.'

Tears prick Starling's eyes as he leaves Emile and edges out of the tight space.

'Emile, come out!' shouts Claudette.

'Stay down, Claudette,' calls Starling, his voice hoarse. He cannot bear to look at her as he searches for the pistols.

Peeking through the broken rear window, he sees the bright headlamps of two vehicles following them, one behind the other. The front vehicle is a Kübelwagen, containing at least four soldiers. Wiping his eyes, Starling shoots, but the bullets seem to go wide. A volley of return fire forces him to take cover and wait until they reload their weapons.

When the shooting stops, Starling is on his knees at the rear window and with a steady hand takes out one of the headlamps. He needs to concentrate; he can see the Kübelwagen getting closer. Taking two deep breaths, he aims calmly and directly at the silhouette of the driver. With his pistol's sight locked on to its target, he can almost see the driver's grim expression as he shouts at his colleagues to hurry and reload. Starling squeezes the trigger and is satisfied to see the driver's jaw explode in spray of what looks like dark ink. The Kübelwagen swerves off the road, spinning and crashing into a copse of trees and exploding in a ball of fire.

The dog whines.

Starling hears Claudette call Emile, her voice trembling.

'You must keep your head down!' says Marie-Antoinette.

The second vehicle – which seems to be a Peugeot cabriolet – is gaining ground. He can see the silhouettes of three shaved and hooded heads. Monks. One is hanging over the passenger door taking aim with a machine gun. Starling wastes no time and fires two bullets. One chips the wing mirror, the other hits the man's temple. He slumps dead over the car door and drops the weapon on the road below.

Starling takes aim at the headlamps. He is about to shoot but tumbles across the back seat when Marie-Antoinette swerves the car onto a different road with rougher terrain. The dog yelps as its small frame slams against the side of the door. Starling sets its trembling body on the floor.

There are tall trees on either side of them. Marie-Antoinette has switched off the lights and is driving blindly in inky darkness. She turns left, then right, slows and switches off the engine in a concealed spot off the track. Through the trees, Starling hears the rumble of the monks' Peugeot moving slowly through the woods. He sees the beam of the headlamps disappear up the road they have just turned off. They are safe. For now.

His first thought is what to say Claudette. His stomach is in knots.

'This is where we part company,' says Marie-Antoinette. She is pointing across Claudette to an opening in the trees. 'Take that pathway and you will come to a clearing. He is waiting for you.'

'Who is he?'

'You will know when you see him. He will take you out of here.'

'He will take us out of here,' adds Starling. He turns to Claudette. Her head is turned sideways as if she is looking out of the passenger window. Starling follows her gaze but sees nothing beyond the woods and the entrance to the pathway.

'Claudette, it is time for us to leave.' He steps outside and opens her door but she doesn't move. Her pretty face is pale, her expression serene. There is a wound on her neck from which blood seeps steadily.

'No…' says Starling, his voice choked and broken.

Her eyes that were once so full of mischief and humour are dull and lifeless. The walls of his throat seem to close in as he tries to stifle a sob. He kisses her forehead, which smells of the lavender soap she was so fond of.

'You must leave immediately,' says Marie-Antoinette.

But Starling feels desolate, frozen and unable to budge.

'Will, listen to me. Do not let their deaths be in vain. The plans you carry are important to all of us. We are in terrible danger if you do not complete this mission.'

Starling closes his eyes. He is weary of the life he has ended up with.

'Fight for them. We are not finished yet.'

Marie-Antoinette is right. He shivers and feels a familiar cold rage rise inside him, crushing his sorrow. He looks at the agent. 'Take care of them for me.'

'I promise,' she says.

Starling turns and sprints up the dark pathway, mindful of who might be lurking behind the trees on either side. To his right he catches the beam of the Peugeot's headlamps slicing through the woods and then hears the sound of an unfamiliar engine starting up at the end of the path. The headlamps turn in its direction and begin to pick up speed. Starling increases his pace, pounding his legs on the soft surface of the path. He emerges onto what seems to be a disused airfield. About one hundred yards away is a bi-plane with German insignia. His heart sinks. Has Marie-Antoinette betrayed them, too?

He hears the screeching of brakes and sees the Peugeot spin onto the airfield. The bi-plane is already rolling away. The pilot is beckoning him to hurry. What choice does he have? If Marie-Antoinette was a double agent, surely she would just have surrendered them at the checkpoint.

He starts sprinting towards the bi-plane, which is gathering speed. Pumping his arms, he pounds the ground with his legs until he is running alongside the plane. He edges closer to the passenger seat behind the pilot and leaps into the small pit, hanging on grimly as the plane speeds up the runway and lifts off the ground.

He gasps in the cold air, the muscles in his arms screaming and his feet flailing in the air. His hands grip the worn leather seat fixed inside the cockpit and he pulls himself inside. He hears the crack of gunfire above the bi-plane's puttering engine and, looking down, sees the monks below, watching him disappear from their grasp.

Below is Chartres, his home for the past year. Beyond it, a plume of black smoke rises from the pylon, which lies burning and twisted on the meadow. At this height, it seems like a mere child's toy. The beams of headlamps speed beyond the woods to Marie-Antoinette's Citroën, inside which are the bodies of his dear friends and colleagues, Emile and Claudette, and their unborn child. He feels his soul darkening. His sorrow has left him and all he feels is the cold hard rage that has lain dormant for the past year. Embracing it like an old friend, he swears he will have his revenge and this time he will not spare the life of anyone from VIPER.

Chapter 5

The Acolyte

Rome

The acolyte had been surprised to be summoned so quickly to the highest office by the lady herself. Considering he was a relative newcomer and still had much to learn of their ways, it did seem an honour, albeit a dubious one. He was no fool, and it had occurred to him that this could be some sort of trick and he might be going to his death, but he had come to doubt it. He knew – and the Master knew – he had much to offer them.

It was early evening and warm. A towering figure dressed in his grey robes, the acolyte cuts through the crowds on Via Paola and crosses the Piazza, stopping at the entrance to the Ponte Sant'Angelo to admire the magnificent Castle St Angelo, the broad, round fortress glowing in shades of red and pink as the sun begins its descent. On top of the fortress, overlooking the city, is a striking, bronze statue of the archangel Michael sheathing his sword, a symbol of Pope Gregory's sixth-century vision in which the angel had appeared to announce the end of a plague sweeping through Rome. The irony that his new master had chosen this place as the centre of operations is not lost on him.

With his hood up he crosses the bridge, offering the angel statues on either side a deferential nod. He is met by a suited, thick-set guard with an unprepossessing countenance. A so-called agent of VIPER, the man is without humour or warmth, but then again, so is the acolyte. The guard takes him up the long, dark, stone ramp leading to the first level. They are alone in the lightless space and he wonders if, at any moment, the guard might take out one or both of his weapons and shoot him dead. No one would be any the wiser. The acolyte stays close and watches the guard's every move as they ascend the ramp.

They arrive at the first level, emerge outdoors and cross the perimeter overlooking the Ponte Sant'Angelo and the Tiber River. The guard stops and knocks on a heavy, dark wooden door. Another guard appears, similar looking to the first. Bred from bloated pigs perhaps. He nods curtly at the acolyte and points to another door at the end of the corridor.

The acolyte makes his way towards the door. He can hear music, something brash and loud by Wagner, if he is not mistaken. He can also smell the acrid odour of cigarette smoke. He knocks on the door.

The music stops.

'Come!' calls Ophelia Black.

He has not met her and knows her only by her remarkable reputation. Ophelia Black was born into one of the richest families in the world; into a fortune made by spilling the blood of many. The family mined for gold, drilled for oil, manufactured cars and had recently taken over the manufacture of weapons for the war. Her adored father, a ruthless businessman, took whatever action was necessary to increase their sizeable wealth, whether it meant merely removing his opposition or committing full-scale genocide. Ophelia was following in his footsteps. She was highly educated and shared many of her father ideals – and perhaps even more of his ambition.

The acolyte enters the room, a vast space with an egregious marble floor and garish walls painted in a display of ancient Roman opulence with half-naked nymphs and cherubs. He shudders under his robes and looks out from the protection of his hood at Ophelia Black who, in a cloud of blue cigarette smoke, is closing the lid of a gramophone player. Against the wall above it, he sees a projection screen.

'Kind of you to come,' she says, without looking up.

'Good day, mistress,' he says.

She is not what he expected. Dressed in a steel grey suit and red heels, she is of slender build, in her late thirties: a handsome woman with a strong jawline and blonde hair with threads of silver. Black turns and walks behind a broad, gilded desk, where she sits down and extinguishes her cigarette. She looks at him and beckons to the chair opposite her. 'Sit, please.'

Moving towards the chair, the acolyte notices a movie projector on top of the desk and a cardboard box on the marble floor next to her chair.

With hooded, appraising eyes, she watches him approach and sit. After a moment of silence, she asks, 'How are you adjusting to your new routine?'

'It serves me well, mistress.'

The woman's face betrays no emotion, her expression is unreadable. 'Do you have any idea why you are here?'

'No, mistress.'

'I have a project for you. But first I would like you to watch this.' She reaches over to the projector and switches it on. A beam of light shoots across to the screen. Some numbers count down from five and then the image of a girl appears. She is perhaps ten or eleven years old and oddly, but not disagreeably, strapped to a steel throne. She seems to be waking up. She is talking but there is no audio with the film. He glances at the VIPER queen who regards him with interest.

'Keep watching,' she says.

The girl seems to be angry. Nothing much seems to happen for a moment until suddenly everything changes. The acolyte watches with both revulsion and excitement. How was that possible? He breaks into a sweat and feels his breathing increase. This is why he has been chosen. He swallows.

The film ends and the VIPER queen switches off the projector.

'She's quite something, isn't she?'

'Indeed, mistress.'

'That was three years ago. She's changed a bit since then.'

He is unsure what she means by this.

'In the box at your feet is a cat. It belongs to the girl in the movie. Her name is Rose. Rose Starling. I would like you to return this cat to the owner.'

'Yes, mistress.'

'She is kept in the old Pope's Apartment at the top of the tower.'

The acolyte feels a frisson of dark pleasure at what may lie ahead.

'Do not harm the cat. Keep it safe. I want you to befriend the owner. You both have a shared history that we can use to our advantage.'

'Very good, mistress.'

'Change out of those robes and wear something less intimidating. No one seems to trust the Cerastes. I can't imagine why,' Black adds, dryly. She takes a shiny silver case from her jacket pocket, removes a cigarette and lights it. 'That will be all.'

'I am happy to serve, mistress.' The acolyte bends down to pick up the box. He hears a frightened meowing sound from inside and turns to leave the room. He feels a shiver of excitement as he imagines his hands round the neck of animal, squeezing the life from its wretched body.

Chapter 6

A Drop in the Ocean

When the plane is fully airborne, Starling hears a scratching sound coming from the panel at his knees, where a small brass-mesh speaker is fixed. He hears laughter and then an older man's voice.

'Ha, ha! I say, that was a close one.'

It is the pilot. Starling looks up at him, but only sees the back of his head, which is covered in a battered leather helmet.

'Can you hear me?' calls Starling.

'In case you ask, I can't hear you. Only you can hear me. One-way communication, I'm afraid. Our mutual friend said you might need some convincing once you saw the Nazi insignia.'

Starling wonders who the mutual friend is – the agent codenamed Marie-Antoinette, or the mysterious Owl?

The pilot continues. 'Just so you know, they are a disguise. Don't want to risk being shot down by the buggers, do we? That said, let's hope we don't fly into a squadron of Spitfires, eh?'

For some reason the pilot thinks this is hilarious and laughs a raucous, chesty, choking laugh, which does not fill Starling with confidence.

'We'll fly north, skirt around Paris, swoop over Dunkirk and cross the Channel. Sit back and enjoy the flight, old man. I'll let you know when it is time to get off.' He roars with laughter again, his chesty laugh filling the small cockpit, and Starling wonders exactly what he means by getting off.

It has become unbearably cold in the exposed passenger seat of the bi-plane. Starling's teeth are chattering. He rubs the sides of his arms and regrets shedding the jacket he stole from the Kübelwagen driver. He checks his wristwatch, holding his trembling arm up to the stars for a clearer view. It is almost midnight. He hears the scratching sound of the speaker.

'Dunkirk below, old boy. Not long now.'

Starling peers over the side and sees the long stretch of Dunkirk's famous beach below, its pale sands littered with the ghostly wreckage of war: a twisted Spitfire and a charred and shattered ship – a paddle steamer. He wonders if it is the famous *Crested Eagle* that left London on the 28th May 1940 to bring home British soldiers trapped on the beach.

The rasp of another plane draws his attention. He looks to the west and sees a second bi-plane flying nearby. It is a smart new Tiger Moth, painted cream and equipped with two sets of guns. For a moment he thinks it might engage them in battle. However, it flies alongside them and both pilots give each other the thumbs up. The Tiger Moth's pilot looks towards Starling, his face obscured with large goggles, his gaze lingering long enough to make Starling sit up. Despite the night's gloom, there is something familiar in the pilot's face that he cannot quite place. Before he can see any more the Tiger Moth cranks up its engines and flies off into the night, leaving them in a reeking wake of burning diesel.

Who was that?

They fly across the Channel. The dark waters sparkle dangerously under the stars. Deep in thought about his next move, Starling no longer feels the cold, as if his body has adapted to the icy temperature. After a while, he hears the familiar scratching noise from the speaker followed by a guttural, chesty cough. The pilot clears his throat and says, 'Look below at nine o'clock.' Starling peers down to see a boat below with a single light flashing on it.

'Hang on tight!' says the pilot. The plane picks up speed then turns wide, circling the boat below.

'Unstrap your harness now!'

Starling does as he is told and gasps as the plane plummets towards the boat.

'Make sure you have everything you need!'

Starling peers over the side, not at all sure that jumping into the water from this height is a good idea.

'Goodbye, son, and best of luck!'

The plane levels off.

'Sir?' shouts Starling at the top of his voice. 'Is this really a good idea?'

He hears the sound of something cranking under his feet and then feels cold air sweep up his trousers. There is a gaping hole where the floor beneath his feet had been. Way below are the choppy waters of the Channel.

'What the…?'

Before he can say anything more, his seat flips down and he falls, arms waving furiously. He plummets hard and fast, feet first into the freezing water. As he sinks, the echo of a memory flashes in his mind, disorientating him. In it, he is falling helpless into the icy cold waters off Hastings. Colonel Frost has shot him in the chest. As the water closes over his head, two overbearing silhouettes of evil flash into his mind. Enclosed in their shadow are the faces of people he once knew and loved: his mother, his father, Rose, Chittlock. There are others too: faces from VIPER – faces he is not supposed to know about. He feels his rage rising, but in a split second they all disappear and there is just the ice-black sea.

Starling kicks his legs, swimming to the surface.

Crashing through the surface of the water he swallows the air greedily and looks around. The bi-plane is disappearing back towards France and the chugging engine of a tugboat is approaching. A torch beam sweeps the waters and lights Starling's face. Two dark figures in long heavy coats look his way. He swims towards the boat and, in the starlight, catches the boat's name and smiles. *The Outcast.* He knows this boat and once knew its owner, Skipper, the fisherman who had pulled him from the sea near Hastings after he had been shot. As he reaches the side he hears a familiar voice.

'Nice of you to drop in,' says Eoin.

Starling reaches for the hull, gripping a rope fastened around a cleat. He pulls himself up and Eoin helps haul him onto the deck. As soon as he has found his feet, Eoin throws his arms around him, hugging him, not caring that Starling is sodden. The Irishman steps back and looks him up and down.

'Look at you. War agrees with you.'

Before Starling can respond, the second figure, wearing a long coat tied with a belt at the waist, steps forward and smiles warmly.

'Hello, stranger,' says Anna.

Chapter 7

The Peace Ray

Starling is alone, below deck in *The Outcast*'s cabin, where the faint, reassuring smell of sweet tobacco makes Skipper's absence all the more painful. It feels good to be here, despite the sad memories that surround it. The old man had saved his life. It had been the first real act of kindness he had experienced since losing his memory. Deep inside, he suspects it was an act of kindness he'd not experienced in a long time. Skipper had witnessed Frost's attempt to kill him and watched as Starling plunged, apparently to his death, into the sea. If it hadn't been for Skipper, Starling would have perished, the Stones of Fire would not have been found and London would be no more. Who knows at what stage the world and this damn war would be? For his kindness and faith in Starling, Skipper had paid with his life, and it did not stop there. Violet, little Sam and many students from Beaulieu had been murdered in the pursuit of Starling and his notebook. The world owed Skipper a large debt.

Starling had tried to find Skipper's family but had discovered that he was a widower whose only son had been killed in action at Dunkirk. Skipper had been there too, hoping to find his boy. Sadly, that reunion never happened. However, he had saved the lives of fourteen other soldiers that day by ferrying them across the sea to the safety of home. The old man had been a hero long before Starling had known him.

He sighs at the memory. The world could be a cruel and unforgiving place. He knew this all too well.

The cabin has not changed much since he rescued the boat from St Katherine's Dock two years back. The little oven is still there, along with the bed he had woken up on and Skipper's table. There is a brown leather briefcase on top, the only object that does not seem to belong here. Before leaving for France, Starling had asked Eoin to look after the little boat. 'It may be useful one day,' he had said, and he had not been wrong.

From his pocket he takes out the cigarette case and the tin soldier and places them by the old sink. Removing his damp clothes, he dries his wet, salty body with a rough towel. Anna and Eoin have provided a casual, blue shirt, grey tweed trousers with braces and a navy sports jacket, all dry and neatly folded for him to put on, with some shiny black brogues alongside. The fabrics are smooth on his rough skin and feel almost foreign.

There's a knock on the door.

'Come in,' he says.

Anna and Eoin enter the small cabin and sit down. Anna discards her overcoat, revealing a smart, blue trouser suit. Her shiny, wavy brown hair reminds him of Rita Hayworth's. Her lips are full, her make-up skilfully applied to accentuate the beauty of her face. Starling swallows. He has missed her. She seems different. Older, more grown up. She is very much a woman now and not a girl.

'It's really good to see you, Will,' says Eoin, smiling.

'It's good to see you, too.' He looks at Anna. 'Both of you.' Their eyes lock for a moment, before Eoin breaks in.

'Did you bring it?'

Starling hands the cigarette case to Eoin, who breaks the wax seal and opens it. Inside is a small box. He opens it and Starling sees a row of microfilm.

'What are they?' asks Starling.

'Over the past two years, VIPER have been recruiting. Their numbers have doubled, as has their power and wealth. They stole the plans for a new super-weapon, which their scientists have apparently developed.'

'What kind of weapon?'

'Nikola Tesla was a US-based Serbian scientist – a physicist and a futurist,' says Anna. 'He drew up plans for what the US press – without irony – termed the "Peace Ray".'

'It is anything but a peace ray,' says Eoin. 'It was designed to be powerful enough to stop wars. A weapon capable of destroying tanks and tearing planes from the sky. A death ray, in truth.'

'Just what the world needs. Thank you, Mr Tesla.'

Anna continues. 'In his defence, he was not a warmonger. He was an ideas man, an inventor, the archetypal mad scientist. He created plans for the "Teleforce," but he never built the weapon; it was always just a theory. However, VIPER have made the theory a reality. They have built Tesla's Death Ray.'

'This microfilm contains the plans for it,' says Eoin.

'And we need to destroy it?' asks Starling, although he already knew the answer.

'Correct,' says Eoin. 'When we return to London, I will get these developed and we will work out what to do next. In the meantime, you two get some rest. I'll get us home.' Eoin gets up to leave.

'Wait. Have you heard anything about a red storm?'

Eoin wrinkles his brow. 'Doesn't ring any bells. Why do you ask?'

Starling tells him about his fight with the monk and his warning.

'I'll look into it,' says Eoin.

'One more thing... is there any news about Rose?'

'I'm afraid not, Will. Sorry.'

Starling sighs as Eoin shuts the door behind him. He realises finding Rose is not a priority for the Secret Service, but still he cannot help but feel resentful and disappointed.

'It's been almost a whole year since I saw you,' says Anna, when the door has closed.

'Three hundred and seventy-one days,' says Starling.

'Oh? You've been counting...' She seems surprised and he wonders why she looks away.

Starling reaches for her hand, and she allows him to hold it for a second before freeing herself and folding her arms. She seems uncomfortable.

'There is other news that Eoin did not mention.'

The Outcast's engine chugs into life.

Anna opens the briefcase, removes a folded newspaper and hands it to him. It is a copy of *The Times*, dated 27th December 1942. The headline reads: WANDSWORTH PRISON BREAKOUT LATEST.

Starling feels his stomach contract as he begins to read. 'At 6 am, on Christmas morning 1942, eight prisoners escaped from south-west London's Wandsworth Prison...'

He looks up at Anna, who gazes back with a serious expression. Starling reads on, scanning the article until he finds the list of escaped prisoners. He feels his shoulders tighten when he sees two he recognises: Victor Francis Frost. Rupert Jefferson Van Horne.

The final paragraph claims the escapees had help from unknown outside sources. Starling tosses the paper on the table. VIPER again.

'I'm sorry, Will.'

'Those two should have swung for what they did.'

'We will find them. I promise.'

Still raw from the deaths of Emile and Claudette, Starling walks to the porthole window and stares out to sea, losing himself in the shiny, vast blackness of the water and the soporific rhythm of the boat. He feels Anna's breath close by and realises she is inches behind him. He turns to face her, but she is looking down, avoiding his gaze.

'I've thought about you every day,' he says.

'We need to talk.'

He moves closer but she steps to the side and folds her arms again.

He feels a fluttering in his stomach. 'Anna. You're not telling me something.'

She rubs her arms. 'There's someone else.'

Starling steps back. He feels like he has been punched. He turns back to the porthole, wishing to be lost in the waters again. He does not know what to say or how to respond.

'You have no idea what I have been through,' she says.

Tensing, he feels his face flush and whirls round. 'What *you* have been through? Let me tell you a little bit about my day, Anna. I and my two best friends – Emile and Claudette, recently married and already expecting their first child – blew up a pylon on orders from London. VIPER knew where we were. We were betrayed and Emile, Claudette and their unborn child were murdered in cold blood…'

'I'm so sorry…'

'…just like Violet, like Skipper, like Sam: because of me – because of what is hidden up here,' he points to his head to illustrate the point.

'Will…'

'I escaped, leaving their bodies for an unreliable stranger to bury, and I'm wondering: is she actually going to do it, or will she toss them onto the roadside?' He feels his eyes welling up at the thought. 'And then I'm flown across the country and dumped unceremoniously into the sea by some crazy pilot…'

'I thought you were dead!' shouts Anna.

The tension in the air between them is heavy. Starling can almost feel it pushing against his chest.

'What are you talking about? I'm clearly not dead.'

'When I returned to London last year I – *we* – were all told you had been killed in action. The great Starling captured by the Nazis and sentenced to death by firing squad.'

'It was clearly a fabrication.'

'There were pictures, Will. Photographs.'

'How? That's just not possible.'

'I know what I saw.'

'Well, it wasn't me. As you can see. Did you see my face in those photographs?'

She shakes her head. 'I didn't believe them at first. I asked for proof and all they could say was "look at the pictures". All doors were closed to me.'

'Why didn't you speak to Eoin?'

'I did. He wouldn't deny it… because it was his lie.'

Starling swallows. 'Why would he do that?'

'He did it to protect you.' Anna sits back at the table and looks at him at last. 'Yesterday he called me for a meeting – a mission I was to undertake immediately. The first thing he did was apologise. When I asked what for, he told me that your death had been a cover-up. I felt sick. I didn't know what to think.'

Starling sits back at the other side of the table.

'VIPER were regrouping and they had undercover agents operating in the Secret Service. Eoin had heard whispers on the grapevine that Starling was alive. He knew this news would reach the wrong ears and your life would be in danger again.'

Starling leans on the table and rubs his face. Here he was back in the same game with the same villains. Emile and Claudette's dead faces flash in his mind but he pushes them away. The time to mourn would have to wait.

'You don't know what it did to me. I had to move on. I had to live.'

He tries to process what Anna had just told him. He knows he cannot blame her. What choice did she have? Yet the thought of her with someone else makes him go cold inside. It is better that way, he thinks. His love for her – this stupid emotion – was a distraction he could do without. The time was right to bring VIPER down and he had to be the one to do it. He is ready to start again and this time he would bring the fight to them.

'I understand,' he says.

Chapter 8

The Office at Puddle Dock

Starling stands on the deck watching the sun rise over east London as Eoin steers *The Outcast* along the Thames and towards a wharf called Puddle Dock. A group of fishermen are selling their haul to market traders, restaurateurs and whoever else has the money to buy their catches.

'We keep an office here,' says Anna. 'It allows us to keep an eye on who is coming and going.'

Two warehouses are separated by a narrow street. The warehouse on the left has been ripped in half, its charred remains open and exposed like the toothless mouth of a corpse. The building on the right is untouched; there are four floors of tall, wide leaded windows where people are going about their jobs.

Starling stares down the narrow street and sees something silver and gleaming parked at the top of it. He smiles and feels his mood lifting. It is Eoin's Embiricos.

The Irishman moors *The Outcast* and they step onto the jetty. Glancing up at the surviving warehouse, Starling sees a slim, suited man looking down at them from the top floor window. He thinks he knows him. He follows Eoin and Anna across the jetty, threading through the fishermen and their lively banter, with his head down.

He hears a voice that sounds familiar.

'…and I says to him, you listen right 'ere, I says. *The Lazy Turtle* is my boat. No one else's and you ain't got no business showing your old face round here. Now clear off…'

There is a grumbling response from the men.

Starling stops, his eyes focusing in on the face belonging to the voice that had grabbed his attention. The man must be in his forties, with thinning grey hair, a pot belly and blotchy skin on a pinched face with an expression carrying an air of smugness about it.

One of the fishermen speaks. 'Well, I never. What did he say to that, Ned?'

Ned! Of course. The same 'treacherous' Ned that stole Skipper's haul the morning after he saved my life.

'What is it, Will?' asks Anna.

Eoin is already at the top of the jetty and hasn't noticed that Anna and Starling are lagging behind. Starling scans the moored boats and sees *The Lazy Turtle.* It is a shiny, brand-new fishing boat that barely looks as if it has one day's fishing behind it.

'Anna, that man holding court. I need you to distract him for a few minutes.'

Anna looks at him questioningly.

'Trust me.'

She shrugs and walks towards the men, the hem of her coat flaring dramatically as she turns. When she gets close, she strikes up a bubbly patter, praising the men for their bravery in taking to the dangerous waters during these troubled times. Ned and his fellows seem captivated by her.

Who wouldn't be?

Starling hurries towards *The Lazy Turtle*, glancing back to check that Ned isn't watching. Moments later he is walking back towards Anna and the men.

'Gentlemen?' he calls. The fishermen turn.

'Which one of you owns *The Lazy Turtle*?'

'That'll be me. She's mine,' says Ned, gruffly.

Starling points across the water. 'She seems to be making a run for it.'

'What the hell?' cries Ned.

Starling had started the engine and untied her from the dock. *The Lazy Turtle* is now making what seems to be a drunken reverse attempt to leave the dockside.

The fishermen roar with laughter as Ned hurries down the jetty, the blotches on his face glowing a pillar-box red. He pushes past Starling to the empty spot where his boat was moored only moments back.

'Oi! Come back 'ere!'

Starling is soon behind him. 'That one was from me and this one is from Skipper.' He kicks the man's backside, sending him toppling off the jetty and into the soupy brown water below.

The other fishermen roar with laughter while Starling walks back up the jetty to the sound of Ned splashing in the water.

'Help, I can't swim!'

This causes the men to laugh louder and some even slap Starling's back as he joins Anna.

'What was that about?'

'I'll tell you later.'

With the laughter and Ned's splashing and bleating behind them, they walk to the warehouse and take the wide concrete stairs to the top floor. As they reach the top, Starling hears the tapping of fingers on typewriter keys.

The office contains just two desks, facing each other. Looming over their typewriters are two identical, red-haired, female secretaries dressed in dark green suits. They look up at Anna.

'He's in a shocking mood!' says the one on the left, rolling her eyes.

'Unbearable,' says the other. 'He just doesn't like Eoin doing his own thing,' she adds.

'Hello,' says Starling.

Their attention turns to Starling and their eyes roll up and over him, lingering for longer than is comfortable.

'Will, meet Daisy and Alice,' says Anna, gesturing half-heartedly so that Starling is not quite sure who is who.

'Don't ask me which one is which. I have no idea.'

'State secret,' says the one on the right, who winks quickly at him.

Clearly they are twins and Starling can't help but notice the outline of pistols beneath their jackets. These ladies are guards as much as they are secretaries.

'You two need a medal for what you put up with,' says Anna.

'Don't we know it,' says the one on the left.

'Go on through,' they say in unison.

'Beaulieu, Class of 1942,' whispers Anna to Starling as they walk past the penetrating eyes of the secretaries. 'Both have earned their gold badges.'

He looks back and sees them both smiling sweetly at him. He smiles at them and they turn back to their typewriters without another word.

'Neither of them can type for toffee,' Anna adds. 'It's all just a front.'

There is a second office with a frosted glass door. Starling hears raised voices. One is Eoin's. Anna knocks.

'Come,' calls a voice. Starling recognises the tinny tone. He has met this person before.

The office behind the door is large and sparse with a filing cabinet and a mahogany desk holding just a telephone. It seems to Starling that not much work happens here. Standing at the window is a slender man with a serious face and a long, hooked nose: Nicholas Morrow of MI6. His unreadable eyes linger over Starling for a moment.

'So, the rumours are true then,' he says, folding his arms.

'Sorry to disappoint you,' says Starling, noting the flare in Morrow's eyes at his insolence.

Eoin tosses the cigarette case onto Morrow's desk. 'I need this film developed and the pictures enlarged as soon as possible.'

Morrow looks at the insignia on the cigarette case with a sneer. 'You're a fool to trust the Owl. You paid a fortune for these and they could be pictures of anything.'

'He has never let us down.'

'As long as the price is right.'

Starling is intrigued about this mysterious Owl. 'Who is he?' he asks.

'No one knows,' says Anna.

Morrow snorts. 'Owl indeed. I prefer to think thieving magpie.'

'The Owl is a rogue spy,' says Eoin. 'He is very good at his job and has no love for the Nazis or VIPER.'

'Unless they are paying more than we are,' says Morrow.

'I think he was trying to send me a message,' says Starling.

'What are you talking about?' says Morrow, frowning.

Eoin's brow is furrowed too. 'Why do you think that?'

Starling removes the tin soldier from his pocket. 'At the cathedral I found this.'

'A toy soldier?' Morrow shakes his head.

'Why is that important?' asks Eoin.

'Because it was mine, and the last time I saw it was when I lived at Tim Chittlock's house in Pimlico.'

Eoin says nothing for a moment.

'I'd like to go back there. It might jog some memories.'

'I agree. We should go there now.' Eoin gets up immediately, clearly eager to get away. 'Tomorrow morning at the latest for those pictures, Morrow,' he calls.

As Starling turns to follow, he notices that Morrow picks up the telephone.

Chapter 9

Morrow's Lack of Caution

The Embiricos is as shiny and glorious as it was when he last saw it two years back. Starling caresses the bonnet absent-mindedly and catches Eoin watching him from the driver seat.

'She's quite something, isn't she?'

Starling nods his head.

The Irishman gets out of the car, smiles and tosses the key to Starling. 'You drive.'

Starling catches the key in one hand, a wide grin spreading across his face.

'Wait for me!' calls a voice.

He turns to see Morrow hurrying towards them.

'What do you want?' asks an unimpressed Eoin.

'I'm coming with you.'

'Oh, that's just friggin' wonderful, so it is!' says Eoin.

Morrow's lips tighten and his eyes narrow at the Irishman.

'It might be good to have a perspective from MI6,' says Anna, clearly trying to placate both men.

'Exactly, Miss Wilder. Thank you.'

'Whatever!' says Eoin, who drops his large frame into the passenger seat and slams the door behind him.

Starling hops into the driving seat as Anna and Morrow climb into the back.

'Why is he driving? This is not his car,' says Morrow.

'*He* has a name! This is my car and I decide who drives it,' Eoin replies.

'This is highly irregular!'

'Lighten up, Morrow. Starling is a very competent driver, as you will see.'

Starling starts the engine.

'Do you remember the way?' asks Eoin.

'I remember where Pimlico is, but I can't quite recall the house.'

'I'll direct you.'

Starling reverses away from the warehouse and lets the engine roar for a moment before pressing the accelerator, perhaps a little too hard. The wheels spin and the Embiricos takes off. Starling's heart leaps as he controls the steering wheel and swerves around, overtaking two other cars in front.

'I think we can slow down a little,' Eoin says.

'Yes! We don't want to draw attention to ourselves, do we?' says Morrow.

Starling drives through the mid-morning London traffic, easing off the accelerator as he approaches a red light. He glances at Anna through the rear-view mirror. She is unusually quiet, her eyes down, focusing on something he can't see. He hears the clicking of metal and glances round to see her pulling apart a Walther PPK pistol made from polished steel. The barrel is engraved with beautiful feathers – a stunning piece of craftsmanship. It is both beautiful and dangerous. Just like her, he thinks.

'Is it necessary to play with that thing, here in the back of car?' says Morrow.

'I'm cleaning it,' Anna responds.

'It had better not go off!'

'If it does, I'll try to make sure it's not pointing at you.'

'That's hardly reassuring.'

'Idiot!' growls Eoin, under his breath.

'What was that?' says an indignant Morrow.

Eoin does not respond.

Starling turns his thoughts to the Embiricos and wonders how someone like Eoin could own such an expensive car. Despite being well-groomed, the Irishman usually dressed in the same clothes: a grey, three-piece tweed suit, white shirt and blue tie. Hardly the garb of a rich man. Starling's curiosity niggles at him; he needs to know.

'Eoin, the Embiricos. It's an expensive car.'

'Yes…'

'How did…?'

'How did someone like me come to own such a fine motorcar?' asks Eoin, finishing the question.

'That's not what I meant.'

Eoin laughs. 'Don't worry. I know what you meant.'

'If I may…' interrupts Morrow.

'I won it in a bet,' says Eoin, ignoring Morrow again.

'It used to belong to Sir Hugh Coleridge,' says Morrow, 'who happens to be our chief of staff. As it happens, I phoned him before we left. He told me he will meet us at Chittlock's house.'

'What the hell, Morrow? This is a private mission. No one is supposed to know about it.'

'Since when was it private? May I remind you we both report into him. He is your superior.'

Starling hears Eoin swear under his breath. 'Well done, Morrow. You seem to forget that other people are listening in on our phone calls. It is possible your indiscretion will compromise our safety.'

Starling feels a tremor of excitement in his stomach. He glances in the rear-view mirror and catches Anna's gaze. She smiles briefly and he knows she is excited too.

Chapter 10

The Cerastes Strike

It is almost 11 am when they arrive at Westminster. Despite the war, people are going about their business. Some stand gossiping on street corners and others watch the world go by through the windows of tea rooms and cafés. Starling catches admiring eyes drawn to the Embiricos's impressive styling.

Following Eoin's directions, Starling navigates slowly through the bomb-damaged Pimlico streets, now a vast open space with stacks of rubble, the remains of the once grand and beautiful Regency townhouses that had stood for over a hundred years.

'This part of Westminster has recently been hit heavily by parachute mines and high explosive bombs,' says Eoin, grimly.

A harrowing sight, Starling thinks. Despite the felled houses and barren streets he feels a frisson of recognition. He knows he has been to Chittlock's house. He may even have lived here for a time before his move to VIPER. Frustratingly, he just does not remember.

'Straight up, turn first right and find somewhere to park,' says Eoin.

Starling drives towards an area of undamaged homes and shops and takes the first right turn into a street called Warwick Way. He pulls up at an empty space outside a beauty salon. The windows are gone, blown out by the force of recent bomb blasts, but business still goes on. There are three ladies, drinking tea and sitting under hairdryers, while another is getting her hair styled by a slender woman with silky, blonde hair curled on top of her head, and horn-rimmed spectacles dominating her face.

Eoin opens the glove compartment, takes out a black Beretta pistol and hands it to Starling. 'Just in case.'

'Thank you.' It is heavy and loaded. Starling slides it into the side pocket of his jacket.

Starling and his passengers get out of the car. His stomach flutters with vague memories, like dreams that can't quite be grasped. He notices the stylist look in their direction. With one hand she pushes her spectacles up her nose and cranes her head at Starling. A look of surprise forms on her face.

'Let's move on, Will,' says Eoin.

Starling looks away and follows Eoin. He hears the tinkling of a bell. Turning, he sees the windowless door to the salon open and the stylist staring at him with one hand on her chest.

'It's really you, isn't it?' she says, her accent has a distinct South London ring to it.

Starling freezes. He is in no way prepared for meeting someone who knew him in his previous life. He is at a loss for words.

'Young Starling,' she says, hurrying towards him, with open arms.

Starling notices Anna and Eoin reaching for their weapons and he shakes his head discreetly at them.

The woman wraps her arms tightly around him and he is engulfed in a cloud of powder and floral perfume. The scent is familiar, but he cannot place it. She pulls away from him and places her hands on his cheeks. Starling smiles politely and glances above the door of the salon where it states: 'Proprietress – Miss Millicent Kallender'.

'Hello Millicent,' says Starling.

She stares into his eyes as if reading his soul. He wants to look away. 'You've still got those sad eyes,' she says, 'and how did you get that scar?' She runs her finger across the scar on his left cheekbone.

He shrugs and swallows. This is his first contact with anyone who knew him before he lost his memory.

'Miss Kallender, if you don't mind, we have some important business, so we do,' says Eoin.

She glances at Eoin and nods. 'Of course you do. It's just I thought you were…'

Dead

'I'm fine.'

Her face brightens suddenly and she squeezes his shoulders and arms. 'Good. Look at you now. Not a boy any more. You're a man.'

'It's nice to see you again, Millicent.'

'Milly.'

'I'm sorry?'

'You used to call me Milly,' she says.

'Yes… of course… Milly.'

Her bright face slackens and she tries to smile but Starling can see she is hurt.

'I better get back to my ladies,' she says.

'Bye, Milly.'

'Oh, I was so sorry to hear about your Mr Chittlock. Terrible business, especially after your fam…' She stops herself before saying any more.

'Thank you.'

'Are you visiting the old house? It's strangely busy in there today. I even saw two monks go inside.'

Starling freezes, his muscle tighten. 'How long ago, Milly?'

'Only a few minutes ago, I reckon,' she says, looking across the road.

Starling follows the direction of her gaze towards a tall Regency townhouse, its yellow bricks layered with the dark soot of fire and destruction from neighbouring streets. He knows the house. It is Timothy Chittlock's.

He turns to the stylist. 'Milly, go inside and lock the doors.' He glances at the missing shop-front windows and frowns. 'Do you have somewhere you can hide?'

The stylist seems confused and looks from Starling to Eoin, Anna and then Morrow.

'It's for your own safety,' says Anna.

A blast of gunshots from inside Chittlock's house kills the awkward silence. Milly pales.

'Go, Milly, and take your ladies,' says Starling urgently.

'I have a shelter.'

'Perfect.'

She hurries nervously back to the salon. Despite the door having no glass she locks it anyway and turns the 'Open' sign to 'Closed'.

'We approach the house with caution,' says Eoin, removing his pistol, a Browning Hi-Power semi-automatic.

Starling feels his pulse racing and nods his agreement.

'I don't have a gun,' says Morrow, nervously.

With his free hand Eoin removes a battered and old, small Walther PP from his inside pocket. 'You do now.'

Morrow regards it with a look of distaste and reluctantly accepts it.

They follow Eoin across the road, hastily ducking behind the shelter of a blue Ford 7Y parked outside Chittlock's house. Crouching with their backs to the vehicle, pistols at the ready, Starling whispers 'Good luck' to Anna.

'You too.'

They hear the sound of glass breaking and a man's voice calling out in distress.

'I go in first,' says Eoin, who leaps to his feet and sprints to the front door. Starling can see it is ajar. Eoin kicks it open, glances inside and then runs in brandishing his pistol. Starling hurries after him with Anna and Morrow following. He stands to the side of the entrance and peers inside. Anna stays close; he can feel her breath on his neck. The hallway has a checkerboard-tiled floor and upon it are the scattered remains of pictures and frames pulled from the walls. Someone has been searching for something. There is a door to the drawing room. Eoin darts out of it, knocking over a hat stand and startling Starling. Hopping over the debris, he slides into the kitchen, his gun sweeping around the space. He glances back at Starling and shakes his head. They hear a groan from upstairs.

'Ready?' Eoin mouths, nodding at the stairs.

Starling's pulse races.

Eoin points at Starling and himself and then up the stairs. He looks at Anna with his palm out, indicating that she should stay down here, at least for the time being.

Anna nods once.

Eoin begins the countdown from three and, at one, runs at the stairs with Starling sprinting beside him.

To Starling's relief there is no one at the top of the stairs. Old memories of this floor flash in Starling's mind, impeding his concentration for a second. Shaking out of it, he sees the landing is in a similar mess to the hall downstairs. To their left, the door to the bathroom is open and a man with dark hair, dressed in a tailored, blue suit, lies on the floor, pale, with a bloody lip. There is a broken walking stick at his feet. He is conscious and watches them, his eyes lingering with curiosity on Starling. The bathroom window is broken, the glass shattered from the inside out. Eoin steps over the man and looks outside and down below. His fixed expression suggests there is no one there.

'Where are they, Hugh?' asks Eoin.

The man weakly lifts his arm and points his finger at the room behind Starling. Starling swallows. He knows the room. It was where he slept for the short period he had lived with Chittlock. He slides along the landing wall to the entrance of the room. Peering round the doorframe, he looks inside. He sees the single bed he used to sleep in and the wooden desk at which he used to sit. Above it, fixed to the wall, is a painting he remembers: an obscure and depressing landscape. He cannot recall the artist's name. He narrows his gaze at it, thoughtfully, but is distracted by a creaking floorboard. Through the open door, he can see a figure blocking the light of the sash window. It is a hooded monk dressed in grey robes tied at the waist with a red rope. The Cerastes. Starling notices three steel globes, the size of cricket balls, hanging from the rope tied around his waist. Ether bombs?

The monk is standing at the tall sash window overlooking Warwick Way. He raises the sash.

'There is nowhere for you to run,' says Starling, the Beretta pointing at the man's back.

The monk turns to face him, his arms at his side. Starling's memory stirs and the room spins for the briefest of seconds.

'Everything alright up there?' calls Anna, her voice waking him from distraction.

At that same second he sees two knives leave the monk's hands and hurtle towards him. He ducks out of their path and, with relief, hears them thud into the wall behind him.

He rights himself in time to see the monk fall backwards out of the window. Starling runs over to the sash and peers down, expecting to see another suicide, but the monk has landed nimbly on his feet and is sprinting up Warwick Way.

'He's on the run!' he shouts and hops down the stairs.

'I'll stay with Hugh,' calls Eoin. 'Make sure you catch him alive!' he adds.

Chapter 11

Death on Westminster Bridge

Anna is nowhere to be seen as Starling hurtles past Morrow in the downstairs hallway.

'What's happening?' shrills Morrow.

Starling only half hears him as he skids onto the pavement looking for Anna. He sees her coat flapping behind her as she pursues the monk towards Pimlico. They are already making ground despite the short head start. He looks at the Embiricos, hurries towards it, jumps into the driver seat and fires up its fierce engine. Steering out of the parking space, he slams the accelerator and speeds up Warwick Way.

The roads are thankfully clear of traffic but Anna and the monk are nowhere in sight. He swears under his breath, scans the area, then sees the tails of Anna's coat disappear over a pile of dusty rubble. He swings the car to the right and follows her, skirting the perimeter of the devastation. Frustratingly he does not see either of them.

Driving slowly, eyes peeled, nerves on fire, he turns into Belgrave Road, cruising steadily as he scans the pedestrians on either side and the entrances to the ornate houses. He passes Warwick Square on his right and slows, peering at the bushes and trees. It is then he sees the dark form of the monk charging towards him. He slams the brakes and pulls out his pistol, but the monk flips over the bonnet of the Embiricos and runs up Belgrave Road.

The passenger door opens and, with relief, he sees Anna jump in, her cheeks rosy with exertion.

'You took your time.'

Starling smiles. 'Nice to see you again.'

Pressing on the accelerator he pursues the monk, who is remarkably fast. Starling sees him turn left into Lupus Street, narrowly avoiding a man on a bicycle who calls out in anger. The monk disappears amongst the pedestrians on Vauxhall Bridge Road.

'I can't see him,' says Anna.

Starling scours the crowd but there is no sign of him. He notices the crowd's attention focused ahead and follows their gaze in time to see the monk haul the driver of a black cab from his vehicle. He punches the driver twice and throws him to ground.

'There!' says Starling.

The monk is on the move, ploughing the black cab through innocent pedestrians as they cross the road. There are screams and shouts as two men fly across the bonnet and tumble on the roadside. The cab disappears down Rochester Row.

Starling blares his horn and edges the Embiricos through the crowds and traffic onto Vauxhall Bridge Road. There are cries of protest and horns pressed in anger but Starling ignores them.

They cross to Rochester Row, but there is no sign of the taxi. Starling presses the accelerator and dodges through the morning traffic.

'I see him,' says Anna, pointing ahead.

Almost three cars ahead of them Starling can see the black cab threading dangerously in and out of traffic.

'Hold on!'

Anna grips the dashboard as Starling swings over to the wrong side of the road, slamming the accelerator. A red bus is heading right for them and Starling registers the look of terror on the driver's face.

'Move, you fool!'

As if he has heard him, the driver swings the bus to his left, mounting the kerb and smashing a blue police box to pieces. Glancing back, Starling is relieved to see no one is injured.

With his eyes fixed on the cab, Starling is gaining ground. He feels cool air and sees Anna unwind the window with one hand. In the other she holds the steel Walther. She leans out the window and fires two shots at the taxi, shattering the rear window. Starling steadies the wheel as Anna takes aim again, but the taxi disappears behind traffic. Starling presses on but with a long line of oncoming cars is forced to return to the left side of the road. There are six cars between him and the monk and Starling is forced to decrease his speed.

'Shit!' he says, his hands tightening on the wheel. He sees the taxi turn right into Great Peter Street. It drives out from the left-hand side and roars down the right, forcing oncoming traffic off the road and leaving a clear trail for Starling. He turns to the right and speeds after the taxi, flying past the ugly, steel North and South Rotundas, where the cabinet war rooms operate during an air raid.

Starling is beginning to gain ground when the taxi swings a hard left where the road widens and the traffic seems to thin out. He slams on the accelerator and speeds past the Houses of Parliament, which seems like a great Gothic blur.

Anna hangs out of the window again. She lowers her arm and fires twice at the taxi's wheels. The right-hand tyre blows and causes the speeding taxi to swerve and collide with a Post Office van before slamming into a lamppost.

People instantly crowd round the vehicle obscuring the view. Starling parks the Embiricos and both he and Anna jump out, moving cautiously towards the gathered onlookers. Starling conceals the Beretta under his jacket and pushes his way through.

'I never seen anyfink like it,' says a man. 'Driving like a maniac, he was.'

'I know!' says a woman. 'And him a man of the cloth. The war does some queer things to people.'

Reaching the taxi, Starling is dismayed to find the driver's seat empty and the monk nowhere to be seen.

'I'll see if he's close,' says Anna, but Starling fears the monk may already be gone. He leaps on the taxi's bonnet, holds on to the lamppost with one hand and searches over the top of crowd towards Big Ben.

'Do you see him?' asks Anna.

'Yes!' Starling spots the hooded figure hurrying towards Westminster Bridge. He takes out his gun and, ignoring the gasps from the crowd below, he aims. But the monk is in the thick of it and Starling risks injuring an innocent person. Instead, he raises the Beretta in the air and fires two shots.

The crowd screams and scatters and the monk crouches, turning back to look behind him. Starling jumps off the bonnet and runs with Anna towards the bridge, dodging the panicking bystanders. With pistols drawn, they arrive midway across the bridge, alongside a bus full of people who are watching intently. A breeze cools Starling's hot face. What a strange sight this must be, he thinks fleetingly, him and Anna armed and chasing what must seem like an innocent, holy man. The traffic has stopped as people duck in front of cars and cower at the side of the bridge at the sight of Starling and Anna, their pistols pointing at the monk who faces them, twenty feet away. His face is obscured in the shadows of his hood, he is rolling the three ether bombs between his palms. Behind the monk, to his right, Starling sees a young mother cradling her toddler, a little girl, desperate to free herself from her mother's clutches and pick up her doll, which has fallen to the pavement. Starling feels a pang of anxiety.

'We need him alive,' Starling whispers.

'I'll do my best,' Anna replies.

The monk begins to juggle the ether bombs as if he is some bizarre street entertainer.

'You do realise you will be dead before those things reach us,' Starling tells him.

The monk seems unfazed and tosses a bomb at the upper deck of the bus. It smashes through the window causing people to cry out in shock.

'What's he doing, Will? What was that?'

'A VIPER invention. An ether bomb that will render people unconscious for a short period of time. I don't know what he is playing at.'

The monk throws the second bomb far behind him. Starling hears the heavy steel globe crunch the bodywork of a car.

'What the hell is going on?' someone protests.

The monk tosses the third up and down in his palm.

'Drop it,' says Starling.

Starling hears screaming from the bus; his blood goes cold, but he keeps his eyes and gun focused on the monk.

'Oh Starling,' cries Anna.

Starling feels his heart pounding. And then he sees it. Rising behind the monk, from where the second ether bomb was thrown, is a red mist. His mouth dries. He hears more screams that make his skin crawl. The upper deck of the bus is engulfed with the same mist. The passengers howl in pain, choking, their eyes red, their mouths frothing. Blinded and disoriented, they beat against the windows in their desperation to get outside. The monk holds the final bomb – not an ether bomb, but something vile and horrible.

'Anna, get off the bridge. There is nothing to be done here. Go.'

'I'm not leaving you!'

'Go!' he commands. 'Please, Anna.' He feels her retreating and is relieved. Trembling with rage, he hears the toddler cry and sees the tearful expression of horror on the mother's face. His eyes blaze at the monk whose finger hovers on the release button of the final bomb. Starling squeezes the trigger. The blast of his pistol is lost in the screams of those dying on the bridge. The bullet hits the monk squarely in the chest and he falls back, lying deathly still on the road. The final bomb rolls from his hand towards the mother and toddler. The mother screams.

'No! No!' Starling runs towards it, scoops it up and runs to the side of the bridge. The breeze picks up and he hears the bomb click and hiss. Had he pressed the button accidentally?

'Get out of here,' he says to the mother, who wastes no time in running away, clutching her toddler tight.

Starling throws the bomb into the dark water of the Thames, inhaling what seems like the sweet odour of decaying fruit. A trail of red mist follows the bomb as it plops into the water and sinks. He turns to look for Anna, but his head begins to spin. He can see her. She is calling to him but he cannot make out what she is saying. She seems so far away. He feels his throat swell and coughs into his fist. His hand feels wet and warm. Blinking to focus, he sees blood on his palm. He groans, unsure what is happening, and then everything goes dark.

Chapter 12

Rose

Rome, 15th July 1943, morning

Rose Starling stirs in her sleep. In her dream she is naked and lying on a cold steel slab in a brightly lit room. Her lips are numb, her jaw is frozen shut and she is unable to move, scream or call for help. She hears voices and rolls her eyes downward. Blinking to focus, she sees figures wearing white coats huddled around her feet.

Their voices seem familiar.

Men's voices.

Murmuring.

In the dream she is drugged, but the effects are weakening and it feels like her body is thawing. Her blood is warming and she can feel every goosebump erupt on her skin. She feels her backside shifting and her legs parting. Through half-closed eyes she sees her feet have been raised and placed in leather stirrups.

No! No! No!

She is still too weak to move and wishes the drugs would disappear from her frail body. She hears a familiar female voice. It is flat and emotionless, yet firm and authoritative. It seems to be further away, as if it is in another room.

Ophelia Black. Rose feels her stomach twisting.

The white-coats huddle closer. One of them is bending down between her legs. Frustration and shame overwhelm her and she shudders as something cold is inserted into the private place between her legs. She tries to scream, but no sound comes. Trembling inside, a rage ignites in her soul and surges through her thin, cold body.

'She's coming round!' says a man, his voice raised in alarm.

Sick with humiliation she tries to pull her knees together, but she is still not strong enough.

'More ether. Quickly!' someone shouts.

Adrenalin hurtles through her body and she forces herself to lift her head. She glares at their shiny faces, half obscured by surgical masks, their eyes wide with panic and fear. She reaches her mind across the room and senses their heartbeats quicken to a gallop. There are four at her feet. Two behind. Six in the room beyond. Including *that woman.*

'Where is that bloody ether!' shouts a harsh voice.

An anaesthetist mask appears above her face. She can smell the gluey, sweet smell of ether as it spits angrily from the gaping black rubber hole. Holding it is a hand belonging to a semi-masked face with frightened eyes. She tries to warn him, but she cannot speak. Her body is weak but her mind is strong.

The mind is strong.

Focusing her thoughts she pushes against the mask with her mind. It trembles in the air above her. She pushes harder and stops when she hears the snapping of bone and a scream. She hears scuffling in the theatre and watches as the white-coats retreat clumsily.

The mind is strong.

She closes her eyes and, with her mind, caresses the heart of each man in the theatre as they clamber over each other to get out. With one merciless stroke she squeezes each beating organ until it beats no more. One by one the men drop dead to the floor.

'Rose. Stop! What have you done?' cries Ophelia Black.

She is beginning to feel movement in her legs and arms now. She pushes herself up to her elbows and lifts her feet off the stirrups. Her mouth is dry, as if it hasn't tasted water in weeks, but that's not important now. They have put something inside her. Fury envelops her and she focuses her mind across to the next room. Then she hears something clang on the floor beneath her. Looking down she sees a spherical object – an ether bomb, hissing and filling the theatre with its gluey smell. More drugs.

You cowards.

She feels herself weakening once more as the ether claims her. Curling into a foetal position, she lets the gas take her.

She has had enough.

She just wants to sleep.

Chapter 13

The Experiment

Rose jolts from her dream, waking to the sound of her nursemaid, Sofia, scuttling around the apartment, unbolting the shutters and throwing them open. Sunlight floods the room, sweeping away the gloom of incarceration. She blinks and lets her eyes adjust slowly to the light.

Sofia's round and kind face smiles down at her. She is wearing a black dress with a snug white apron pulled tight around her broad waist. 'Did you have the dream again, *bambina*? I heard you talking in your sleep.'

'I have it every night, Sofia. I am cursed.'

'No, *bambina*, you must not say that. You are a miracle, a gift from the Almighty.'

Rose rolls her eyes, uncurls from the foetal position she has woken in and pushes herself up into a sitting position. Sofia hurries to help, plumping pillows behind her back and kissing her on the forehead as she does so. 'I make you breakfast. Your favourite: soft boiled eggs with army.'

'Soldiers,' corrects Rose.

Sofia bellows a wheezing laugh. '*Sì*, but lots of soldiers make an army, no?'

'If you say so,' replies Rose, content to humour her nursemaid, the only real friend she has in this prison.

Sofia hurries out of the bedroom, her laughter trailing to the kitchen at the other side of the small apartment.

Reliving the events in this same dream is always visceral and horrible, yet somehow, rather than breaking her, they strengthen her resolve. Not only that: something wonderful and pure has come of the whole experience. Casting her eyes downward, she rests her hands on her swollen belly and whispers good morning to the child growing strong inside her. She will be a mother any day now and the fact that it has been put there against her will, Rose knows, is not the child's fault. It is still her baby – hers alone – and she will love it and take care of it like any mother would.

The warm morning sun soothes her pale skin and she yawns, stretching her limbs. They burn at the effort, two hundred or so half-healed cuts begin to pull apart before they have had time to close. She lets out a muffled cry and slowly relaxes her arms and legs.

There are no mirrors in her apartment and no glass in the windows, just empty frames with heavy duty shutters. The glass had been removed a long time ago after she had smashed it and used the sharp edges to cut her arms and legs. At first it had been an accident. One day, three years ago when she was only eleven, she had woken in a strange room, cold and numb and facing a mirrored wall. She was strapped to a steel chair as if she was some sort of mass murderer facing death by electrocution. At her feet were eight large leather medicine balls lined up in a neat row. Behind the mirrored wall lurked the ice queen and her white-coats, watching and speaking to her in silky tones through a round speaker fixed to the wall on her left.

'Rose, please try and lift one of the balls,' Ophelia had ordered.

'I'd rather not,' Rose had replied tartly. She hated Ophelia Black so much. *Evil witch.*

'Rose, dear. Please try. It is important we carry on your father's work. It is what he would have wanted.'

Rose had bristled at the mention of her father. 'My father would never have drugged me and tied me to a chair!'

Ophelia's tone had lightened then and she had spoken to Rose like a well-meaning governess. 'It's for your own good, Rose. We've talked about this. Remember?'

Rose had gritted her teeth and then caught sight of her reflection. Her heart had sunk. She had watched her mouth open in surprise as if it were not her own. There were dark rings under her eyes. She was pale and drawn with unkempt hair and wearing a dirty nightdress. How long had she been like this? She had wanted to cry but suppressed all emotion, knowing the ice queen enjoyed her misery as if it somehow nourished her black soul. She had once caught her smiling as Rose wept inconsolably at the loss of her brother Starling and her parents.

Ophelia had said, 'We will look after you now. Your parents left you in our care. It's what they wanted.' And so she had been taken away without attending their funerals and saying goodbye to them properly.

For almost a year after the death of her family she had felt a crippling desolation and was unable to talk with anyone. She had cried herself dry and succumbed to everything Ophelia Black asked of her. What choice did she have? She was a child and had no one else in the world. Besides, being here was, after all, what her parents had wanted.

It was just so hard.

She had thought about Starling then and wondered what he would have done if he were in her position. Perhaps he would not have cried so much, or at all. He would have been sad but he would have been brave and strong. He was always so brave. How she missed him.

'Rose. Are you with us?' said a faceless white-coat.

She had still been so young then and had just wanted to sleep, not lift heavy objects. 'I'm tired. I want my pills,' she'd told them.

'You can have your pills once we finish.'

This had irked her and her hands had gripped the edge of the steel armrests.

'Rose, please try and lift one of the medicine balls.'

'No.'

She heard the murmur of their voices from the speaker and imagined them all huddled in discussion wondering what to do with her. A wicked thought had entered her mind. Through hooded eyes she had smiled at her reflection across the room, reached out and pushed it with her mind. The mirror had rippled like a millpond swallowing a pebble.

The voices in the speaker had gone quiet.

A moment passed.

'Rose, did you do that?'

She had begun to scratch the armrests.

'That was wonderful, Rose. Now could you please try and lift one of the balls?'

She had decided to play their game. They would reward her with her pills and then she would be able to go back to her apartment. Focusing on one of the balls she had extended an invisible hand from her mind and lifted it into the air. After spinning it around she had let it thud back to the floor. She had heard an audible gasp from the speaker.

'I'd like my pills now, please.'

She recalled that the calming effects from her last dose of pills had been wearing thin and her desolation and remorse was returning.

'Can you do that again?' said the voice.

Rose had rolled her eyes.

'My pills!' she shouted.

Rose heard Ophelia's voice. 'Get out of my way! Rose!' she demanded. 'Stop being as worthless as your father. Lift the balls!'

Rose had felt her stomach twisting and her neck flushing. Two of her nails had broken against the edge of the armrest. She had never felt such rage.

One by one she had lifted the balls into the air, spinning them clockwise on either side of her.

'Good Lord!' said a voice from the speaker.

Rose had sensed the weight, shape and density of the balls as if they were part of her. She'd imagined her mind as a great octopus with eight tentacles stretching across the room controlling the balls. They zig-zagged past her, flying inches from her head and face.

She'd had enough of the witch and her monkeys. Looking down at the thick leather straps around her wrists, she'd lifted the buckle with her mind and yanked out the strap. She'd done the same with the second.

'Rose, you can stop now,' the faceless white-coat had said.

She had been in control. Her expression was fixed but, inside, her heart had felt as though it had been pounded by a butcher's hammer. She'd stood up and walked towards the mirror staring at the reflection of a girl she did not recognise. The balls spun and flew behind her bending to her will. And then she'd made them stop. They'd hung vertically in the air at the back of the room, four on each side, twitching as if their work was not yet done.

'Rose, please sit down,' Ophelia had said.

Rose had closed her eyes. The loneliness, the desolation, the cold fear had returned to her like ghouls in the darkness of her mind. It was just too much. She'd screamed. The medicine balls had shot like bullets across the room and shattered the mirror. She'd heard the voices from the other room rise in alarm and the sound of chairs falling over and feet shuffling rapidly. She'd then felt a sharp pain in her right forearm. She'd opened her eyes and looked down. Her arm and hand were dripping in blood. The pain was intense.

The bitter whiff of cigarette smoke had invaded her nostrils and, looking up, she'd seen that the mirrored wall was no more – just a pile of glittering shattered glass lying on the floor. In the room beyond had been six white-coats, huddled at the back, staring back at her with a mixture of awe and horror. Ophelia Black stood in the middle of the room, arms folded, her body shrouded in a cloud of blue cigarette smoke. Beside her was a movie camera. Ophelia had grinned calmly at Rose.

'I think it is time for those pills, Rose, dear.'

The pain in Rose's arm had dominated her thoughts. She'd watched the blood drip and splash to the floor, suddenly aware that with the arrival of this physical pain and the spilling of blood, the ghouls had been released from her mind.

For two years after that she had secretly cut herself. She had no idea how she'd managed to hide it from them, but she had. And then one day all the glass and the mirrors and all the sharp objects had been removed and her drugs had been increased. She had not complained. Her limbs were now hideously ugly, and the drugs kept her ghouls at bay.

That had been three years ago, although it seemed like a lifetime.

The sound of Sofia singing to herself and clanging pots and pans from the little kitchen at the other side of the apartment distracts Rose from her memories. She sighs and rubs her scarred arms. A moment later the nursemaid calls from the living room.

'Rose, I forget the bread. I lose my mind! I run quickly and be back soon. *Ciao, bella!*'

Rose hears the bolts sliding, the key turning and unlocking the apartment door. The same procedure is repeated in reverse as Sofia locks the door from the outside and hurries off to wherever she is going.

Chapter 14

Find Charlie

Rose pulls herself from her oversized four-poster bed and experiences an odd feeling that makes her skin prickle. The scars on her arms and legs begin to itch as they always do when she becomes anxious.

On the bedside table is a small jar of ointment. She notices the two white pills she was supposed to swallow before bed, and makes a mental note to flush them down the toilet before Sofia sees them. Opening the ointment jar, she rubs her arms and legs softly with the lemon-scented salve and shudders at the self-inflicted lines and grooves that disfigure her thin limbs.

Something feels different. What is it? She glances around the sparse bedroom looking for Charlie but does not see his shape or hear his snore.

'Charlie,' she whispers, but hears no response.

She hears Sofia come back in and begin to lay the table for her breakfast. Rose grabs the pills and hides them under her pillow. Cradling her belly, she leaves the bedroom and steps onto the cool, red tiles in the living room of her prison apartment. The room is long and sparsely furnished with an old sofa, a dining table for two people and some shelves to store books. Charlie is nowhere to be seen.

Morning sunlight floods the small but cosy space. She peers through the glassless windows to see if Charlie is on the ledge outside, but the ledge is empty. In the distance she sees the gleaming dome of St Peter's Basilica and the rooftops of the Vatican City. Car horns honk across the Tiber and, closer to home, within the confines of her apartment prison, she hears the sound of men's voices barking and hollering.

'Please, *bambina*, eat,' says Sofia.

'I'm not hungry. Where's Charlie, Sofia?'

'Who knows? He'll be back, I'm sure.' Sofia's arms rest on her hips as her eyes scan the living room. 'You must be keeping up your strength, child. You are eating for two now, remember?'

'I wish you would stop saying that.'

Rose wants to lose her temper but Sofia is one of the few people who is kind to her. The men in the castle both loathe and fear her after what she did. Even the ice queen, Ophelia Black, the one person everyone fears, is wary of her. None of them understands that Rose could not stop herself. They had invaded her. She wanted to make them pay and she just couldn't stop. Her thoughts turn back to Charlie.

'Charlie?'

Rose feels her heart break into a gallop. Charlie never leaves her side. Where could he be? Her belly is so heavy her back hurts, yet she hurries out of the apartment and down the worn stone steps without a thought that this is forbidden.

'Charlie! Charlie!' she calls, her voice trembling with fear. Has something happened to him? At the bottom of steps the thick, heavy door is closed. She turns the handle and pushes it, but it does not give. It is locked. There are men's voices from the tower walkway on the other side.

What if they see Charlie and don't know who he is? What if they hurt him? Her heart begins to race and she focuses on the door. Her body is weak but her mind is not. She wills the door to open. It shudders and then begins to warp inwards and outwards, the ancient wood creaking in protest.

She hears the men's voices raised in alarm and pushes the door with the force of her mind. It splits into pieces, as if punched with a mighty, invisible fist. Two guards in dark blue suits stand in the walkway gaping back at her, eyes wide with astonishment. Both have their hands inside their jackets, poised to remove their pistols.

She glares at them, daring them to try, and watches with satisfaction as their olive-skinned complexions turn white. She screams at the top of her voice and both men scarper. Composing herself, Rose charges through the shattered doorway with one hand holding her belly. The heat from the afternoon sun dries her clammy face as she runs down the walkway. Her eyes dart around, searching for Charlie on the red-tiled roofs above the walkway and inside the rooms and offices. He is nowhere to be seen.

She hears a man holler a warning to his colleagues. Word is spreading that she is out but she doesn't care. She must find Charlie. He is all she has left from her old life. She runs and runs, ignoring the people who jump out of her way. She feels the scars on her arms and legs opening one by one, tears in her flesh that sting and bleed. There is warm blood on the soles of her feet that causes her to slip and almost fall. Behind her she hears Sofia's wheezing calls.

'Rose! Rose! Stop, please!'

Rose reaches the steps leading down to the Courtyard of the Angel, where Montelupo's marble sculpture of the angel Michael, with its magnificent bronze wings, watches over a gathering of people below. She sees monks and men and women in dark suits. All at once they look up at her. She swallows and remembers that she is still in her nightdress, her scarred bloody limbs bare and exposed for all to see.

Sofia reaches her side, her face red and sweaty with exertion. 'Rose, *bambina*. Come back with me,' she says softly, removing her apron and draping it around Rose's arms.

-

With the cat on his lap, the acolyte sits quietly in the Courtyard of the Angel on a stone bench under the angel Michael's watchful gaze. He has shed his robes in favour of an innocuous Catholic priest's cassock. He wears dark glasses and by his side is a white cane. To the world at large he is a blind priest, a role he has thus far relished. People defer to him, rather than recoil. They say '*Scusami, Padre*' if they walk in his path.

With this disguise comes a power that he can use to his advantage. She will take to him, the girl. She will feel sorry for him and befriend him. The cat's heart beats slowly, steadied by a small measure of opiates, which he'd administered one hour earlier.

He knows she is there. The VIPER rabble are gawping at her like frightened children. His head down, he shifts his gaze to peer up through the dark glasses. She is standing at the top of the steps, thin and pale, her arms and legs scored with a thousand cuts. A slither of pleasure ripples through his sinewy body. With one hand he softly strokes the cats back; with the other he squeezes his nails tightly into its hind legs. The creature lets out a low squeal.

-

Rose hears a meowing sound from the crowd below. Her eyes widen and she scans the courtyard. A man she doesn't recognise, a priest wearing fingerless gloves, is cradling her beautiful black cat, instantly recognisable with his white socks and white eye patch.

Rose feels her heart melting and, breaking away from Sofia, runs down the steps to the courtyard, ignoring the pain of her open wounds. The crowd retreats but she ignores them, her eyes focused only on Charlie. She hurries towards the priest and lifts Charlie from him. She buries her face in his fur, taking in his hot musty scent, kissing him and gently squeezing him.

'Oh sweetheart. You frightened me. Don't ever do that again.'

The acolyte watches her through the dark lenses of his spectacles. 'I think he missed you,' he says, chuckling like a kindly grandfather. He can see the girl's eyes appraising him.

'Yes. I think he probably did.'

He reaches for the cane and rests his hands upon it. 'What is his name?'

'Charlie.'

'Oh. Like Charlie Chaplin?'

The girl hesitates. He bristles inside and curses himself. What would a blind man know about Charlie Chaplin? For a moment he thinks he has lost her.

'Rose, *bambina*. Please come now,' calls the fat nurse as she scurries across the courtyard.

The girl turns to leave.

'My name is Father William.'

The girl stops and cuddles her cat. His chosen name has done the trick. 'My brother is called William,' she says, sadly.

'Oh, that's nice. Is he here too?'

'He's dead,' she replies.

'Oh, I am sorry. So, so sorry.'

'Rose, quick now,' says the nurse. '*Scusami, Padre.*'

Scusami, Padre.

'Your name is Rose? Now how about that,' he chuckles. 'What a coincidence.'

'What do you mean?' The nurse begins to usher Rose away.

'My sister was called Rose, too.'

'That is quite a coincidence. Is she dead too?'

'Rose!' admonishes the nurse.

'That's quite alright, good sister. My dear Rose died a long time ago. I still think of her every day.' His head dips and he affects a sad expression. 'She was only sixteen.'

The girl gasps. 'I'm sixteen!'

'Oh, are you now? Well, I'm sure you will live a long life.' He smiles with what he hopes is an approximation of warmth.

'Rose, we must go now,' says the nurse pulling her close. 'Come, child.'

'Thank you for my cat,' calls the girl.

'My pleasure.'

'Maybe we could have tea sometime. You can tell me about Rose and I can tell you about Will.'

'Yes, I'd like that.' The acolyte sits back and smiles to himself. He has aroused the girl's curiosity. She will be open to talking to him again and perhaps again after that. Ophelia Black had plans for her, but that was of no concern to him. He does not serve the VIPER elite, despite what they think. He is here for other reasons. He watches the girl climb the steps with her intoxicated cat lying limp in her arms. He catches the fat nursemaid frowning at him and he looks away.

That one might be a problem.

He pictures his hands around the nursemaid's neck and feels his skin prickling under his cassock.

Soon he would have the girl.

Soon.

Chapter 15

Return to St Ermin's

London

In his dream Starling is free falling through the night. Red angry storm clouds herd through the skies spitting fire at the land below. Voices cry out as thousands of people choke and die in the midst of a bloody apocalypse. A smoking tree interrupts his fall, the crackling branches cushion his crash to the scorched ash that was once earth. He hears his name being called and pushes himself up. A cluster of people are choking to death in a cloud of red smoke on a stone road lined with the statues of angels, the kind you would see in a graveyard. At the end of the road is a tower and he sees Rose looking down from it. She is waving at him. Three shadowed figures, one woman and two men, stand imperiously behind her, watching her.

'I'm sorry, Will. I'm so sorry,' she cries as the three pull her back engulfing her in darkness.

'Rose,' he calls.

'Will!' calls Anna. He looks around the hellish scene but cannot see her.

'Anna, where are you?'

He feels a hand on his shoulder and stirs from his dream, waking to a blinding white light, his body aching, his mouth dry as if he has not drunk water in weeks.

'Will,' says Anna.

'Anna...' His voice is hoarse and weak. His eyes adjust to the light and he sees her peering down at him, her face full of worry, her hand gently squeezing his shoulder.

'You were having a nightmare.'

'Where are we?'

'In the hospital wing of St Ermin's.'

It had been two years, just after he had found the Stones of Fire, since he was last at St Ermin's, a luxury Victorian mansion-block hotel in Westminster where the Secret Intelligence Service operated under the noses of the hotel guests. His wounds had been cleaned and bandaged and it was in his room in the hotel that he had first kissed Anna. That memory alone made St Ermin's a special place for him.

'Drink this,' she says, placing a glass of cold water to his lips.

He sips it at first, then drinks it greedily and begins to feel better. 'Thank you.'

Glancing down, he sees he is fully clothed.

'Do you remember what happened?' asks Anna.

Starling recalls the events that led him to the bridge. He closes his eyes. 'They were not ether bombs… The people on Vauxhall Bridge?'

Anna shakes her head and Starling feels a stabbing anger. He sits up but his head begins to throb.

'The mother and her child?' he asks.

'They got away. You saved them.'

Starling closes his eyes, sighs with relief and lies back. He is happy for them but devastated for the innocents who died. He should have killed that monk the moment he laid eyes on him.

'You almost died in the process,' says Anna.

They hear the sound of approaching footsteps, leather-soled shoes echoing on a hard floor and a tapping sound, like a cane. He hears Eoin's voice and those of two other men.

There is a polite knock on the door and a bespectacled man with a shock of grey hair and wearing a white lab coat enters. Starling recognises him as Doctor Jones, the doctor who had treated his wounds during his last visit; Starling had thought him more a mad professor than a doctor. Eoin and the man he'd seen at Chittlock's house follow behind him, the latter leaning on a sturdy walking stick.

'Hello again,' says Doctor Jones, picking up the clipboard at the foot of his bed.

'Hello.'

Eoin gestures at the other man. 'Will, you may recall Sir Hugh Coleridge from Chittlock's house.'

Starling nods.

Coleridge smiles broadly at him. 'It's so good to see you again, Will, after all this time.' He grabs Starling's hand and shakes it vigorously.

Aside from seeing Coleridge bruised and beaten in Chittlock's house, Starling has no other memory of him.

'You and I…'

'How are you feeling?' says Eoin, interrupting the exchange.

'Like I have been hit by a truck,' says Starling.

'It'll pass,' says Coleridge. 'The good doctor tells us you were not as badly affected as those poor buggers on the bus. Terrible business.'

'Will,' says Eoin, 'Anna gave us a rundown of what she saw. However, we need to understand why you were not so affected. Tell us what you remember in the seconds before you blacked out? Perhaps there is some clue there.'

The throb in Starling's head increases as he tries to relive those last few moments. He recalls the monk lying dead on the surface of the bridge.

'I remember picking up the bomb and throwing it over the side of the bridge. There was an odd smell, like sour apples.'

'Was the air clear of red gas?' asks Doctor Jones.

Starling's head is fuzzy. He tries to remember. 'Yes, I think it was.'

'Did you inhale any of the red toxins?' asks Doctor Jones.

'No, I don't think so. The red gas did not appear until the bomb was falling towards the Thames. I remember the bombs had two buttons: one red, the other black.'

'Both buttons must be pushed to activate the red gas,' says Coleridge. 'One must have clicked when the monk dropped it and perhaps you activated the other moments later.'

Starling rubs his head and thinks that seems a plausible explanation.

'It is possible that there are two gases, both unpleasant, but not life threatening until they merge,' says Doctor Jones.

'Which means you are very lucky to be alive,' adds Coleridge.

Starling's mind fritters back to entering his old bedroom at Chittlock's house where the monk had been waiting. He had noticed that something had changed but in the heat of the moment he had not seen what it was. Remembering now, he can see it clearly but he decides to keep it to himself for now.

'What happened at Timothy Chittlock's house?' he asks.

'After I received the call from Nicholas,' Coleridge answers, 'I went over to Warwick Way to meet you. When I got there the house was being ransacked. I thought it was a few local urchins but to my dismay found it was not. I fought a feeble and losing battle but, to my good fortune, you arrived just in time.'

'How did they know to go there?' asks Starling.

'We don't know yet,' says Eoin. 'Perhaps someone from Baker Street intercepted Morrow's call. It could be we have another mole.'

'Did the monks find anything?'

'There was nothing on the body of the monk on the bridge. As for the one who got away, I could not say.'

'They were wasting their time, Will. There has not been anything at Tim's house for a long time,' says Eoin.

Starling notices Coleridge's expression turn to a frown.

'What do you mean by that?' says Coleridge.

'I had all of Chittlock's files moved shortly after he died.'

'You did what?'

'I moved them for safekeeping, which was evidently the right thing to do if Baker Street has another mole.'

'Where are they?'

'Safe. For now.'

The exchange between Eoin and Coleridge has become tense, much to Starling's surprise. They might be old friends, but there is something else – a rivalry? Anna glances at Starling, her eyebrows arched.

'We'll talk about this later,' says Coleridge.

Starling cannot figure out if Coleridge is angry or just disappointed.

'Please give those files to me at your earliest convenience.'

Eoin's expression is impassive. 'Of course, Hugh.'

There seems to be a lot going on that Starling does not know about. His head begins to throb as he tries to absorb everything. He closes his eyes, shutting out the glare of the hospital light.

'We should let Starling rest,' says Anna.

'Indeed we should,' says the doctor. He turns to Starling. 'I suspect right now you feel the worst you have ever felt. I would liken it to a most terrible hangover. Some sleep will do you good.'

Starling recalls his dream and the city he was free-falling into. Something in it has tapped into his lost memories. He feels his hand being squeezed by Anna and he gently returns the affection.

'Right,' says Coleridge, 'we need to look into this red gas business. Can't have monks running around the city dropping bombs everywhere!'

'I think it is called Red Storm,' says Starling.

All heads turn to look at him.

'It's a gas manufactured by VIPER to wipe out factions of the world's population.'

Coleridge's cheery expression falters. 'I'm sure we can handle a few monks.'

'I think there is more to this than the Cerastes and a handful of small bombs tied around their waists.' Starling says nothing more for a moment as his fractured memory tries in vain to piece together his past.

'Tell us, Will,' says Eoin eagerly.

'I'm really not sure. I had a dream. There was an apocalypse. Imagine what happened today but on a scale a thousand times bigger.'

'We need more than dreams, Will,' says Coleridge.

'Let's not discount this,' says Eoin. 'Will has VIPER intelligence hidden in his memories. It returns to him in flashbacks and dreams.'

Starling is keen to get back to Chittlock's house. He is certain there is something there. A clue perhaps. He swings himself off the bed but feels his head spinning.

'You're not going anywhere just yet,' says the doctor. 'One more night's rest will do you good.'

Starling tries to protest but his head begins to bang and spin faster.

'Listen to Doctor Jones,' says Anna. Bending over, she eases him back gently and he does not protest. He feels overcome with tiredness and within moments he forgets everything and is fast asleep.

Chapter 16

Assassin

Starling wakes to the sound of something clanging outside. The door to his hospital room is slightly ajar, spilling a small measure of light from the corridor outside into the darkness. He sees his clothes folded neatly on the chair next to his bed. He has been dressed in blue and white striped pyjamas.

For a moment there is silence and then he hears a thud followed by a groan. His heart begins to race, but he tells himself he is just being paranoid. This is a safe place, isn't it? Maybe one of the other patients has fallen over? He slips out from under the covers and is instantly relieved to discover that the dizziness is gone. From the doorway he peers up and down the corridor. The light is bright, the walls are white and bare and the floor is a pale parquet wood. He sees the nurse's desk and, standing with his back to him, Dr Jones dressed in his white coat, his grey hair wild and sticking up. Starling starts to walk towards him and stops when hears the unmistakable *phut phut phut* of a silencer pistol.

'Doctor Jones?'

Doctor Jones is reloading the gun as he turns around. Behind him, in a pool of blood, is a hospital porter. The porter must be a VIPER spy or assassin, Starling thinks, though there is something in the doctor's expression, a coldness in the eyes, that worries him. Starling takes a step back, not taking his eyes off the doctor. Neither speaks. Starling isn't consciously anticipating the shot but when it comes he is already diving to the floor and rolling for protection behind a stainless steel trolley. Two more shots clang off the trolley as the doctor comes towards him. Starling has nowhere to go. He kicks the trolley towards the doctor, slamming it into his legs. It stops him for the moment but he manages to land deftly from a near-fall. For a man his age, Doctor Jones is certainly nimble.

Starling is on his feet now, and charges him, pushing the doctor's gun hand towards the ceiling and kneeing him in the balls at the same time. The man groans and doubles over still trying to point the gun at Starling. Starling launches a punishing kick at the pistol, sending it spinning down the corridor. He grabs the doctor's wild hair, determined to finish him off, but the hair comes away in Starling's hand. It is a wig. The man looking up at him is wearing a black hair net. He is not Doctor Jones.

For a second Starling is caught off guard. The imposter seizes the moment and punches him hard in the stomach. Blunt pain stabs his abdominals. Winded, Starling drops to his knees, his face close to the wall. The man is on him instantly, straddling his back. A strip of red cord passes over his head and instantly he is choking. Gasping for breath, he manages to get one hand up to his neck where a cord is tightening. He just gets his fingers under it. Starling can feel the blood trapped in his head as the rope gets tighter. The man is squeezing the life from him. He tries to pull the rope with his fingers but the lack of oxygen weakens him. Is he going to die here? Black spots appear in front of his eyes. He thinks of Anna, Emile and Claudette. He thinks of the red gas and the people trapped in the bus. *Many must die.*

But not him. Not yet. With one last desperate effort, he pushes himself up, the man still clinging to him. With his free fist he rains punches at his opponent's head and takes satisfaction at the man's pained grunting. Leaning his weight into the man, Starling raises his feet and pushes them against the wall with all his strength. They tumble backwards and Starling slams his elbow into the man's solar plexus. He groans as the wind expels from him. The rope loosens at last and Starling pulls it from his throat, feeling glorious oxygen fill his lungs. Spinning around, he sees the man remove a viper-shaped dagger from his sleeve. Starling pulls back just in time, his throat inches from the blade. Without a weapon, he knows his chances are slim. He turns and runs, slipping clumsily on the blood of the unfortunate porter at the nurse's desk. It covers his hands and pyjamas as he tries to stand up. His assailant is coming. Starling scrambles to his feet, sprints down the corridor and crashes through a set of double doors. On the other side is some sort of tapestry blocking his exit. He pulls it up and tumbles forward.

For a moment he is confused. It's as if he has stepped into an alternate world of luxurious decadence. There are enormous glittering chandeliers, ornate walls and ceilings painted a soft white like the icing on a cake. The floor beneath his feet is cool marble. There are people. All heads have turned to look at him, their eyes wide with disbelief. It is the lobby of the St Ermin's Hotel – and he is barefoot and dressed in bloody pyjamas.

His eyes catch those of the hotel receptionist, a West Indian gentleman, perhaps in his late twenties, who watches him impassively over the head of an irate hotel guest, a round lady stuffed into a green suit with fox furs draped over her shoulders. Starling remembers the receptionist from his last visit. His name is Joseph and he is also an MI6 operative.

Starling pads towards the reception desk, ignoring the eyes that follow him.

'Hello again,' says Joseph.

The lady turns to look at Starling. She gasps, and her complaints cease as her hand flies to her chest.

'Excuse me, madam,' says Starling, politely, before turning to the receptionist. 'There's some trouble in the ward, Joseph.'

'I see,' replies Joseph. 'How can I assist you?'

Starling turns away from the lady and makes a subtle gun signal with his hand.

Joseph's eyes flick towards the tapestry. 'Very good, sir.' From under the desk he removes a Colt 45 and hands it to Starling.

The woman gasps again.

'Thank you, Joseph.' Starling does not want to alarm any other guests so he tucks the Colt under his pyjama top.

'Be careful, sir. I will alert the others.'

Starling is already halfway back to the tapestry. Behind him he hears Joseph addressing the lady, 'Now, Mrs Christchurch. Where were we?'

'You… you gave him a gun.'

'It appears we have a rodent problem.'

'Oh, I see…'

More of a snake problem, thinks Starling, as he lifts the tapestry. There is no one there. He slides behind it to the double doors and pulls one open a fraction. Up the corridor, he sees the dead porter and the circular pool of blood that surrounds his corpse, staining the parquet floor. He can see his own red footprints running down to the lobby – and the killer's leaving a trail in the opposite direction.

Cautiously, he scurries down the corridor, leaping over the blood and following the congealing footprints. They lead to a ward with six empty beds. He sees an office further down the corridor. The door is open and inside, slumped over his desk as if he is sleeping, is Doctor Jones. Starling cannot tell if it is the real one or the imposter. He goes in with the gun pointing at the man and prods him, but there's no response. He pulls at his hair, which appears to be real. Feeling for a pulse, Starling is relieved to find one and notices something small and metallic lodged in the doctor's neck. He pulls it out. It is a dart of some sort, no doubt containing a narcotic.

Leaving the office, he sees a white panelled door next to it. Despite the killer's footprints disappearing under a door marked 'Exit' at the end of the corridor, Starling pushes it open. Beyond it is an empty stairwell.

At the end of the corridor, he kicks the exit door open and stands with his back to the inside wall, out of any line of fire. Cold night air sweeps inside, a cool relief. Light from the corridor reveals a small walled yard used for storing crates and boxes. There is no one there. The footprints, now faint, stop at a back door on the wall opposite. Starling tiptoes across and pulls it open. The street outside is dark, seemingly unoccupied but for several parked cars.

'Oi!' comes a stern voice.

A man in a uniform has turned the corner. His tin hat marks him out as an Air Raid Warden. Starling holds the Colt 45 out of sight, behind his back.

'Turn that blimmin' light off! Don't you know there's a war on?'

'Apologies,' Starling replies, hurrying back and closing the door quickly, not wanting to attract any further attention.

He walks back to his room, half disappointed his would-be assassin had escaped, half relieved. From back down the corridor he hears the doors to the lobby opening and sees Joseph, Eoin and Anna hurry through them, armed and ready, albeit a little on the late side.

After a summary of what had happened Starling and Anna watch Joseph bolt and lock the exit door where the fake Doctor Jones had escaped. Eoin is crouching down examining the bloody footprints.

'I saw Doctor Jones arrive in the hotel lobby not twenty minutes back,' says Joseph. 'He nodded hello to me and then entered the hospital wing under the tapestry. I thought it strange. As a rule we do not use that entrance because it makes our hotel guests ask questions.'

'With the real Doctor Jones in his office and the porter going about his duties there was less chance of him being challenged,' says Starling.

'Correct. Poor Smith, the porter, is also the hospital guard. He must have been doing his rounds when he bumped into the fake Doctor Jones.'

Starling feels the comfort of Anna's hand as it brushes close to his.

Eoin is on his feet. 'We have a meeting later this morning. We can discuss what to do next.'

'I will take care of this mess,' says Joseph.

'Thank you, Joseph,' says Starling, and hands back the Colt 45.

'A pity you never got to use it.'

'Yes, a pity,' Starling responds, noting the coldness in his own tone. As he returns to his room to gather his things, he reflects on how different he is now compared to two years back, when he was unsure of who or what he was. His memory is still fractured, but the truth he has learned about who he is and what he has lost has only fuelled his rage and desire for retribution. This knowledge has bubbled quietly like the lava of a dormant volcano waiting for its moment to explode into the world.

Chapter 17

The Revelation

Rome

The following day Rose is alone in the apartment, resting on her bed. Turning over, she smiles at Charlie lying curled up on the pillow next to her. His eyes are open and he seems to be staring across the room. Rose follows his gaze, but there is nothing extraordinary, just the polished walnut dresser with her brush on top and her daily dose of pills. She nuzzles him with her face, taking in his familiar and comforting musty scent.

'What's the matter, Charlie boy?'

He lets out a weak meow, which worries her. She lifts him onto her chest and cuddles him. 'Maybe you should eat something? Keep your strength up. That's what Sofia tells me to do when I'm poorly.'

She hears a knock on the apartment door and wonders if Sofia has forgotten her key. She remembers the nursemaid locking it and waits for a moment. The knock comes again, harder this time. Rose feels a flutter in her stomach and sits up, wincing at the pain in her arms and legs. Carrying Charlie, she hobbles to the apartment door and places her ear to it. Charlie hisses.

'Hush, Charlie.' She bites her lip and wonders what to do.

'Sofia?' she calls.

But there is no answer.

She shrugs and, overcome with curiosity, stares hard at the empty keyhole and uses her mind to twist the cogs and open the lock. It makes a satisfying clicking sound. Easy stuff. She has done it many times before – before pills, that is, after which she had given up hope of ever escaping. There are two bolts built inside the door. One at the top and one at the bottom. With little effort she slides them across and then pulls the door open. For a moment she sees nothing but the dark shadowy passageway leading away down from the apartment.

'Sofia?'

As her eyes adjust to the gloom the shadows seems to merge, gather form and move towards her. She gasps and steps back, squeezing Charlie a little too tight.

'Rose, is that you?'

She sees the white cane first, then the hands with fingerless gloves belonging to the blind priest, who is looming in the doorway. She is surprised at how tall he is and how powerful he seems now that she sees him on his feet.

'Father William, what are you doing here?'

'Hello, child. I was passing and thought I might drop in and say hello.'

Charlie begins to squirm in her arms.

'But it's forbidden. I am not allowed to see anyone.'

He chuckles. 'And what is so wrong with an old priest visiting one of God's children?'

Charlie's claws sink hard into her shoulder and she yelps.

'Charlie, what is the matter?' She loosens her grip letting him jump to the floor. He runs drunkenly back to the bedroom. Rose shakes her head. What has got into him?

'May I come in?' asks Father William.

'Yes, Father, do please come in. I've never had a friend visit.'

The tall priest steps into the room, clicking his cane on the stone floor, checking for obstacles or steps.

Rose closes the door. 'I'm surprised the guards let you through. They're normally so rude.'

'Guards – now is that what they were? How odd. They seemed very polite.'

Rose frowns. 'Polite? That's a first. Perhaps you worked some magic on them.'

'I was polite also. I told them I was here to do God's work.'

Rose shrugs. The guards were mostly locals who were all God-fearing men, according to Sofia.

'Would you like to sit down?'

'Yes, please.'

'Shall I guide you?'

'Thank you, child.'

Rose takes his arm and leads him to the little sofa in her living room. He lowers himself, his long fingers wriggle in the air by his side searching for the arm rest.

'Would you like some tea?'

'No, thank you.'

She stiffens suddenly, blushing, as she realises her scarred arms and legs are bare and she is still wearing her nightdress. He cannot see you, you fool, she thinks, and relaxes. Nevertheless, she excuses herself for a moment and runs to the bedroom to pull on her pink, floral, silk dressing gown. A gift from Sofia, apparently. Rose did not believe that for one moment. Where on earth would Sofia get the money to buy such a fine garment. No, this was bought with Ophelia's money. No doubt a way to make Rose happier and more comfortable during her twenty-four-hours-a-day, seven-days-a-week confinement.

Tying the belt around her waist, Rose sits beside the priest on the edge of the sofa.

'I thought we would carry on where we left off,' says the Father.

'We can talk about your sister, if you like?'

'That would be nice. But I think I would like to hear about your brother.'

Father William's response catches her off guard. 'Of course. If you would like.' She pauses and tries to gather her thoughts but it's harder than she thinks. Despite wondering about him every day she struggles to form a sentence. After a few moments the words come.

'We lived with our parents in a leafy street in Highgate, London. Will was older than me. He had dark hair like our mother and clear, blue eyes like our father, and he was determined like him, too. That's what mother used to say anyway. He was a typical boy, always kicking a football, climbing trees or getting into scrapes with other boys. He was fiercely competitive, which was a never-ending source of worry for Mother, but he was also kind and funny. He made all of us laugh all the time. I tried to be like him and would follow him around. I wanted to kick balls, climb trees and fight boys, too, and Starling would let me.'

'He let you fight other boys?'

'Oh, no. He would sit in the garden with me and I would punch his palms like a fierce boxer.' Rose smiles at the memory and pauses. Tears threaten to fall but she holds them back and blows her nose on a handkerchief she finds in the pocket of her dressing-gown.

Father William sits quietly and nods his head. After a moment he speaks. 'You must miss him.'

Rose casts her eyes downward. 'I do. Every day.'

She turns at the sound of someone at the apartment door.

'Rose, why is the door not locked?' asks Sofia. The nursemaid stands at the entrance with a loaf of fresh bread in her hands.

Rose ignores the question. 'Sofia, look who's come to visit.' She sees the nursemaid stiffen and her face frown.

'No one allowed here. Not even you, *Padre*. I am sorry. You must leave.'

'But…' says Rose.

'That's quite alright. I must be on my way.' Father William struggles out of the sofa. He reaches for Rose's hand. She takes it and pulls him gently forward, ignoring the stinging pain it causes in her arm. There is something in his palm. It feels like paper. His other hand covers hers as he surreptitiously slides the paper into her hand.

He leans towards her and whispers, 'Tell no one. These walls have eyes and they have ears.'

Rose is too surprised to know how to react or what to say. She slips the paper into her pocket and walks the padre to the door.

'Goodbye, Rose.'

'Goodbye, Father. I hope to see you soon.'

'Oh, you will. I can promise you that.'

As he disappears into the shadows Sofia closes the door and turns to Rose. 'You mustn't open the door when I am not here. You don't know what these men are like.'

'He's just a priest doing his rounds.'

Sofia bolts the door and turns the key. 'There's something about that man I don't like.'

Rose rolls her eyes. 'I'm going to my room.'

'I bring you breakfast soon.'

Rose walks quickly to her room and takes out the piece of paper. She unfolds it and reads the single line. She feels her stomach somersaulting; her head turns light and giddy.

Written across the page in neat, blocked letters are the words:

> YOUR BROTHER IS NOT DEAD. I KNOW WHERE HE IS.

-

The acolyte smiles to himself as he makes his way down the steps of the dark passageway, keeping up the guise of the blind priest. The girl had opened up to him; he had seen her emotions begin to stir as he watched her from the corner of his eye through the dark glaze of his spectacles. He had made her reminisce. It had hurt her and that pleased him immensely. The revelation in his note was a risk. If the VIPER fools discovered what he had done, they would have him killed. But they would not find out because the girl despised them. She would keep her counsel and confide only in him – he was her saviour now. The seed had been planted. He pictures her now, full of hope and desperate to be reunited with her guttersnipe brother. His work was done here.

For now.

He would keep his distance and, in time, her patience would wear thin and she would seek him out. Then, he would take her.

He hums aloud to himself, a familiar old tune, passes the guards and wishes them a good day in fluent Italian.

Chapter 18

Dressed to Kill

London

With the real Doctor Jones still recovering from his shock, Starling discharges himself from the hospital ward. Filthy with dried blood and sweat, all he wants to do is get cleaned up and take some time to think things over. Joseph has given him the same room he stayed in two years back. Despite its grandeur and luxury it is with mixed emotions that Starling stands there now. After the Stones of Fire, he and Anna had spent two days and two nights alone together. She had shared his bed and helped him forget. It was then he had fallen in love with her. All that is over now.

He showers and scrubs the blood from his hair and body. His thoughts turn to Emile and Claudette, his friends, who were alive and well less than twenty-four hours ago. He wonders if Marie-Antoinette has done the decent thing and arranged for the burial they deserved. The thought of them being ditched on the side of the road or in a pauper's grave with no stone was too much to bear.

He dries himself and tidies his hair with a comb embossed with the grand logo of St Ermin's. There is a knock on the door. Wrapping the towel around his waist, he walks into the bedroom and opens the door.

'Hello again, sir,' says Joseph, who is carrying a large paper bag.

'Hello, Joseph.'

'May I come in?'

Starling steps aside for Joseph, who removes clothes from the bag and places them on the bed. There is a dark blue tweed blazer, a red flannel shirt, grey trousers with braces and clean underwear and socks. A pair of oxblood brown leather Derby boots are set down on the floor.

'First things first,' says Joseph. 'You have a meeting with Sir Hugh, Mr Heaney, Mr Morrow and Miss Wilder at 11 am.'

'Where will that be?'

'Somewhere in the hotel. I will confirm the venue closer to the time.'

Joseph takes out a black case and opens it. Inside is a small pistol engraved with oak leaves and finished in a high polish steel.

'A Mauser,' says Starling.

'A Mauser HSc,' corrects Joseph. 'Easy to carry without being noticed.' Joseph's eyes light up. 'This one is one of a kind. A beautifully crafted pistol, quite rare and very expensive.' He hands it across. 'A gift.'

Starling looks down at the weapon and can't help but admire its compact size and lovely craftsmanship. 'This must be a mistake.'

'No mistake.'

He accepts the case and runs the tips of his fingers over the cold steel. 'From whom?'

'From Mr Heaney.'

'How did he get this?' But Starling suspects he might already know.

'From a card game, I believe,' says Joseph, confirming Starling's suspicions.

'Did it belong to Sir Hugh, by any chance?'

Joseph shoots him a wry smile. 'It's not for me say. However, your intuition serves you well, sir.'

Joseph picks up the blazer, removes a brown leather shoulder holster from the inside pocket and drops it on the bed. He holds the collar of the jacket and tries to bend it, but it seems solid.

'Concealed inside is a flexible saw that can cut through wire and steel, if time is on your side.' Turning the left sleeve cuff, he points to four pen-like items secreted in the lining. 'The first one is a three-in-one multi-purpose tool containing a screwdriver, a scalpel and a lock pick – just unscrew them to get the one you require. The second is a Time Pencil with a thirty-second blast time. It's a new model and quite powerful, so do be careful. The third is a pen.'

'Just a pen?'

'Yes, and no. The top has a button that will dispense the ink into a liquid – a cocktail or cup of tea, for example. The ink will clear instantly. It is a poison that will render the drinker unconscious in minutes. Also, if you write with the pen and someone touches the ink, they should suffer a reaction that will paralyze them temporarily.'

'How long for?'

'Hard to say. We've had mixed results. We're trialling this model. It has not passed our high-quality standards because some of our candidates have remained conscious while others just seemed happily inebriated.'

'That's reassuring.'

'Either way, it may help you. The fourth is a torch with a small glass dome that will widen the beam.'

Joseph lifts the right-hand sleeve. 'I do think you will like this one. The cuff contains a spring action pipe with two steel poison darts. Similar to VIPER's blow pipe, however, the velocity is greater: they have a range of twenty feet and will penetrate at least two layers of clothing. Quite impressive, don't you think?'

Starling smiles. 'If you say so.'

'We call it the Velo-Dart.'

'Catchy.'

'To shoot a dart, simply straighten your arm, turn up your wrist and swing your arm towards the target,' Joseph demonstrates by swinging his rigid arm fast at the room's door. A dart shoots out and penetrates the wooden surface, splitting the white painted wood.

Starling is impressed. 'You're right. I like it.' He pulls the dart from the door and examines it. 'A dart like this was used on Doctor Jones.'

Joseph nods grimly. 'We cannot rule out the fact that the assassin might be one of our own.'

'Hard to know who to trust in this game.'

'Quite so, sir.' Joseph points to the middle button of the blazer. 'This button is made from reinforced steel. Its thread is a thirty-foot extendible and retractable wire.' Joseph demonstrates by pulling it back and forth. 'Any questions?'

'None. Thank you, Joseph. I feel ready to take on the world.' Starling pulls on the red flannel shirt, which is soft and warm.

Joseph regards him thoughtfully. 'If you don't mind me mentioning something, sir…' The receptionist-come-agent pauses, waiting for Starling to respond.

'Of course.'

'Some years back I met a man: a kind man, a scholar and a scientist. We worked together briefly, just before he passed away.'

Starling lifts the underwear from the folded pile of clothes and puts it on. 'I'm sorry to hear that, Joseph.'

'He told me that I reminded him of his son.'

Starling pulls on the trousers and slips the braces over his shoulders.

'When I asked why, he looked at me, smiled and said, "Don't take this the wrong way. You are over-protective, impetuous and too quick to use yours fists." I explained to him it was my job to be that person. He told me he understood and that his son was just like me.'

'Sounds like he did not like his son very much.'

'Not at all. He was very proud of him, very proud.'

Starling pulls on his socks and the Derby boots and ties up the laces. 'What was your job?'

'I was his guard.'

'Why did he need a guard?'

'Because his life was in danger, as were the lives of his wife, his son and his daughter.' There is a tremor in Joseph's voice.

Starling stares hard at his boots and wonders how on earth a colour could be called oxblood. Wasn't all blood the same shade of red and not this brownish rust colour?

'I did all I could for them. It wasn't enough. I am sorry.'

Starling puts on the shoulder holster and checks the cartridge of the pistol. It is full.

'There are more bullets in the bag.'

Starling nods absentmindedly as he turns Joseph's revelations over in his head. Standing, he pulls on the blazer and feels the weight of the flexible saw around his neck, stiff but not uncomfortable.

'Sir…'

'You don't need to say any more, Joseph.'

'But I do. I feel responsible and I know your father would want me to tell you that your chosen profession is not one he would have approved of. Let others fight this fight. You are young and you have so much to live for. Walk away, before it is too late.'

Starling meets Joseph's gaze. The agent's eyes are red, holding back tears, his expression pained.

'I never chose this profession, Joseph. It chose me. I am merely the sum of what others have made me. VIPER are afraid of me. I have been made an aberration, a monster, a nightmare. Not just because of what secrets I hold in my head, but because I am coming for them and they know it.'

Joseph's expression changes and Starling thinks for a second he sees a flicker of fear.

'Thank you for what you did for my family.' Starling picks the spare bullets from the bag and the tin soldier from his old trousers. He puts them into his jacket pocket. 'Thank you for everything, Joseph.'

'I wish you all the luck in the world.'

Starling nods his thanks and turns to leave. In the corridor, he wonders where Anna could be. Before their meeting with Eoin and the others, he wants to return to Warwick Way. If he is right, then another clue has been left for him. When he stepped into the bedroom, there was something that had seemed irregular. Before he'd had a chance to figure it out he was chasing the monk across London. That was yesterday, and now he was eager to get back and investigate.

Chapter 19

The Menin Road

Starling makes his way down the marble staircase and sees Anna with a man he does not recognise talking in the lobby. Dressed in a blue pin-striped suit, he is tall and clean-shaven with sharp cheekbones and a chiselled jawline. Starling wonders if he is Anna's new man. His eyes catch Starling's and he leans across and says something to Anna. She turns and looks up at Starling. Did the man just inform her he was on the staircase? Who is he? The man exits the hotel and Anna meets Starling at the bottom of the stairs.

She has shed her coat and blue trouser suit and is wearing a dark red jacket with matching skirt and a crisp white shirt underneath. Under her arm she carries a dark leather purse that no doubt contains her Walther PPK. He swallows and tries to suppress the unwelcome desire that makes his throat dry suddenly. He is torn. He wants to spend time with her but what is the point? She is with someone else now – someone with penetrating cheekbones and a pin-stripe suit? Perhaps it is better for their working relationship. Easier to step away and become less attached.

'How are you feeling?' she asks.

'Fine. Who was that man?'

'What man?'

'That man you were just talking to.'

Anna smiles. 'Oh, him. He's just another stooge. Someone I worked with once.'

'Not your new boyfriend, then?'

Anna's eyes widen and she scoffs. 'I don't think so.'

It is so easy to mistrust anyone in their line of work that Starling regrets his suspicion and thinks nothing more of the chiselled man. Anna and he had spent a year apart and she had worked on several other missions. She would know many people.

'Fancy an excursion?'

'Where are we going?'

'I'll tell you outside.'

They cross the lobby and go out into St Ermin's front courtyard where the sun is shining and the sky is a clear blue. The doorman, a stocky man dressed in a dark suit, red waistcoat and top hat, bids them good morning.

'Morning,' replies Starling, noting the strap of a gun holster under the doorman's unbuttoned jacket.

'May I get you a taxi, sir?'

Starling is about to say yes but decides against it. He does not want anyone to know where he is going. No one can be trusted for certain.

'We'll walk, thank you.'

'Have a good day, sir, miss.'

'You too.'

Anna loops her arm into Starling's, a warm smile on her face. He can feel the heat from her body and smells an exotic fragrance that she does not usually wear. He can't help it. He wants to spend more time with her, despite her new relationship.

'Where are we going?' she asks.

Starling glances behind him, ensuring they are not being followed. The doorman tips his hat and Starling nods.

'Let's get out of here and I will tell you.'

They stroll casually, like two lovers, down Caxton Street, turning left towards Victoria and making their way through the locals going about the business of the day.

'What is that scent you are wearing?' asks Starling.

'It's new. Do you like it?'

'Yes.'

'It's called Soir de Paris. It's what all us good girls with a "dangerous" side to their nature wear.'

Starling laughs. 'I can see why that might be.'

'Why do you ask?'

'I met someone recently who was wearing it?'

'Was she beautiful and dangerous?'

Starling thinks about the agent codenamed Marie-Antoinette. It had been difficult to make out her face behind the make-up and veil, but from what he remembers, she was beautiful. As for being dangerous, he reckons she was just that and more – reckless.

'I didn't really get to know her,' he says.

In reverse of the previous day's car chase, they turn down Rochester Row and Starling explains about the message left for him at Chittlock's house. He does not say more than that as they cross over Vauxhall Bridge Road and on to Warwick Way. Starling looks towards Milly's hairdressers and sees the shop has been boarded up and Milly's name is no longer above the door. Perhaps the sight of their guns and the news of the horrible deaths on Westminster Bridge was enough to make her leave. Who could blame her?

Chittlock's door has been bolted and locked, presumably on orders from Eoin. Starling removes the multi-purpose tool from his sleeve and, using the pick, opens the lock as Anna watches the street. Moments later they are inside.

They wade through the debris that litters the floor and climb the stairs to Starling's old bedroom. Standing by his desk, Starling gazes at the painting, a grim oil-on-canvas depiction of a landscape from the First World War. There are trenches and bomb craters flooded with dirty rainwater and tree stumps, devoid of foliage, pointing towards an oppressive red sky full of clouds and plumes of smoke. There are two shafts of odd green sunlight that seem more like gun barrels. There is something deeply unsettling about the whole scene.

'I know that painting. I've seen it at the Hall of Remembrance,' says Anna, '*The Menin Road* by Paul Nash.'

Starling had seen the picture in his flashback, though he couldn't remember the title and artist. He studies it in silence for a few moments.

'It's a copy,' he says.

'Yes, of course. The original is enormous.'

'It has been tampered with.'

Anna leans forward for a better look.

'The original does not have red sunlight or a red sky,' Starling says.

'You are right!'

In the centre of the painting are two soldiers navigating their way through the troubled scene. Starling points to them. 'Look.'

The soldier on the left wears a long green coat and a helmet typical of the period, however the soldier on the right is different. He is a fusilier from the Victorian era, dressed in dark blue trousers and a red jacket, just like Starling's tin soldier. He has been painted in tones sympathetic to the oil colours of the rest of the painting so that he does not stand out.

Starling reaches across and runs his finger gently over the fusilier. The paint is thick and hard. He presses the soldier and frowns. 'There's something underneath.' Lifting the canvas from the wall, he uses the scalpel to cut it away from the frame. There is nothing there. Laying the canvas on the desk, he crouches down and runs his eyes across the flat surface. Anna hunches beside him and follows his gaze. The paint used for the fusilier is button-thick. The painter had done an expert job of making it seem flat.

Using the scalpel Starling begins to cut gently around the shape of the fusilier until it comes loose. He picks it up and turns it over. Concealed behind the body of soldier is a rolled-up piece of paper. He looks at Anna, his eyebrows raised.

'Bingo,' she says.

'Bingo,' he replies, with a grin. He unrolls the paper and frowns. It is blank. He turns it over and holds it up the light of the window but there is nothing. 'Could be invisible ink?'

'Give it to me,' says Anna. She sniffs the crisp paper, her eyes closed in concentration. She nods and hands it back to him. 'Hold it open, please.' She removes a small ioniser from her purse.

'Soir de Paris?' asks Starling.

Anna smiles. 'Not quite. People would run a mile if I wore this on my skin.'

She stands at arm's length from the paper and sprays the surface. A sour acidic smell fills the air and Starling recoils. 'You're not wrong there.'

A moment passes while nothing happens, and then brown dots start appearing randomly on the paper. Within minutes four lines of symbols and hieroglyphics become visible on the page.

Starling studies it and tries to make sense of it.

'Any ideas?' asks Anna.

'No. I don't recognise the code.'

'We'll try and figure it out. If we can't, I know someone who can help.'

Starling folds the paper tightly, inserts it through the spine of the tin soldier and puts the soldier back inside the pocket of his blazer.

They leave the bedroom and Starling stops at the entrance to the bathroom where he and Eoin had found Hugh Coleridge yesterday. It is a square room, roughly seven feet by seven feet, with a large white Edwardian bath, a toilet, a sink and rectangular white tiles on the walls. There is a pale green, round rug on the floor spotted with Coleridge's blood and broken glass. Starling squats down and examines a piece of the glass, curiously. Turning to the sink he sees the mirror is intact. A draught turns his attention to the broken window. Outside there is a gully below, closed in by tall walls. There is nothing out of the ordinary.

It would not have been so easy to escape over those walls. How did Eoin not see him?

'See anything?' says Anna.

Starling shakes his head and checks his wristwatch. It is almost 11 am.

'I think we are running a little late.'

'Morrow will be most upset,' says Anna.

'I do hope so.'

-

They arrive back at St Ermin's almost twenty minutes late. Joseph is at the reception desk and he directs them to the MI6 tea room.

MI6 has its own tea room?

'Mr Morrow isn't happy,' says Joseph.

'Mr Morrow is never happy,' says Anna.

Joseph smiles. 'Isn't that the truth.'

They thank the receptionist for the warning and Starling follows Anna through a grand hallway and into the Caxton Bar, where several agents and customers take their mid-morning tea. He recognises Mrs Christchurch, the lady from reception who saw Joseph handing him a gun. She stiffens when she sees him and then seems to scan the floor for rodents. Starling smiles politely and carries on. He feels another set of eyes watching him and looks across the tea room to see the chiselled jaw and sharp cheekbones of the 'stooge' Anna had been talking to earlier. He looks away as Starling meets his gaze and nonchalantly picks up a newspaper and turns his attention towards it. There is something about him that Starling cannot put his finger on.

At the end of the bar is a black door with a table for two outside it. Seated at it, sipping from cups of fine china, are Daisy and Alice, Morrow's twin red-headed guards.

'Hello, ladies,' says Anna.

Daisy, or Alice, shakes her head. 'He's not happy.'

'We know,' replies Anna.

'He's also in a spot of hot water.'

'What do you mean?'

'You'll find out. Hello Starling,' Daisy and Alice say in unison, in an almost musical fashion.

'Hello Daisy… Alice.'

'You can go on through,' they say.

The door swings open before they can knock and a furious Morrow appears.

'You are twenty minutes late!'

'Sorry,' says Anna.

'It was my fault,' says Starling. 'I took Anna for a stroll.'

'A stroll! We are at war and you go for a stroll!'

Anna and Morrow disappear inside. The door closes behind them.

'Daisy, Alice, who is that chap in the tea room – pin-striped suit, cheekbones, square?'

'That'll be Roland Cooper,' they say.

'And he is?'

'Handsome,' says one of twins, with a wry smile.

'US Intelligence,' says the other. 'Office of Strategic Services. They're like us, but… American.'

'What's he doing here?'

'Lord knows. Top secret, apparently.'

'Isn't everything? Thank you, ladies.'

The door opens again and Morrow's furious face appears.

'Good Lord, Morrow, get him inside and let's crack on!' says an exasperated Coleridge.

Morrow stands aside. 'Of course, Sir Hugh. Far be it for me to delay this meeting anymore,' he says in an obsequious fashion, still glaring at Starling.

The MI6 tea room is circular, with green walls and a single narrow window overlooking a small garden. There is a round dark wood table in the centre, where Eoin and Sir Hugh wait.

'Where have you two been?' asks Coleridge.

'We went…' says Anna, but is cut off by Starling.

'Back to St James's Park,' says Starling, who meets Anna's gaze. 'We haven't been in quite some time. We went there for a stroll to take in some air and lost track of time. It was my fault. Sorry.'

Both Eoin and Coleridge look through narrowed eyes from Starling to Anna. They know he is lying, but don't press the issue.

'I hope you are feeling refreshed after yesterday's near misses,' says Coleridge.

'Very much so,' says Starling.

'Are you hurt in any way?'

'No, I am not.'

'No, I am not, sir,' hisses Morrow.

'Pipe down, Nicholas. Starling has narrowly survived two attempts on his life and I have no doubt there have been many in the past and will be more to come. I think we can cut him some slack.'

Morrow grumbles under his breath.

'I'm glad you are unhurt,' says Coleridge to Starling. 'All in a day's work for one of our most promising spies.'

Starling can feel Morrow's eyes bore into him but ignores him.

'First things first. We have a problem. A big problem, in fact,' says Coleridge, turning to Morrow.

Starling looks at Morrow, who seems to shrivel under the gaze of those around the table.

'Nicholas, tell us your news,' says Coleridge.

Morrow coughs and squirms in his chair. 'The plans are missing,' he says so quietly that Starling has to strain to listen.

'What? How?' says Eoin.

'Someone broke into my office,' he replies.

'Jesus Christ, man! Why didn't you lock them up?'

'I did! Everything was secured. I followed all protocols.'

A flush of heat storms through Starling's body. 'My friends died for those plans!'

Morrow straightens, his lips purse. 'I followed protocol,' he says again.

'Where were they?' asks Eoin.

Morrow says nothing.

'He locked them in his desk,' says Coleridge.

Eoin slams his hand on the table. 'How is that following protocol? Why didn't you just post them direct to VIPER HQ, love from Nick with a big kiss? You could have saved the thieves some bother.'

Morrow's eyes flare. 'How dare you! I warned you not to trust the Owl. Nothing good will come of anything to do with him.'

Starling can see Eoin's fists balling.

'Will and Anna,' says Coleridge, 'I'd like you to look into this break in. Nicholas give them access to all areas.'

'Yes, Sir Hugh.'

'What's done is done. However, there will be repercussions.'

Starling notices Morrow's face drop.

'Let's move on. Next on the agenda,' says Coleridge.

Morrow holds a manila file in his hands. 'We have reason to believe VIPER spies have infiltrated the Secret Service.' Morrow glances at Starling through hooded eyes and suddenly it dawns on him what Morrow's problem is. He thinks Starling is the VIPER spy.

Morrow continues. 'One of our agents has been tailing a VIPER spy. Someone known to all of us: a Beaulieu alumni and resident of Wandsworth Prison, until recently.'

Starling's interest is piqued. It must be Horne. Was he about to be given the chance to search for him and get his revenge for Sam?

'Rupert Van Horne was spotted in Manchester two days ago. We were alerted by the local constabulary. We sent an agent to investigate but he was murdered before he left London.'

'How was he killed?' asks Eoin.

'His car was planted with a Rolling Ticker.'

'What's a Rolling Ticker?' asks Starling.

'An incendiary device fixed to a car. It kicks in when the car engine starts and blows when it stops.'

'A vile VIPER invention,' says Coleridge.

'What about Horne?' asks Anna.

'We don't know. We assume he is still in Manchester, or has moved on.'

Morrow consulted his folder again. 'It seems likely that someone within our ranks knew and either leaked the information or carried out the deed themselves. Either way, we need someone to go to Manchester immediately to see if Horne is still there.'

'I'd like to go,' says Starling.

'I understand your feelings about Horne, Starling, but I need you to investigate the breach of security at Nicholas's office,' says Coleridge. He looks to Eoin. 'Could you head up there, old boy?'

Starling conceals his disappointment and notices Eoin seems surprised.

'Of course. I will drive up there today.'

'Thank you all. That will do for today.' With some effort, Coleridge stands and rests on his stick. He seems to be in pain. 'Report back to me, all of you, as soon as you have news.'

Everyone stands and turns to leave.

'Nicholas, please remain seated. You and I have not finished.'

Starling watches Morrow's face pale.

'Yes, of course, Sir Hugh.'

Chapter 20

The Rolling Ticker

Outside the hotel, Eoin pulls Starling and Anna to one side. 'There was something I wanted to bring up at the meeting, but Sir Hugh overruled me. He did not think it was important. I… disagree.' Eoin looks at Starling. 'My contact at Bletchley Park has acquired some intelligence that you should be aware of…' The Irishman hesitates. 'It's about your sister.'

Starling feels the blood drain from his face. 'Is she dead?' he asks.

'All we know is that the Russians have despatched one of their most elite spies to find her.'

'She must be alive then.'

'One must assume they have information that we don't.'

Starling feels his gut churning. 'Why do they want her? What is she to them?'

'My guess is that Rose is more valuable than any of us imagined.'

Starling processes what Eoin has told him. He has worried about Rose for the past two years. He has waited and waited for news but to his frustration nothing has ever come; not one tiny bit of covert intelligence that might lead to finding her. In his darkest moments he has thought she might be dead, perhaps overcome by the demands of her oppressive captors, and therefore there was no intelligence to report. She was, after all, just a child. He feels a surge of resentment. So it seems the Russians are ahead of them and have acquired VIPER intelligence on Rose. Eoin's news both appals and fuels him. He is relieved that she may still be alive, however, the truth is he feels completely powerless and even more anxious. Not only is she at danger from VIPER, but now from the Russians too.

'It's fair to say we are on the same side,' says Eoin. 'We're allies. However, as far as the Russians are concerned, Rose is part of VIPER. They are unaware of her history and probably wouldn't care much if they did know.'

'Do we know anything about this agent, or even where he is?' asks Anna.

'We only know him by the name Sedova. He is in the field right now but that could be anywhere, even here in London. We are looking into it. We'll find him, I promise.'

'Do you know what he looks like?' asks Starling.

'We only know his second name. Nothing else. Our people are looking for whatever they can find. Hugh and I will keep you up to date.'

-

Starling and Anna say their goodbyes to Eoin. Before he leaves he tosses something to Starling. It is the key for the Embiricos.

'Look after her for me. I'm going underground and don't want her blowing my cover.'

As Starling drives Anna, Daisy and Alice back to Puddle Dock and Morrow's office, he barely notices the Embiricos or the conversation; his mind is focused on the Russian agent, Sedova. So many questions fly through his mind: why is he looking for Rose? What do the Russians want with her? Could they be working with VIPER, or, like him, are they against them? The Russians may be allies yet everyone knows the Secret Service does not trust them. Whatever the answers, Starling has to assume that the threat to Rose has doubled. Nothing will stop him in his efforts to bring down VIPER, but at the same time he must do whatever it takes to find Rose before the Russians do. He doesn't know what to expect from this agent Sedova, but he has no doubt their paths will cross.

'Are you with us, Will?' asks Anna, interrupting his thoughts.

'I'm sorry. I was miles away.'

'Come back to us!' calls one of the twins. Which one, he has no idea. He glances in the rear-view mirror at the two guards.

'Daisy,' he says.

The twin sitting on the left behind Anna looks up and smiles.

'Alice.'

'Present,' says the twin behind him.

Traffic stops at the lights and Starling looks closely at the two of them. They are so alike they are almost indistinguishable. Both faces are round and freckly, the lips thin and noses long. Daisy, however, seems to have more of an abundance of freckles around her nose.

'Morrow's really in the dog house, isn't he?' says Daisy.

'I think so,' says Starling.

'It's that film Eoin brought, isn't it?' says Alice.

'Yes.'

'The Tesla Death Ray,' says Daisy.

'What's that noise?' says Alice.

'How do you know about the Tesla Death Ray?' asks Starling.

'We developed the film,' says Daisy.

Starling catches Alice's expression. She is frowning, clearly thinking hard about something.

Anna turns to the twins. 'Did you see the plans?'

'Of course. We studied them at length.'

'But Morrow said he locked them away,' says Starling. He turns on to the Embankment and glances over at the Thames on his right side. The waters are murky and rippling from the wake of the boats going about their journeys.

'He locked away his copy. Not ours.'

'You have a copy?' asks Starling.

'We weren't going to trust that idiot, boss or no boss.'

'Daisy, Alice, you are amazing! We need to see those plans.'

'We thought you'd ask. When we get back to the office we'll show you.'

Starling shifts gears and presses the accelerator.

'I can still hear it,' says Alice.

'Hear what?' says Daisy.

Up ahead Starling sees the traffic lights turn red.

'Listen,' says Alice.

The Embiricos purrs along the Embankment and no one says anything as they listen. There is a ticking sound. Starling's throat dries and he looks at Anna. Her face is ashen. Glancing in the rear-view mirror, he sees the twins, their eyes wide with the realisation that the Embiricos has a Rolling Ticker fixed underneath.

There are many people around and the traffic slows for the lights. He beeps the horn in a vain attempt to move things along, but the traffic ahead is obstructed by a bus, which is hogging the lane.

'We have to get out of here,' says Anna.

Starling knows this but does not respond. He listens carefully to the noise and swallows when he hears the ticking slow as he eases gently on the brakes to avoiding hitting the car in front.

'Don't slow!' shouts Alice. 'When the ticking stops, the car will blow.'

'We're in a bit of a jam – pardon the pun,' says Starling as he focuses on the car ahead, trying to keep enough distance between them without being forced to stop. The traffic light goes green and the cars and buses begin to move.

Now is the time.

'All of you. Get out of the car. Jump!' shouts Starling.

'Will…' says Anna.

'Just do it. Go. I will think of something.'

The doors fly open and Anna, Daisy and Alice scramble out as the Embiricos rolls slowly forward with the rest of the traffic. Focusing on the road ahead, with his foot resting lightly on the accelerator, Starling prays the cars in front will not stop, but the sudden glare of the red traffic light makes his stomach lurch. He sees a gap in the cars on the opposite lane and swings the Embiricos across, blasting the horn and trying his best to avoid the pedestrians who leap out of his way. He crashes through the iron barrier. The bank is almost six feet below. He throws open the door mid-air, leaps from the driver's seat and falls on his hands and knees onto the wet shingle. Scrambling to his feet, he hears the Embiricos crash behind him. He hurries up the bank to get as far away as he can, but the car blows in a mighty blast that lifts him off his feet. He lands face first in the mud.

His heart pounding, he pulls himself up and looks back at the Embiricos. Fire rages inside where, only moments back, he, Anna, Daisy and Alice had sat. He shudders. The windows have blown and flames lick and slap hungrily at the car's body, charring and blistering the fine silver paint. Smoke rises in black clouds. Once again he has survived, but he cannot help feel a pang of regret that he will never drive the extraordinary Embiricos again.

'Will?' he hears Anna call.

Anna, Daisy and Alice are looking down at him. A crowd has gathered on the pavement around them. There is rusty iron ladder fixed to the wall. He climbs up.

'Are you hurt?' asks Anna.

He is shaken, but does not say anything. In the distance he hears a police siren. 'I'm fine. The police will be here soon. We should get away.'

They push their way through the thickening crowd and hurry on foot.

'Without stating the obvious, that was rather close,' says Alice.

'Someone wants you dead,' says Daisy.

'Many people want me dead, but that bomb was not meant for us. It was for Eoin.'

'We need to warn him,' says Anna.

'He's not going to be happy when he discovers what's happened to his beautiful car,' says Alice.

'At least he's alive,' says Daisy.

'For now,' says Starling. 'This is only the beginning.'

Chapter 21

A Nest of VIPER Spies

When they finally reach the office at Puddle Dock, Starling watches Daisy and Alice pull their desks apart and unscrew a section from one of the floorboards. Underneath is a safe. Alice turns the dial and takes out folded sheets of paper the size of a book. Block letters at the top left of the paper say: TESLA PARTICLE BEAM DEATH RAY.

At the heart of the schematic is a diagram of a tall pyramidal shaft with a sphere on top. Inside both parts are various electrical circuits and some pipework. There are callouts with descriptors and numbers but none of it makes any sense.

'What do you make of it?' asks Anna.

'Alice is a bit of an electronics buff,' says Daisy. 'She's the brains; I'm the beauty.'

'I think you'll find I'm both,' says Alice, her tone playful.

'It doesn't look like a weapon,' says Starling.

'I think this is only one part of a greater schematic.' She points to the base of the pyramid. 'These pipes and circuits lead on to something else.'

'What could that be?'

Alice shrugs. 'Possibly another one of these things, or perhaps the death ray itself.'

'Is this diagram of any value then?'

'Absolutely it is. We just need another pair of eyes. Obviously someone technical who understands this kind of thing.'

'I know someone,' says Anna, reaching for the phone on Alice's desk. 'I'll call him now.'

Alice takes the receiver from Anna and puts a finger to her mouth. 'All of our phones are being listened in on.'

'By who?'

'The Secret Service, of course. We trust no one. Not even our own people. Wait until we leave and use a call box.'

Starling folds up the schematic. Anna takes it from him and puts it inside her purse.

'This is hot stuff, isn't it?' asks Daisy.

'Yes, it is,' says Starling.

'I assume it is why Eoin's car was rigged?'

'Yes.'

The phone on Alice's desk rings suddenly. Neither Daisy nor Alice moves.

'Shouldn't you answer it?' asks Starling.

Alice picks up the phone. 'Good afternoon. Minimax Fire Extinguishers,' she says in a jolly tone. 'Oh, hello, Sir Hugh... Oh my!' Alice's expression darkens. 'Mr Morrow has been arrested! Why...?'

Starling and Anna exchange worried glances.

'I'm afraid I don't know where Mr Heaney is... Starling and Anna...?' Alice looks to Anna and Starling and Starling shakes his head.

'No. They have just left... They found nothing... There's nothing here... Yes, of course, we will try and find them... I'm so sorry to hear about Mr Morrow... None of us is safe, that is true... Goodbye.'

Alice places the receiver down. 'Morrow was the VIPER mole. He's been arrested. Sir Hugh sounds in such a state. He doesn't know who to trust. He said that Puddle Dock is a high-risk location and we should leave immediately. He thinks Morrow might have other secrets hidden here.'

'I doubt that,' says Daisy. 'Yet, to be honest, I'm really surprised. I did not believe Morrow had it in him to be a double agent. Puzzling.' She walks into Morrow's office, folds her arms and looks out the window. 'They're here.'

'Who?' says Alice.

Daisy snorts. 'Four men, dressed as fishermen, wearing thick jumpers with neatly ironed trousers and brand-new shoes. Amateurs! I don't recognise any of them and none of them look like they've done a day's fishing in their lives. They're watching the building.'

'VIPER,' says Starling. He sidles into the office and, keeping out of sight, looks through the window. He sees the four men on the jetty. Beyond them, moored to the quay, is Skipper's boat, *The Outcast.*

'Coleridge wants us to take you in,' says Daisy.

'That won't be necessary.'

Daisy looks at him with a frown and, for a moment, Starling thinks she might just try.

'Daisy,' says Anna, 'we have to leave. The Secret Service has become a nest of VIPER spies. We can trust no one.'

'Anna is right, Daisy,' says Alice. 'The best thing we can do is help Starling and Anna get out of here and keep our heads down.'

Daisy shifts uneasily before nodding and rubbing her palms together. 'We must do this.'

'Good. We need a plan,' says Starling. 'How are you all fixed for weapons?'

'I am a walking armoury,' says Alice.

'Me too,' says Daisy.

'Me three,' says Anna.

'Good. Is there another way out of here?'

'That might not be an option,' says Daisy. 'Two of our fishing friends are on the move. They're coming up. You two stay in here. Alice and I will take care of them.'

Daisy shuts Morrow's door behind them and Starling and Anna stand on either side of it, their backs to the wall, listening. Starling hears the scraping of chairs on floorboards followed by the furious fake tapping of Daisy's and Alice's fingers on their typewriters.

Then he hears the door being kicked open.

The typing stops and he hears the thudding of two bodies falling to the wooden floor. His heart sinks. He removes his Mauser from the holster and watches Anna as she retrieves the Walther from her purse.

Footsteps approach the door of Morrow's office. Starling moves away from the wall and gets ready to fire.

'You can come out now,' comes a voice. It's Alice.

Starling and Anna breathe a sigh of relief. Opening the door, Starling sees Daisy and Alice drag the unconscious bodies of the two men away from the entrance. He wonders how they went down so quickly and then sees a steel dart lodged in one of their necks. 'Velo-Darts.'

'Life savers,' says Daisy.

Alice has found some rope and they all work together to tie the two men securely.

'They'll be out for a few hours at least,' says Alice.

'We need to hurry before the other two get suspicious,' says Starling. 'Daisy and Alice, there is a boat outside called *The Outcast*. Take it and get away from here. Perhaps go to Beaulieu until we figure this out.'

'We can come with you,' says Alice.

'We need to get away from those men. It would be safer if we split up.'

Daisy and Alice agree, and Starling and Anna lead the way cautiously down the wide concrete steps, Mauser and Walther at the ready.

Starling peers through the exit door, down towards the jetty. There is no sign of the men. Glancing to the other side, he sees it is clear. He beckons to Daisy and Alice, who hurry through and run down the jetty to *The Outcast*. He watches Alice untie the boat and waits until he sees it reverse and move safely away.

'Let's go,' he says, wondering where on earth the other two men are.

They hurry up the narrow path between the ruins of the old warehouse and the building that contained Morrow's office. Glancing back, he is relieved to find they are not being followed. They turn the corner and immediately collide with the two men, who reach under their jumpers for guns. Before they can aim, Starling and Anna work as if on the same wavelength, delivering unforgiving kicks to each man's groin.

The men's faces contort in pain and they slump forward. Anna slams her purse down on her assailant's head. He grunts and falls to the ground, his gun slipping from his grip. She kicks it into the gutter and out of reach.

Starling's assailant has managed to take out his gun but pain has made him clumsy and slow. Starling grabs his arm, pointing the gun in the air. A shot rings out, followed by a second.

Anna kicks the man twice in the ribs and Starling, his teeth gritted, slams his arm back with all his might until he hears a bone crunch. The man screams, dropping the gun to the ground. Starling picks it up and shoots him in the chest.

'Run, Anna,' he says.

Anna runs away from warehouse and on into the centre of the road dodging the traffic and ignoring the blare of car horns. Starling follows her, holding the pistol pointing down at the ground. Anna's man is hobbling after them, his face red. The traffic is thinning out and speeding up. Starling sees a bus ahead of them and Anna is sprinting towards it. She leaps onto the platform and spins round, holding the post and reaching out to Starling with her free hand. He grabs her hand and hauls himself onto the bus. The man is now running to catch up with them. Starling raises the pistol and points it at their pursuer, who is only feet away. 'You get to live today,' he shouts. 'Tell your masters I am coming for them.'

The man stops running and stands in the middle of the road, catching his breath. Starling watches him get smaller as the bus gathers speed.

Chapter 22

Edward and Clifford

The bus takes them as far as Fleet Street, where they dismount. Anna finds a phone box and Starling watches over her, his eyes profiling every passer-by from the shadows of St Bride's Church. Anna is deep in conversation, her face turned away from view. She puts the receiver down and then picks it up and dials again.

Why is she calling someone else?

Moments later she steps out of the box and makes her way towards Starling. She seems agitated and does not meet his gaze. 'He's agreed,' she says.

'Good.'

'He said he owes you. You saved his life.'

Starling isn't used to praise or compliments and does not know what to say. He shrugs. 'It will be good to see him again.'

Anna flags down a black taxi and they climb inside. 'Euston Station, please.'

'Right ya be,' says the driver.

The *he* in question is Edward Simms, Starling's overweight, frightened ex-roommate and reluctant friend from Beaulieu. He had last seen him two years before when Starling, Anna and Edward had escaped the terrible siege of Beaulieu, pursued by the agents of VIPER. Starling's plan had been to go to London and stop the Stones of Fire decimating the capital, but, at the last minute, Edward had lost his nerve and run off into the night. But it was Edward's breaking of the code that had helped save them all.

He had seen him briefly one more time at the memorial service for the pupils and staff killed during the siege. Starling had wanted to thank him for his help, but Edward had avoided him and Starling recalled a haunted look on his face – was it guilt or fear? He could not discern. It didn't matter anyway. Edward did not have the mettle to be a killer, or a spy. There was no shame in that. He had other skills and they needed him more than anyone else now.

In the taxi, Starling senses that Anna is distant. She is quiet, seeming to prefer to look out the window rather than talk.

'Is everything alright?'

'I'm fine,' she says, without looking at him.

The driver pulls up at Euston Station and Anna pays him. Starling steps out and scours the area for signs of a threat, but the station is quiet with just a handful of people around. Anna loops her arm into his and they walk towards the ticket office, smiling and casual on the outside but alert and ready to kill on the inside.

The ticket office is a stuffy, warm, square, wooden room painted a pale green and smelling of stale cigarette smoke and bleach. There is a small window with a ticket agent seated behind it and another larger window looking out on to the concourse and platform entrances.

'Two second class tickets for Bletchley,' says Starling.

'Next train is noon,' the ticket agent tells them.

Anna goes to stand at the bigger window, watching the concourse outside.

'Anyone we need to watch out for?' Starling says.

'It seems clear to me.'

The station clock says 11.55, so they hurry to the platform, board the train, find a quiet carriage and sit opposite each other by the window.

Anna still seems distant and preoccupied and Starling does not know what to make of it. He thinks back to anything he might have said or done that was out of turn, but he can think of nothing.

The guard's whistle blows and the train begins its journey.

'Anna...'

She looks at him with a pained expression and opens her mouth to speak just as the carriage door swings open and a couple of about their age fall inside giggling to each other.

''Ere, don't mind us,' says the young woman.

Anna smiles politely and the two lovebirds sit next to her, huddled together petting and kissing.

Starling leans forward. 'Anna, talk to me.'

'Not now,' she replies, head bowed and eyes down.

Starling sighs heavily, sits back, folds his arms and tries to sleep. He has no idea what is going on in Anna's head and wishes he didn't care. After all, she is someone else's problem now, not his.

An hour later the train stops at Bletchley station. The young couple had left at the previous stop leaving an awkward silence between Starling and Anna. He still has no clue what is troubling her.

They step onto the platform, the guard already blowing the whistle to encourage passengers to board quickly, as the train is about to leave. At one end of the platform two men are looking back at them. One of them seems familiar.

'Will, I'm sorry. I've been a fool.'

'Anna, what's the matter?'

'He's here. At Bletchley.'

Starling frowns. 'Who…? Edward?'

'No… Yes…' She sighs. 'Someone else…'

'Darling!' comes a voice.

Starling turns to see one of the men hurrying towards them, his eyes only on Anna. Anna smiles and opens her arms and the man pulls her close, kissing her full on the lips. They hold each other.

Starling cannot take his eyes off them. He swallows and feels himself go cold.

He takes stock of Anna's lover. He is tall, square-jawed with high cheekbones and slick blond hair. He is dressed in a smart, expensive, blue suit.

Extracting himself from Anna's embrace, the man turns to Starling. 'And you must be the famous Starling, returned from the dead.' He extends his hand. Starling hesitates and then lifts his hand slowly.

'Clifford Meadows,' Anna's man says ebulliently, shaking Starling's hand. His grip is at odds with his enthusiasm. It is non-committal, his skin soft. 'So good to meet you. Anna never stops talking about you. At times I thought I would never win her heart. But I did!'

Starling glances at Anna, who seems mortified.

'I do believe you know our resident genius.' Meadows tugs his hand from Starling's and gestures at the other man.

'Hello, Will.'

Standing beside Meadows is a smiling Edward Simms. Not the round, awkward eighteen-year-old; this Edward is two years older, slimmer and more confident.

Starling smiles. 'Edward, I didn't recognise you.'

'I've been learning to box, and I've been running. With Cliff.'

'Clifford,' corrects Meadows. 'He's quite the sprinter. He's beaten me a few times.'

Edward beams at Meadows and blushes. 'I got lucky, Cliff… Clifford, you know that.'

'We should get some lunch,' says Meadows, 'and you can tell us exactly why you are here.'

'We don't have much time,' says Starling. 'It's Edward we need to see.'

'All in good time, old boy. Besides, I have not seen my girl in weeks and I bet she has missed me terribly.' Meadows puts his arm around Anna and leads her out of the station.

Edward watches them walk away with a sullen look on his face.

'How is life at Bletchley?' asks Starling, as they follow Anna and Meadows across the road.

'Terrific. Exciting. We're doing some incredible work. Cliff is wonderful, too. Don't you think?'

'Is he?'

'He's so clever and funny. He does make me laugh. Even Alan thinks so.'

'Alan?'

'Alan Turing. He's our mentor. A great man.'

Starling is keen to bring the conversation to the point.

'Edward…'

'Call me Eddie. Everyone does.'

'I thought you hated that name.'

'Cliff uses it all the time and it just stuck. Now everyone calls me that and I like it. Cliff and Eddie. It has a ring to it, don't you think? Cliff seems to think so.'

Starling does not respond. His eyes follow the slick, blond hair and expensive suit of the man who has captured Anna's heart – and Edward's too, it seems.

Bletchley Park is opposite the railway station, an immense Victorian Gothic house set in almost six hundred acres of land where rows and rows of huts had been built for the encryption experts, analysts and mathematicians to work in. Meadows signs them in through the heavily secured gates and then leads the way towards the staff canteen in the main house. The interior walls are panelled in dark wood, and accusing eyes stare from the grim portraits that dominate the walls. The canteen is buzzing with activity. There is a strong aroma of meat stew and hot tea in the air.

'The place is quite something, isn't it?' says Meadows. 'Look around. Where else would you find so many boffins and debutantes in one place?'

'Is there somewhere quieter we can go?' asks Starling.

Meadows gently punches Starling's arm. 'I would never have put you down for such a stiff. Let's eat.'

Starling has to bite his tongue. He looks at Anna, who mouths a sorry to him.

They find a table to themselves. Starling and Anna have no appetite and choose a mug of tea each. Meadows and Edward tuck into the stew.

'Terrible news about Morrow, eh?' says Meadows, slurping his food. 'And the Irishman. What's his name?'

Starling sits up, his stomach tightening.

'Eoin Heaney?' says Anna.

'That's the fella.'

'What about him?' asks Starling.

'He came a cropper this morning. Someone planted a Rolling Ticker in his car. Terrible waste…'

Starling and Anna exchange glances but say nothing.

'…I always liked that car,' adds Meadows, with a snorting laugh.

'Cliff!' says Anna. 'Eoin was our friend.'

Starling grits his teeth, stares at Meadows' throat and imagines planting his fist in it, right here and now.

Meadows raises his arms in an apologetic gesture. 'Bad taste, I know. I'm sorry.'

An awkward silence hangs over the table for the remainder of lunch. Eventually Meadows breaks it. 'Let's go to my office. We can discuss what you need there.'

Leaving the canteen, Meadows and Edward guide them through the wooden huts and cabins where the code breakers work. Meadows' office sits among a block of huts at the rear of the main house. Inside, it is sparse and neat, containing a small desk with a stack of worn notebooks. There is a map of Europe on the wall and a window overlooking a gravel path.

Meadows sits down at the desk, leans back and rests his feet on the desktop. 'Now, how can we be of assistance?'

Starling thrusts his hands in his pockets and curls his fists. There is something about Meadows he doesn't like. Is he jealous?

'Could we speak to Edward? Alone?'

'Sorry, old man. Eddie is my responsibility. There are no secrets between us,' he replies, winking at Edward, who blushes in response.

Starling hesitates. He really wants to tell Meadows to clear off but doesn't want to risk upsetting Anna or Edward. Besides, they need answers quickly.

As if sensing his reluctance, Anna says, 'Will, you can trust Clifford.'

Starling meets Meadows' gaze and for a second sees his eyes flare. Perhaps Starling's hesitation has offended him. All eyes look towards Starling and after a moment he relents. He takes out the schematic and unfolds it on the desk.

They all crowd around it.

'This is a diagram for the Tesla Death Ray,' says Starling.

'Very interesting,' says Edward. 'Is it operational?'

'We don't know.'

'Where did you get this?' says Meadows.

'That's not important,' replies Starling.

'What can you tell us about it?' Anna asks Cliff and Edward.

Meadows and Edward pore over the schematic. Edward keeps having to push his spectacles up as they slip down his nose.

'What exactly do you want to know?' asks Meadows.

'How does it work? Are there any weak points? Can we destroy it?'

Meadows snorts. 'There is very little here to go by.'

'I don't know,' says Edward. 'It would be helpful to see the actual weapon, however, what we have here is arguably more useful.' Edward says nothing for a moment as he studies the schematic.

Starling leans in, hungry for information. 'Tell us, Edward.'

Edward places his finger on the pyramidal base. 'This is the link between the weapon and the power source. The power is somehow contained in the sphere. Destroy the pyramid and you break the link. Destroy the sphere and you destroy not just the weapon but much more. That is my assumption. What do you think, Clifford?'

Meadows looks at the diagram through lidded eyes. 'It's possible,' he mumbles.

'What can power something like this?' asks Starling.

'There may be some sort of generator, which would need to be immense. That suggests to me the weapon is not transportable but is at a fixed spot.'

Starling feels a surge of excitement. 'So, if the weapon is operational then all we need to do is find the power source and destroy it somehow?'

'Is there any clue about how we might do that?' Anna asks.

'There's nothing obvious from the diagram. I will need time to study it a bit more. However, this is an unconventional weapon and I have no doubt it will be very difficult to disable never mind destroy.'

'How much time do you need?'

'A day, maybe less.'

'Can you do it quicker?'

'I'll try… Oh, I have something for you.' Edward removes a photograph from his jacket pocket and gives it to Starling. 'Eoin sent me this. It's a close up of the serial code from one of the gas bombs on Westminster Bridge.'

'You never mentioned this!' says Meadows, clearly rattled.

'It was information given out on a need-to-know basis. If something happened to Eoin then I was to tell Starling or Anna. Those were his orders. He asked me to find out what I could about the serial code. From my research I was able to determine that the bomb was manufactured in a plant situated in the Swiss Alps.' He points to the schematic on the desk. 'Look, the same number is on the bottom right here.'

Meadows takes out a silver case and lights up a cigarette. Smoke surrounds him, filling the air.

'The plant is owned by the Teleken Black Corporation,' says Edward.

'It's owned by the Black family,' says Anna, 'one of the richest families in the world. They manufacture all sorts of weapons. The war has made them even more powerful and wealthy than they were before.'

'Teleken are also funded by VIPER. I think we have our strongest lead yet. Great work, Edward,' says Starling.

Edward smiles and shrugs.

Starling takes out the paper from his blazer pocket and gives it to Edward. 'There's something else. I need you to decode this.'

Edward studies it and Meadows stands over him, his brow furrowed, smoke streaming from his flared nostrils.

'We have a new super-machine. It's called Colossus. I can run it through that. What do you think, Cliff… ord?'

'Where did this come from?' asks Meadows, ignoring Edward.

'I can't tell you that,' says Starling.

Meadows scratches an eyebrow and smiles a hard smile. Starling can feel the distance between them growing wider, but doesn't care. It might be jealousy. Or it might be something more. He can't be sure.

'Clifford, I can run to Colossus and sort this out,' says Edward.

Meadows smiles. 'Of course. We're all here to do our bit for the war. You run ahead, Eddie, and I'll look after our guests. I'll make a quick call to the Machine Room and tell them you're coming.'

'Thanks, Cliff,' says Edward.

'Clifford!'

'Erm… sorry,' he says, turning to leave.

'One more thing,' says Starling, taking Edward to one side and out of earshot. 'Did Eoin mention anything about a Russian agent called Sedova?'

'Yes. He asked me to find out whatever I could about him.'

'What did you discover?'

'Not as much as I'd like. His name is Pyotr Sedova. He worked for the Russian secret police. He was married to Inga and they had two daughters: Anastasiya and Elena. One day his family were sent to a gulag. No one knows why. They spent two months doing hard labour and then suddenly they were released. After that, Pyotr went missing. It's possible he negotiated their freedom in exchange for doing the Russian government's dirty work.'

'I don't suppose we have a description?'

'I'm afraid not.'

'What are you two chatting about?' asks Anna.

'I'll tell you later,' says Starling, aware that Meadows is leaning across his desk and trying to listen in.

Meadows looks at Anna. 'Darling, why don't you and Starling wait outside and get some air. I'll be with you in a second.' He kisses Anna brusquely on the cheek.

Starling and Anna follow Edward out and stand outside watching him hurry off to the Machine Room. Starling glances through the office window and sees Meadows putting down the phone receiver.

'I'm sorry about Cliff. He can be a bit territorial. What do you think of him?' asks Anna.

Before Starling can answer Meadows appears and seems in happier mood. 'I left a message for Edward telling him to meet us at the Eight Bells.'

'I'd rather stay here and wait,' says Starling.

'Let's go have a pint and get to know one another. I fear we may have got off on the wrong foot.'

'That's a nice idea, darling,' says Anna. 'Come on, Starling. I could do with a drink after what we have been through.'

'Come on, old man,' says Meadows. 'I'll drive us and I'm paying!'

Starling shrugs and agrees for Anna's sake.

'Eddie can meet us there, once he's decoded the cipher.'

Meadows' car is a striking red Alfa Romeo sports car with four seats. He winds down the roof and offers Starling the front passenger seat. 'Let's talk as I drive.'

Starling frowns at Anna, who shrugs and climbs into the back.

Meadows starts up the car, spinning the wheels too fast, and flies out of Bletchley and through the security gates. 'A lovely mover, the Alfa Romeo, but not a patch on the Embiricos. I had my eye on that for a while. Damn shame.'

Starling wonders what he means by that, but doesn't press it.

They drive through the country roads, the sun beating down their faces, the wind blowing through their hair. Starling is actually enjoying the ride. Meadows slows as they approach a junction. Looking for traffic on either side, he moves forward to the centre of the junction but the engine cuts out.

'Bloody thing!' says Meadows. He hops out and tries to open the bonnet.

'Will, could you turn the engine over when I say so?'

Meadows lifts the bonnet. 'Darling, could you hold this open for me while I try and fix this blasted thing.'

Anna gets out and holds open the bonnet.

'Turn her over now!' calls Meadows.

Starling leans across and turns the ignition key, but nothing sparks.

'Keep turning!' calls Meadows.

The engine is churning and choking and making quite a racket. Above the din, Starling hears Anna call his name. There is something about the tone of her voice that makes him sit up straight. She is screaming at the car. In his peripheral vision is a large shadow. He turns. Hurtling towards him is another car. He thinks he sees a hooded figure at the wheel, the face almost visible. He lifts his arms to protect his head as the car smashes into the side of Alfa Romeo.

Everything goes black.

Chapter 23

The Red Storm Is Coming

Starling wakes to a blinding headache and aching ribs and muscles. Groaning, he blinks open his eyes and shuts them quickly as bright light dazzles them, doubling the pain in his head. He is lying cheek down on cold, dusty wooden floorboards in a strange room. His hands and feet are tied, secured with some sort of rough cord. He tugs and pulls but the cord is tight. His blazer has been removed and he cannot feel the comfort of the Mauser strapped to his chest. He is helpless. He recalls the last few moments before everything went blank: Meadows' car breaking down at the junction, another car speeding towards them. A hooded figure. A face…

He takes a few deep breaths and lets his eyes adjust to the light. The room is small, square in shape, with low ceilings: a room in a cottage. It seems soulless and devoid of any human touches, as if no one lives here. There is a window with the curtains drawn and a table where his and Anna's pistols and jackets lie. Lying on the floor next to the table is Anna. She is staring at him, her eyes wide with concern.

'Are you hurt?' he mouths.

She shakes her head and he is relieved she is unharmed. He hears voices and twists his head to look in their direction. The door is partially open and he can see a hooded monk dressed in black robes with a red trim on the cuff of his sleeves. A memory stirs: a name. He has seen those robes before. The man underneath them is no ordinary monk. He is the head of the Cerastes. Proatheris! His name is Proatheris and he is holding the schematic and talking to someone. Starling sits up to get a better view, ignoring the stabbing pain in his head and his protesting bruised muscles. He sees the monk pointing aggressively at Meadows' chest. Meadows is nodding.

'If I had a lot of money I would have gambled all of it on you being a treacherous VIPER swine,' Starling shouts.

Proatheris and Meadows turn to look at him. Starling narrows his gaze at the shadowy hood and tries to pick out the face but Meadows frowns and shuts the door. He wonders if he imagined seeing the monk's face before he blacked out, as he cannot for the life of him remember who it was he saw.

The two men walk further away and Starling hears a door open and close. Then, outside, a car door opens then closes too. An engine starts up and he hears the sound of the car driving away.

Another door closes, which he guesses is the front door of the cottage. There are footsteps in the hallway. The door to the room swings opens and Meadows stands for a moment, framed in the doorway. Then he approaches Starling, crouches down, reaches across and pulls Starling's hair up so that their faces are inches apart.

Starling grits his teeth.

'I now have the great privilege of torturing you to find out what you know and who you have spoken to. Both of you,' he adds, glancing at Anna. 'Sorry, darling. This is not quite what I had in mind for us, but hey ho – plans change all the time, do they not?'

Anna glares at him but before she can speak Meadows raises his hand. 'Don't answer that. It's rhetorical.'

Starling hears Anna muffle a reply.

'We know nothing,' says Starling. 'You'll be wasting your time.'

'You know more than you should already, thanks to that zealous little queer, Simms.'

'Where is Edward?'

'He'll be here soon with whatever he has decoded from Colossus.'

'Then what? Are you going to torture him too?'

'I've thought about it many times. Fantasised in fact. I'll probably just kill him and pin his death on you. One less of his sort in the world can only be a good thing, don't you think?'

Starling hears the sound of a different car pulling up outside.

'Talk of the devil,' says Meadows, with a wicked grin.

There is a frantic knock on the door. Meadows removes a handkerchief from his pocket and ties it tightly around Starling's mouth, gagging him. He leaves the room, shutting the door behind him.

Starling tries to wrestle free of his bonds and sees Anna doing the same. He hears Edward.

'Oh, Cliff. I got your message and then I saw your car! I was so worried.'

'Nothing to worry about, old son. Come in. Starling and Anna will be delighted to see you.'

'Where are they?'

'They're a little tied up at the moment. Did you crack the code?'

'Can I see them?'

'If you must...'

And then Starling hears something heavy fall to the floor. His heart sinks. He feels sorry for Edward and continues to pull at his bonds until the door swings open. Looking up he can't quite believe his eyes. Edward is staring down at him. *How can this be?* Edward hurries towards him and, with a penknife, cuts his gag.

'What did you do?'

'I punched him in the temple. I don't think he was expecting it.'

'Cut the bonds on my wrists,' says Starling.

Edward reaches behind Starling and begins cutting, but Starling hears a roar as Meadows rushes in and pulls Edward away from Starling by the collar. The knife slips from Edward's grip and Starling catches it with his fingers. Deftly he turns it over and begins sawing at the cord. Edward stumbles and falls on his back and Meadows rains his fists down hard on him.

'You think you are so clever, you duplicitous shit.'

That's rich. Starling cuts through the cord and turns the knife towards the bonds on his ankles, but now Meadows sees what he's doing and scrambles from Edward to the table, reaching for the guns on top. Anna slides forward and kicks him with both legs and Meadows falls forward, smashing his nose on the edge of the table. Blood sprays onto the floor.

Free of the bonds, Starling leaps to his feet and runs at Meadows, who is pulling the Mauser from its holster while Anna continues to kick at his shins. Starling wraps one arm around Meadows' throat and grabs the hand holding the pistol. He slams Meadows' hand several times on the table – a bullet fires, blowing a hole in the plaster on the wall. Starling squeezes Meadows' neck tighter and the Mauser falls to floor. Meadows makes a choking noise and moments later Starling feels his body go limp. He tosses him to the floor in disgust and picks up the Mauser.

Starling cuts Anna's bonds; her wrists are red raw.

'I'm so sorry, Will,' she says. 'I trusted him. I feel such a fool.'

Without thinking, he rubs Anna's wrists. 'We're fine. That's the important thing.'

'Edward…' she says.

Edward is on his knees nursing a bleeding nose and one rapidly swelling eye with one hand and putting his twisted spectacles on with the other.

'Edward, you're a bloody hero,' says Starling. 'Where did you learn to fight?'

'I told you I'd been boxing,' he says.

Meadows begins to stir, so Starling checks his body and pockets for hidden weapons. There is nothing. Starling and Anna put on their holsters and jackets as he comes round.

'Get up!' says Starling, the Mauser pointing firmly at Meadows' chest.

Meadows pushes himself up and glares viciously at Edward. 'You little bastard. You tricked me.'

'I'm afraid so. I spent a year at Beaulieu and learnt more than just code-breaking, you know. I trained to be a spy. I am a spy. I might not be at Starling and Anna's level but I am a spy, nevertheless. We've suspected you for quite some time now. You think you're so clever. I was playing you, getting to know you. Did you not think I could see through your pathetic act?'

Starling is quite impressed. 'You fooled me too.'

Edward looks at Anna. 'I'm sorry I couldn't tell you, Anna. Those were my orders.'

'I understand, Edward,' says Anna, brushing the dust from her jacket, her eyes downcast. Starling can see she is hurt. It is a double blow: not only was Meadows lying to her, but so were her close colleagues and friends. She stands in front of Meadows.

'How about a tumble for old times' sake?' he says, sneeringly.

What happens next is almost a blur as Anna swings her fist at his face. The force of it lifts him of his feet and he falls back against the wall and slides down to the floor.

'That'll be a no, then,' he mumbles.

Anna rubs her fist and looks at Starling. 'We need to lock this vermin away.'

'We can take him to security at Bletchley,' says Edward.

Starling grabs Meadows' collar and hauls him up, digging the Mauser into his ribs.

Meadows snorts. 'Why bother? You might as well finish me now. We're all going to die very soon, anyway.'

Starling frowns. 'What do you mean?'

'It's coming.'

Starling pushes him into the hallway. 'What's coming?'

Meadows looks at him and laughs.

Anna leads the way outside where Edward's car, a green Mosquito Morris Minor, is parked. The cottage is isolated, somewhere deep in the countryside. There is a road at the end of the driveway that leads up to the cottage. Starling sees a blue car slow and the window wind down. It is dark inside the vehicle. Suddenly rapid gunfire explodes from inside. Edward and Anna are behind the Morris Minor. Anna fires her Walther at the vehicle. Shielded by Meadows, Starling fires the Mauser at the blue car but it speeds off and disappears from view. Meadows slumps to the ground, with two bullet wounds in his chest, his breathing laboured.

'You're all going to die,' he mumbles. 'It's coming.'

Starling crouches down. 'What's coming?'

'Die… you're all going to die…'

'What's coming, Meadows? Tell us,' Starling says urgently.

'The Red Storm…' Meadows exhales a final breath and then his eyes become glassy and lifeless.

Starling feels a chill running through him.

'What does he mean?' asks Edward.

'I still don't know.' But he senses Meadows is telling the truth. Something is coming. Something evil and deadly.

'We should get out of here.'

'There's a tea room just out of town. We can talk there. I'll call security later and they can deal with Meadows,' says Edward.

Starling drags Meadows' body back into the cottage.

All their eyes are focussed on the road as Edward drives them through the Buckinghamshire countryside to a sleepy village of thatched cottages with a grocer's, a post office and a café called Betty's Cosy Tea Room.

A bell rings as they enter the café. The tables are neatly laid out and aromas of tea and coffee fill the air. It's not busy. One older gentleman sits reading *The Times* while two ladies stir tea in china cups. No one pays them any unusual attention.

Edward orders three teas and takes them to a table that's quiet and out of earshot at back of the café.

'How is your eye?' Anna asks Edward.

'I'll live.' He hands the original paper with the code across to Starling. 'This wasn't as difficult as I thought it might be. I almost cracked it myself, however

Colossus beat me to it.' Edward beams like a proud parent and gives Starling a lined sheet of paper torn from a jotter.

Written in Edward's scrawl are four lines of different letters that don't make any sense to Starling. Frowning, he looks at Edward. 'I don't understand.'

'The code was created using two different ciphers – hieroglyphics and an advanced pigpen. Let me show you.' Edward begins to sketch a grid on the paper.

'Actually, Edward, perhaps just tell us what it says.'

Edward looks from Starling to Anna and back to Starling. He smiles and shrugs. 'Sorry, I do get a little carried away sometimes. So, each word is an anagram.' Edward flips the paper over. On the other side are four lines of what seems to be a poem or a riddle.

Ares ruin lies hidden far and wide
but the orphan sleeps
where the fledgling knights joust and spar
buried deep in a dungeon black

'What does it mean?' asks Anna.

'I haven't had time to work that out,' says Edward.

Starling turns it over in his head. Ares ruin. The fledgling knights. He knows exactly what it means. He smiles at Anna.

'You know, don't you?' she says.

'You're a bloody hero, Edward!'

Edward shrugs. 'There's just one more thing. The single hieroglyph on the fifth line.'

Starling takes a closer look. 'It's a bird.'

'Not just any bird. It's an owl.'

'This message came from the Owl. I assume it is his signature.'

'That's correct. The owl in the Egyptian alphabet translates as M in the English alphabet. I'm not sure if it is important but I thought I'd mention it.'

Starling is unsure of what to make of it. 'Thank you, Edward. It might well be important.' He pauses before saying, 'Edward, can we borrow your car?'

'Of course. It's not really mine anyway. It belongs to MI6.'

'I'll drop you back at Bletchley.'

They leave the café and Starling gets into the driver's seat of the Morris. He takes Edward back to the front gates of Bletchley. They all get out of the car and Starling embraces Edward. 'Thank you, for everything.'

'If you need me, I'll be here.'

Anna hugs Edward warmly.

'I'm sorry about Meadows,' he says.

'I'm not,' she responds, kissing him on the cheek. 'You take care.'

Starling starts up the Morris Minor and honks the horn at Edward. As they drive away Starling says, 'I'm sorry, too. About him. Meadows.'

'What's done is done. I'm glad it's over.'

'Do you want to continue on this… mission… quest, whatever it is?'

'Yes.'

'I'm glad.'

They say nothing for a moment until Anna changes the subject. 'Where are we going now?'

'We're going back to Beaulieu.'

Chapter 24

Return to Beaulieu

Starling feels an unnerving sense of nostalgia – a sensation foreign to any amnesiac – at the thought of returning to Beaulieu House, one of the Government's secret residential training facilities for spies. Two years before, when he'd lost his memory, he had found himself at Beaulieu searching for answers about who he was. The masters, including Eoin, and most of the students had welcomed him and had taken him in when he had nowhere else to go. It was also where he and Anna had first met. He has a fondness for the place and in an odd way it feels like he is going home.

Starling pulls up at the entrance to Beaulieu where the same old soldier of the Home Guard, Private Tom Fletcher, stands dutifully at the entrance.

'Hello there, young Starling, and Miss Wilder too. This is a nice surprise.'

'Hello, Tom. We're here to see the Major.'

'She's not expectin' any visitors today, but I'm sure she will be pleased to see you two.' Private Fletcher opens the gate.

Starling and Anna wave as they drive inside and up the wide winding gravel drive to the imposing stone house, with its stained-glass windows and a turret at each side.

The front door opens and a stocky woman with short curly brown hair and wearing a green tweed suit steps outside. It is the principal of the school, Miss Clews, or as she prefers to be known, the Major. She smiles warmly as Starling and Anna get out of the car.

'Will Starling,' she says, grabbing his hand and squeezing it. 'I'm so pleased to see you. I had heard… Well – we thought you were dead.'

'I'm very much alive. It's good to see you, Major.'

The Major embraces Anna and stands back to admire her. 'You look wonderful, dear. Spying clearly suits you. Come to my office, both of you, and tell me why you are here.'

They follow the Major to the Great Hall and along the familiar stone flags through hallways lit with sconces and decorated with educational pictures of aircraft bombers, rifles, pistols.

They pass a common room where several students lounge on two large leather sofas, poring over their textbooks. He notices a girl of around sixteen with a strong, wiry frame and mousey brown hair cut just below the ears looking back at him through narrowed eyes. He slows to a stop, his stomach in knots. It's Kitty from Fenchurch Street in London, the leader of a gang of orphans who were trying to stay alive during the Blitz. Kitty and Sam had been friends and it was because of Starling that Sam had been killed.

'Kitty?'

Kitty's eyes flare. She stands, gathers her books and walks out of the common room, passing him without saying a word. Starling rubs the back of his head, still not quite believing she is here in Beaulieu. *How did that happen?*

Anna and the Major are at the end of the hallway, standing outside the principal's office, watching him.

'That girl,' says Starling. 'How did she come to be here.'

'You mean Kitty? She found us. Just like you did. It has occurred to me that we might not be as secret as we think we are.'

Starling wonders if Sam had confided anything about him and his connections to Kitty.

The Major's office is much the same as he remembers. It is a spacious room with maps pinned to the walls, a mahogany leather-topped desk and two threadbare sofas on either side of a small fireplace. On the walls are photographs of the Major driving speeding cars, flying aeroplanes and attending a garden party at the palace with the royal family, the Prime Minister and Hugh Coleridge. Pride of place in the centre of the wall is the photo of the Major sitting closely, hand in hand, with a tall handsome woman. They are both smiling.

'How is Miss Davenport?' asks Starling.

'She's very well, thank you. Teaching shooting out at the range today. She'll be pleased to see you.'

'I'm afraid we cannot stay very long,' says Anna.

'Oh, that is a shame. So tell me. Why are you here?'

'I need something of Eoin's. Something that once belonged to Timothy Chittlock.'

'I'm afraid Eoin isn't here. I heard this morning he was in the field somewhere.'

'Who told you?'

'I had a telephone meeting with Sir Hugh Coleridge this morning. We are in a dire situation, it seems.'

'Is Eoin in trouble?'

'I'm afraid I don't know.'

'How is Sir Hugh?' asks Anna.

'There have been two attempts on his life, but he is otherwise fine.'

'Where is he now?' asks Starling.

'He's in Baker Street. Working long hours trying to put an end to this situation.'

'We should talk to him,' Starling says to Anna. 'He…'

The Major looks from Starling to Anna with curious eyes. 'Are you going to tell me what this is all about?'

Starling and Anna exchange glances and nod an informal agreement. They both know they can trust the Major. Starling tells the Major everything up to the point of receiving the decoded message from Edward.

'Well, that's quite a story. Life is never dull with you two, is it? Are you going to tell me what this hidden thing that you want from here is?'

'I can't,' says Starling. 'It's just vital we find it and leave without anyone knowing that we've been here. I don't want to put you and the pupils at any risk.'

'*Does* anyone else know you are here?'

'No one. Not even Edward.'

The Major twiddles her thumbs and stares at them, deep in thought. 'I don't like it. I have a feeling that you have put us all in great danger. But you are here now and I can only do what is best for the country.' The Major sighs. 'Where is this thing?'

'It's hidden down in the dungeons.'

'Do you remember the way?'

'Yes.'

'Very well. Come with me.' The Major switches on the desk lamp, stands and draws the curtains hanging at the windows in her office. She walks to the wall where her many photographs hang and pushes a piece of wood panelling level with her waist. The wall opens inwards, revealing a dark corridor behind it. A slight breeze of musty damp air cools Starling's face.

'You know your way there and out again?'

'We do.'

'Please find whatever it is you need and leave quickly. It'll be dark soon. Good luck, both of you.'

They say their thanks and goodbyes to the Major as Starling removes the small torch concealed inside his sleeve and flicks it on. For something so small the beam is indeed wide, as Joseph had claimed. They hurry down damp stone steps and through the dark passages. Grimy cobwebs hang everywhere and brush against their faces and hair. From the other side of the walls they hear the sound of voices and laughter as they pass the various dormitories and classrooms, which invokes in Starling another wave of nostalgia. He wonders what it would be like to have all his memories back. Part of him wants to know everything, to remember his family and previous life, but the other part of him wants it to remain dormant. He knows that regaining all his memories would bring grief and even more of the anger that he has since learned to tame. Two years back when he had lost his memory, he was driven by a rage that he could not quite explain. Though he had mastered it, his desire for revenge has never been so great. VIPER would pay for what they had done to his family and his friends, or he would die trying to make them. First, he had to put a stop to their plans for the Tesla Death Ray and whatever the Red Storm was.

Starling leads the way into the dungeon, where the air becomes significantly colder and the walls are dripping with moisture. The perfect environment to store the unstable artefact that was the fragment from the Stones of Fire.

'Did you hear that?' says Anna.

'Hear what?' says Starling.

Anna is looking behind her. 'I thought I heard something.'

He shines the torch behind them – it reveals an empty passage.

'Perhaps it was a mouse,' says Starling.

Anna removes her Walther from the holster.

Starling carries on until he sees the end of the passage and the heavy wooden cell door with its steel reinforcement bands and small barred window.

'There,' he says.

Shining the torch through the window, they peer inside. The cell is bare, as he had left it two years back. Starling pushes the cell door, but it does not move. He swears under his breath. How could he be so stupid!

'What is it?' asks Anna.

'Eoin had a key to get into the cell.'

'Perhaps it's hanging up somewhere,' says Anna.

Starling runs the beam around the outside of the cell door but there is no key. It was stupid even to think that it might be hanging there.

'Shit!' he says.

And then something heavy slides across the floor and hits his boots. Anna swings her gun behind her as Starling peers down at the object. It is a large iron key, the same one Eoin had used to open the cell door.

'You might need that,' comes a voice.

'Stay where you are,' says Anna.

Starling shines the torch down the passageway and sees the wiry frame of a Beaulieu student with her hair cut just below the ears. 'Kitty. Is that you?' he says.

The girl turns to leave.

'Kitty, wait.'

She stops.

Starling steps towards her. 'How come you have the key?'

Kitty still does not look at him and hesitates before answering. 'I was given a message from Eoin.'

'What did he say? Is he alive?'

'I don't know! He said that if you showed up I was to give you the key. That's it! That's all I know.'

Kitty has not lost any of her attitude. He had always admired her for taking in all of those orphaned boys and ensuring they had a home and were fed.

'What happened to you, and to the others?'

'They were all taken away from me and rehomed, no thanks to you,' she says. 'Except for Sam, of course, who was killed.' She glares at him. 'It's because of you he is dead.'

Kitty's last statement was like a blow to Starling's stomach. He feels his mouth dry. He has no words to defend himself because she is right. Starling should have done more to protect Sam. But he failed. 'I'm sorry, Kitty.'

A moment passes with nothing more said and then Kitty leaves.

Starling feels Anna squeeze his arm. He picks up the key and unlocks the cell door. Without wasting any more time he pulls up the flagstone in the corner of the cell where the fragment is hidden. Underneath is a shallow hole. From it he lifts an old wooden box and sets it on the table. It looks like something a cobbler might house his tools in.

The box begins to tremble, he hears a humming sound and notices flickering movements as insects begin crawling out from the cell walls. He opens the box and the same unearthly blue light as he has seen before erupts from inside, flooding the cell and the corridor beyond. Starling and Anna both raise their hands to shield their eyes from the glare. When his sight adjusts he sees the glowing shard of blue stone, about two inches long.

'It can feel our presence, our energy, our emotions.'

'How dangerous is it?' asks Anna.

'I saw it turn a table to ash in seconds.'

'But how can we use it?'

'I have no clue. Right now I need to learn how to calm it down.'

'How do you do that?'

'Soothe it and stroke it and remain calm, I think. It responds to emotions and violence.'

Starling holds the stone between his thumb and index finger. Small lights like miniature fireworks begin sparkling around them, stinging him like tiny electric shocks. He takes three deep breaths and begins to calm himself down as he strokes the fragment. The lights begin to spiral and snake around his hand. They spread up his arm and around his neck and back, causing his hairs to stand on end. He gasps and closes his eyes, his thumb running gently over the stone. He feels the tickling sensation subside.

'It's working,' says Anna.

Within moments the fragment has stopped shining and is no longer blue, but an unremarkable shade of grey like any other stone. It is sleeping. Starling does not know how he knows this. It is more like he feels it.

'We should go,' he says, and wonders how he will carry the stone. An idea comes to his head. He takes out the tin fusilier and unscrews the screwdriver from the multi-purpose tool concealed in his left sleeve. He wedges the flat of the tool into the spine of the tin soldier and opens it up. There is just enough room inside to house the fragment. Starling places it inside and pushes the two sides of the soldiers back together again.

'Nice idea,' says Anna.

Starling places the soldier into his inside breast pocket and buttons it for extra safety.

They leave the passage following a different but still familiar route to the fireplace that leads to the Great Hall. The smell of soot is choking as Starling removes a brick and peers through the hole. The Great Hall is empty; the students will be in the mess hall. He pulls the metal catch above his head and the wall turns inwards.

Closing it behind him, Starling and Anna hurry outside, dusting the soot from their hands. Standing by the Morris Minor is Kitty.

'Kitty, no one must know we have been here,' says Starling.

'I know,' she says.

Starling nods his thanks and opens the driver door.

'Make them pay for what they did,' says Kitty, her eyes locking firmly on to Starling's.

'I will. I promise.'

Kitty thrusts her hands into her blazer pockets, turns and goes inside.

Chapter 25

Moonlight Squadron One

With his hands firmly gripping the steering wheel and his brow furrowed, Starling navigates through the Buckinghamshire countryside, his mind fixed on what their next move should be. Should they go to Secret Service HQ in Baker Street or head to Manchester to seek out Eoin?

Anna can sense his agitation. 'We should call Sir Hugh. He can advise us on what to do next.' She is clearly on the same wavelength.

'You're right. Let's find a phone.'

They pass through a small town and park near a telephone box. They both squeeze inside it and Starling keeps a lookout as Anna phones Baker Street.

'Hello. Sir Hugh Coleridge, please.'

Starling moves his head near to the earpiece so that they can both hear.

The phone rings for a few moments, before a man's voice answers, 'Sir Hugh Coleridge's office.'

'May I speak to Sir Hugh?'

'He's not here. He's not been here in days,' the voice says dryly.

Starling and Anna exchange nervous glances.

'Could you give a number or address where I might find him?'

'No. Who is this?'

Starling shakes his head.

'Thank you,' says Anna, replacing the receiver. She places her thumbnail in her mouth and bites on it absentmindedly. 'The Major said Sir Hugh was spending all his time in Baker Street. Why would she lie?'

Starling scans the street outside. 'I really don't know. Perhaps she didn't.'

'I'll try his home number. He told me to use it if ever we were in trouble.' Anna dials the number and they both listen. After a moment the phone is picked up.

'Hello,' says Sir Hugh's voice.

Starling smiles at Anna who sighs with relief. 'Sir Hugh. Thank God.'

There is a hesitation before Coleridge answers. 'Anna?'

'Yes. It's me. It's good to hear your voice. We thought the worst.'

'Is Starling with you?'

'Yes, he's here; we are both fine.'

'Marvellous. Where are you? I'll send someone to pick you up.'

'No, don't worry, we have transport. Listen, we have intelligence on VIPER.'

'What intelligence?'

'I'd rather not say on the phone.'

'My line is safe, Anna. Tell me what you know.'

Anna tells him about the schematic, Edward, Meadows and the photograph of the serial number linked to the Teleken Black manufacturing plant in the French Alps. Sir Hugh listens without interrupting.

'You should go there,' he says at last.

'But how?' asks Starling.

'I will need to make some calls. Phone me back in ten minutes.'

'Will do.'

They wait outside the phone box, both deep in thought.

'I wonder if we'll need to go tonight,' says Anna.

'It's possible.'

Anna folds her arms and leans against the Morris Minor.

'Are you sure you want to do this?' asks Starling.

'We started this together. We'll finish it together.'

Their eyes lock for a moment and then Anna looks away. Something is troubling her. He thinks it might be Meadows and does not press the matter.

Ten minutes later Anna redials Sir Hugh's number. The receiver is picked up and Starling hears the scrunching of paper, as if a sheet is being flattened out or held up.

'Will, Anna, can you hear me?' says Sir Hugh.

'We hear you,' replies Anna.

'I've just spoken with Group Captain McFarland at the RAF base in Southend. He is leading a moon squadron into south-west France tonight. I have persuaded him to take both of you with him. He will drop you close to Lyon. Have you had parachute training?'

'Yes,' says Anna.

'Good. Teddy – Captain McFarland – will give you everything you need. How long do you think it will take you to get there?'

'Two hours possibly,' says Starling.

'He leaves at midnight. You'd better hurry. Do you know the way?'

'No.'

Starling hears paper shaking.

'I have a map. Take the following route…'

Anna pulls a notebook and pencil from her handbag and jots down Sir Hugh's directions.

'Try and get there as quickly as you can. Excellent work both of you and good luck.'

They say their goodbyes and get back into the Morris Minor. Starling is relieved and full of renewed determination now that they have a clearer plan ahead.

–

On what seems like a thimbleful of petrol, Starling and Anna arrive at Southend airfield fifteen minutes before midnight. There is a runway with a Lockheed Hudson light bomber and two Westland Lysanders. Starling pulls the car up alongside a security guard at the airfield gate and winds down the window.

'Group Captain McFarland is expecting us,' says Starling, handing across their ID.

'Starling and Wilder. Yes. We were expecting you earlier.'

'This is not the easiest of places to find.'

The guard points to two men standing outside an art deco building near the runway. One is a tall man in a blue pilot's uniform; the other is a dressed in overalls and holding a clipboard. They are deep in discussion.

'Group Captain McFarland in uniform,' says the guard.

'Thank you.'

The guard opens the gate and Starling drives the car through under the watchful gaze of the pilot.

Starling gets out of the car and introduces himself and Anna to Group Captain McFarland, a handsome man in his thirties, clean shaven with neatly combed brown hair. 'You're a little late,' he says, frowning.

'I'm sorry, Captain McFarland. We tried to get here as quickly as we could...'

'Not easy to find. Yes, I know,' he says, his face relaxing. 'Both of you are with me tonight in the Hudson, replacing Rowden and Lefort, who are a little disappointed not to be heading to France to do their duty, I might just add. I assume you've both jumped before?'

'Yes, we have,' says Anna.

'Splendid.' McFarland looks towards the art deco building. 'You'll find the ladies' and gents' changing rooms inside. There are protective jumpsuits hanging up with your papers in the breast pocket. Put the suits on and come straight out to the Hudson.'

Five minutes later, Starling and Anna are walking towards the Hudson, dressed in loose-fitting khaki jumpsuits on top of their clothes. The rumble of the Hudson's and Lysanders' engines kills the silence of the night and leaves the air thick with diesel fumes.

'Nervous?' asks Starling.

Anna is pulling her collar up. 'Yes. I suppose. Excited too. What about you?'

'The same.'

They say nothing more as they climb through the side door of the Hudson. The cabin is like a large steel tube painted green with two fixed metal benches under two rows of five small square windows. At the rear of cabin, six parachute backpacks are fixed securely. On the benches are two other passengers dressed in the same jumpsuits: a smiling thin-faced man and a woman in her twenties with short dark hair.

'I'm Ron,' says the thin-faced man.

'And I'm Barbara. Lovely to meet you.'

'Nice to meet you too,' says Starling.

'This is our first mission. Isn't it, Ron?'

'First one, yes.'

'We're ever so nervous.'

'And excited, Barbara.'

'Yes, of course. Excited too.'

Starling can see Barbara is anything but excited. This is probably her first time in an aeroplane not to mention her first jump.

'Is it your first time too?' asks Barbara.

'Not quite,' says Anna.

'Oh,' says Barbara. 'That's nice.' She rubs her thighs, smiles politely and casts her eyes to the floor.

With the pleasantries seemingly over, Starling looks towards the cockpit and sees McFarland poring over a map with a man he assumes is the navigator. They finish their conversation and the map holder climbs down to the navigator cockpit. McFarland looks back and smiles.

'Me and old Pikey make a great team. We'll get you there in double time. You wouldn't mind shutting the side door for me would you, old chap?'

Starling pulls it closed as McFarland addresses his passengers. 'Make yourselves comfortable, ladies and gentlemen. Moonlight Squadron One is about to hit the clouds.'

The putter of the Hudson speeds up as it rolls forward on the runway. Starling settles beside Anna, facing their fellow passengers. Barbara's head is bowed, her lips moving quietly, her fingers parse through a set of rosary beads.

The Hudson's engine roars as the aircraft lifts off and begins the ascent. The cabin trembles inside as if being shaken by the hand of an invisible giant. Ron fumbles for something to grab hold of.

Moments later they are flying above the clouds with the moon lighting their way. Glancing through the windows, Starling sees the Lysanders flanking the Hudson on either side. He settles down for the flight and, without thinking, he moves closer to Anna, feeling the warmth of her body. She, in turn, relaxes into him.

Two hours pass and Pikey, a small man with an eager mouse-like face, climbs from the navigator's cockpit and into the cabin. He looks at Starling and Anna. 'We're approaching your drop area—' His voice is interrupted by a sudden blare like a mighty klaxon that fills the plane.

'Stone the crows! What on earth was that?' says Pikey.

A blinding flash of red light follows. Starling's stomach clenches.

'Pikey! Pikey! Get up here now,' shouts McFarland.

'What's going on?' asks Anna.

'I don't know.'

Starling peers behind Ron and Barbara, looking for the Lysander, but it is nowhere to be seen.

The klaxon sounds again, an unsettling and horrible noise. Starling looks through the window behind him and sees the other Lysander, but then, from the clouds, a violent red streak of lightning strikes the small plane. It shatters into four pieces and falls.

'Oh my God!' says Anna.

'What the hell!' says Ron, his voice trembling, his face pale.

Barbara is sitting rigid and silent, frozen by panic.

Starling gets up towards the cockpit. 'Captain McFarland, what's happening?'

'Look!' says Pikey, pointing ahead.

Starling looks though the cockpit windows and swallows. Something dark is rising from the silver clouds. His first impression is that it is some sort of massive whale.

'Good Lord,' says McFarland.

Surfacing above the clouds is an enormous airship. Dwarfing the Hudson, it must be more than five hundred feet long and two hundred feet wide. It rises further, crossing their flight path, and Starling can see the gondola fixed underneath at the centre of the airship's body. There are windows lighted from the inside with the silhouettes of people looking in the direction of the Hudson. Painted on the undercarriage of the airship cabin is a snake, its jaws wide open to reveal a long tongue. It is unmistakably a viper. The tongue seems to be growing, as if it is telescopic. Starling sees that it is a tube, turning to point in their direction – it's some sort of cannon.

His heart rate begins to increase. *The Tesla Death Ray. They have made it.*

He turns back to his fellow passengers. 'Get your parachutes on now!' he shouts.

The klaxon sounds once more, the sky flashes and from the cannon red lightning snakes its way towards the Hudson. But McFarland has anticipated the strike and veers the plane off course, causing the tail of the death ray to hit the body of the Hudson with a ferociousness that makes it shake violently.

'What the hell?' cries McFarland, battling to control the plane.

Starling hears cries from the cabin and turns to see Ron on his knees and Barbara wrestling with her parachute backpack. Anna has her parachute on and tosses another to Ron. Anna seems calm but he knows, like him, she is terrified. She pulls another parachute from the cabin wall and throws it towards Starling, but in that same second they hear a horrible cracking sound followed by the fast whoosh of cold wind. There's a long loud creak and, as if in slow motion, the cabin begins to split in two. With his heart in his mouth, Starling reaches for Anna. And suddenly the rear of the Hudson shears and is wrenched away. It spins into the night leaving a hole gaping to the heavens through which the contents of the cabin are now being sucked out. Clinging with all his strength to the plane, Starling watches as Ron and Barbara tumble, helpless and screaming, into the night, their unfixed parachutes flying ahead of them before they disappear into the clouds. It is too cold to hold on to the steel girder for much longer. He reaches for his parachute but it is whisked away before he can get close. With his free hand, the tips of his fingers reach for the strap of Anna's parachute backpack, a hair's breadth away. He hears incomprehensible shouts from McFarland and Pikey and sees Anna's feet lift off the floor, her grip on the plane loosening.

'Don't let go, Anna!' he cries.

Her eyes are wide with terror and fixed to his. He inches closer but can do nothing as her strength fades and she is sucked out into the night.

'Annaaaa!' he cries, but she is gone.

Chapter 26

Into the Abyss

Starling hears the klaxon shake the night sky once more, announcing another blast of the cannon – enough to destroy the Hudson. He closes his eyes and exhales. There is nothing more he can do here. Opening his eyes he stares down into the abyss and swallows. He releases his grip of the girder and gives himself up to the blackness.

Tumbling through the air, he catches a brief glimpse of the Hudson as it explodes in a ball of flame and then he falls into the clouds. His life – what he remembers of it – races through his mind. He had always wondered how he would die. He'd thought he might be shot, or poisoned, or tortured to death even, but falling to his death from twenty thousand feet was never on the table. It seems odd to him that he'd never considered it as an option. He had, after all, flown quite a lot.

He clears the clouds and sees land far below, his eyes squinting in the cold, his cheeks pinched and his lips dry.

This is it. This is the end.

He looks around for signs of Anna and sees her, spreadeagled in the air, her head turned back, eyes staring in his direction. She is still holding the spare parachute. His heart begins to race. Is there still a chance? Can he reach her in time? But how? She is almost directly below him. He is the heavier of the two but she is almost two seconds ahead of him – it's not much, but there might as well be a gulf between them. He tries the only thing that he can think and flips his body, straightens it and plunges like a dart through the air. Anna turns over and faces him.

He gains speed and closes on her, but the critical time has passed: she must open her chute.

Just one more second.

Starling urges his body forward, his arms reaching, hands inches from the backpack flapping about in the air. He grabs the canvas strap and Anna releases it, but the force of the wind pulls it from his grasp and it slips from his fingers and tumbles off into the night.

His heart sinks. And then he feels something tugging at his collar. Anna is pulling him towards her, straddling his lower back with her legs.

'Anna, no! It's too dangerous.'

With all her strength, she hoists him up and wraps one arm under his and around his chest. She pulls on the cord of the parachute and Starling feels the sharp tug on his body as he and Anna are jerked upwards. She wraps her other arm firmly around his chest and locks her legs around his waist.

'Grab the steering line and take control. You'll have to be the legs for landing,' she shouts.

Starling reaches up and takes hold of the steering line straps as he and Anna drop faster than is comfortable with a one-man chute. Above them, the clouds part and the moonlight casts a silvery sheen on the landscape below. He sees a forest to the left, thick with trees that could break their fall. Pulling on the left cord he guides the chute towards it.

'Get ready!' he calls as his feet skim the trees and they drop through the foliage, their body and faces smacked by unforgiving twigs and small branches. They stop with a jolt midway down a tree as the chute becomes entangled. The impact forces Starling from Anna's grasp and he falls through the branches, tumbling as if falling down stairs. He takes a bang to the head and lands on his back on damp wet ground, his head spinning. He sits up, rubbing his head and looks up the tree. Anna has cut herself from the parachute and is climbing down. It is a miracle they have survived.

'Will, are you hurt?' she calls.

'I'm fine,' he replies as a shadow appears above them. It is the airship descending. The klaxon sounds and a prolonged blast of the cannon lights up the forest a hundred feet away, destroying six ancient trees all at once.

'Hurry, Anna!'

She jumps down and they run away from the airship and the light. They hear voices and pause for a moment to get their bearings. Peering up through a gap in the trees Starling sees long ribbon like drapes – seven in total – rolling out from either side of the gondola to form what seems to be a dark curtain blazoned with the VIPER insignia. Soldiers are climbing down the ribbons, scurrying like rats, with rifles on their backs. He swears under his breath.

'Let's go! Just run,' he says.

They sprint through the shadows of the forest without knowing where they are heading.

'That was it,' says Anna, 'the Tesla Death Ray.'

Before Starling can respond the klaxon blares and a streak of green lightning spirals above the treetops, twists down and scorches the ground almost two hundred feet ahead of them. Trees crack and splinter in the fire and there is almost enough light to give them away.

'This way,' says Starling, turning right heading deeper into the darkness and out of sight. He hears the sounds of heavy boots behind them.

'There!' calls a voice.

A volley of gunfire ripples through the woods and Starling and Anna dive for cover. The riflemen are close behind.

'We have no option but to fight,' says Starling, ripping off his jumpsuit. Anna is already free of hers and she crouches behind a tree holding her Walther ready. With his back to the tree opposite, Starling holds his Mauser firmly and listens for approaching footsteps. Slowly they come. Just two men, if he is correct. Anna is watching him and he holds up two fingers. She nods an acknowledgement.

Two soldiers, dressed in black uniforms with the VIPER insignia, stalk into view. Starling straightens his arm and swings it up as he hears Anna's Walther fire. He feels the Velo-Dart shoot from his cuff and sees it hit the man's cheek. Both men fall forward.

Dipping behind the tree, Starling looks quickly out and sees two more men approaching.

'Look!' says a voice.

Starling crouches down and fires at the soldiers. He misses his target but Anna takes hers with a shot straight to the forehead. The second man ducks behind a tree and begins firing in Anna's direction. Starling circles around behind him and slams his temple with the side of the Mauser. The man crumples to the ground and Starling takes his rifle.

He hears more boots running towards them and begins shooting at random. Anna has picked up the rifle from the other VIPER soldier and together they fire at the approaching men.

Then Starling hears the sound of more voices behind them. He turns and sees shadowy figures moving through the woods. They are trapped.

'Anna! Behind us!'

The figures behind them close in and Starling looks around desperately for an escape route, but they are surrounded. There is no way out.

Chapter 27

Reunion

Starling hears the stomping of boots and turns to see the figure of a large man running towards them. He roars; his voice is deep and guttural. Starling points the Mauser but the man, eyes dark and angry, sprints past them. He charges like a bull, a pistol raised in each hand, and shoots the VIPER soldiers one by one. From the darkness two soldiers leap on him and try to wrestle him to the ground, but he is too strong. He slams one of them against the tree. The soldier slumps to his knees, arms wrapped around his ribs as the big man up-ends the second soldier and smashes him head first into the ground, crunching his neck. The big man spins round to the first man, who is now raising his pistol to fire at him, but Starling has the soldier's chest in the sight of the Mauser. He squeezes the trigger and the VIPER soldier falls backwards with a look of horror on his pale face. The big man looks at Starling with a wary expression.

Starling hears yet more footsteps behind him and sees more armed people emerging from the shadows. He pulls Anna behind a tree and prepares to defend himself but the new arrivals ignore them and begin shooting at the VIPER soldiers surrounding them. A small battle begins, with Starling and Anna lying low in the crossfire.

In the near distance Starling hears the rumble of the airship. The shooting quietens and Starling hears voices shouting beyond the trees. There is no sign of any more VIPER soldiers. The large man from the woods approaches and with him are the other figures from the shadows. They are not VIPER soldiers but men and women, young and middle-aged, dressed in casual civilian tweeds and flannel shirts, typical of rural France. He thinks of Emile and Claudette. Like his much-missed, departed friends, these must be French Resistance. Pointing their rifles at Starling and Anna, they rally around the big man, who seems to be their leader. Starling takes stock of him. He is a grizzly bear of a man who wears a heavy shooting jacket with a matted fur collar. His face is as broad as a football, adorned with a large grey moustache curled at the ends.

'Who are you?' the man says gruffly in English, his accent French, his voice deep.

'We are British agents,' says Starling.

'Prove it!'

'I can vouch for them, Sebastian,' comes a familiar voice.

'Eoin?' says Anna.

And emerging from the trees, wearing a cap and looking every bit the French Resistance fighter is Eoin, smiling. '*Bonjour, mes amis.*'

The Resistance fighters redirect their weapons to the surrounding woods.

'How is it possible you are here?' asks Starling.

Eoin laughs. 'Well, I'm very pleased to see you too.'

'I'm sorry, I didn't mean it like that.'

Anna embraces Eoin. 'I can't believe it's you. We thought the worst.'

'It'll take a lot to bring me down. Anna, I'm sorry about Meadows.'

'You knew?'

'We had a suspicion.'

The sound of rasping static and a tinny voice from a radio receiver interrupts their exchange. 'Red Leader, this is V Command. What is your status?' All heads turn to look in its direction. The radio's owner is the soldier Sebastian up-ended. The receiver lies beside his body. 'Repeat. Red Leader, what is your status?'

Eoin picks up the radio. 'Come in V Command. Red Leader is down. Repeat Red Leader is down. We have lost several men and taken out most of the Resistance.'

'Excellent! What news of the parachutist from the plane?'

'Dead,' says Eoin.

'Good work. Head back to the ship. We are returning to base.'

'On my way,' he replies and switches off the radio. Then Eoin cuts the wire of the radio, killing the communications and the static.

'How did you know we would be here?' asks Starling.

'I'll explain all later. In the meantime you two need to get out of here and head to Lyon to meet your contact.' Eoin pulls out a folded sheet of paper from his jacket pocket. 'This will help get you out of the forest and into Lyon.' He points behind him. 'Follow that trail. If you keep heading east you should get to Lyon by morning. Look for a place called Café Parisien. It's marked out on the map. Wait there and your contact will be in touch.'

'But what about you?'

'We have unfinished business to take care of. Another drop to pick up. I will look for you sometime tomorrow. Now go.'

'Eoin, the Tesla Death Ray...'

'I know. Things are worse than I expected.'

'How?' asks Anna.

'I will explain everything when I see you tomorrow. Good luck both of you, and stay out of trouble. A lot to ask, I know,' he adds, squeezing a shoulder of each.

'Same to you,' says Anna.

They watch as Eoin, Sebastian and the other Resistance fighters disappear into the gloom of the woods.

Anna and Starling follow the trail as directed, stopping occasionally to look at the map using the torch from Starling's sleeve.

The sun rises early, the sky is a clear aqua blue and in the distance, almost two miles away, they can see the historic city of Lyon.

'We should make sure we don't look like we've just dropped from the sky and been walking through the countryside all night,' says Anna.

'You're right,' says Starling, brushing down his sleeves and running his hands through his hair. 'How do I look?'

Anna tilts her head and arches her eyebrows. 'I've seen you look worse.' She reaches across and fixes his hair, combing it with her fingers on top and on the sides.

She bends over, shaking out her own hair and running her fingers through it before standing up again and straightening her dark red suit, which is still intact – and eye-catching.

'How do I look?' she asks.

'Stunning,' says Starling.

She rolls her eyes. 'I doubt that.'

'We should separate,' says Starling.

Anna looks at him quizzically.

'It will be safer. If we are stopped as a couple there is a risk we could both be arrested as strangers, suspected of being spies. There's less chance of that if we make our way to the café at different times.'

'You're right.'

They look at the Lyon street map and memorise the route to the Café Parisien. Starling leaves the map with Anna and goes first, making his way up the pathway that runs along the Rhone. The locals are up and about and occasionally cast fleeting suspicious glances his way. Lyon is occupied by Nazis and every now and then a Kübelwagen with an officer or a soldier in it drives by. They observe him, but Starling ignores them and walks casually along the river with a confident air, as if he has lived in Lyon all his life.

Chapter 28

Madeleine

16th July 1943, morning

Starling turns right into Rue de Bonnel and sees the small coffee shop called Café Parisien. There are a few scattered tables and chairs outside with an old woman nursing what must be her grandchild. She glances at Starling as he approaches. '*Bonjour*,' she says, tending to her baby.

'*Bonjour*.' He hesitates for a moment, waiting for her to say something else. Could she be his contact? She says nothing and Starling moves on quickly, making his way inside where the smell of hot coffee and freshly baked bread makes his stomach rumble. He's not entirely sure of the last time he ate.

Café Parisien is small and pleasantly rustic, with a bar and well-worn wooden chairs and tables stained with the rings from red wine glasses. It reminds him of the places he had frequented with Emile and Claudette during his year in Chartres. His hands ball into fists and he pushes the thoughts from his mind. Sitting at corner table near the window he orders a coffee and a bread roll with cheese from the waitress, a roundish woman with pleasant face.

Almost twenty minutes pass and he is still alone. He glances at the clock above the bar. It is 10 am. Where is Anna? He peers outside and is relieved to see her walking towards the café. She enters without looking at him and sits at a table by the wall on the other side of the room.

The waitress appears. '*Bonjour, Mademoiselle*.'

'*Bonjour. Un café, s'il vous plait*.'

The waitress nods and disappears behind the bar to pour the coffee.

Starling hears the sound of men's voices approaching. German! He freezes and looks down into his coffee.

Two men enter the café talking and laughing loudly. He looks up for long enough to see that their black collar patches bear the SS insignia. Black shoulder straps and double-striped arrows on their sleeves mark them out as

Rottenführers – corporals of the Waffen-SS. They are young men, perhaps in their early twenties. Both are tanned. One wears his cap over dark hair; the other removes his cap to reveal a full head of Aryan blond hair that would make Hitler himself stand to attention. Their talk stops as they look from Anna to Starling.

Starling nods at them. '*Bonjour.*'

They do not reply and sit at a table in the centre of the café resting their feet on the tabletop.

The soldier with the blond hair looks over at Anna and wolf whistles.

'*Bonjour, Mademoiselle,*' he says in a thick German accent.

Anna says nothing for a moment before replying, '*Bonjour,*' quietly and without looking at them.

Starling feels his muscles tense.

The one with cap leans across and pokes Anna's arm. '*Parlez-vous allemand?*'

Anna shakes her head and Starling can see her back straightening.

The waitress appears from behind the bar.

Anna stands and drops some coins on the table. '*Merci,*' she says to the waitress.

'*Au revoir,*' says the waitress.

'*Au revoir,*' the soldiers mimic in unison, before bursting into laughter.

Anna's eyes find Starling's and she nods at the door as the soldiers order coffee. This might be the best time to leave. Starling stands as Anna opens the door.

'*Attend!*' says a voice. It is the Aryan corporal.

Anna hesitates at the door and Starling levels his gaze at the corporal. Which one of them was he talking to?

'Mademoiselle, you may leave,' he says to Anna, without taking his eyes from Starling. The corporal with the cap turns his attention to him. The blond one appraises him with a frown and talks to his friend in German. '*Ich mag sein Gesicht nicht.*' *I don't like his face.* Starling understands every word. He remains calm but can feel the shard tremble slightly in the confines of the fusilier tucked inside his blazer pocket.

The blond corporal approaches Starling and his colleague swings around to watch the exchange.

'How may I help you, Corporal?' asks Starling, his French crisp and fluent.

'Your papers,' the German says, in his thick accent. 'Show me them.'

Starling searches his inside pocket and cannot find his papers. He had placed them with the map and given them to Anna. He curses his bad luck and glances through the window where Anna is standing pretending to wait for someone.

Starling smiles at the corporal and wonders if he is too close for a Velo-Dart.

The corporal frowns and Starling sees his hand inching towards the Luger strapped to his waist.

Suddenly, the door flies open and someone shouts, '*Cherie!*' at the top of her voice. Before Starling can turn to see who it is, the arms of a young woman are wrapped around his neck and he is being kissed full on the lips.

'Darling, I can't believe you are here at last!' She kisses him more, pushing her tongue deep into his mouth and hugging him, urging him to respond. With nothing to lose, he hugs her and lets her kiss him. Then he buries his face in her neck, which is pleasantly fragranced with Soir de Paris. She pulls back and looks at him, her face beaming. She looks to be in her early twenties with dark wavy hair, full cherry-red lips, olive skin and brown eyes with glittering flecks of green. She is quite beautiful and wears a fashionable green trouser suit that would not look out of place in Paris.

She turns to the corporal. 'Hello Franz. I see you two have met. That is so nice.'

The corporal remains tight-lipped and greets her informally. 'Good morning, Madeleine. It is nice to see you. I have asked the gentleman for his papers and he appears not to have any.'

Starling notices the corporal's eyes rolling hungrily over Madeleine's body.

Madeleine turns to Starling with a teasing frown. '*Cherie*, have you not checked your pockets?'

She reaches inside his blazer and takes out a wallet that is not his. Starling is impressed with her sleight of hand. She hands it to the corporal, who checks the papers and hands them back, seemingly satisfied. He looks at Starling with hooded eyes; Starling can tell he is not quite convinced.

Madeleine wraps her arm around Starling's waist and through the corner of his eye he sees Anna sitting outside, furtively looking in at the scene.

'Please tell me you are coming to the garden party tonight, Corporal?' says Madeleine.

'I am afraid I have other important business.'

'Oh, I am sorry to hear that.' Madeleine sounds quite convincing.

The corporal nods formally, replaces his cap and bids her goodbye.

'*Au revoir*, Corporal,' she says, and sits down at Starling's table. They watch the two soldiers leave and Madeleine waves and blows kisses at them. When their backs are turned her expression turns to stone.

'Thank you,' says Starling.

She shrugs and smiles. 'Thank you for the kiss.'

There is something familiar about Madeleine. 'Have we met before?' he asks.

'No, I don't believe we have.'

'My name is Will.' Starling hears the door to the café open and a shadow appears over the table. It's Anna.

'Two coffees,' says Madeleine, without looking up.

Starling looks from Madeleine to Anna and back again. 'Madeleine, this is Anna.'

Madeleine glances at Anna and merely says, 'Please bring sugar.'

Not looking very pleased, Anna walks to the bar and orders the coffees.

'Who is she?' whispers Madeleine.

'She's an agent, like me.'

Madeleine rolls her large dark eyes, pouts and folds her arms. 'I was expecting only one person.'

Anna pulls up a chair and sits at the table. Madeleine forces a smile. 'I apologise. I thought you worked here.'

Anna remains tight-lipped.

'It must be your outfit,' adds Madeleine.

Starling feels the air between the two women ice over. The waitress appears with coffees and Starling is glad of the distraction.

'Madeleine, we are pleased to meet you, and thank you for getting me out of that difficult spot. We need to get out of here, away from any more prying Nazi eyes.'

'You are safe with me. For the time being.' Starling wonders what she means by that. 'We will take my car to my uncle's house. He is the mayor and he is hosting a garden party for a very special guest. That is where we will need your help.'

'To do what?'

'To kill the very special guest.'

Chapter 29

The Resistance

Madeleine's car is a sporty red Mercedes Benz 770, parked on the roadside by the Rhone. There are only two seats so Starling and Anna squeeze into the front together, with Starling sitting in the middle. Madeleine turns the engine over and drives them away from the river.

'The Gestapo headquarters is on the Avenue Berthelot, which is five minutes from here,' says Madeleine, switching to English. 'The soldiers mostly stay around that area. It was unlucky those two showed up at the same time.' She glances at Starling, with a wry smile. 'I hope you are not always this unlucky.' Her spoken English seems flawless, and he wonders if she has ever lived in England.

'Luck is not something I've ever been blessed with,' says Starling.

'Correct. You have been blessed with much more. You are a fighter, a survivor.'

Starling shoots a quizzical stare at Madeleine and ignores the snorting from Anna.

'You are wondering how I know this, no?'

'It had crossed my mind.'

'The Irishman talks about you with great fondness.'

'How do you know Eoin?' asks Anna.

Madeleine leans across to Starling. 'I do not understand her accent. What did she say?'

Starling feels Anna tensing. 'Anna was wondering how you know Eoin.'

'We have worked together before,' she says, nonchalantly.

They skirt past the gated entrance to the Parc de la Tête d'Or, where two red swastika flags flutter in the morning breeze. Madeleine curses under her breath and speeds past heading north-west to a wide bridge over the Rhone and on through narrow streets lined with tall ornate French townhouses and ancient squares. For a moment Starling gets lost in the atmosphere and colour of the city until he catches sight of the grey uniforms and jack boots of the occupying Nazi forces, threading their way through the streets and crowds like vermin.

The mayor's house is on the outskirts of the city, in one of Lyon's most affluent communes, Saint-Didier-au-Mont-d'Or. Madeleine drives through a large double gate and into the grounds of a stone mansion house set within beautifully kept French gardens, where decorators and gardeners are at work preparing for the party tonight.

'This is my uncle's private residence. You will be safe here until tomorrow when you will have to leave.'

'Madeleine, we cannot stay. We have to make our way to the Swiss Alps as soon as we can.'

Before Madeleine can respond, the front doors open and Sebastian, the burly resistance fighter with the thick moustache, appears looking very different from how he did in the forest. His hair and moustache are combed neatly, his grizzly cheeks are clean shaven and his flak jacket has been replaced with a smart brown suit. 'Madeleine. *Cherie*,' he calls. He opens his arms, his face beaming at Madeleine, and pulls her gently to his broad chest.

So Sebastian is her uncle – and the mayor.

Starling sees Eoin appear behind Madeleine's uncle, dressed casually with his sleeves rolled up.

'Good to see you made it without any hitches.'

Sebastian turns his attention to Starling and Anna. '*Bonjour, mes amis.* I am pleased see you again.'

Starling extends his hand. '*Bonjour*, Sebastian. Thank you again for rescuing us,' he says. The mayor's hand is hard and thick with calluses.

'Think nothing of it.' Sebastian smiles warmly. 'Come inside. Everyone. We have much to discuss. But first we eat.'

The interior of Sebastian's house seems a strange setting for the rough and ready strongman who had mercilessly killed half a dozen VIPER soldiers only hours earlier. The hallway is laid with smooth sandstone tiles, the walls are painted an elegant white and adorned with four oil paintings depicting French rural life. Sebastian takes them to a dining room where his housekeeper, a brittle and grey lady, is laying silverware and napkins on a glossy oak table in preparation for lunch. There are tall and wide French windows leading out to the garden where carpenters are sawing wood and banging nails. The ceiling is high, with ornate coving and hanging chandeliers that glitter in the morning sun.

'Please sit wherever you like,' he says.

Starling and Anna sit opposite Eoin and Madeleine. Sebastian sits at the head of the table.

'Edward tells me you have had quite the adventure,' says Eoin.

'He was very helpful,' says Starling.

'He's quite the wizard with communications. He was listening in on radio transmissions and heard you two were at Southend making the drop to Lyon. If it wasn't for him, we wouldn't have been there for you.'

'We assumed Sir Hugh had been in touch with you,' says Anna.

'I'm afraid Sir Hugh did not make it.'

'Oh no,' says Anna.

'What happened?' asks Starling.

'A VIPER spy murdered him.'

'I'm sorry. I know you two were old friends,' says Starling.

The Irishman sighs and seems lost in thought for a moment. 'I will miss him.'

The silence is broken by the housekeeper, who returns with a younger assistant carrying trays of food and drink. Lunch is fresh bread, cheese, ham, artichokes and red wine. Simple but delicious. When the eating is done, the housekeeper clears up, serves strong coffee and then leaves.

Starling takes this moment to tell them what he has learned. 'Eoin, Sebastian, we have intelligence that VIPER has a manufacturing plant in the Swiss Alps. The airship you saw yesterday – that weapon – it was made there. This morning we all heard the radio receiver. The airship captain said he was returning to headquarters. I believe the manufacturing plant and the headquarters are the same place. We need to go there as soon as possible and destroy that place and the weapon.'

No one says anything for what seems like a long time, until Eoin speaks.

'This is going to sound odd, Starling, but VIPER are not our priority for the time being.'

'But why?' says Anna. 'They have never been so dangerous. You saw what that weapon did in the forest. You must have seen what it did to the aeroplane that was flying us here?'

'We were given orders from Sir Hugh just before he died,' says Eoin.

'But…'

'There is a war on,' says Sebastian. 'My country is under Nazi occupation and our people are starving and dying.'

'We know that,' Starling cuts in, 'but there are dark forces at work here. This isn't just about that weapon. Something worse is coming.' Starling notices that Madeleine is watching and listening to him intently. But she says nothing.

'What exactly is coming?' asks Sebastian.

'They call it the Red Storm.'

'They?' asks Sebastian.

'VIPER.'

'And what is this Red Storm?'

'I am not sure. They have grenades that carry a deadly red gas.'

'If they come to us with those grenades, then we will kill them. But before that we have a man to get rid of.'

'Uncle,' interrupts Madeleine, 'perhaps I can take Starling to the Swiss Alps?'

'No, I forbid it. We are all needed here.'

'But—'

'Madeleine, I said no.'

'Why is this visitor so important?' asks Starling.

Sebastian leans forward, his elbows on the table, his fingers interlaced. 'Hans Krüger is an Obergruppenführer, a senior ranking officer in the SS. He is man without a soul. A man with the blood of thousands of innocent men, women and children on his hands. A creator of death camps and destroyer of families, livelihoods and dreams. He is coming here to Lyon, to my home, for a party to celebrate his illustrious career. It will be the last visit he makes before we send him to Hell.

'We owe it to all the people who have died because of him to carry out this mission. This assassination will be a blow for the Nazis and a major win for the Allies.'

'What do you expect from us?' asks Starling.

'Let me show you,' says Sebastian. He stands, gesturing for them to follow him, walks towards the French windows and looks outside. 'They are building a platform, a stage if you like. At 8 pm this evening there will be a break in the party and Krüger will take to the stage to be applauded and revered by his Nazi colleagues. Except Krüger will not make it to the party.'

'What do you mean?' asks Starling.

'I expect by 7 pm you will have killed him, Monsieur Starling.'

'Me?'

Eoin speaks. 'Will, there is something else about Krüger. Something very important. He is also a key figure in VIPER's military wing. He has worked on many of their weapons programs, including the Teleken project your father worked on.'

Starling feels a clawing at his throat. 'He knew my father?'

'He betrayed your father. His treachery led directly to your parents' deaths and Rose's kidnapping.'

Starling feels a cold hollowness inside.

'Eoin and me,' says Sebastian, 'we are old-fashioned men. We believe in revenge. Killing Krüger will help your head.' He taps his own temple to emphasise his point. 'So, two birds with one stone, no?'

'Sebastian has used his influence with the local soldiers to throw a party in Krüger's honour. We were going to kill him ourselves tonight; however, when we heard you were coming I put the suggestion to my friend, the mayor, that you would be a better choice and he was agreeable. What about it Will?'

'I will do it,' Starling says, without hesitation.

Sebastian smiles. 'I am very pleased to hear that.'

Starling watches the men outside building the stage. It reminds him of a hangman's gallows.

'You are special, Starling. I know you can do this. I am aware of your reputation. Your history, your exploits in London and more recently in my beloved country, are well known.'

Starling hates the idea that he has been discussed and analysed by people he does not know. He shoots a sideways glance at Eoin, his brow furrowed.

'Uncle, that is enough, I think,' says Madeleine.

'You are right, my dear. Forgive me, Starling. But please, do not blame Eoin for these indiscretions.'

'Who should I blame?' asks Starling.

'We have another mutual friend. You may know him as the Owl.'

'The man with a thousand faces,' says Anna.

'You know him?' asks Starling.

'No one has ever met him,' says Anna. 'He's a rogue spy who cannot be trusted.'

'No spy can be trusted, my dear. They are all skilled in the art of deception,' says Madeleine.

'The Owl has no morals. He works for whoever has the biggest wallet.'

'Everyone has their price,' says Madeleine.

Anna looks icily at Madeleine. 'Really? What's yours?'

Starling catches Madeleine's eyes flaring. She folds her arms.

Sebastian speaks. 'Please, let us deal with the matter at hand. Starling, you will work with Madeleine tonight. She knows the area and can help you. Like you, she has much experience. It pains me to bring it up but she has had as difficult a life as both of you. I think you three have much in common.'

Anna and Madeleine snort almost at the same time.

'My niece will sort you out with suitable attire for tonight's party. In the meantime, Eoin has something to show you and I have much to prepare for this evening.'

'Come with me, both of you,' says Eoin.

Eoin takes them back into the hallway and through a door under the staircase where there are more stairs leading down to a cellar.

At the bottom of the steps Eoin flicks a switch and the room lights up. The cellar is cold with damp air and contains rows of wine racks. 'This is Sebastian's pride and joy,' he says.

There is also a bench and a table where an open suitcase containing a Whaddon Mark VII radio transmitter lies. On the floor are two khaki green trunks. Eoin flips the lids open. One of them contains six Lanchester submachine guns and boxes of ammunition, while the second contains a dozen or so gas masks. 'This was our unfinished business this morning. After finding you we had another drop to pick up. I had Edward despatch these masks for me. Sebastian was expecting more weapons and was not very pleased. He is dangerously indifferent to the VIPER threat despite what happened this morning.'

'The death ray, on the airship, is more powerful than I ever imagined,' says Starling. 'It tore our plane apart in seconds.'

'For VIPER it is a magnificent addition to their arsenal. I fear we have only seen half of what it can do.'

'Do you know how we can destroy it?' says Anna.

'I'm afraid not. I have asked Edward to try and remember as much as he can about the schematic we had – and lost. He is sketching it from memory. I'm hoping he'll come up with something soon; we don't have a lot of time.'

Starling sits down heavily on the bench. His limbs still ache from the fall and his body feels battered and bruised.

'You two have had a long night. You should get some rest. The housekeeper has prepared rooms for you. Get some sleep and we'll talk more later.'

-

Starling lies with his eyes closed on a soft bed on the first floor of the mayor's house. The curtains are closed, the room dark and warm, yet sleep is impossible amid the relentless hammering of nails into wood. Nevertheless he feels oddly calm. The shard is warm and pulsates quietly like a snoozing puppy on his chest. He feels himself drifting off, the hammering becomes a distant memory and he seems to float in a swirl of blue light.

Am I dreaming?

His body tingles and his eyes flicker open. The room is bathed in an unearthly blue luminescence. Small blue lights, like miniature fireworks, fly from his face and body and penetrate every fibre of his flesh and bone. Writhing on the bed he feels an extraordinary power that is not of this world and he doesn't know whether to laugh or cry. His body feels hot and clammy and he feels a howl deep within his soul. He opens his mouth to cry out but his voice is silent. His heart burns as the dormant emotions of sorrow, pain and rage shatter the blue lights like fragments of glass. The room trembles as if there is a storm. The curtains rise and flap noisily, pictures fall from the walls and a wind whirls around the room like an angry spirit. The shard trembles, rattling in the confines of the tin soldier. Starling places his palm over it and soon it quietens down, resuming its slumber.

He hears knocking on the bedroom door. The handle cranks open and Madeleine and Anna rush in.

'Will! What happened?' says Anna.

Starling swings his legs round and sits on the edge of the bed. 'I think I know how we can destroy the death ray.'

Chapter 30

Les Collègues

In a bathroom at the end of the hallway, two rooms down from his bedroom, Starling dries himself after a warm shower and shave. Wrapping the towel around his waist he heads back up the hallway to the bedroom. The curtains are closed, but a line of sunlight slices through a chink in the curtains and casts a golden glow over the bed.

His clothes have been tossed carelessly on top of it. Lying next to them is a clean, freshly pressed tuxedo, a white shirt, a black tie and some socks. Resting on the floor is a shiny pair of black brogues. A surge of anxiety scratches at his spine; someone has been in the room. He curses his carelessness and searches the inside pocket of his blazer. The tin soldier is still there. He takes it out, peers through the gap and relaxes when he sees the shard still lodged inside. He places it upright on the dresser and unfurls his towel, dropping it on the floor.

'I hope everything fits you,' says a voice. It is Madeleine's.

He can't quite determine why he is not surprised. He turns to see her standing in the shadows watching him. She steps forward wearing a low-cut black dress with a lace trim on the chest and shoulders. Shimmering from the hem and around her waist and ribs are a thousand silver sequins sewn into the shape of a roaring dragon. A diamond necklace sparkles dangerously around her neck.

'I'm sorry if I startled you.'

Starling glances at the tin soldier. 'What are you doing here?'

'I wanted to drop by and give you your clothes for this evening. I saw you were not here, so I decided to wait.'

'Considerate of you.'

She smiles. 'Most Englishmen blush when they are naked in front of a lady.'

'I am not "*most Englishmen*".' He lifts the shirt from the bed and pulls it across his back. Madeleine moves towards him, standing inches from him so that he can feel the heat from her body. She begins to button his shirt, starting from the top and working her way down. Her breath is warm and sweet, her full lips glossy, red and smiling. Stopping at his navel, she meets his gaze and with the palm of her hands slowly brushes his chest and fixes the shirt. He feels his blood warming and rushing to his loins. She steps back, appraises her work and unashamedly glances at the hemline of his shirt.

'Just perfect,' she says.

There is an element of danger to Madeleine's brazen attention that fires up desires he has not felt in a long time. His feelings for Anna are still there but they had to change when she confessed to having taken another lover. Meadows had been a traitorous VIPER swine, now deceased, but things are no longer the same between them. He pulls on the trousers and watches Madeleine watching him.

'She is your lover?' asks Madeleine.

Starling hesitates, thrown by the question. 'At one time.'

'Do you love her?'

Sitting on the edge of the bed, Starling puts on the socks and shoes, his eyes focused on the shiny leather. He does not respond.

'She still likes you.'

'I'm not sure she does.'

'I can see it. Women know these things.'

'We're colleagues now. Nothing more.'

'Are you?'

'Yes.' He picks up the tie and wraps it around his collar.

'Let me,' says Madeleine, taking hold of it. She ties it gently. '*Les collègues*,' she says, in a mocking fashion.

'*Oui. Les collègues.*'

'*D'accord*.' Madeleine finishes tying the bow tie.

'Tonight you will be my partner at the party. The Nazis will think you are my lover. It is the perfect cover for you. Because of this, some of them may resent you; however, my uncle's position in this town keeps them at arm's length. That will all change tonight.'

'What about Anna?'

'Who?'

Starling arches his eyebrows at Madeleine.

'Oh. Is that her name? Do not worry about her. I have made sure she has the perfect dress.'

'I'm glad to hear that.'

'You must excuse me. I have some last-minute party arrangements to take care of. We will meet in the dining room for the final briefing in ten minutes.'

Starling pulls on his shoulder holster. '*D'accord*.'

She pauses before opening the door and looks back. 'Thank you for helping us.'

He nods and Madeleine smiles and leaves the room, shutting the door behind her.

He checks the Mauser, which feels lighter than it should. Sliding out the magazine he sees it is short of bullets. There are spares in his blazer and he pops them one by one into the magazine.

The hammering has stopped at last. Walking to the window Starling peers through the curtains and looks down at the garden. The carpenters have finished building the stage and are in the process of dressing the backdrop with a Nazi flag. There are two long tables covered in white cloths on either side of the garden. The mayor's staff are laying out bottles of wine, jugs of water, bread, cheeses, hams and cakes. In times of rationing there is nothing but the best for the master race.

His eyes look beyond the stage where he sees Madeleine walking towards what look like a small gîte. Narrowing his gaze he sees a paint-splattered easel leaning against the wall outside. Madeleine looks behind her before disappearing inside.

Curious.

Chapter 31

Kill Krüger

It is almost ten minutes later when Starling slides the Mauser into the holster and pulls on his tuxedo. It is a snug fit with just enough room to stop the Mauser's outline from being visible. Combing his hair back with his hands he hurries down to the dining room and hears the voices of Eoin, Sebastian and Madeleine inside. He is about to knock when he hears Anna's voice behind him.

'What are you wearing?' she says.

Starling turns, expecting to see her dressed in a beautiful gown.

'Oh…' he says.

Anna is wearing a loose fitting and unflattering black and white maid's outfit. He bites his lip in an effort not to smile – or laugh for that matter.

'The housekeeper brought this to my room. This is *her* doing, isn't it?'

Starling is on the verge of bursting into laughter and coughs to hide it. 'I'm sure there must be something else you can wear.'

Anna's face turns red with anger. 'Oh forget it!' she says marching past him and into the dining room, where Eoin, Sebastian and Madeleine are sitting around the table. The room goes quiet and all heads turn to look as they walk in. Eoin and Sebastian's eyes widen as they gaze at Anna's outfit.

'My dear, why are you dressed like a maid?' asks Madeleine.

'I have been asking myself the same question.'

'It must be the housekeeper. Perhaps she misunderstood my request.'

'I'm sure she understood every word.'

'I must say, you make a very convincing maid,' says Madeleine. 'The Nazis will never suspect you.'

Anna does not respond. Instead, she sits down and looks to Eoin and Sebastian. 'I'm ready.'

'Superb,' says Sebastian.

Starling sits down next to Anna as Sebastian slides a sheet of paper across the table. It contains a roughly sketched layout of the garden with the stage and two banqueting tables. Around the tables are dozens of circles representing people. In between the two tables and in front of the stage are more small circles with swastikas inside. Sebastian points to the middle where the swastikas are.

'At 8 am the officers will gather here to listen to Krüger. Before then word will get out that he has not arrived. It is not possible that they will know he has been assassinated. If so, all hell may break loose. If that happens we will assemble at the tables. Hidden under both banqueting tables are the Lanchester submachine guns: two at each table. Starling and Madeleine, if you make it back in time, you will take the table on the right. Eoin and Anna will take the table on the left. I will organise my people to pick out the strays.'

'What happens if they do not make it back in time?' asks Eoin.

'Two of my men will take their place. Keep your eyes on me and the clock above the stage and also ensure your watches have the correct time. Just in case.'

Starling glances outside at the clock on the stage. It is almost thirty minutes past six. He checks his Timor wristwatch, which is two minutes slow, and adjusts it. He hears the sound of vehicles approaching; among them is a car blaring its horn like a trumpet, as if announcing their arrival.

Sebastian's face darkens. '*Merde*,' he mutters. 'They are early.'

Starling feels his arm being squeezed.

'We should go,' says Madeleine. 'I will brief you on the way.'

'Thank you, Madeleine,' says Sebastian. 'Does anyone have any questions?'

'None from me,' says Starling.

'Nor me,' say the others in turn.

'Very well. I will greet our guests. *Bon courage!*'

Starling, Anna, Madeleine and Eoin leave through the French windows.

'Anna,' says Starling.

She turns to look at him with a concerned expression.

'Be careful tonight.'

Eoin and Madeleine are out of earshot. 'I'm not sure about this, Starling. Something feels wrong.'

'What do you mean?'

'It's just a feeling. I can't put my finger on it. It just seems so convenient that we are all here at the same place and unable to move on to the most important place in our mission.'

'I know. But this is such a good opportunity.'

'For what – revenge?'

'Will!' calls Madeleine.

'We will leave tonight. I promise.' He hurries after Madeleine, who takes him to a gate at the rear of the garden where a black Citroën is parked. He sits in the passenger seat as Madeleine drives them out of town and along an isolated tree-lined country road. Anna's words echo in his head, but he pushes them away as the thought of confronting Krüger releases a spark of adrenaline that begins to surge through his body.

Almost twenty minutes later Madeleine eases on the brakes and stops the car in the middle of a road.

'There are two Lanchester submachine guns hidden under the back seat,' says Madeleine. 'Krüger will be coming along this route. He will not be alone; he will be guarded.'

'I don't doubt that.'

-

Starling hides behind the trees at the side of the road, with a Lanchester machine gun in one hand and binoculars in the other. Madeleine is peering under the bonnet of the Citroën, which blocks the narrow road. To a casual onlooker, she might appear to be a driver with no idea of how to fix her broken vehicle – a damsel in distress. She is anything but that, Starling thinks. Only moments ago she had casually and confidently taken out the machine guns and tossed one to him without a thought. The way she held hers, feeling its weight, extracting the magazine and checking the contents revealed a little more about the mystery of this French Resistance spy. Starling had no doubt this kind of mission was not new to her. She knew precisely what she was doing. On the surface she appeared to be spoiled and rude, to Anna certainly. She was also brazen, courageous and definitely dangerous. He is intrigued by her. She reminds him of someone and he smiles to himself as he realises who it is. Two years ago he and Anna had gone to watch *Gone with the Wind* at the Empire in Leicester Square. In many ways Madeleine was like Scarlett O'Hara, the over-privileged and seemingly immoral heroine who overcomes war and poverty with her courage, intelligence and grit.

He sweeps the area with binoculars. The rolling hills and meadows are serene and glow in the simmering red evening sun. For a moment he is overcome with a sense of peace before the rumble of a car engine tears through the country calm. Through the lenses he sees a shiny black six-wheel Daimler-Benz with two small red Nazi flags flapping above each of the headlamps. It is an impressive vehicle designed for military officers who require comfort and space, and this one belonged to Obergruppenführer Hans Krüger. He would be here in minutes.

Starling catches Madeleine's dark eyes. She nods once. He dips into the cover of the trees and watches the Daimler slow behind Madeleine's car. The driver is frowning, clearly unhappy at being slowed down. Krüger sits in the rear of the vehicle, his attention focused on the driver. The two men exchange words. Madeleine is smiling sweetly, beckoning the driver to help her. The driver says something to Krüger, who nods and folds his arms. The driver gets out. Madeleine smiles a wicked smile.

Starling walks out of the woods, the machine gun fixed on the man who betrayed his father and whose actions caused his parents' murders and his sister's kidnapping. He hears the driver's pitiful broken French as he tries to question Madeleine about her car.

Krüger is rounder than he expected and is squeezed into full uniform with several medals and ridiculous Nazi symbols. With an eager audience waiting, he was intending to put on a show tonight. *Shame.*

Starling sees his own reflection appear in the windows of the car like a dark spectre of death, an unwelcome vision of the future he was turning towards. He hesitates as an overwhelming sense of unease prickles his skin. Joseph's words stab at his conscience. '*…I know your father would want me to tell you that your chosen profession is not one he would have approved of.*'

Frozen, he stares blankly at the man whose actions devastated his life.

Krüger looks up and sees him. His pudgy jowls frame confusion. He calls to the driver but it is too late. Madeleine's machine gun rattles and the driver cries out in fear.

'Will. Do it!' cries Madeleine.

Krüger's expression contorts in anger, sparking Starling's desolation and rage. There is no going back now. Gritting his teeth, he squeezes the Lanchester's trigger and sprays the car with several rounds of bullets.

A strange smoke fills the air before him.

The smoke clears and he looks at the car waiting for that unspoken sense of achievement, but all he feels is cold inside. Krüger is nowhere to be seen. Starling imagines him lying bloody and dead on the back seat of the car, but something is not right. There are no holes in the car nor is the glass broken. He sees Krüger sitting up, his face deathly white and clammy with shock. *Why is he not dead?*

Madeleine is looking his way, frowning.

'The bullets are blanks. We've been betrayed. Again!' he says. He sees that the driver is on the ground, unharmed and reaching for the Luger at his belt, but Madeleine runs at him. Starling is distracted by goading laughter and sees Krüger pointing a pistol at him. A bullet cracks through the window, narrowly missing Starling's shoulder. Dropping the Lanchester, Starling spins around, pulls out the Mauser from its holster and, through the rear window, shoots Krüger in the side of head. Blood sprays the interior of the car. Madeleine is beating the hapless driver half to death with the Lanchester. The man is unconscious.

'What the hell is going on?' she cries.

Before Starling can answer, the thunderous klaxon sounds from the skies shaking the ground beneath their feet. Above them, the VIPER airship – like an enormous blood-red cigar – flies towards the town.

'The Resistance! The party! My uncle! We've been betrayed!'

'Get into the car!' shouts Starling, taking the driver seat. The skies flash with a horrible red lightning that scorches the ground ahead. He knows it and Madeleine does too. The target is the mayor's party. His heart sinks as he thinks of Anna and Eoin left alone to defend themselves with machine guns that are as much use as water pistols. He prays that they are both safe.

Chapter 32

Poison Cyclone

The airship flies across the sky with all the stealth of a shark as Starling skids the Citroën to a stop outside Sebastian's home. Mercifully the house is still standing. Beyond it in the distance is a wall of black smoke. He hears gunfire. His heart sinks. A battle is underway. If all the ammunition is made up of blanks then the Resistance are horribly ill-equipped.

'*Merde!*' cries Madeleine as she runs towards the house.

'Madeleine, wait!' But she does not listen.

Sprinting after her, Starling takes out his Mauser and watches the airship as it circles around, casting a shadow and blocking out the sun. Long red drapes unfurl from the gondola's base and flutter together to reveal the blood red VIPER flag with the image of the black snake curled around the planet.

He sees Madeleine peeking around the side of the house at the rear garden. The battle seems to have stopped. There are a dozen bloodied bodies scattered on the grass, including the carpenters who built the stage, Sebastian's old housekeeper and several other French civilians he does not recognise. Most of the Nazis are alive and are gathered at the stage in a circle, facing out with their Lugers ready. There is no sign of Anna, Eoin or Sebastian.

The airship blares its terrible klaxon again and begins to descend. A red flash blinds him for a second as the Tesla Death Ray cuts through the air and scorches across the ground like a giant crooked scythe. Trees split and explode and the Nazis scream and scatter like mice to avoid the beam that slices through their circle. Two soldiers are caught as they run past Starling and Madeleine. Starling pulls Madeleine to him as the bodies of the two men light up and sizzle and, in seconds, become clouds of ash and dust. Starling coughs as the dusty remains fill his nostrils and coat his face.

The ray cuts through the right side of the mayor's house like a knife through butter. The brickwork begins to crumble, falling around them and exposing the inside. Starling tries to pull Madeleine away but she sprints across the garden, dodging the death ray and its lights that have split into a dozen separate blades of death.

'Madeleine, stop!' he cries, but she does not listen. *What is she thinking? It's a bloody suicide run*. She is making for the artist's studio at the end of the garden.

'Will!' comes a voice. His heart skips. It is Anna.

There is a break in the firing of the death ray. Eoin, Anna and four members of the Resistance are hauling two black trunks from the front of the house. Starling hurries towards them. He is relieved to see Anna and he can see from her smile she feels the same way too.

'Where's Madeleine?' asks Eoin.

'She ran to the artist's studio.'

'There is stash of hidden weapons inside it. Sebastian is there too.'

Eoin opens the black trunks. Inside is an array of old rifles and pistols.

'Look!' says Anna, pointing upward.

Red dust clouds are emerging from beneath the gondola and are falling towards the house. A sickening sensation grips Starling's stomach as he recalls the poison he almost succumbed to on Westminster Bridge.

-

From the viewing balcony of the gondola, the acolyte watches the battle unfold. The slaughter intoxicates him. He is moments from being there among them and is hungry to open flesh and spill blood. As the airship descends, the soldiers on either side of him kick out the rolls of thick material that unfurl beneath. They fasten their gas masks and begin the drop to the garden.

He puts on his gas mask and kicks out the red roll of material at his feet.

He is ready.

He is his old self.

Gone is his priest's cassock, the white cane and the dark glasses. In their place, a long dark coat and a fedora. He prays he will find the Starling swine and carve the life from him once and for all. The thought of it arouses him and he swallows.

And when he is done with him, he will take the sister. She is an abomination; a daughter of the devil himself. Without mercy he will do God's work, squeeze the life from her and her unborn spawn and send them back to Hell.

–

'The gas masks are in the basement!' cries Eoin.

Starling runs into the house with Anna close behind him, past a gaping hole cut by the death ray. In the basement they grip one end of the trunk each and clamber back outside.

The base of the gondola has four large fans, which are spinning, pushing out the dust clouds to form them into a gruesome deadly red cyclone. At the same time, armed soldiers in gas masks are hanging from the drapes waiting for the ship to reach a safe distance so they can drop to the ground. Starling thinks of Madeleine and Sebastian. They have no masks. He straps on his, securing it tight to his face. Grabbing two spares, he runs, his rapid breathing resonating through the rubber mask. The door to the artist's studio is open and Madeleine and her uncle are loading the magazines of two Beretta submachine guns.

'Madeleine! Sebastian!' he calls, but his voice is muffled. Sebastian sees him and swings the Beretta in his direction. He doesn't know who he is behind the mask. Starling freezes, his arms in the air, and – thank God – Madeleine realises it's him and pushes Sebastian's gun down.

Starling hands across the masks, pointing at the sky. A look of horror crosses Madeleine's face and she tosses the machine gun to Starling.

'No blanks,' she says, pulling on her mask. Starling scans the studio and pauses at an oil painting of a battlefield lying against the wall. Starling has seen it before. One of them is a very talented painter.

He watches Madeleine as she crouches at an open trapdoor in the floor and reaches down, pulling out rifles, pistols, grenades and another submachine gun.

'Hurry!' shouts Starling, pointing to the front of the house. 'We need to join the others.'

Madeleine and Sebastian nod their agreement.

Starling steps outside, cautiously looking up at the approaching red storm. He sprays bullets blindly through the billowing clouds, hoping to take out some of the soldiers climbing down the drapes. With satisfaction he watches two of them fall dead to the ground as Madeleine and Sebastian run to the front of the house.

The cloud swirls around his head and shoulders. Daylight diminishes as the thick red dust envelops the garden and the house. Starling hears feet thudding onto the grass. The VIPER soldiers are here. Overhead the airship's engines kick into gear as it begins its ascent, the fans' steady whirling spreads the dust far and wide.

Starling moves forward blindly, heading in what he thinks is the direction of the front of the house, and collides with a dark figure. Through the churning red mist he makes out a VIPER soldier dressed in black combats. The mask makes him look even more sinister. The man raises his pistol but Starling swipes the butt of his machine gun, knocking the pistol from his hand. He then rams his elbow into the man's windpipe and the soldier falls to his knees clutching his throat.

Gunfire sounds from all directions. The battle has resumed.

Suddenly he feels an arm around his neck and a hand attempting to prise off his mask. Dropping the Beretta, Starling tries to pull the hand and arm away but they are too strong. Gasping, he reaches behind him and wraps both his arms around his assailant's neck. Using all his strength, he pulls him up and flips him over his shoulder. As the man tumbles through the air Starling rips the mask from his face. He lands on his back, his arms clawing at Starling begging for the mask. His body trembles violently, his eyes desperate, the blood already beginning to fill them. Starling tosses the mask away just as the first man runs at him with a knife. Swiftly he grabs the man's wrist, twisting his arm to straighten it before slamming a fist hard into the man's elbow, forcing it inwards. Above the din, he can just about hear the snapping of bone and the muffled howl of pain from beneath the soldier's rubber mask. Still holding the man's wrist, Starling slams the knife point into the man's chest. As his victim falls, Starling scrambles forward feeling across the ground for the machine gun. To his great relief, his fingers find it.

There is a movement on the edge of his peripheral vision. He shivers as if someone has walked over his grave. Through the red cloud he sees a tall slim figure wearing a fedora and a long dark coat that flaps behind him like the wings of the angel of death. Something long and sharp glimmers in his hand. Starling feels the hairs on his neck stand on end. The figure disappears among the billowing red clouds.

Who is that?

There is humming. Someone is humming a tune, a hymn he has heard before. The shard trembles against his chest. Something in him has triggered it. Or was it the man who just walked by? Starling scans the area but the man has gone. Perhaps he saw a ghost, but logic bucks that thought from his mind. Perhaps he imagined him, yet still he is gripped with a strange uncertainty.

With the blood pounding in his ears and the machine gun pointing ahead Starling heads in the same direction, cautiously navigating through the swirling poisoned clouds and across the garden, stepping on and over the corpses of the dead. The man is nowhere to be seen. Pushing on, he nears the house, its side now open to the air. Two soldiers are shooting at the front of the house where Eoin and Anna were moments before. Starling squeezes the trigger and takes them down.

The red dust is still falling thick and fast. The drone of the airship is distant but still the poison cyclone swirls. *Is there no end to it?*

Chapter 33

The Man in the Fedora and the Long Dark Coat

The shard is trembling harder now against Starling's chest. It begins to spark and a hole burns blue in his tuxedo. He shivers as a blue light snakes across his chest, down his arm and onto his hand. Sparks pop from his fingers and around them the red dust begins to disperse.

What on earth?

He waves his hand and, in wonder, watches the red poison dissipate as if he has cast a magical spell. He takes out the tin soldier, which is oddly scorched yet cold to the touch. He prises it open, pulls out the shard and drops the soldier to the ground. The shard is glowing its familiar unearthly blue but it seems to be getting fainter. Soon the blue light fades and the red dust gathers again around the shard and his hand.

No!

He recalls the first time Eoin showed him the shard and demonstrated its power. The Irishman had placed it on a table and slammed the butt of his pistol onto the stone causing it to ignite and burn the table to ash. He had never seen anything like it before. He stares at it, wondering.

Is it possible?

Placing the shard on the path, he lifts a rock from the rubble of the house and smashes it down hard. A booming sound like a thunderclap roars through the air and the ground shakes beneath his feet. The house wobbles and the glass in the windows shatters. Starling ducks to avoid the flying fragments. The shard begins to shake angrily. Like a firework, it fizzles a blue flame that grows to eye level, shining so bright he has to stave off the glare with his hand. Lights begin to shoot from the shard in all directions, eating through the red dust and clearing the air. Behind him he sees Madeleine and Anna shooting at three VIPER soldiers at the other side of the stage. Starling fires off a few rounds from his magazine, killing one of the soldiers. Realising they are exposed, the soldiers run behind the stage but Madeleine and Anna are already ahead of them and pump them full of bullets. He sees Sebastian snapping the neck of another soldier and wonders where Eoin could be.

Looking up, he sees the airship wobbling precariously as the shard's blue lights snake around the gondola searching for more poison to consume. However, it seems they are not enough to bring the ship down. Instead, it retreats. *Until next time.*

The red dust has cleared but Starling keeps his mask on in case the air is not yet clean. He senses someone beside him and turns. Madeleine's black curls frame her mask. In her hands is the tin soldier and she is pushing the shard back inside the spine. She shoves it into his hand and he feels its satisfying weight. He frowns at her. How did she know? But already she has gone to help Sebastian and Anna.

With the soldiers at the rear of the house dead and his friends safe, Starling makes his way across the rubble, eyes fixed ahead, machine gun ready. He sees a soldier sitting up and leaning against the rocks, blood seeping from a bullet wound in his chest. The man sees Starling and reaches for his pistol, which lies at his feet, but he is too weak to get to it. He can't have long to go, thinks Starling. He reaches down and pulls off the man's mask. He is dark-haired with olive skin, Italian perhaps. His face is gaunt, pale and glistening with sweat. He looks at Starling with a pained expression.

'Kill me,' he croaks.

Satisfied the red poison has cleared, Starling pulls off his own mask and crouches down, levelling his gaze at the man. 'Where is the airship going to?'

The man frowns and coughs. 'Kill me… please.'

'Tell me where the airship is going.'

Starling places the machine gun on the ground. The soldier begins to sob. Starling holds his gaze like a seasoned poker player. After a moment the soldier lifts his arm and points into his chest. Starling reaches across, unbuttons his jacket and sees a map tucked inside. He unfolds it and lays it out. The soldier points to a location in the Swiss Alps.

'Schöllenen Gorge?'

The soldier nods, his face contorted with pain.

A memory flashes in Starling's mind. He is cold and climbing up a sheer rocky cliff face. Around him are snow-capped mountains. He hears a voice barking commands. It is Frost. Starling feels dizzy. He swallows and puts his hand on the rubble to steady himself.

'Please,' says the soldier.

Taking two deep breaths, Starling stands, removes the Mauser from its holster and points it at the man's chest. He recalls his dark spectre-like reflection in the windows of Krüger's car. There is no going back now. This path has been chosen for him and he must follow it.

'Blessed Virgin, forgive me,' says the man, speaking in Italian.

'I'm sorry,' Starling says and, stepping back, he puts a bullet into the man's heart. The Italian's body jerks and sags as the life leaves it forever.

Starling regards him pityingly and thinks about Schöllenen Gorge. He has clearly been there, but why, when and for how long he has no idea. This information is hidden somewhere in his fractured memory.

'Will!' comes a voice.

Starling turns to see Eoin carrying a rifle in one arm and waving with the other. He smiles, relieved to see the Irishman is fine. Placing the Mauser back in its holster he notices the bodies of three of Sebastian's men lying on the front path. The oxygen tubes on their gas masks have been cut in two with a knife. *Strange.*

A shadow appears at the corner of his eye. He sees the man in the fedora and long dark coat glide towards the Irishman as if weightless. Starling feels his spine icing over. *It can't be.*

'Eoin… stop… no!'

The Irishman looks at him quizzically and smiles. At the same time the man in the fedora swings his arm up and points a pistol at Eoin's back.

Starling feels his stomach lurch and sees Eoin frowning, an expression of not quite understanding. A single shot shatters the air and Eoin's face contorts in agony as a bloody hole appears on his chest.

'No!' cries Starling, desperately reaching for his Mauser.

The man in the fedora looks up. A small tongue darts out of his mouth and wets his lips. His one remaining eye blinks three times. The other is a scarred empty socket.

It's the Pastor. Returned from the grave.

Starling fires the Mauser, torn by grief, rage and fear as Eoin crumples to the ground. His bullets go wide, his aim and concentration rocked by his emotions. The Pastor is nimble and darts to the gated entrance, laughing maniacally. Starling tries to focus and fires four more times in succession but all he does is chip the gatepost as the Pastor disappears behind it.

When Starling gets to the gate, the Pastor has gone.

He runs back and kneels by Eoin's side. The Irishman is trembling and trying to talk. Blood seeps from his wound. Starling presses down on it and hears rapid footfalls on the grass. Anna, Madeleine, Sebastian and two of his men arrive by his side.

'Get some towels and fetch the doctor!' he hears Sebastian barking at someone.

Starling looks down at the man who had taken him under his wing two years ago. This man who believed in him and became a mentor and replacement father. His face is grey, his lips dry, moving as if he is trying to speak.

'I'm sorry. I'm sorry,' says Starling.

Eoin looks up at Starling and, smiling weakly, says, 'I'm not gone yet.'

Chapter 34

Aftermath

Later, while Sebastian's remaining men gather the bodies of the dead, Starling stands over Eoin's bed as the newly arrived doctor cleans and patches up his wound. Having briefed the Irishman on what happened, he watches on as guilt begins to prickle his inner voice. If only he'd acted sooner Eoin might be in a better state. To make matters worse there are no painkillers – only whisky – and the Irishman flinches as the doctor stitches his flesh.

'You're lucky to be alive, Monsieur.'

'This is not what I call *alive*,' croaks Eoin, wincing as he reaches for the whisky, his brow sweaty with the pain.

'You must go easy on that,' says the doctor. 'It will thin your blood.'

'I have work to do, Doc. The only way I will get through it is to numb the pain.'

'The bullet went straight through you, Monsieur Heaney. Bed rest for you, nothing else. Understand?'

Eoin swears under his breath.

'The doctor is right, Eoin,' says Starling.

'I will come by tomorrow,' says the doctor, as he walks towards the door. 'Take care of yourself. *Au revoir*.'

'Thank you,' says Starling.

Eoin tries to sit up. 'The feckin' Pastor. How can he still be alive?' He swigs back a generous helping of whisky.

Starling recalls the last time he saw the Pastor. It was two years back when they fought at the hidden crypt below St Mary le Bow. The German bombs had fallen and destroyed the little church. Starling and Anna had escaped and he'd really thought the Pastor – already half-blinded in their earlier fight – was dead and buried in the rubble. He was clearly wrong.

'The truth is I never actually saw him die.'

'He's as slippery as an eel that one.'

'I have no idea how he escaped the crypt. He must have found another gap to the surface. But why is he here and why now?'

'VIPER can be very persuasive. I can only imagine the offer of employment includes first choice on killing off his old enemies. You and Anna must watch your backs.' Eoin's eyes begin to flicker and close. He is tired.

'We'll be careful.'

'Make sure you are.' The Irishman takes another slug of whisky and winces. 'I see you brought the shard. Good thinking. At least we now have a way of killing the red gas. As for that bloody death ray – Christ knows how we can destroy it.'

'There is a way. But I – we – need to go to Schöllenen Gorge. Tonight.'

The Irishman frowns, shakes his head slowly and fights to keep his eyes open.

Starling continues, 'I've been there before. I think it's a VIPER military base and it must also be where the Teleken-Black manufacturing plant is based.'

'But…' Eoin's voice grows fainter, '…but how can you destroy the weapon?'

'I don't know the finer details yet. I'll work it out.'

The whisky bottle slips from the Irishman's grasp. Starling takes it from him and places it on the bedside table.

'Good work today,' mumbles Eoin. 'Now disappear. I need to rest.'

Starling turns to leave and stops at the door. 'I'm sorry I didn't stop him… the Pastor that is.'

But the Irishman's eyes are closed and he is already fast asleep. Starling leaves and closes the door quietly behind him.

In the landing outside his own bedroom he pauses to look at the night-time panorama of French countryside through the immense hole created by VIPER's death ray. The weapon was so powerful. How on earth could it be destroyed? He really has no clue. *I'll work something out.*

The sound of Madeleine's Citroën springs into life and distracts him from his thoughts. He wonders where she could be going. Perhaps to get some supplies for the wounded – he had overheard earlier they were short of medicine and bandages.

He changes out of his tuxedo and pulls on his red flannel shirt and dark grey trousers with braces. Sitting on the edge of the bed he laces up his

Derby boots and then stands to pull on his MI6 jacket. He hears a knock on the door.

'Come in.'

Anna enters.

'We were betrayed again!' spits Starling.

'I know.'

'Eoin said Sir Hugh died sending us the intelligence on Krüger's visit. VIPER must have intercepted the call for more guns and sent us those duds. This whole scenario with Sebastian's party and Krüger's visit was a set-up. They knew we were here.'

'We have a VIPER mole in London. Someone with influence who can pull strings.'

'Who could it be? Morrow is out of the picture and Coleridge is dead.'

'There are others. I will get in touch with Edward using Eoin's transmitter. See if he has heard anything.'

'Good idea. Thank him from me. Without those masks we would be dead, too.'

There is something different about Anna, Starling thinks. He looks at her, up and down, trying to work out what it is. She looks more confident, taller. He thinks it must be the clothes: high-waisted blue trousers with a matching jacket. It is stylish – like something Madeleine would wear.

'You look… different,' he says.

'Her ladyship warmed to me and gave me some of her very expensive French *haute couture*.'

'She has good taste.'

'I'll take that as a compliment, I think.'

'I'm sorry, I didn't mean it like that.'

'It's not important.'

After a moment, they sit on the edge of the bed and Anna says, 'I just spoke to Sebastian. He told me you are going to Schöllenen Gorge.'

Starling has deliberately not discussed this with her. He stares at the hard-wood floor, unsure what to say. 'He is gathering his remaining arsenal. He and his men are going also.' Starling reaches across and takes her hand.

'When were you going to tell me?'

'Anna… I want you to go back to London.' He feels her stiffen.

'Why?' she asks, curtly. But before he can respond she goes on, 'You think I am incapable of seeing this through.'

'No! It's just dangerous. Now the Pastor is back from the dead, I have no doubt you and I are high on his kill list.'

'And?' she replies, standing.

The words take moments to form in his mouth. 'I've lost everyone Anna. Everyone. We almost lost Eoin. I… I can't lose you too.'

'You don't get to make that choice, Starling. Neither of us does. This is our job. It is what we do.'

Starling gets up from the bed. He'd known it was futile to ask and that Anna would not take it well, but still, he'd had to try.

'Very well. We leave tonight.'

-

Starling and Anna look for Sebastian in the hive of quiet activity in the gardens. The corpses are gone, the bodies of the Nazis and VIPER soldiers have been covered with sheets and laid respectfully in a row underneath the stage. Despite who they represented, they were still human beings and – Starling thought – had been acting under orders, just as he, Anna and Eoin were.

Passing by the open side of the mayor's house, he sees the deceased Resistance members laid out on the table in the dining room, where they had sat that afternoon. The fingers of the dead are interlaced as if in prayer. Standing over them is a priest, shaking holy water from a vial and saying a prayer aloud. Starling thinks of Emile and Claudette, their deaths still so raw in his heart. The dead lying on the table are strangers to him yet he feels a choking sensation in his throat and looks away.

Sebastian appears by his side as a truck drives through the gateway.

'We'll travel in that tonight,' he says. 'It contains enough weapons to blow them from the face of the planet, the bastards!'

'I'm glad to hear that,' says Starling, coldly.

The truck is large and green with the Nazi cross painted on the side doors. A large canvas covers the rear.

'We acquired it from our German friends,' says Sebastian. 'I knew it would come in useful one day.'

The driver gets out. Starling recognises him as one of the carpenters. He is tall, fair-haired and unshaven. A cigarette hangs from his mouth.

Sebastian beckons to him. 'Luca!'

Luca takes the last draw from his cigarette, throws it down and exhales as he approaches.

'Luca is half French, half Swiss. He grew up as a shepherd in the Alps before moving to Lyon to follow the love of his life, Sabine, who'll be with us too. He knows the area around the gorge and how to get there.'

Starling shakes his hand. 'Can you speak German?'

'*Ja*,' replies Luca, 'but I am told I have a slight French accent.' He nods politely at Anna.

'I am fluent and will ride up front with you.'

'As you wish.'

'Let's look inside. Luca, do you have that inventory?'

Luca removes some folded sheets of paper from his jacket pocket and hands them across to Sebastian as they walk back to the truck.

Inside are trunks of rifles and explosives, some German and some from the Allied forces. There are two long green metal containers with an American star on them. Inside each one is a portable rocket launcher.

'Bazookas! How did you get these?' asks Starling.

'I have friends,' replies Sebastian and leaves it at that.

'If we get close enough, we can destroy the airship.'

'Exactly my thoughts.'

Buoyed by this unexpected addition to their armoury, Starling asks, 'How many Resistance fighters are coming with us?'

'We are low on numbers, I'm afraid. There is just me and Luca, Thierry and Sabine.'

Starling frowns. 'Madeleine?'

Sebastian shakes his head. 'She has gone.'

'Typical,' mutters Anna.

'But why?' asks Starling.

'Do not worry about my niece.'

Starling can't help but feel horribly disappointed. How could she leave now when they needed her skills more than ever? No matter. They would have to do without her.

'We should take three of the German uniforms. One each for me and Luca. Sebastian, you can wear the other one. This should keep us free from prying Nazi eyes until we reach the Swiss border. Thierry, Anna and Sabine can pose as captured Resistance spies.'

'I think that might just work,' says Sebastian. 'The Swiss borders are heavily guarded. Luca, however, knows a back route. He has a cousin in Lauterbrunnen, which is close to Schöllenen Gorge.'

'It's our best and only option,' says Starling. 'Let's get to it.'

Chapter 35

Trouble on the Road to Switzerland

They leave at four in the morning. The night sky is a charred black and the air is cool and fresh. Luca is driving and Starling is sitting in the passenger seat wearing a Nazi officer's cap and jacket. Sitting in the back of the truck is Sebastian, squeezed uncomfortably into the biggest uniform they could find. Opposite him is Thierry, a tall gentleman of mixed race: African and French, Starling guesses. Beside him are Anna and Sabine, who is a quiet cat-like woman with dark hair. They each wear makeshift bonds and sit patiently, with their weapons concealed under their jackets. Hidden under the benches are trunks of weapons including guns, bazookas and explosives. Starling feels a surge of excitement. They are bringing the battle to VIPER and he will have his revenge.

They drive out of Lyon, heading east into the countryside as the darkness fades and the summer sun rises and warms Starling's face. They pass local folk who look away at the sight of a German truck navigating its way through their towns and villages. On occasion another German truck, or a Kübelwagen or two, pass them by, their passengers offering a nod or a salute. As they drive deeper into the countryside Starling begins to feel a small sense of achievement. At last they are making progress and getting closer to VIPER.

On the journey so far, Luca has been a man of few words, preferring to drive quietly and not indulge in small talk. That suits Starling. Only after several hours does Luca finally speak.

'We are almost one hour from the border,' he says. His accent is unusual – mostly French with a trace of Swiss from where he spent the first half of his life. 'We will take the next turning and head into the mountains.'

'That sounds good.'

'There are no Germans there. We will pass through an unmanned border that is known only to a few.'

The countryside expands into miles of rolling hills and fields like a wonderful green ocean with the Alps floating on air in the distance. Starling feels a sense of remoteness that he has never felt before. It makes him feel oddly safe.

As Luca turns left, heading up the narrowest of roads, Starling sees a black car driving towards them. It flashes its lights. His stomach begins to clench. 'Slow down,' he says to Luca.

The car is a Peugeot 202 with French registration. Inside are what seem to be three male civilians: two in the front, one in the back. They are casually dressed as if on a day trip but there is something about them that makes him nervous. Three men. As they get close, he sees that the two in the front are young, perhaps in their early twenties, with cautious and humourless expressions. Starling zones in on the passenger in the rear but cannot make out his face.

'There are three men inside the car. They look like military to me,' he says.

The car stops ahead of the truck and the two men in front get out. They stretch their legs and light up cigarettes. The rear door opens and the man in the back seat steps out. He is thin, tanned and Aryan blond. Starling freezes. He knows this man. It is the German corporal who asked for his papers in the café. The one Madeleine had called Franz. So this is why he could not make the mayor's party.

'They could be Swiss Army,' says Luca.

'Or German spies watching over the Swiss.'

Surreptitiously Starling pulls his cap lower over his forehead.

The corporal nods in a formal manner, reaches back inside the car and takes out his jacket. Doing up the buttons he reaches in for his cap and fixes it on his head, checking his reflection in the side mirror. Starling unbuttons the Luger that came with his borrowed uniform from the holster at his waist.

The corporal approaches the truck and indicates for Luca to wind down the window. The man has an officious air about him.

'*Guten Tag*,' says Luca, in his not-so-perfect accent.

The corporal frowns.

'*Guten Tag*, Rottenführer,' says Starling, deflecting attention from Luca.

The major's eyes slide across to Starling and blink a few times as if he is trying to place his face. After a moment he says, 'Where do you think you are going on this road?' The man clearly likes to be in control.

'We are delivering three French Resistance spies.'

The corporal frowns. 'To where?'

Starling swallows. *Good question.*

'To L'Étournel,' says Luca.

The corporal glances from Starling to Luca with narrowed eyes. 'This road leads to Switzerland. L'Étournel is the opposite direction.'

Starling slaps Luca on the arm. '*Dummkopf!* I told you we took the wrong turning.'

Luca swears under his breath, laughs and shakes his head.

'We'll reverse back,' says Starling. 'Thank you!'

Luca turns the ignition; the cabin trembles as the engine fires up.

'Wait!' commands the corporal. 'I want to see these spies.'

Starling grits his teeth and smiles. 'Of course, Rottenführer.'

The other two German soldiers watch on with a trace of amusement. Through the driver-side mirror, Starling can see Franz is already walking along the side of the truck inspecting it closely with his hands behind his back.

What on earth is he doing?

'Get ready for those two. If it comes to it, take no prisoners,' says Starling, quietly. 'I will take care of our officious friend.'

Luca smiles at the two men. 'I am ready,' he says.

Starling hops out of the truck and walks to the rear where he meets the corporal. He hears the driver door opening and Luca stepping down to the path.

'Do you have a light?' Luca asks the two men.

The corporal looks at Starling again, with a frown, as if he trying to place his face.

Starling smiles. 'Hello again, Franz,' he says in English.

The corporal's eyes flare and he reaches for the Luger at his waist but Starling is fast and launches his fist at the man's face, knocking him back against the truck. Sebastian appears from behind the green canvas with a thick piece of cord, which he loops around the man's neck, choking him. As his face turns purple Starling hears the blast of gunfire and sees Luca putting a bullet into the chest of one of the soldiers. The second is unarmed and making a run for it across the fields.

Starling aims the Luger but its unfamiliarity makes him clumsy. His first shot misses but the second hits the man's thigh. The soldier cries out, stumbles but limps on. He turns at the sound of Luca's rapid and heavy footsteps and sees the Resistance fighter pointing his stolen Luger at him.

The soldier hops to a stop and raises his arms. 'I surrender! I surrender!' he cries in German, his voice desperate.

Take no prisoners, Starling had instructed. Luca shoots him in the head. The force of the bullet propels him backwards and he lies deathly still on the green grass. Starling feels his mouth drying. He turns away and slips his Luger back into its holster, clipping it shut as he scans the area for a place to conceal the bodies.

Working together, it takes them almost ten minutes to hide the corpses.

'We can take this car. It might be useful,' says Starling. 'It's best we ditch the Nazi uniforms in case we bump into the Swiss Army.' Removing his stolen jacket he retrieves his Mauser, MI6 blazer and civilian clothes from under the seat of the truck and puts them on.

'Sabine and I both know the way to my cousin in Lauterbrunnen. I can drive the car and she can drive the truck. If we meet any more obstacles and are forced to part company, then at least we have a better chance of getting both parties to safety.'

'Good plan,' says Starling.

'We should stay on this trail for another hour or so,' says Luca.

'At some point we will need to ditch this truck. The Swiss Army will not take kindly to a Nazi truck in their country,' says Sebastian.

'Some might. There are many Nazi sympathizers in Switzerland,' says Luca.

'How far away are we from Schöllenen Gorge?' asks Anna.

'Perhaps two hours. We'll stop at Lauterbrunnen first and meet my cousin, Max. He can hide the truck and perhaps provide an alternative.'

As Luca explains the plan to Sabine, Starling and Anna find themselves alone, standing by the Peugeot.

'How're you doing?' asks Anna.

'I'm doing alright.'

Anna pauses. 'Since you came back from France, you seem different.'

He wonders what she means and looks at her questioningly.

'When you killed that wounded soldier at the house…'

'He was dying.'

Anna folds her arms. 'You killed him without hesitation.'

He mulls over her point for a moment. 'He asked me to. I wanted something from him and he wanted something from me. This is our job, Anna. These people are our enemies.'

She shifts uneasily and averts her eyes. 'You just don't seem yourself.'

'They have taken everything from me, Anna. And along the way they have murdered hundreds, if not thousands, of innocent people, robbing families of their loved ones, and it is only going to get worse. They have to be stopped. I have to stop them.'

'I understand that. I just don't want you to be consumed by your need to destroy them. We should be cautious and methodical.'

'Eoin said that two years ago. I agreed to do it his way and look where it got him. I acted under his and bloody MI6's orders. I gave him that promise and nothing happened the way it should have. For two years we've been caught up in this stupid war and what have we achieved? We killed a few Nazis. Great! We blew up their trains, their cars and we brought down a French pylon here and there. Good for us! And what has happened in that time? VIPER have grown. They have an airship with a super weapon and a red gas capable of wiping out lives in any village, town or city, horribly and quickly. And what about Rose? She could be dead for all I know.' Starling feels himself trembling inside. 'We've been played. Someone in the Secret Service wanted us out of the way and I have no idea who. Morrow and Coleridge are dead. Eoin is lucky to be alive. We are alone, Anna. Alone.'

Anna leans against the car and tilts her head back. 'We really are.'

'This time we will do it my way.'

'Our way. We are in this together.'

Leaning on the car next to her, Starling breathes. 'Our way,' he concedes. Despite asking Anna to return to London, he knows he needs her.

'I just want you to know I am here for you. Always.'

He shoots her a sideways glance and sees her looking across the rolling hills, her eyes misty.

'Thank you,' he whispers. He wonders if he should mention his brief memory of Frost and Schöllenen Gorge, but decides not to. There is nothing concrete to tell.

Chapter 36

Rose's Mistake

Rose has not seen Father William since he left her the note with the surprise revelation about her adored brother Starling. She has not slept with the excitement of knowing he was out there alive and well. She wonders what he is doing. Does he still live at their old house? What a thrill that gives her, the thought of being back in her own bed. Rose wants answers, but the blind priest is gone as fast as he appeared.

For two days she has demanded a meeting with Ophelia Black, but typically the ice queen has ignored her requests. Rose has thrown tantrum after tantrum and been horrible to Sofia, which she bitterly regrets. She has threatened to leave her apartment and march straight down to Ophelia's office, stopping hearts and pushing open doors and walls if she has to, but the truth is she is feeling tired and weak and does not have the strength to venture anywhere. Her baby is due any day now and, despite the fact that *they* put it inside her, it is still hers. It is part of her – her child – and she wants it.

But this morning Sofia comes back with the breakfast loaves and the news that Ophelia will be here at the apartment very soon. For a moment Rose thinks to cancel. She was not expecting this. Flustered, she gets dressed and washes her hot face with cool water.

Sofia serves breakfast at the little table by the window, but Rose has no appetite. 'I can't eat.'

'You must. You are…'

'…eating for two. I know.' From the corner of her eye Rose sees something move, and looking outside sees a man on the terracotta-tiled roof opposite. He looks away when her head turns, and she thinks no more of it. No one ever looks at her; they are all too terrified.

Sofia sits beside Rose and places a soft chubby hand on top of hers. 'Why do you want to see that woman? She will do you no good.'

'I only want to talk to Father William. Just once more.'

Sofia tuts. 'I ask around about this blind priest and no one has heard of him. I tell you I no trust him.'

'Priest or no priest, Sofia, he told me a secret.' Rose trembles with excitement at the memory.

'What secret?'

'I can't tell you. Not yet.'

There is a knock at the door.

'Is it eleven already?' says Rose, who is both nervous and excited. Soon she will be able to speak to Father William and learn where Starling is and perhaps run away with the baby to be with him.

Sofia opens the door and Ophelia Black walks in with smoke streaming through her nostrils. She drops her cigarette to the floor and kills the flame with the toe of her pointed shoe. She folds her arms and looks at Rose. 'What is it?'

Rose bristles but stands up. 'I want to speak to Father William.'

'Why?'

'That's none of your business.'

'Tell me what you want to say and I'll pass it on.'

'No. I want to talk to him in private.'

'That won't be possible.'

'Why not?'

'He's not here.'

'Where is he?'

'I don't know.'

Rose grits her teeth. 'You're lying.'

Ophelia sighs and rolls her eyes.

Rose's eyes flare; her fuse is lit. With her mind she pushes out at Ophelia. The ice queen trembles and frowns. Blood begins to pour from her nostrils, rolling over her glossy red lips and dripping on to her white silk blouse.

'Rose, stop!' says Sofia, with a quiver in her voice.

Rose pictures snapping Ophelia's neck. The thought excites her and she grins.

Ophelia can barely move but she is looking beyond Rose's shoulder and out the window. She manages a slight nod.

Rose feels her skin prickle. She turns to look out the window and sees the man on the roof aiming a rifle at her. All she can think about is her baby. She makes to run out of the way but a sharp pain cuts into her arm and she feels coldness race through her veins.

'Catch her before she falls and damages that child!' yells Ophelia.

Rose sways, her head is swimming.

'Rose! *Bambina!*' cries Sofia pulling her into her warm soft arms.

Rose falls into them and feels herself almost floating to the ground. Blinking, she looks up to see Ophelia looking down at her. The blood on her nose makes her face almost clown-like. Rose wants to laugh but tears prick at her eyes.

'You can't be trusted, Rose. From now until that baby is born this is how you will be. You're a danger to that child. I will not let you...'

The sound of her voice trails off as Rose's eyes grow heavier. All she wants to do is sleep.

Chapter 37

Lauterbrunnen

Starling sits in the front beside Luca as he navigates the Peugeot through the mountainous roads of the Alps. Lying across the back seat, an exhausted Anna tries to sleep.

It is a warm, sunny afternoon. They wind down the windows and breathe in the gloriously clean mountain air. Through the rear-view mirror he sees Sebastian and Thierry, free of their too-snug Nazi uniforms, scanning the countryside carefully as Sabine concentrates on driving the heavy German truck on the trail of the Peugeot.

It is almost one hour later when they clear a narrow mountain pass that opens out into a valley between steep, lusciously green hills scattered with chalets and lodges. He sees a tall white church spire amongst them.

'Lauterbrunnen is a thriving municipality here in the Alps,' Luca tells them as he drives down towards the small town. 'Do you hear that?' He points to the right where a giant waterfall roars down a rocky cliffside. 'The Staubbach Falls,' he says.

Lauterbrunnen seems like a green and peaceful paradise. Starling cannot help but be bowled over by the beauty of the place.

'We're here,' says Luca, as he steers off the road towards a lodge-style house. Beside it is a large barn with a farmer's lorry parked outside. 'And there is Max and his family!' On the hillside running up from the house a man with dark hair, a blonde woman and three children – two boys and a girl – rake hay in the mid-afternoon sun. Luca honks the car horn three times for their attention and waves out the window.

The family turn to look in their direction.

'Uncle Luca!' cries the smallest of the children, a golden-haired girl of around six years old, holding a rake twice her height. She smiles and waves as Luca eases the Peugeot to a stop at the bottom of the hill.

'Maria, my beautiful girl!'

She drops the rake and runs down the hill towards the car.

'Maria!' scolds the deep voice of the man, but she ignores him and runs with her arms open. The others follow her down. Luca gets out of the car and embraces the girl. 'Your father has you working hard, I see.' He tickles her and she giggles and then runs to embrace Sabine.

The man called Max wears a white collarless shirt and a threadbare brown waistcoat. He embraces Luca and Sabine and, when the introductions are over, all except the father and Maria return to their chores on the hillside. Max seems pleased to see them, but his eyes keep being drawn back to the Nazi truck and when the others are out of earshot he asks, 'Luca, what have you brought here?'

'Max, we need your help.'

Max looks suspiciously at Starling, Anna, Sebastian and Thierry.

'These are my friends, Max.'

Maria leans against her father and watches Starling. He smiles at her and she beams back, revealing two missing front teeth.

'We don't want any trouble here,' says Max.

'Max, hear us out. We are all of us in great danger.'

'This is not our war, Luca. Switzerland is neutral, remember?'

'It's not just about the war, Max. There are others worse than the Nazis. They have an airship with weapons that can kill thousands.'

'It is true, Max,' says Starling. 'There are powerful people who will stop at nothing to get what they want.'

'And what might that be?'

'Power. Control. Oppression. They will control people with their weapons and with fear.'

'I have seen the airship,' says a little voice.

Starling and the others had forgotten Maria was still there.

'Maria, go to your mother!' says Max.

'But Papa!'

'Now!' he scolds.

Her face drops and tears threaten to fall, but she spins around and stomps up the hillside.

'You've seen the airship?' says Starling.

Max sighs. 'Come inside and please hide that truck in the barn before someone sees it.'

As Sabine and Thierry sort out the truck, Starling and the others follow Max into his home, where the aroma of wood smoke, coffee and spice welcomes them. Max's kitchen is neat and well-kept with tall windows on all sides opening on to the views and the farmland.

'Please sit,' says Max, gesturing to a long wooden table. 'We can talk without interruption.'

Starling, Sebastian and Anna sit as Max and Luca prepare coffee and talk in hushed tones. Starling can hear Max explaining the events of yesterday evening. Max shakes his head, his expression grim. Starling hopes their presence doesn't threaten him and his family.

When they each have a hot cup of coffee, Starling begins, 'Max, we will not stay long. I… we don't want to put you and your family in danger – but you must believe me when I say these people must be stopped. They intend to kill us all.'

Max cradles his coffee and seems to consider Starling's words.

'We have seen their ship,' he says. 'It flies overhead sometimes. The children chase after it. They dream of one day flying in it.' He looks outside at his family raking the hay on the hillside. 'I have heard talk,' he says. 'There are whispers in the village.'

'What sort of whispers?' asks Starling.

'People have gone missing. There have been "accidents", or at least that is what the factory say.'

'Which factory?'

'The Teleken-Black plant in Schöllenen Gorge. They make weapons of all kinds, including chemical ones. They employ local people, but sometimes there are accidents and workers die in mysterious circumstances. The rumours are that the chemicals are dangerous. Families have lost fathers, mothers, sons and daughters.'

'Why does no one involve the police?' asks Anna.

'Because Teleken-Black are very rich. They pay the police off. They pay the families off too and no one says anything.'

'How do you know all of this?'

'They go to all the towns and villages looking for workers. They employ local people to do their dirty work. They pay well and people need money.'

'Can't the Swiss government intervene?' asks Anna.

'In return for setting up a "peaceful" hidden factory in the Alps, Teleken-Black give the government a generous rental. They turn a blind eye to any complaints of people who die there.'

'Have they asked you to work there?' asks Luca.

'Yes. My wife too. But we refused. They were not happy. They told us they would return.' Max looks outside at his family hard at work on the hillside. 'I do not trust them. I fear that one day it will be impossible for us to turn them down. And, if we don't return, who will take care of our children?' Max slumps into an armchair, head hanging down.

'We will not let that happen. I promise,' says Starling.

'In that truck we have a lot of explosives,' says Sebastian.

'We are going to wipe that place from the Alps, Max,' says Luca.

'How do these workers get to Schöllenen Gorge?' asks Anna.

'There is a bus that takes them there and takes them home again. The plant operates twenty-four hours a day. The next bus is due to pick up the night shift workers at 6 pm.'

'Where from?' asks Starling.

'The pick-up point is in a place called Lochbrücke on the other side of town.'

'This could be our way into the gorge. Max, can you show us where Lochbrücke is?'

'Of course.'

'Luca, do you know the way to Schöllenen Gorge?' asks Starling.

'I do.'

'Good. Then you will take over as the bus driver. So, let's figure out what we do from here.'

'You will need passes to get inside the plant,' says Max.

Starling looks at Max and mulls this over. 'We'll cross that bridge when we get to it. Thank you, Max.'

Later, with the plan in place, Starling and Anna take the transistor radio from the truck to the highest point at the top of the hill. Their plan is to send a broadcast to Edward telling him about Eoin's injury, the airship and the operation of the death ray and the red gas in the hope that, if he picks it up, he might relay it to the military. Anna takes over the controls and with the headphones fixed to her ears she begins transmitting.

Two hours pass with no response. Anna shakes her head and drops the headphones.

'We've done all we can,' says Starling. 'Besides, technology is different these days. Perhaps one of Edward's super-machines will pick up the transmission and keep it for him.'

'Let's hope he gets it in time. We're going straight into the nest of vipers.'

Despite himself, Starling laughs. 'I like that pun: the nest of vipers.'

By 8 pm that evening a fine mist has descended over Lochbrücke making visibility poor. This could work to our advantage, thinks Starling, as he, Anna and the others wait at the pick-up point. Parked nearby, and out of sight, is Max in his van into which they have transferred the haul of weapons.

They hear an engine approaching and two headlamps appear like giant cat's eyes in the mist. The bus pulls over. Starling counts the silhouettes of seven passengers. Max believed that the local workers lived in fear and mostly hated working at the Teleken plant. They would do anything to stay out of trouble, he had told them.

The driver, a surly man with olive skin and a dark cap, opens the door.

'*Guten Abend!*' says Starling. 'Please can you help me with my bags?'

The driver growls something impenetrable and gets out. Starling retreats into the mist, drawing him away from the eyes of his passengers.

'*Scheiße!* Where are you?' snarls the driver.

'I am behind you,' replies Starling, and pulling the man's head back he squirts a solution of poison ink from his pen into the man's mouth. The driver struggles for a moment before his body weakens and slips to the ground.

Luca removes the man's jacket and puts on his driver's cap.

Starling boards the bus with his Mauser to hand. The passengers comprise two women in headscarves and four men. One is wearing a dark brown fedora. Two of the men have backpacks and one of the women holds a large bag. They each carry a gas mask box hanging from string around their shoulders. They glance at him and then quickly look away.

Speaking in German, Starling says, 'Leave your passes and your bags, get off the bus and go to your homes. Do not speak of this to anyone. Do I make myself clear?'

Without hesitation they mumble agreement, drop their bags and hand their passes to Starling as they get up and leave the bus. Starling places a hand on the chest of the gentlemen in the fedora. The man's head dips.

'Do not be alarmed. Your hat, please.'

The man pulls off his hat without question, hands it across and slides quickly past Starling and off the bus.

As the passengers hurry down the misty road, Starling helps the others load the weapons inside and under the seats. No more than ten minutes later, they say their goodbyes to Max and continue towards Schöllenen Gorge.

Chapter 38

Schöllenen Gorge

The road leading into Schöllenen Gorge is narrow. The sheer granite looms high as they descend into what seems like a rocky hell. At this height they are still above the mist and visibility is good.

Starling stands at the front as Luca steers the bus around a corner. He sees a line of buses below them in the distance driving towards an old stone bridge.

'Teufelsbrücke – Devil's Bridge,' says Luca.

Starling has the sense they are going deeper into the earth and thinks the bridge is aptly named. They are soon joining the other buses and behind them are four more. Luca drives them across Devil's Bridge and into a dark tunnel where Starling takes a seat next to Anna.

'Checkpoint ahead!' Luca warns.

Starling and Anna stand to get a better look. There are two buses ahead of them at the tunnel exit where VIPER guards, dressed in black, man the checkpoint.

It takes approximately four minutes to check passes and get each bus through.

'*Schnell!*' calls a guard to the bus in front, waving it through with the beam of a torch.

With the guards distracted as they usher the bus forward, Starling begins the first phase of their plan. 'Now Luca!' he says, removing Joseph's Time Pencil from his sleeve. He snaps the copper end of the pencil cracking the glass vial inside. The acid releases and the countdown begins.

Luca pulls the lever and opens the bus door. Cold night air sweeps inside. Starling hangs down at ground level and tosses the Time Pencil back up the road and under the bus behind them. Slipping back inside, he sits beside Anna and puts on the fedora, tilting it slightly so that it covers his face. Turning to look at her in the gloom he sees her breath steaming.

'Cold for the time of year,' she says.

'Not long now.'

Anna smiles wanly. 'I must admit defeat and say these fashionable threads of Madeleine's are not suitable apparel for an excursion to the Alps.'

Starling meets her gaze and covers her hand with his. 'Good luck and stay safe.'

'You too.'

The bus eases to a stop and the guard boards, shining the torch in their faces. 'Passes!' he commands. As he walks to back of the bus to check Sebastian's pass first, Starling notices he wears a thick utility belt with a pistol attached and a knife and gas mask hanging from it.

'*Guten Abend*,' says Sebastian, handing him his pass.

The guard ignores him and checks his pass under torchlight before examining the others one by one. He comes to stand by Starling, his gloved hand extended.

'*Guten Abend*,' says Starling, handing across the pass. He wonders about the Time Pencil. It should have detonated by now.

The guard grunts and shines his torch on the paper. He looks at Starling for longer that is comfortable and frowns. 'I know your face,' he says.

Starling's stomach clenches. Is it possible his face was on some kind of VIPER Wanted list? Starling smiles politely. 'I work here.'

The guard breathes heavily through his nose. 'Which division?'

Before Starling can respond there is an explosion far bigger than Starling had anticipated from the Time Pencil.

'What the hell?'

The base of the bus behind them is engulfed in flames. Thankfully the door is open and all the passengers are able to escape.

The guard hurries out of the bus and waves at Luca. '*Schnell! Schnell!*' Luca wastes no time in driving through the checkpoint. The guards have their rifles raised, stopping anyone from leaving the tunnel. In seconds the engine of the bus is on fire, and it explodes in a ball of flame. Abandoning protocol, the guards and the passengers run through the exit together.

Joseph was not wrong about the Time Pencil being powerful. Starling can't quite believe he has been carrying that thing around. What if there had been an accident while he was wearing it? He pushes the thought from his mind. It's bad enough carrying the shard, which on its own makes him a potential weapon of destruction. It occurs to him he has not felt a pulse from the shard since they left France. He rests his palm on his breast pocket and feels the reassuring outline of the tin soldier. It is still there inside the fusilier. Sleeping.

Luca drives them quickly through a car park where dozens of buses are parked and the occupants gather in droves to watch the scene at the checkpoint. Starling and the others sit at the front of the bus taking in their first view of Schöllenen Gorge.

Starling feels his throat drying. There is an unsettling familiarity to this place. He has clearly been here before. The gorge is vast, like a valley fit for the gods, with stunning and oppressive granite rock faces that stretch high into the sky. A long and steep stairwell runs from the car park and leads almost a quarter of a mile up to a stark three-storey building built into the side of the rock face. The Teleken-Black weapons plant.

'*Merde!* It is much bigger than I expected,' says Sebastian.

'The length of four football pitches,' says Starling.

He feels the eyes of his companions rest on him curiously and pretends not to notice.

Carved in stone at the centre of the building is the ominous Teleken-Black logo: a T overlapping a B with a viper coiled through the letters. There are twenty-four small windows on each level, however on the top floor at the far end is a large window with a balcony overlooking the gorge. He swallows and his pulse races.

I know that place. But how? I have stood there. Once before. No, more often than that.

He shakes the thought from his head. With no time for retrieving lost memories, he looks beyond the plant at the bottom of the gorge where there is a vast flat landing pad, big enough to hold an airship.

Their plan had been to split into two teams, one led by Starling, the other by Sebastian. The goal of Starling's team, comprising Anna and Thierry, was to attack the factory from within. Sebastian's team of Luca and Sabine was to find a secluded spot where they could fire the bazooka rocket launchers at the airship and factory.

But there was no airship to be seen.

'*Merde!* Where is the airship?' says Luca.

'Damn it,' says Starling. 'Sebastian, we need to adjust our plan.'

Chapter 39

Bon Courage

With the airship absent Starling has to think fast. 'Sebastian, you'll have to use the rocket launchers on the factory. We may not get the opportunity to get to the first and second floors so aim for the top two floors if you can.'

'That is a good plan but I would suggest holding back with the rockets in case the airship returns,' says Sebastian.

'Agreed. Remember everyone, this mission is about sabotage and subversion. This is our best chance of blowing this place from the face of the earth. If by any chance the airship appears then be my guest and take it from the sky.'

'Our pleasure,' says Sebastian.

'Will, the workers are heading into the factory,' says Anna.

Starling looks out to see the Teleken-Black employees making the climb up the stone steps with their gas mask boxes. 'We need to go.'

Thierry and Starling take a backpack each. Anna takes the bag.

'Good luck everyone,' says Starling. 'Remember, there will be a mass evacuation. If all goes well, and if, by some miracle, we achieve this without being caught or hurt, then I hope to see you back on the other side of the tunnel. Stay in the crowd and keep out of sight.'

'*Bon courage, mes amis*,' says Sebastian.

'*Bon courage*,' Starling and the others reply, shaking each other's hands.

Starling can't help but feel guilty. These people are risking their lives to join him on what might be a suicide mission. He feels a strong warmth and kinship like none he can remember. He can't thank them enough but now is not the time. Perhaps in another life, if there is one.

Starling, Anna and Thierry leave the bus and melt in with the crowd trudging up the stone steps. Turning back he sees the fire has been tamed in the tunnel and there are a dozen or so guards investigating the scene. Some are questioning the civilian workers at gunpoint. Swallowing, he looks at the entrance to the factory in the distance. It is arched, with two ornamental spikes pointing towards the ground. They are walking into a viper's mouth.

Guards on either side of the entrance are making random security checks. His stomach knots and he keeps his head down, only looking occasionally from under the rim of the fedora. Thierry is three people ahead of him and has cleared the entrance without being checked. Starling feels a surge of excitement. Anna is next.

'*Guten Abend!*' she says in a jolly tone.

The guard, a young man with a ferret-like face, whistles his approval at Anna.

Anna smiles at him and with this distraction Starling hurries by, but the young guard has moved forward to speak to Anna and collides with Starling.

'*Entschuldigung*,' says Starling.

The guard does not seem in the mood for accepting apologies. '*Dummkopf!*' he shouts, poking Starling's chest.

Under the shade of the fedora Starling rolls his eyes. '*Entschuldigung*,' he repeats, and tries to bypass the man, but the guard grabs his arm.

'What is in your bag?' he asks, as people file past.

Starling looks up and sees the guard smiling quickly at Anna. This show of authority is clearly for her benefit. He grits his teeth as the guard squeezes his arm and shakes it.

'Your bag!' he commands.

Cursing his luck, Starling glances to the side. The other guard is caught up with his own security checks and is unaware of what is going on with his colleague. Starling wonders how he can solve the problem of this irritant without attracting attention. He levels his gaze at the guard. The man's ferrety eyes take in his face and focus on the scar on Starling's left cheekbone. For a second he seems confused and then he steps back, reaching clumsily for the pistol on his utility belt. But before Starling can spring into action he hears a nearly inaudible whoosh. The guard stiffens, eyes wide. Starling sees something small and metallic lodged in the guard's neck. A Velo-Dart. He turns to see Anna's arm drop to her waist.

The guard falls back and Starling eases him to the wall leaning his stiff body against it. Starling furtively snatches the dart from his neck, tosses it to the floor and joins Anna. They merge with the crowd.

'Reassuring to know that France's finest *haute couture* comes equipped with the latest in Velo-Dart technology,' says Starling.

'I must admit, I did make a few adjustments before leaving France. A girl is just not safe in these troubled times.'

'I like your style.'

'What's our next move?'

Starling is loath to admit he really does not know. Their intelligence on Teleken-Black's factory is next to nothing.

'Still trying to work that one out.'

'Is it possible you have been here before?'

'I can't be sure. Some things seem to resonate but I haven't any details.'

Looking around him none of it seems familiar. The ground floor lobby of the building is immense, with tall ceilings and functional grey concrete walls, and four lifts that lead up to the upper floors. Queues of people wait patiently by the doors.

'Look,' says Anna, nodding at the wall opposite the lifts.

Starling sees Thierry looking at a diagram on the wall. It is a layout of the building. He feels his adrenalin pulsing. They thread their way through the crowd and join him.

The ground floor is marked in three coloured zones: white, yellow and grey. The white zone is a weapons building facility – rifles; the yellow zone is pistols; and the grey contains an lightening symbol. Pointing to it Thierry says, 'The power generator.'

The first floor is split into a blue zone – Teleken research – and a red zone marked with a skull and crossbones, the symbol for toxic substances. Starling's hands ball into fists. So that is where they manufacture it. He sees what looks like two staircases on either side of the plant, each with a 'Restricted' sign.

The second floor is a green zone comprising offices, meeting rooms, classrooms and training facilities. His memory stirs and his mind spins. Unsteady on his feet, he leans against the map.

'Will, you have been here before, haven't you?' asks Anna.

He nods. 'Yes, I believe so. This is the main training facility.'

'Are you feeling alright?'

He takes a few breaths and feels better. 'I'm fine.'

'I can take the ground floor and blow the generator,' says Anna.

'First thing we need to do is evacuate the building,' says Starling. Looking up he sees red alarm bells dotted around the walls. 'I'll set off the alarms when you two are out of sight.'

'I can take the first floor,' says Thierry.

'Good, but be careful there. It is inevitable the red gas will be released, so make sure you both keep your masks close. Set your explosives to detonate at 11 pm.'

To lessen his load, Starling removes the mask from the box and straps it to his backpack as Thierry wastes no time and runs to the open doors of the lift, jumping the queue, much to the consternation of those before him.

As they part company Anna reaches for Starling's arm. She pulls him close and kisses him warmly on the lips. 'For luck,' she murmurs, and then turns quickly and disappears into the crowd before he can say anything to her.

'Good luck,' he whispers, his stomach fluttering.

Chapter 40

The Training Ground

Hearing raised voices back at the entrance, Starling sees some new guards milling around their stiff, unconscious colleague who has slid to the floor on his back.

The queues for the lifts are still three people deep, the doors firmly closed as the latest batch of workers ascend to their respective floors.

According to the map, further along the lobby is a corridor with a staircase, where he catches the glow of a light as a door opens. A stern-faced woman dressed in a grey suit with a Teleken-Black badge emerges clutching a batch of manila folders. Behind her he sees the staircase. As she walks away he hurries towards the door noting the sign written in German on the outside: 'Teleken-Black badged personnel only.'

A risk worth taking, he thinks, and slips through before it closes. The steps are concrete, painted a clinical white like the walls. There are two flights of stairs per floor. He hurries up the first one two steps at a time until he reaches the landing and the entrance to the top floor. On the wall next to the door is an alarm activator.

Slinging off his backpack he crouches down and begins to undo the straps to get his mask. So far so good, he thinks, opening the flap of the backpack, but at that moment he hears men's voices. The door swings open. He swallows and looks up to see three guards frowning down at him. The door closes behind them.

'Hello!' says Starling, in a disarming tone.

'What are you doing here?' says the guard on his right, a broad man, the largest of the three.

Starling stands to face them, smiling politely, his hands raised in an appeasing gesture. 'I'm sorry. I wandered up here by mistake.'

'Your pass. Show it to me now!'

Starling's eyes slide to the guard on his left who is leaning across and looking down at the contents of his backpack on the floor behind him.

'What is in the bag?' he asks.

Starling smiles and shrugs. 'Explosives.'

The first guard snorts and glances at his colleagues in what seems like the longest of seconds. Starling can sense their next move and feels his hybrid martial arts training and survival instincts switch into gear. He lunges his fist at the throat of the large guard to his right. The man topples back against the wall behind him.

The second guard is canny. Growling, he swings his fist at Starling's face, but Starling leans back, narrowly missing the blow. Pain sears his ribs as the third guard hits him hard. The second guard swings a fist at Starling's stomach winding him and forcing him back, his feet knocking the backpack of explosives.

Holding his ribs and stomach he smiles at the guards. 'You'll have to do better than that.'

They run at him and, pushing back from the wall, Starling deflects their fists with skilful Aikido hand-blocks that confuse his opponents. The first guard quickly edges behind Starling and locks his arm around his throat. Leaning back Starling swings his feet onto the second guard's shoulders. The man drives forward unwittingly giving Starling the power to propel himself head over heels behind the first guard. Landing on his feet Starling picks the guard up by the belt and tosses him over the bannister. He scrambles at the bannister rail but misses and cries out as he plunges to the concrete steps below. The large guard has made a recovery and, despite still clutching his throat, has removed a knife from his utility belt. The second guard has unfastened his pistol and raises it. Starling grabs the second man's arm and swings his pistol at the first. The gun fires twice, shooting the large guard who drops the knife and tumbles down the white stairs in a bloody mess.

Starling slams the second guard's hand on the bannister, cracking his bones until he releases the pistol, which clatters onto the stairs below. The guard is strong and with his other hand claws at Starling's eyes and mouth, pushing him against the bannister and forcing him over with all his might. Grunting, Starling feels his feet slipping beneath him. He cannot escape this. The guard forces him harder. Starling's feet lift off the ground. He wraps his arms tight around the guard's neck, pulls the man to him and together they flip over the bannister. With a keen sense of what is around him, Starling twists his body over the guard so that he is on top as the two of them fall through the air to the steps below. The guard slams and crunches on the steps, cushioning Starling's fall. They slide down the flight of stairs like a man on a bobsleigh, making a stop beside the first guard, whose neck is twisted in a gruesome way. The bobsleigh is verging on unconsciousness, breathing erratically and groaning.

'What the hell!' Starling hears from the landing above. A pair of boots begins to tread carefully down the steps. Starling pulls out his Mauser and ducks out of sight.

'Hello?' calls a voice.

'Help me,' Starling responds in a weak voice.

Standing out of sight, he waits for the new guard to show. A moment later a figure in black combats appears with a rifle pointing before him. As he examines his groaning colleague Starling shoots him in the chest. He topples down the stairs and Starling darts past him up to the landing and the bag of explosives. Pulling on his gas mask as a disguise, he smashes the alarm glass with the butt of his Mauser. One by one alarms begin ringing across all floors in the plant.

People flood into the stairwell below. Starling steps into a corridor lit only by the flashing of red warning lights. Teleken-Black employees are still emerging, their faces terrified, fumbling with their gas masks and pushing their way past each other. The red gas takes no prisoners, thinks Starling, not even those who create it, process it, bottle it and ship it.

He sees men in white lab coats hurry from a doorway like frightened mice. In the room they have left are rows and rows of glass cabinets containing jars and bottles of chemicals. He has no idea what is inside but reckons they might boost the effect of his explosives. He takes the first batch from his backpack and places them carefully behind one of the cabinets.

Checking his watch he sees it is twelve minutes to eleven. He has precious little time. He sets the timer for eleven and hurries out of the room. The crowd in the corridor has thinned to a trickle of masked people moving towards the stairs. Starling is drawn towards the far right of the building, though he is not sure why. His mind swirls and he hears voices from another time. Among them is Colonel Frost's barking orders. Starling remembers men in training gear running down this same hall. He can't quite recall what is down there. Taking off his mask, he goes down the hallway where there are large green double doors.

He opens them.

The smell of stale sweat fills his nostrils, evoking old memories of sparring and gruelling workouts. Inside is an enormous, brightly lit gymnasium with a shiny hardwood floor, French windows and a balcony overlooking the gorge. Around the walls are weights, duelling daggers, chains, nunchucks, swords, gymnast hoops, climbing bars. At one end is a boxing ring and a martial arts floor. He feels the hairs on his neck stand up. This space had been his training ground. He has spilled blood here, his own and that of others. He takes out the remaining explosives. Hearing gunshots outside, he goes to the window, wondering if Sebastian, Luca and Sabine are in trouble. Opening the glass doors he steps onto the balcony. The cold night air prickles his hot face. The car park has been lit with flood lamps and the floor of the gorge resembles a giant runway. The car park is full of people and he is too far away to pick out any individuals. The base of the landing pad has been lit and, as he watches, a great shadow appears blocking out the night sky. It is the airship.

His heart racing, he scans the area for any sign of Sebastian and his team but is distracted by the rasp of a second engine. To his right, beyond the tunnel, a bi-plane flies towards him and sweeps over the car park. It is a cream Tiger Moth. He has seen it before. Could it be the same one that flew past him on the way to his drop-off point over the Channel?

The guards fire at the plane but it dives quickly, spinning and dodging and shooting off several unforgiving rounds in their direction. The Moth loops over the car park and across the factory, passing close to Starling on the balcony. The pilot smiles as she pulls upwards, all guns raging at the gondola of the descending airship. It is Madeleine. He laughs. He thinks back to when he flew from Chartres to deliver the microfilm. Was she the pilot who flew alongside him?

As he sets the timer on the explosives a glance at his watch shows he has three minutes left. *Shit!*

Chapter 41

Frost

Picking up his mask, Starling hurries out of the gymnasium, runs up the hallway of flashing lights and ringing bells and down the stairs, leaping over the still bodies of the four guards. As he reaches the second floor he stops at the unsettling blare of the death ray's klaxon. Red light flashes through the small windows as the scorching blast roars and people scream in terror. He thinks of Madeleine and his stomach clenches. Has the death ray just finished her off?

On the ground floor he runs towards the exit, shouting to the crowds, 'Get out of here! Run for your lives!'

The airship hovers high above the landing pad. There is no sign of the Tiger Moth. His heart sinks. Search beams on both sides of the gondola sweep through the skies. The beams swing down to scan the crowds below. One stops on Starling. He raises his hand against the glare and then hears the buzz of the Moth as it swoops up from behind and spins like a corkscrew in the air firing at the gondola, killing the lights and plunging him into darkness. Two bodies drop from the gondola to the rocky surface below.

The cannon spins around searching for the little plane. The klaxon blares and the death ray whips through the night sky lashing angrily at the Tiger Moth.

Around him people watch in wonder as the plane loops and dives, dodging the murderous ray, which misses and slashes the surface of a nearby cliff skimming off a flurry of rocks and dust. The cannon tracks the plane as it flies over the car park, across the landing pad and up the gorge.

Starling feels his heart pounding. *Get out of here, Madeleine. It will take a miracle for you to survive this attack.*

The klaxon blares and the cannon fires. The red ray spirals through the air. Madeleine steers the Tiger Moth close to the granite walls of the gorge, darting from one side to the other like a mouse being pursued by a snake. The heat ray hits the surface, missing the little plane by inches as it disappears over the gorge.

Starling starts to move, scanning the tops of heads for any sign of Anna or the others, but there are too many people. 'Anna!' he calls, but there is no answer.

Suddenly a thunderous roar bellows through the gorge as the plant blows in six simultaneous explosions. Debris flies through the air as people scream and swarm towards the tunnel. Starling reaches a bus. Using it as cover, he watches the Teleken-Black building crumble in on itself. He feels a surge of adrenalin; a grim smile creases his face.

He hears Anna's voice. 'Will!'

She is running towards him, pushing her way through the panicking people.

'Anna!' Without thinking, he embraces her and feels relief wash over him. 'Thank God, you're safe.'

'I saw Thierry run ahead of me from the plant. Have you seen him?'

'No. Perhaps he's with Sebastian and the others. We have to find them. I want those missiles to blast that airship from the sky.'

'Look!' says Anna, pointing beyond him.

Starling turns to see six or more VIPER soldiers shooting in the direction of a pathway cut into the granite and leading to the landing pad. Halfway along, poorly protected by some rocks, are Sebastian and Thierry trying to provide cover for Luca and Sabine as they run the gauntlet towards the landing pad with the bazookas.

Starling takes out his Mauser. 'We're not finished yet.'

The buzz of the Tiger Moth has not returned. He hopes Madeleine is safe.

A second search beam from somewhere at the top of the factory sweeps downward and picks out Sabine and Luca. They shoulder the bazookas and lift them towards the airship as the blare of the klaxon sounds. Starling sees the cannon below the gondola swing around and point downwards. The VIPER soldiers turn from their battle with the mayor and Thierry and begin to scatter.

'No!' says Starling, grabbing Anna's arm.

'Luca! Sabine!' he screams pointlessly.

And then it comes. The flash of red light, whipping like a glowing tentacle as it lashes at Sabine and Luca.

It is too late. The two Resistance fighters and the bazookas light up and explode in a cloud of grey dust and ash.

'Oh Starling,' says Anna, her voice trembling.

Boots stomp behind and around them. They swing around, their guns ready, but there are too many VIPER guards surrounding them. They are trapped.

'Remove their guns,' says a familiar voice that makes Starling go cold. It is Colonel Victor Frost, the man who was his VIPER trainer and leader for four years – the same man who murdered his parents and kidnapped his sister. Starling had last seen him two years ago when he was captured by Eoin, just before he was sent to jail.

One of the guards snatches Starling's Mauser and Anna's Walther and cuffs them both.

Then Frost makes his way from behind the VIPER guards. Starling's hands curl into fists as the muscular figure comes near.

'The prodigal son returns,' says Frost. 'I would say welcome home, William, but there is nothing left of it. You've made quite a mess here, haven't you?'

'It's the first of many home improvements I intend to make.'

Frost smiles wanly at Starling, then assesses him. 'Look at you. All grown up and the fire in your belly is still raging. Despite our history, William, I am pleased to see you.'

'Because of our history, Vic, I am pleased that soon I will get to put a bullet between your eyes.'

Frost snorts and turns to Anna, looking her up and down. 'Have we met?'

Anna levels her gaze at Frost, her expression fixed and unafraid. He walks around her, leaning towards her and sniffing the air. 'I remember you, missy. London, May, 1941. What a rollercoaster of a night that was.'

'Fun times,' says Anna, coldly.

'Maybe when the dust settles you and I could grab a drink somewhere.'

'I'd rather go on a date with a fetid corpse.'

Starling hears some of the VIPER soldiers stifle a laugh and notices Frost's nostrils flare.

'That could be arranged,' says the Colonel, glancing upward. 'For now we are all going on a little trip.'

Guards and some of the workers are making a quick job of sweeping the debris from the surface of the landing pad. Above them the airship begins its descent. The painted viper on the base of the gondola gets bigger and the cannon retracts and disappears inside the snake's mouth. The gondola is larger than it seemed, perhaps a hundred feet wide and two hundred feet long. Starling can see the front window and, through it, the hooded shape of Proatheris, leader of the Cerastes, looking his way.

Who are you?

'It's time for you to atone for your sins, William,' says Frost.

Chapter 42

Proatheris

The airship hovers unsteadily twenty feet above the landing pad. The engines chug relentlessly, the cooling fans swirl and expel mini tornadoes of warm air, raising dust and pushing it into the faces of everyone below. Starling squints and watches as a rope falls from the centre of the gondola and is grabbed by several guards who hold it firmly, tethering the ship to *terra firma.*

A hatch opens from the belly of the snake and lowers to the surface of the landing pad: a walkway to and from the airship.

Frost points at two of the guards. 'You and you. Come with me.' He pushes Starling and Anna towards them. 'Put a bullet in their backs if they try anything.' Frost leads them towards the airship. On either side of the pathway workers and guards watch. Starling sees Sebastian, and the mayor takes a step towards him. Starling shakes his head. *No, Sebastian! There is nothing you can do here.*

As if reading his thoughts, the mayor halts and jerks his head at something behind Starling. Confused, Starling keeps his eyes trained ahead and walks on a few paces before quickly glancing back to see what Sebastian was trying to indicate. A familiar face is shaded by the visor of a guard's helmet. Thierry! The Frenchman shoves him in the back. 'Move!' he orders, and Starling stumbles forward, hiding a smile inside.

Up the ramp, all Starling can see is a rectangular bright white light. The ramp wobbles as the guards fight to control the tethering rope.

'Faster,' snaps Frost.

With Anna beside him, Starling steps onto the unsteady ramp and ascends into the gondola, sandwiched between Frost and Thierry and another armed guard.

A line of armed VIPER soldiers awaits them at the top of the ramp. It leads to what seems to be the deck, which is more than ten feet tall and almost thirty feet wide. As well as being the access and exit point for the airship it also seems to be a storage area. Stacked high along the walls are dozens of yellow barrels marked with a skull and crossbones. The red gas.

'Raise the ramp,' calls Frost.

As the ramp is pulled up the engines accelerate and Starling feels a lurch in his stomach as the airship rises. Frost walks ahead to the front of the ship. The two guards shove Starling and Anna, urging them to follow the Colonel.

The inside of the ship is a hive of activity filled with maintenance people, soldiers, guards and engineers with grease-covered skin. Starling notices two sliding windows that run from floor to ceiling on either side of the deck. Beyond both are slatted balconies with angled windows overlooking the world below. At the base of each window are the red rolls of material that together combine to make the VIPER flag, and which are used by the soldiers to climb down to the ground.

Frost leads them to a steel door where two grim-faced guards stand like sentinels. Passing through, he is greeted by a warm blast of steam hitting his face from two giant fans in the ceiling above them. There is no floor, only a narrow steel lattice bridge, wide enough for two people. Steam rises around and through it and below it he sees the Tesla cannon, hidden from the outside world, like a sleeping dragon. Around it men in heavy overalls spray water from hoses to cool it down.

Crossing through a flurry of steam Starling steals a glance at Anna, who surreptitiously nods to her left. Starling follows her gaze and sees a walkway from the bridge leading to what looks like a bank of machines the like of which might be used at Bletchley. Operators turn dials, flick switches and write notes on clipboards. They make him think of Edward and he imagines his pal would love the opportunity to play with this equipment. A steel pipe runs under the walkway and connects to the cannon. *The power source. Does the machine control it all?*

'Move!' says the guard behind him, prodding him with the barrel of his gun.

At the end of the bridge there is a white door, which slides open to reveal a dimly lit navigation room. Two uniformed men stand with their backs to him at a control panel with a wooden steering wheel. Curved front windows run from floor to ceiling to enable them to navigate the ship.

He sees a familiar face. Tall, with pale pockmarked skin, thin lips and oiled red hair: Rupert Van Horne looking every inch the model of smug superiority.

'Child killer,' spits Starling, through gritted teeth.

A smile appears like a scar on Horne's face.

And then he hears Anna say, in a bewildered voice, '*Sir Hugh?*'

Horne is standing beside a brown Chesterfield sofa. Seated upon it, with a cane resting by his leg, is Sir Hugh Coleridge. His hair is ruffled, he looks pale and gaunt with dark rings under his eyes. He does not seem to notice them. Behind him is a guard holding a pair of hair clippers. Gently he tilts the chief's head back and begins to shave his dark hair right down to the skull. Coleridge says nothing and lets the barber get on with it.

Has he been drugged?

Moments later, Coleridge's hair has fallen to the floor where it lies by his feet in small wisps and tufts. Prisoner-like stubble is all that remains on his head. But there is something else. A shadow beneath the stubble, like a tattoo of something Starling can't quite make out.

Anna turns to Frost. 'Why are you doing this? Hasn't he suffered enough?'

Frost does not respond.

Starling glances at Horne, whose eyes have never left him since he walked into the navigation room.

The guard lifts a bowl from behind the sofa and begins to lather Coleridge's head with soap and water. With a shaving blade he begins skilfully to cleave through the stubble, leaving streaks of bare white skin and revealing the tattoo. Starling feels his stomach fluttering. The tattoo is a viper rising from the base of his skull: the symbol of the Cerastes, the Order of VIPER. He glances at Anna, who watches, frowning in confusion. The barber finishes and pats Coleridge's head with a towel. Coleridge blinks, rubs his eyes and looks from Anna to Starling.

'We thought you were dead,' says Anna. 'Perhaps it's a shame you are not.'

Coleridge smiles grimly and sits up. 'Sir Hugh Coleridge is long gone, my dear,' he says, as the cane slides away from the sofa and falls to the floor. Rolling up his trouser leg to the knee, he reveals his wooden leg. Starling can now see three silver clips running up the calf. Coleridge undoes them one by one and pulls the wooden limb apart, revealing his real leg underneath.

'*You're* the mole!' says Starling.

'Deception is king in our line of work, Starling. Ten points to you, although I'm deducting eight for not working it out sooner.' The MI6 Chief of Staff stands, his eyes levelling with Starling's. He wobbles for a moment before emitting a low hoarse laugh. 'Forgive my theatrics. I can't help myself sometimes.'

Horne lets out a sycophantic cackle. Coleridge gives him a disdainful look and Horne's face drops, his cheeks flushing a deep red.

Coleridge lifts what looks like a black blanket resting on the back of the sofa and pulls it around him. But it is no blanket. It is a monk's robe with a red trim around the hood and cuff. It is the robe of Proatheris – the leader of the Cerastes.

'You are Proatheris?' The parts of the jigsaw begin to fall into place. Coleridge had fooled them all.

'You have cost us quite dearly today, Will.'

'It's been you all along. That night in the hospital, it was you who tried to kill me.'

Coleridge pulls a platted red rope around the waist of his robe. 'Regrettably, I did not succeed.'

'You framed Morrow. You planted the Rolling Ticker under the Embiricos. You employed Clifford Meadows to spy on Anna and Edward. You sent us to France on a plane that you shot down.' Starling glances at Horne, who smiles coldly from the shadows. 'You freed that treacherous child killer and sent a murderer after your best friend! You betrayed him. You betrayed us and you betrayed your country!'

'It was all necessary for the greater goal. Besides, as detestable as Horne is, he is my nephew and I made a promise to look after him.'

'So many people have died because of you!'

Coleridge smiles. 'I'll take that as a compliment. Thank you.'

'You disgust me.'

'And you disappoint me. I thought you were better than this. I really believed my time was up when we met at Chittlock's house. Dear sad old Nicholas mentioned that the hairdresser told you two monks had entered the house, but only one had left it. You went back and did not even find the hidden robe. You're not as bright as Eoin thought you were.'

Starling steps forward, his face inches from Coleridge's. 'You treacherous scum!'

A punch hits his ear and Starling falls to his knees, nursing the burning ear with his cuffed hands.

'Watch your mouth!' says Frost.

'Try not to damage the goods, Frost. She wants him in one piece, remember.'

'Let's just kill him now, Uncle. She doesn't have to know. Let me do it!'

'Be quiet, Rupert!' bellows Coleridge.

Starling pushes himself up. 'Who is *she*?'

'She is the *Lady*. You will meet her. Soon enough.'

'Where is my sister?'

'In cloud cuckoo land!' laughs Horne, almost deranged.

Starling's fingers dig into his palms. He looks from Horne to Coleridge. 'What does that mean?'

Coleridge ignores the question and whispers something to Horne. Horne's face pales. 'Yes, Uncle,' he says and immediately leaves the navigation room.

'Captain Smythe, are we on course?' asks Coleridge.

'Yes, sir. The winds are on our side. We may arrive thirty minutes early.'

'Not a minute less, Smythe.'

'Yes, sir.'

Starling steps towards Coleridge, but is held back by Frost.

'Just what are you expecting to achieve with this bloated flying contraption? Do you really think one airship with a fancy gun and some red gas is enough against the Spitfires and Messerschmitts of the world?'

Coleridge folds his arms inside his sleeves. He hesitates and then smiles slyly. 'If it were up to me you would be dead with a bullet between your eyes. But there is a reason you are still alive.'

'Because you are an incompetent idiot who can't seem to kill me?'

Frost raises his fist, but Coleridge gestures at him and shakes his head. Turning to Starling he says, 'You have something we want.'

The shard.

'In Lyon, something destroyed the red gas. Something extraordinary. Something blue.'

'I don't know what you are talking about.'

'The Stones of Fire were allegedly destroyed. But a fragment of them still exists and I think you have it.'

Starling does not know what to say to that. It seems futile to deny it considering he is carrying the shard in his blazer.

'Search them,' says Coleridge.

Frost uncuffs Starling and Anna and nods to the guards. Acting out the role Thierry manhandles Starling, copying what the other guard does to Anna, who does her best to ignore the indignity. They wrench out the Velo-Darts and toss them to a nearby bin. Thierry checks the collar of Starling's blazer where the flexible saw is kept.

'Check the sleeves. There are all sorts concealed there,' says Frost.

Ignoring the saw, Thierry moves to the cuffs and removes the tools. Starling knows he has to do this and lets him get on with it. Thierry begins to empty his pockets, finding only a packet of bullets, some coins and, of course, the tin soldier. Starling pulls back when Thierry's fingers brush the soldier. The Frenchman reads the signal and pulls his hand away.

'Wait!' says Frost.

He pushes Thierry out of the way, reaches into Starling's pocket and pulls out the tin soldier. He glares at Thierry. 'Eyes open, private! Leave no stone unturned.'

'Yes, sir. Sorry, sir,' replies Thierry.

Frowning, Coleridge takes the fusilier from Frost and studies it. He shakes the tin soldier and smiles at the rattling sound. 'That was easier than I thought.'

Behind his stony expression Starling tries to conceal his fury. He glances at Anna; her eyes linger on his. He wants to reassure her, but he can't. VIPER will now own the shard. Lord knows what they might be able to do with it.

Coleridge prises open the spine of the fusilier, takes out the stone inside and holds it up in the light, his expression full of awe. 'Is this really a piece of the Stones?'

It is now Starling's turn to frown. The stone that Coleridge is holding is not the shard. It is a long piece of gravel. Just like the gravel on Sebastian's drive.

Chapter 43

The Owl

Coleridge's expression turns sour. 'This is not a piece of the Stones of Fire!' He throws the gravel to the floor and crushes it with his boot. 'Where is it?'

'I have no idea what you are talking about.'

Coleridge exhales. 'Very well. Frost, kill the girl.'

'Pleasure, sir,' says Frost, raising his pistol and pointing it at Anna's head. The colour drains from her face.

'Wait!' cries Starling.

'Shoot!' says Coleridge.

With his heart in his mouth, Starling springs at Frost and pushes the pistol away. 'Wait, I'll tell you!'

'Let's hear what he has to say, Colonel Frost,' says Coleridge.

The Colonel shrugs and slips the gun back into its holster.

'Don't tell them, Will,' says Anna.

Starling looks desperately from Anna to Coleridge. The truth is, he has no idea where the shard is.

'On the count of five I want the answer or she dies. Five, four, three, two…'

'I had it! I did. It was in my pocket concealed inside the tin soldier but now it's not and I don't know why. I swear to you!'

'You'll have to do better than that.'

Starling tries to think, recalling the battle at Sebastian's house. 'I last saw it at the mayor's house. The red gas was everywhere. I used the shard. The gas dissipated. Madeleine was there. She picked it up and gave it back to me.' He feels his stomach churning.

'Ah, the wily Madeleine. Always two steps ahead of the game. Impossible not to admire her,' says Coleridge.

'How do you know Madeleine?' asks Starling.

'I know everything about everyone and Madeleine is no exception. What you don't know is that before Chittlock coerced you into joining his crusade, there was someone else. Another protégé. You were not his first.'

'What do you mean?'

'Madeleine was Chittlock's first experiment. He was a friend of her family and, after her parents met with a fatal accident – regrettably, caused by us – he offered her a way to exact revenge. He recruited her and trained her to be a spy.'

Starling is finding it hard to swallow what Coleridge has just told him. But what did he have to gain by lying? Besides, Madeleine's story was almost the same as his. He wonders why she never mentioned it.

Coleridge continues. 'As time went by, Tim started getting involved with all sorts of weird and wonderful things. The Stones of Fire was his pet project. Madeleine, however, betrayed him and sold his research and precious notebook to the Fellowship of Fire. Ultimately, that led to his death. So you could say Madeleine killed him.'

'You killed Timothy Chittlock. You and your ridiculous organisation.'

'Well, yes. But thanks to Madeleine…'

'You'll never get the shard now,' interrupts Starling.

'I wouldn't be so sure about that. She is following us right now in that little bi-plane of hers. She thinks we don't know but we do. Our scanners are keeping track of her. It is my guess that she will bring along the shard with the absurd notion that it will help defeat us. Except we will be waiting.'

'She's smarter than you think,' says Starling.

'Is she?' Coleridge responds, dryly.

Coleridge turns and walks towards the navigation desk, making it clear he has finished with them. 'Colonel, take them to a holding cell for now. Miss Black can deal with them when we reach Rome.'

'Yes, sir.' Frost marches them back through the machine room.

Starling looks at Anna with concern. She nods quietly, indicating she is fine, but he expects she is not. Even if you are trained to be shot at on a daily basis it is another matter to be defenceless and have a gun pointed at your head by an unpredictable psychopath acting under the orders of another unpredictable psychopath. They cross the bridge and the deck in silence and reach a small windowless cell at the rear of the ship.

They sit down on the only bit of furnishing: a hardwood bench. Starling's head reels with the revelations about Madeleine. 'Always two steps ahead of the game,' Coleridge had said, and he was right.

'Are you thinking about Madeleine?' asks Anna, interrupting his thoughts.

'Is it that obvious?'

'She's quite something. I'll give her that.'

'Yes. She is.'

'She has her price like all rogue spies.'

'Does she?' asks Starling, sceptically.

Anna looks at him with a quizzical expression. 'She stole the shard from you and has probably sold it to the highest bidder like she did with the Stones of Fire notebook.'

'She's not interested in money. Her parents left her with plenty.'

'It's because of her Timothy Chittlock is dead.'

'Maybe, but that was something she could not have foreseen.'

'What do you mean?'

Starling is lost in thought for a moment and thinks back over the past few days. Standing up, he begins to pace the cell. 'I can see it now.'

'See what?'

'Madeleine has been two steps ahead of the game. That's what Coleridge said and he is right. Damn it. Why did I not see it before?' Starling continues pacing as he remembers. He laughs and shakes his head.

'Will, you're worrying me!'

Sitting down he turns to Anna. 'A few days ago at Chartres Cathedral I met a liaison to pick up the microfilm. Her codename was Marie-Antoinette and she had been set up by the Owl to make the drop.'

'I know this. What is your point?'

'Indulge me. We escaped in Marie-Antoinette's car. Emile and I hid in the boot. There were painter's canvases inside. Emile…' He stops for a moment, sighs and closes his eyes. He recalls Emile's body jolting against his as he was shot and the image of Claudette in the passenger seat, her eye's lifeless and her neck pouring with blood. 'We didn't all make it.' He takes a deep breath and continues. 'Flying across the channel we were overtaken by a Tiger Moth. The same one that attacked this airship tonight.'

'I'm still confused.'

'Remember when we went to Chittlock's house alone?'

'Yes.'

'The painting on the wall of my bedroom – *The Menin Road* – with the red fusilier from another century painted on top and concealing the coded message underneath.'

'Are you saying she painted it?'

'She has a studio in Sebastian's garden, where she also stores weapons.'

Starling thinks of Milly, from the hairdresser's opposite Chittlock's. She had seemed familiar to him. Had Madeleine disguised herself as Milly? Of course! 'Things are becoming clear to me now, Anna. Marie-Antoinette, the pilot in the Tiger Moth, Milly from the beauty salon: they were all Madeleine.'

'That's ridiculous.'

'Is it?'

Anna furrows her brow, clearly doubting her own statement. 'Sounds like she's competing for the Owl's reputation as the man with a thousand faces.'

'How do we know the Owl is a man?' says Starling.

'You can't be serious!'

'The Owl's signature is an Egyptian owl. Edward told us it translates to M in the English alphabet. M for Marie-Antoinette. M for Milly. M for Madeleine. She has the perfect front already. Spoiled attention-seeking rich girl.'

'That's an understatement.'

'It's an act, Anna. Madeleine has had her parents taken from her in the most terrible of circumstances. She wants revenge, just like we do.'

'You seem quite taken with her.'

Starling looks away. 'She's following us and she has the shard. There's still a chance we can win this.'

'And what then? If we destroy this ship what's to stop them building another?'

'I don't know the answer to that.'

They sit in silence for a few moments listening to the sound of the engine's rhythmic chugging.

'We should try and get some sleep. We'll need all our strength tomorrow,' says Anna. 'This is far from over.'

Starling rests his head against the wall and closes his eyes. He tries to zone out, to think of other things, but all he can think about is the Tiger Moth out there, dipping in and out of the clouds and following them.

Chapter 44

The Hangman's Noose

Starling does not sleep. He sits with his eyes closed, mulling over the revelations and their current captured state. Any thoughts of breaking for freedom seem futile. Even if they could disarm the guards and find parachutes, escaping from an airship with a particle beam death ray and killer red gas is unlikely to be a resounding success. After two hours or so the cell door rattles. Both he and Anna sit up.

Frost's broad silhouette appears in the doorway. He is carrying a pistol. Starling shifts uneasily seeing the barrel pointing directly at him but, in spite of it, he is not frightened.

'Morning, Colonel. Must be odd being the jailer and not the prisoner. By the way how was your little sabbatical at His Majesty's pleasure? Did you have fun?'

'Shut up,' snarls Frost.

'I thought you might at least have sent a postcard.'

'Get up. Both of you.'

'It's a little early for breakfast. But that's fine. Bacon, eggs and hot buttered toast? Yum. I could do with a hot bath too. Could you arrange that? I'll make sure you get a generous tip.'

Starling can see his old foe gritting his teeth but, to his disappointment, Frost holds back and gestures for them to leave the cell. Starling can smell whisky as he passes the colonel. A guard is waiting outside but there's no sign of Thierry. Starling has an uneasy feeling and wonders where he could be. Glancing at his watch, he sees it is just after 3 am. Frost orders them forward through the gloom of the deck; the only light is from the moon and stars glittering from the viewing gallery outside. They walk through the grey doors and over the lattice bridge. A cold breeze pinches his skin. Beneath them he sees the slumbering Tesla Death Ray cannon.

From across the walkway, by the cannon's power source, a woman in horn-rimmed spectacles and a lab coat looks up nervously.

'Get on with your work and say nothing about this to anyone,' barks Frost, with a slur in his voice.

The woman pales, quickly picks up her clipboard and turns back to the machine.

Starling feels his shoulders tightening and glances at Anna, who is frowning back at him.

'Down there,' says Frost, pointing to a wooden stepladder at the right side of the bridge.

'What's going on, Frost?' says Starling.

'You'll find out. Get going!'

Starling goes down first, followed closely by Anna. They are in a side passage within touching distance of the cannon. The cold breeze is stronger here, as if powerful fans are pushing wind over the cannon. Looking around he sees no fans other than the two above the machine room which turn slowly. Anna rubs her arms to keep warm.

'I don't like this, Starling. He's drunk and is up to something,' she whispers.

'Agreed. If something happens I will take care of him. Can you deal with the other guard?'

As Frost climbs down the ladder, Anna nods a confirmation.

Starling looks at the cannon. He reaches across and places his fingers upon it. The cold mottled steel reminds him of scales; like dragon skin, he imagines.

Frost prods him with his pistol and nods towards the front of gondola. 'Down there, towards the light.'

White light is coming from an open door at the end of the passage. He and Anna make their way towards it. He wonders if he can destroy the death ray using the power source. Maybe the only way would be to destroy the entire ship from the inside… planting timed explosives maybe? His stomach flutters at the thought. He has no idea.

As he approaches the doorway the wind intensifies and he begins to understand why. He glances at Anna and swallows.

'Move!' barks Frost.

Starling stands at the doorway. The room contains the airship's tethering rope wound around an enormous metal pulley. At the centre of the room is a waist-high safety rail surrounding a hatch in the floor. The hatch is open to the cold night air. Gripping the rail is Horne, who smiles grimly at Starling. 'Do come in,' he says.

Starling notices Horne's knuckles are caked in dried blood. It is not his. Lying on his chest, bruised, shirtless, inches from the edge of the hatch is Thierry. His hands are bound behind his back and he looks up at Starling through eyes swollen like a boxer's, his nose and mouth bloody and almost unrecognisable. Starling hears Anna let out a sharp gasp but keeps his face blank. The Frenchman shivers, coughs and spits blood from his mouth.

'Disgusting,' says Horne, his face contorting.

Frost shoves Starling and Anna forward until they are both at the rail looking down at the vast darkness below.

'Somehow it doesn't seem out of character for you to beat up a defenceless man, Horne. Even one of your own. Bravo,' says Starling.

Horne's thin lips distort into a sneer. 'Except, he's not one of ours. Is he?'

Starling blinks. 'I don't know what you are talking about.'

'I found him snooping around,' says Frost. 'Looking for you two, I believe.'

'I have no idea who this man is,' says Starling.

'He's French for a start,' slurs Frost. 'We don't have many of them here. And he doesn't seem to know his rank or section. I believe that makes him an imposter, Starling, a stowaway – and a guilty one at that.'

Starling swallows.

'He must pay the price,' says Horne.

'You want to kill your own men, that is fine by me.' Pierced with guilt, Starling glances down at Thierry who looks back up at him, a desperate expression on his badly beaten face.

'I'm a fair man, Starling,' says Horne. 'You might not think it, but I do wholeheartedly believe in giving people a choice.' Horne crouches down and hauls Thierry to his knees, so that he's facing over the open hatch.

Starling holds his tongue.

Horne beckons at Anna. 'Come here, Anna, dear.'

'Why?'

Horne's face flushes with anger. 'Because I said so!' he screams.

'Move,' says Frost, nudging her along with his pistol.

Starling feels his spine icing over. He inches back and feels the second guard's pistol in the small of his back. *Just where I want you.*

Frost stands to the side of Thierry, his pistol trained on the Frenchman.

'What are you playing at Horne?' says Starling.

Horne stands behind Anna and raises his hands to her shoulders. Glancing at Starling, he moves his face to the side of her head, burying his face in her hair. He inhales slowly. 'I always enjoyed your scent, Anna. It's such a pity you made the wrong choice.'

Anna shrugs him off but Horne pushes her gently down so that she is kneeling next to Thierry at the edge of the trapdoor. She looks up at Starling and does not seem in any way frightened. If anything, she is angry.

With a flourish, Horne waves his arm above Anna and Thierry. 'You get to choose, Starling.'

Starling feels his pulse racing. In his mind he is calculating how he can take out the guard behind him, and Frost too, without risking a bullet hitting Anna or Thierry.

Horne reaches behind him and lifts the end of the tethering rope. Starling's stomach clenches. The rope has been tied into a hangman's noose.

'You get to choose who swings tonight.'

'You cannot be serious!' Starling glances at Frost, who is laughing at Horne, but at the same time seems unsteady on his feet. Thierry has shot him a sideways glance and notices also.

'Oh yes, I am,' says Horne. 'Who's it going to be?' He swings the noose over Anna. 'Your girlfriend.' He holds it over Thierry. 'Or the Frenchie?'

Starling frowns. 'I told you I don't know who he is.'

'Liar. Liar!' Horne swings the rope back and forth over their heads.

'Stop it, Horne. I want to talk to your uncle. Immediately!'

'Who's it going to be, Starling? You better choose quick or they both get it!'

'Stop it!'

'Choose, damn you!' screams Horne.

Starling sees the muscles on Thierry's bare shoulders tightening. He is looking at Starling and nodding at Frost. He's going to go for him. Not yet, thinks Starling. It's too soon.

'Choose!'

'The Frenchman! I choose the Frenchman.'

Thierry looks up at him in shock at hearing those words. A pang of guilt stabs at Starling.

'Of course you choose him, but it is the wrong choice,' says Horne. He places the noose over Anna's head. Starling nods at Thierry, who lunges at Frost. The colonel's whisky-addled brains have slowed his responses and give

Thierry a temporary advantage. Starling feels the second guard's gun move from his back but, before the guard can shoot Thierry, Starling reels around and snaps his wrist. The guard cries out in pain and the pistol falls to floor sliding through the hatch and out into the night. Starling launches two punches to the man's ribs and finishes him off with a hard uppercut. The guard stumbles backward and falls to the floor.

Horne is trying his best to tip Anna over the edge of the rail. She fights back, punching and kicking him but his eyes are wide, his expression deranged, and he does not seem to feel her blows.

Starling wraps his arms around Horne's neck and pulls him away. His nose wrinkles at the musty smell of unwashed hair forever marinated in stale oil. He crushes Horne's windpipe and, after a moment, feels his grip on Anna weakening. Thierry is raining kicks on the colonel, who has not yet managed to get up though he seems to be rallying. Starling feels Horne's body going limp. His head drops forward as he loses consciousness and Starling is relieved to see Anna get into a safer position. Relaxing his hold on Horne, Starling reaches for Anna. But something's not quite right. Horne is still standing. Starling hears him laugh as he lunges forward and shoves Anna. Crying out, she topples over the rail and falls through the hatch.

'Anna!' shouts Starling, but Horne cuts him off, slamming his elbow into his solar plexus. Starling gasps and crumples to the floor, his heart sinking. Horne begins to kick him and stamp at him, but the thought of Anna, her neck broken, body swinging below the ship fills him with a burning fury. He grabs Horne's foot as it swings towards his face. Holding it firm by the toe and heel Starling uses all his strength to twist the ankle. Horne cries out and yanks his foot away. Starling jumps to his feet and launches a kick Horne's chest. He spirals backwards with the force and tumbles over the pulley. Starling sees the guard has gone. He will return with back-up in minutes, no doubt.

His heart pumping, Starling crouches down, peers under the rail and through the hatch where he sees Anna clinging on to the edge by her fingers. Dawn is breaking and sunlight climbs over the horizon, lighting up green countryside scattered with houses below.

'I'm slipping,' she calls, her face pale and terrified.

Starling uses all his strength to pull her up hauling her on to the floor.

As Anna pulls the noose from her neck he sees Horne scramble from the pulley towards Frost's Browning, which has fallen to the floor behind Thierry.

'Behind you, Thierry!' calls Starling.

The Frenchman's head turns around, but Horne already has the pistol. Grinning, he fires twice at Thierry's broad back.

Two large holes seem to explode on Thierry's upper back. His face contorts and his legs wobble as he slumps forward falling on top of Frost.

Starling dives at Horne as the pistol turns towards him. He grabs his wrist with one hand, wrapping his other arm around Horne's head, gripping his ear and yanking it to the side. Horne lets out a muffled cry. Biting Starling's sleeved arm, Horne squeezes the trigger, firing off several shots as Starling battles to control his gun hand. Anna dives to the ground. Starling pulls Horne's arm to the right. More shots explode. Out of the corner of his eye Starling sees Frost rising. He slides his arm over Horne's eyes and swings the pistol in Frost's direction. The colonel's face is red with anger, but his eyes widen at the gun barrel pointing his way. Starling holds Horne's arms firm as he squeezes the trigger and pumps four bullets into the colonel's chest.

'That's it, Horne. Keep pressing the trigger,' says Starling, sliding his arm away from Horne's eyes.

Horne lets out a shrill cry as Frost stumbles backward, toppling over Thierry's body and falling dead to the floor. Starling feels Horne trembling and slams his gun hand on the rail three times, breaking the bones until he eventually drops it. The Browning falls through the hatch and disappears. Starling pushes Horne forward against the rail. Breathing heavily he recalls the moment he discovered what he was and what his destiny was to be.

Sleeper

'Anna, give me the rope,' he calls.

She picks it up, the noose dangling from her hands, and frowns at him.

'What are you going to do?' she asks.

Liberator

'Give me the rope, Anna.'

He snatches it from her and puts the noose over Horne's head, pulling it tight over his neck.

Executioner

Horne struggles to pull the rope off but Starling slams a fierce punch to his kidney.

'Aaaahh!' cries Horne, lurching and trembling.

'Will, stop! Don't do this. You're not like them,' says Anna.

Starling hesitates briefly but his rage feels so absolute.

'This is for Sam, the boy you murdered two years ago. This is for Thierry, a French hero you tied up and beat with your filthy paws and then shot in the back. This is for all the people you oppressed and bullied, you coward.'

Horne begins to howl and cry. 'Please no. I don't want to die. I'm sorry for everything. I won't do it again.'

'No, you won't,' says Starling, tipping him feet first over the rail.

Horne cries out as he falls but grabs the leg of the rail clinging half in and half out of the airship.

'Enough!' comes a voice. Standing at the doorway and dressed in a black suit, black shirt and tie, is the bald and tattooed Coleridge. Beside him are four armed guards, including the one who had escaped earlier. Coleridge scans the room, taking in the bodies of Frost and Thierry.

'Uncle! At last. Help me.'

'Move away from my nephew, Will,' says Coleridge.

Starling hesitates, but there are four guns pointing at him. He steps away from Horne. Coleridge walks into the room and crouches down, his arms reaching for Horne.

'Take hold of my hands.'

'Thank you, Uncle. Thank you.' Horne reaches across with one hand and then another. Coleridge grips his wrists. He stares hard into his nephew's eyes.

Horne's brow furrows. 'Pull me up, Uncle.'

'You are as weak and as stupid as your father,' spits Coleridge.

Horne shakes his head. 'Uncle, I'm sorry. I just wanted to teach them a lesson.'

'I have done all I can for you.'

Anna gasps as Coleridge releases the hold on his nephew. Horne barely has time to frown in confusion before he disappears through the hatch, screaming until the tethering rope goes taut and there is silence. The only sounds are the airship's engine, the breeze from the hatch and creak of the pulley as the rope swings back and forth.

Coleridge stands and turns to Starling, who shifts uneasily.

'Come with me,' he says, 'both of you.'

Starling and Anna exchange confused glances.

Coleridge addresses one of the guards. 'Have my nephew's body prepared for a full honours ceremony.'

Full honours for being a bully and a murderer. Such is the VIPER way. Starling recalls Anna's words: *You're not like them.* He shudders. But I am like them. I was about to kill Horne in the most brutal of ways. He follows Coleridge and Anna with the guns of the three other guards pointing at their backs. Climbing the ladder and crossing the bridge they enter the navigation room again. The captain is steering at the wheel and his second is manning the controls.

'We taught you well, Will. I have to tell you I do admire you, you know.'

'As much as you admired your nephew?'

'I wish he had been more like you.'

Starling narrows his eyes at Coleridge. His sudden flattery unnerves him. 'What do you want from me?'

'Very soon, you will be meeting the lady herself.' Coleridge pauses.

'And?' asks Starling.

'You should consider where your true allegiances lie.'

Starling laughs. 'Are you offering me a job?'

'Does that surprise you?'

'No. Nothing about VIPER surprises me.'

'We have a lot in common.'

Starling shakes his head. 'I despise you. All of you.'

'Do you? Really? I'm not sure I believe that.'

'You killed my parents. You kidnapped my sister. You murdered my friends.'

'That's all in the past. It's history. You need to think about your future.'

'All I can think about is killing you and wiping VIPER from the face of the planet.'

Coleridge gazes deeply into his eyes. 'The fire in your belly and the drive you have is quite remarkable. I see that now. We are making the world a better place, Will. A safer place. You could be part of that.'

Starling says nothing, too astonished and disbelieving to form words.

'Ironically, Will, you are one of our great success stories. Not only did we make you what you are, but you have something others don't. You survive against all the odds. We could use your skills. Think of what you could bring to the new world.'

'Sir. It is almost time,' interrupts the captain.

'Come to the window,' says Coleridge. 'I do think you will enjoy this.'

As they draw closer, framed in the navigator's window Starling sees a city rise up before them. It is a city steeped in history, with ancient ruins standing majestic among the red roofs of its houses: Rome, Italy's capital city. Was this their destination? Starling has no memory of having been here before, no signals or memories flash in his mind. His knowledge of the city is what he has read in books and seen in pictures. He recognises the Colosseum, the immense amphitheatre that was once the home to gladiatorial battles almost two thousand years ago. He sees the dome of the Pantheon and the grand piazzas of the city. He has an unsettling feeling about this. It is bad enough being prisoners of VIPER but to be taken to the capital city of a country which has firmly aligned itself with the Nazis is another thing altogether.

'A magnificent city, is it not?' asks Coleridge.

Starling does not respond.

The ship flies over the Tiber and turns towards the Vatican City, the smallest country in the world. Unlike Italy – and like Switzerland – the Vatican City, governed by Pope Pius XII, has remained neutral, refusing to align with either the Allies or Hitler, in order, the Pope says, to prevent the city being bombed.

The undamaged dome of St Peter's Basilica looms over the city and Starling is surprised by how close they are to it. The airship turns again and flies over St Peter's Square with its one hundred and forty statues of obscure saints.

'What are we doing here?' asks Starling.

'Just a demonstration,' replies Coleridge.

'Of what exactly?'

But before Coleridge can answer Starling feels his mouth dry. Dotted across the blue sky over Rome are dozens of airships with VIPER flags blowing in the wind beneath their gondolas. His eyes dart over them counting, eight, twelve, eighteen, twenty. More appear overhead and join the others in formation. Three sets of twelve: thirty-six airships. Starling feels Anna move close to him. He can sense her fear.

'Behold my fleet. Behold the Red Storm,' says Coleridge.

Chapter 45

The Red Tower

'You were correct, William. One airship might not fare well against an attack from Spitfires or Messerschmitts. However, a fleet of airships, each equipped with a particle beam death ray and red gas is quite another matter,' says Coleridge.

'Why do this?' says Anna. 'Why do you want to kill innocent people? The world is suffering enough with this damn war!'

'There is no question about that, Miss Wilder. Our cause has benefited enormously from the war and will continue to do so.'

'Your cause? You make it sound like some holy crusade,' says Anna.

'You might call it that. There is definitely something biblical and pure about genocide. Don't you think?'

'You're mad. All of you.'

Coleridge laughs to himself. 'Really? This is the second world war I have witnessed, Miss Wilder, and, once again, I have seen ordinary men rise to become megalomaniacs and cause untold destruction. I have no doubt this will not be the last world war in my lifetime. The Germans and the Americans are already developing atomic bombs. Either this war, or the next one, will see the end of the world. We cannot allow that to happen. The population of the world must reset itself. Many must die for the world to change.'

'And what then? VIPER take over?' asks Starling.

'VIPER, as we know it, will disband. A new world order will be established. The world will become a utopia once more.'

'Why not use your power and influence to work with world leaders and make a change for the better?' says Anna.

Coleridge snorts. 'And you have the nerve to call me mad.'

'One fleet against the rest of the world? What delusions of grandeur you have!' says Starling.

'Sir,' interrupts the captain, 'we are ready for Castle St Angelo.'

Coleridge does not respond to Starling's comment. Instead he turns to the captain. 'Take her down, Captain Smythe.'

'Yes, sir.'

The airship begins its descent towards a vast round tower surrounded by a wall, with a turret in each corner. There are men on the tower's expansive terrace signalling to the navigator under the watchful gaze of a large bronze statue of an angel sheathing his sword. Starling feels Coleridge's eyes upon him.

'There is a rather charming story associated with that statue of the Archangel Michael. Legend has it that in 590 AD Michael appeared on that very spot sheathing his sword as a sign that the plague was over. Many people died and the world changed. And here we are at the eve of a new dawn. I love the irony of it. That's why I chose this place.'

Starling is only half listening. His mind is reeling as the terms *genocide*, *plague*, *atomic bombs* and *biblical* echo in his head.

'Take them to the deck,' Coleridge says to the guards.

As they turn to leave Starling hears a voice from the communication speaker on the dashboard. 'VA1, you are clear to drop the ramp when ready.'

'Thank you, Red Tower. We'll be with you in five minutes.'

'Roger that.'

Starling feels his heart race. Glancing at Anna, he can see she has understood the significance of what they have just heard.

The castle below is the Red Tower. Somewhere inside it is his sister, Rose.

Chapter 46

Ophelia's Proposition

Starling watches the ramp as it is lowered slowly to the roof terrace of Castle St Angelo. The morning is bright and balmy and warm air caresses his face. Down on the terrace half a dozen men pull on the tethering rope, unaware that less than thirty minutes earlier the same rope had choked the life from the treacherous Rupert Van Horne. They hold it firmly as the base of the ramp comes to rest on the terrace floor.

Starling follows Coleridge down the ramp. Anna is behind him, with Coleridge's personal guards watching their backs. He looks up at the statue of the Archangel Michael. It is immense, much larger than it seemed from the airship. Despite not having any religious affiliations, he cannot help but offer up some sort of prayer. *If you did, in some way, put an end to the plague, then I could really do with some divine intervention to prevent a bloody disaster. Please.*

His thoughts turn to Madeleine and he wonders if she made it alive or if her plane was destroyed by one of the other airships. He hopes not. Looking up, he sees the other ships leave Rome's air space in almost single file. He wonders where they are going; they can't fly all the time. He approaches the end of the ramp.

'Is my sister here?' he asks.

After a moment's hesitation, Coleridge replies, 'Yes.'

'I want to see her.'

'You will.'

'When?'

'Soon.'

They leave the terrace and enter a narrow, dark stone staircase that takes them down to a balcony that runs all the way around the outer wall of the castle. They arrive at the steps to a courtyard containing another statue of an angel with bronze wings. Starling has an odd sensation of being watched and looks up to an open window with two wispy white curtains. He squints but can see no one.

'What is it?' asks Anna.

'I'm not sure. Just an odd feeling.'

'Are you alright?'

He nods and they carry on. Passing the angel statue, they enter a hallway with a wide well-trodden staircase that leads down to darkness.

'I'm afraid, Miss Wilder, this is where you leave us,' says Coleridge.

'No!' says Starling. 'She stays with me.'

'Miss Wilder will be in no danger. I can promise you that,' says Coleridge.

'I'll be fine, Will.'

'Where are you taking her?'

'To a suite of rooms we reserve for all our prisoners. The dungeons.'

Starling feels helpless as two of the guards usher Anna away at gunpoint.

'Come this way, Will, please.'

Starling watches until Anna disappears in the darkness. He is taken through a warren of corridors and rooms, some containing tall machines manned by boffin types, others with rows of desk where suited men and women work diligently. They emerge outdoors and cross a perimeter overlooking the Tiber and a bridge lined with statues of angels. Coleridge knocks upon a heavy wooden door. A guard appears and stands to attention when he recognises Coleridge. Starling hears opera coming from somewhere behind the guard. It is thunderous and dramatic and seems to be coming from behind a gilded door at the end of a short corridor. The smell of cigarettes tickles his nostrils. Coleridge knocks the golden door and enters, leaving Starling and the two guards outside. Moments later he returns and beckons them inside.

The room behind the door is a vast space with a glistening marble floor and walls painted with half-naked nymphs, cherubs and Roman generals. The walls must be thirty feet high with a vaulted ceiling covered in ornate golden plaster carvings surrounding several different frescoes and murals.

At the far left of the room is a gramophone player with a large brass flower-shaped horn. Morning sun pours through the open window and a golden desk is engulfed in a cloud of blue cigarette smoke. Lurking within it is a woman with blonde hair wearing a grey suit. She inhales on a cigarette, shoots two jets of smoke from her nose and stares out the window, seemingly lost in the music. Starling shifts uneasily as a scene from his past rolls like a movie reel in his mind. But it is not easy to see. It's like looking through a shattered mirror. He concentrates harder through the broken glass.

He can see her. She is there. He knows her. He has seen her before.

Ophelia Black.

Starling is standing in the rain amongst a sea of khaki green foot soldiers, agents and monks looking up at the landing bay at Schöllenen Gorge. It is a stage with speakers and a microphone. He sees Proatheris, Frost and faceless shadowy figures lurking in the dark behind Ophelia Black, who is bellowing at the crowd and using a fist to emphasise her points. Her audience cheers. They love her. They believe in her. They want what she wants. She is their queen. She is both beautiful and dangerous: a toxic combination.

Queen Ophelia, leader of the new world.

Starling rubs the side of his head and blinks twice. The music has stopped.

'Are you having a turn?' says Ophelia Black, sharply.

It takes a moment for Starling to gather himself.

Ophelia is standing by the gramophone player watching him through a haze of blue smoke.

'Where is my sister?' he asks, ignoring her question.

'The question you should be asking, Mr Starling, is why are you here?' The VIPER queen stands up, extinguishes her cigarette and immediately lights another. She walks from behind the desk and approaches him slowly, arms folded, red heels clicking on the marble. She stands an arm's length from him and studies his face as smoke engulfs him like an out of body spirit. Caught within her blue fog, he takes stock of her. Her straight blonde hair is flecked with grey streaks and is cut below the ears. Her eyes are ice blue with crow's feet that reach beyond her temples. She wears no make-up other than a slash of red lipstick to match her long nails and shoes.

'I had a son once. Took his own life. He was only sixteen. He had everything he could possibly want.' She draws on her cigarette and walks around him looking him up and down. 'Suicide is a curse among the men of my family. It claimed my grandfather, my father, my brother… my son.'

'It's hard to lose those you love to suicide, murder or kidnapping,' says Starling.

'Quite so, Mr Starling. But you adapt. You learn to live with that loss. You move on.'

'Do you?'

Black points her cigarette at him. 'Let me ask you this. Your parents, your sister, do you miss them?'

Starling blinks and turns away from her gaze.

'I thought not.'

Starling feels his muscles tightening. 'Of course I miss them,' he snaps.

'But how could you? You don't remember them. You are an amnesiac, Mr Starling. You have no memory of your parents or your sister. So let me ask that question again: why are you here?'

Starling can feel the heat rising inside him. He glances at Coleridge, who watches him closely with a half grin.

Sleeper. Liberator. Executioner.

Not only had VIPER taken his family away from him, they were also responsible for his amnesia. Deep inside, he never wanted to admit to himself that his memories of his parents and sister were next to none. They were shadows in his mind, ghosts, strangers, really. But for all that he couldn't see or remember, he could still feel; he knew what love was. He knew that his family had loved him and he had loved them. The raw emotion still existed inside him and, despite his being unable to equate it with memories like anyone else, he could still feel their presence and their loss. There was something beautiful about that, but also something terrible and sad. It drove him. It spurred him on.

Starling answers her question. 'I'm here to destroy you. To bring down VIPER. To prevent genocide. To bring my sister home. To avenge my family, my friends.'

'Pipe dreams, Mr Starling.'

'Not for much longer.'

Ophelia smiles drily, drops her cigarette to the floor and stabs the flame with the point of her red heel.

'Let me tell you why you are here.'

She returns to her desk to retrieve and light another cigarette.

'You came here for answers. You want to understand who you are and what your purpose is…'

Sleeper. Liberator. Executioner.

'I can help you with that, Mr Starling. I can provide you with a purpose that would make your parents and your sister proud.'

'Let me guess. You'd like me to join you?'

Her red lips part in a wide humourless smile and expel smoke at the same time.

'You were one of us before, albeit not on our side. You were an exemplary student. A leader. The youngest of your group and as tough as the older men and women you trained with.'

She is wasting her time. Starling feels nothing but contempt for her, Coleridge and everything they represent.

'We are on the verge of creating a new world. You could be part of that. You could lead an army. You could become admiral of my fleet. You can have your own country. Somewhere hot, perhaps? We... *I*... need people like you.' She smiles in an almost matriarchal and caring fashion, which he does not swallow.

'Give it some thought.' She turns to Coleridge. 'Is there any news of the French spy?'

'Her plane was spotted just outside Rome. She should be here soon.'

'I want that shard,' says Ophelia.

'I will make it happen, ma'am.'

'See that you do.' Turning back to Starling, she says, 'The ladies are all chasing after you, it seems, Mr Starling. Join us and I will spare the lives of your two women. Don't say I am not generous considering what you have cost us already.'

Before Starling can respond, there is a knock on the door.

Ophelia smiles darkly at Starling. 'I forgot to mention. We have a visitor for you. Someone who can perhaps persuade you.'

'Come in, Sofia,' she calls.

The door opens slowly inward and Starling sees the back of a short, round woman dressed in rustic clothes. She looks round, catches Ophelia's gazes and blanches.

'*Ciao, scusa*,' she says, nodding in a deferential manner. She eases something gently through the door: a battered wooden wheelchair with large black wheels. Someone is sitting on it. He can see long dark hair, neatly combed in a middle parting. Starling feels his skin erupt in goose bumps. The woman called Sofia turns the wheelchair around to face them.

Starling swallows. Sitting on the chair, dressed in a simple white dressing gown, is his sister.

An image slices through his mind, unsteadying him. He is in the park with Rose and a cricket ball is spinning in the air feet from his mother's head. Other people in the park are watching it and asking questions. His parents quickly gather up the picnic and Starling takes Rose by the hand and hurries away. Their lives had changed from that moment onward.

He blinks and takes stock of her. She looks different. She is thin, pale and… heavily pregnant.

'Rose… how?' Her swollen belly is a shock to him. His throat clenches and his eyes begin to sting. He presses his palm over his mouth and trembles inside. He stares at her for the longest time. How long he cannot be sure.

'Doesn't she look well?' Ophelia's words seem far away and hang in the air like a bad smell.

Rose does not seem to be aware he is here. She stares straight ahead, at nothing. Her mouth opens and drool dribbles from the side and runs down her chin. Sofia crouches by her side and wipes it away with her apron.

'*Bambina*,' she coos, fussing with Rose's dressing gown and fixing her hair.

'Sofia is her nurse and her handmaiden. She looks after her. Gives her everything she needs. Can't have any children of your own, isn't that right, Sofia?' says Ophelia.

Sofia nods once without looking at Ophelia. '*Si, Signora*,' she says quietly, her expression like stone.

'What have you done to her?' Starling says at last, his voice cracking.

'We've kept her alive,' says Coleridge.

'She's a danger to herself,' says Ophelia.

'She's… she's *pregnant*!' Starling can barely bring himself to say it. How could this have happened? Who could have done this to her?

He goes to crouch beside her and looks into her eyes. An image flashes in his mind. Rose with her kitten, Charlie, sitting beside him in the garden laughing. A happy time. Her eyes are blue, like his – but they seem older than her sixteen years. Much older.

'Rose. It's me… Will…' His throat feels parched, as if it has not been moistened in weeks. 'I found you at last.'

She does not respond.

He recalls the family photograph of him and Rose that Eoin had revealed two years back when he discovered the truth about his sister. In the picture Starling looked to be around fourteen years old, which would have made Rose eight. She had been smiling up at him and holding his hand with a firm grip. He takes her hand now, squeezing it gently.

'Rose, I've come for you. We can go home soon.'

But still she does not respond.

'Rose.'

She blinks once and a bubble of spittle appears in her mouth.

Starling bows his head and wipes tears from his eyes.

'We can help her get better,' says Ophelia.

'Help her? She's fucking pregnant!' he roars.

Ophelia's cigarette glows a fierce red as she sucks the nicotine into her bony body. 'If it eases your mind she is quite chaste and has not laid with any men. At least, not to my knowledge.'

Starling takes a moment to gather himself and stands up. 'What have you done to her?'

'We… artificially inseminated her.'

Starling shakes his head in disbelief. 'Why would you do that?'

'We want more like her. A new world is coming, Mr Starling.'

Starling exhales a deep breath and looks upward; his eyes roll unseeing over the frescoes and gold cornicing.

'She is sedated. Nothing more. It helps her sleep.'

'Why do this to her?'

'She is dangerous,' says Coleridge.

Starling's voice rises. 'How can she be dangerous? She is sixteen years old and she's pregnant!'

'She, like you, is another one of our success stories,' says Coleridge.

'Rose is powerful. More so than any of us every expected,' says Ophelia.

Starling looks from Ophelia to Coleridge. 'This is not about me, is it? It's about Rose. You are using me to manipulate her.'

'It's about both of you,' says Ophelia, 'but, more importantly, it is about the child she is carrying.'

Starling glances at Rose's pale face. 'What about it?'

'The seed is from another, just like her. The father was a remarkable but difficult young man. He could start fires by thinking about them. His power consumed him in the end and we lost control of him.'

'You killed him?'

'We did what we had to do. Regrettably he was a danger to himself and to us. Like Rose, he was the first generation of the Teleken Kinetic experiment. Sadly for him, his body was not equipped to deal with the power he was born with. The next generation will be different. Rose's baby will evolve. She will give birth to a god. A messiah for the new world.'

'You're mad! All of you.'

'I can assure you, Mr Starling. We are anything but mad.'

'What about Rose? What happens to her?'

'She is frail. However, assuming she survives the birth she will join us and help mother the child, until a more suitable replacement can be found.'

A cold terror overwhelms Starling. Rose is expendable. It is her child that is important to VIPER. Not Rose. Who else realised this?

'Why are the Russians looking for my sister?'

Ophelia snorts. 'Oh yes. They tried to buy her from us and now apparently they have sent a spy to steal her from us. Quite laughable, don't you think?'

'Hilarious,' bites Starling.

'Understand this, Mr Starling. We are preserving this world. We are taking it away from those who would destroy it. A new world. A new utopia.'

Starling crouches down beside Rose. His heart feels crushed at the thought he might lose her so soon after finding her.

'Join us, Will,' says Ophelia, using his first name as a means to soften him.

'No! You will never have me or my sister.'

Ophelia meets his gaze for a few long moments. 'I am not sure you have quite thought this through.'

Starling leans across and kisses Rose on the cheek. 'Don't give up on me, Rose,' he whispers.

'I'll ask you one more time,' says Ophelia.

'No.'

'As you wish.' She turns to the nurse. 'Take the rest of the day off, Sofia.'

The nurse shakes her head, rests her hand on her bosom and gestures at Rose with the other. '*Scusa, Signora*... Rose...?'

'...will be just fine. Please go home,' demands Ophelia.

Sofia hesitates and nods reluctantly. She then bends down to kiss Rose on the top of her head and scurries out of the room.

'We're ready for you now,' Ophelia calls, and, at the same time, Starling sees Coleridge gesture at the guards and hears the opening of a door. At the top end of the room is a door he had not noticed before, hidden within a mural depicting two large men carrying something on a stairwell. A figure emerges from the shadows behind it. Starling feels the hairs on his neck stand on end. Gliding towards them like a dark spectre is the Pastor.

Starling's muscles tighten; his hands curl into fists and he makes to run at the Pastor, but the guards deliver two swift punches to his ribs and twist his arms behind his back. Crippled with pain, Starling struggles to free himself but they are too strong.

The Pastor looks at him greedily with his one eye. His small tongue darts out and moistens his dry lips.

'Take her to her rooms, Pastor,' says Ophelia.

'Yes, mistress.'

'And be gentle with her.'

'Of course, mistress.'

Starling feels his stomach lurch. 'What are you thinking? You cannot leave her alone with that madman!'

The Pastor wheels Rose out of the room as Starling struggles against the guards.

'Stop!'

'Take him to the dungeons,' says Coleridge.

'Wait!' he calls as the guards drag him to the door.

'You had your chance, Mr Starling,' says Ophelia.

A third guard appears and pushes his way past. 'Ma'am,' he says breathlessly.

'Now is not a good time.'

'I'm sorry, ma'am. This is important. We have reports of an Allied airstrike heading to Rome.'

'How credible is this report?'

'Confirmed by our agents on the inside.'

Starling is dragged down the corridor before he can hear any more. He struggles to break free but two more guards grab his legs. There are too many. He thinks of Rose with the Pastor and his heart sinks, but his rage thunders through and he lets it simmer. They have not killed him yet.

Chapter 47

Prisoners

Starling is carried down flights of dark, cavernous stone stairs and tossed into a small cell secured with a heavy iron gate. One of the guards, an unshaven, thin faced, cross-eyed fellow, locks it with a rusty old key, deposits it in his jacket pocket and leaves with the other three. The cell is nothing but bare stone with a filthy cot for a bed.

'Will, is that you?' says Anna's voice.

Looking through the bars he makes out a similar cell opposite with Anna inside. 'Yes. How are you?'

'I'm fine. What about you?'

He says nothing for a moment. 'She's here, Anna. I saw her.'

'Rose?'

Starling leans his forehead on the bars. 'Yes. They've done terrible things to her.'

'Did you talk to her?'

'They've drugged her. She wasn't even aware I was there... and she's pregnant, Anna. They...' but he cannot finish his words.

'I'm so sorry, Will.'

He shakes his head, his rage simmering inside. 'We have to get out of here.'

'I've tried forcing this lock, but it's too strong. They took all my tools on the airship.'

'Mine too. Except for one.' Starling lifts the collar of his jacket and slips out the flexible saw that runs the length of it.

'Clever you!' says Anna.

'Thank you, Thierry,' he whispers, then, 'Anna, keep an eye on the stairwell while I try and cut through this lock.'

'Right.'

With one hand outside and one inside the bars, Starling begins to saw back and forth against the bolt. The teeth are jagged and sharp and seem to be sawing through. Twenty minutes later, his fingers are raw and his brow is coated in sweat. He removes his jacket and hears Anna call his name.

'Someone's coming,' she says.

He hears footsteps approaching. Quickly, he hides the saw under the mattress and lies on top of it with his hands behind his head, affecting a relaxed look. His eyes narrow in on the floor beneath the lock. There is a small pile of dust, the remains of the half-sawn bolt. He swallows and looks up as the cross-eyed guard appears looking in on him with a suspicious stare.

'Good afternoon,' says Starling, politely.

The guard growls something incomprehensible and turns towards Anna's cell. She is perched on the edge of the bed and rubs her arms. 'Hello. It's very chilly in here. May I borrow your jacket?' she says silkily, with a warm smile.

The guard hesitates, removes his helmet and sweeps back his thinning dark hair. Was he considering her offer? Anna bites her lip and cocks her head.

Starling watches, hoping and praying that her ruse works. Once the guard sets foot inside that cell it will be the last thing he does. He moves closer. Starling sits up, his eyes widening.

'Mario!' comes a voice.

The guard curses under his breath and places his helmet back on his head. He seems unsure what to do and lingers near Anna's gate.

'MARIO!' calls the voice, once more.

'*Merda!*' says Mario as he turns to leave.

'*Ciao*, Mario,' says Anna, softly.

He stops to look back at her and waves delicately with his fingers. '*Ciao, bella.*'

Anna looks at Starling and shrugs. 'It was worth a try.'

Starling continues sawing at the bolt, putting everything he has into cutting through the thick iron lock. An hour passes and sweat drips down his brow and over his nose, but he is making progress; the lock is weakening.

'Someone's coming,' says Anna again.

'Shit!' says Starling under his breath. He is so close. He blows the grainy dust from around the bars and leans against the wall with his arms folded.

The guard called Mario arrives with a friend in tow: another guard, a large man with jowly cheeks and greasy skin. Mario shoots a withering look at

Starling before turning his attention to Anna. '*Ciao, bella,*' he says, removing his helmet.

Starling rolls his eyes.

'*Ciao*, Mario,' says Anna, glancing at Starling. She offers them a welcome smile and they move closer to her cell gate, jabbering to each other in Italian that is too fast to comprehend.

Anna keeps the guards occupied with flirtation and flattery. As the men grow louder and start to compete for Anna's attention, Starling decides to take a risk. He starts to saw slowly at the lock, his eyes never leaving the two men. Anna laughs loudly at every joke and inane comment, drowning out the noise of the slow strokes. The jowly guard reaches through the gate and tries to touch her. She bats his hand away softly and teasingly, but the mood changes. Starling frowns as the man starts to rattle the gate.

Mario shoves his friend's arm. '*Arresto*, Lorenzo!' But Lorenzo shoves him to the floor, pulls a key from his jacket pocket and begins to unlock Anna's gate.

'Lorenzo!' cries Mario.

Starling begins to saw faster. He is almost all the way through; the bolt is weakened and he begins to push at the gate. After the third attempt the gate gives way and he storms towards a confused-looking Mario, who is rising from the floor. With one swift hard punch, Starling knocks him unconscious.

'You took your time,' says Anna. She is standing at the gate of her cell, arms folded. The jowly Lorenzo is lying in a heap, face down, half on, half off her cot. Like his friend Mario, he is unconscious.

'He didn't get very far,' says Starling.

'The big ones are always the easiest to topple.'

'We can use their uniforms as disguises. A small blessing.'

An alarm begins to clang, echoing loudly throughout the castle.

'That can't be because of us, can it?' asks Anna.

Starling looks around for signs of something that might have raised the alarm: a broken wire, a hidden microphone, anything. But there is nothing.

Anna hurries to the steps and looks out. 'There are lots of people running around like headless chickens,' she reports.

Starling pulls Lorenzo off the bed, removes his helmet and begins to unbutton his jacket. 'There's something else going on. Just before I was brought here I heard a guard tell Coleridge that an Allied airstrike was on its way to Rome.'

'So, this might be an evacuation?'

'Or a call to arms.'

Anna removes Mario's jacket, puts it on over her clothes and tucks her hair inside his helmet.

'We have to find Rose,' says Starling.

Anna nods, pulling the visor of her helmet down slightly to maximise her disguise. 'Top priority.'

They pull the two guards into Anna's cell, lock it and toss the key into the shadows of Starling's. Side by side they hurry up the vaulted stone steps, passing monks and guards who do not give them a second glance. As they reach the top of the stairs Ophelia Black's voice fills the air from speakers dotted along the hallways to the left and right. Everyone stops to listen.

'War is upon us. The enemy approaches. This is the eve of the new world!'

A cheer erupts around the castle from the guards and monks.

'We have been preparing for this for ten years. Our time has come. Your time has come. Evacuate the Red Tower and go to your designated ships. Destroy the enemy and bring down Rome!' Ophelia raises her voice. 'MANY MUST DIE FOR THE WORLD TO CHANGE!'

The crowd cheers once more but their voices are soon drowned out by a siren that fills the air. From outside, Starling can hear the drone of bombers and fighter planes. He meets Anna's gaze.

'Here we go again,' she says.

'Fun times.'

'We should split up. We can cover more ground.'

'Good idea,' says Starling. 'Stay safe.'

'You, too.'

Anna takes the left turn and runs off into the crowd. Starling goes right and quickly threads his own way through the throng.

Chapter 48

Rose and the Pastor

Starling sees the figure of a roundish woman pushing her way against the tide of people. It is Rose's nurse, Sofia. She isn't leaving the castle; she must be going for Rose.

'Sofia!' he calls, but she does not hear. He pushes through the crowd and calls again. 'Sofia, wait!'

The woman stops and turns, her eyes searching the crowd. Starling waves his arms and she sees him. Her face drops and she turns and runs, ducking into the crowd.

'Damn it!' He is wearing the helmet. But then, if he wasn't, would she trust him? He fights his way after her through the rising tide of evacuees, recognising the dark narrow stairwell leading up to the courtyard of the angel with the bronze wings. The bright blue afternoon sky is dotted with several airships, floating in a predatory circle.

A guard hurries past and Starling grabs him by the neck, pulling him behind the angel's plinth. He struggles but Starling slams his fist into his stomach. 'Rose Starling. Where is she?' he says.

The guard reaches for the pistol at his belt but Starling snatches it and shoves the gun into the man's mouth, chipping his front teeth. 'Where is she?' he shouts, forcing the barrel down his throat. The man's eyes begin to water and he starts to choke. He lifts his arms in a conciliatory gesture. Starling pulls out the barrel but keeps it firmly pointed at his head. The guard catches his breath and points upward. Starling sees only the walls of the castle beyond the statue. Overhead he hears the rattle of Spitfire guns. He pulls the guard out into the centre of the courtyard. 'Show me!'

The guard points to a window where two white curtains are drawn. Starling had noticed it that morning on his way to see Ophelia. Was Rose behind those curtains? He looks at the guard, who seems terrified and eager to get away. A rare sense of mercy grips Starling and he motions for the man to leave. The guard's eyes widen in surprise. He raises his arms and steps back.

Starling turns towards the steps leading away from the courtyard; however, out of the corner of his eye, he sees a movement and, looking around, sees a knife spinning towards him, thrown by the treacherous guard. He ducks and it clangs off the wall to his left. The guard turns to run but Starling has already squeezed the trigger and a bullet explodes in the man's neck.

Regretting his mercy, Starling does not hang around. He hurries up the steps and halts at the roar of a klaxon overhead. Above, the oppressive shadow of an airship falls as it unleashes a red death ray that lashes across the sky and slices through two Spitfires. The planes break apart, collide and explode. Their remains tumble through the air and into the Tiber below.

With his heart in his mouth, Starling runs up the steps taking two at a time. He races through a doorway and up a stairwell. At the top is the door to what looks like an apartment. There are two dead guards lying on the floor: one has been shot in the head, the other's throat has been sliced open. It seems this could be the recognisable work of his old enemy, the Pastor, or the Russian agent, Pyotr Sedova.

With a firm grip on his pistol, Starling steps cautiously into the room. It is a small lounge with a sofa and a wooden table. Oddly, there are glassless windows overlooking the city. He sees plumes of black smoke rising above the rooftops and turns at the sound of whimpering, coming from a half-open door.

'Rose?'

Peering round the door, he sees Rose's wheelchair overturned, the rattan seat twisted and broken on the floor. Pushing the door open he sees a bed at the top of the room. Sitting on the floor, and crying into her hands, is Sofia. Starling takes off the helmet. There is no sign of Rose anywhere.

'Sofia,' he calls softly.

The nurse looks up slowly. Her lip is swollen and cut, her face is puffy, her eyes red and filled with tears.

'Where is Rose?' he asks in Italian.

Her bottom lip quivers and she seems confused about who he is. He crouches down in front of her. 'Rose is my sister, Sofia. I only want to help her.'

The woman seems terrified, but after a moment she points towards the ceiling.

'The roof terrace?'

The nursemaid nods. 'Please help her,' she says gripping his arm.

'I will. Thank you, Sofia.' He races out of the bedroom, hops over the dead guards and takes the steps leading to the terrace. Outside, the heat smacks his face and the smell of cordite invades his nostrils. A war is raging in the sky. The Allied strike force is outnumbered by the VIPER airships and is losing the battle.

Starling sees the Pastor standing with his arm raised, a blade held tightly in his hand. Backing away from him on unsteady feet is Rose. Barefoot and dressed in a white nightdress, she cradles her belly with one hand and holds a limp and lifeless cat in the other.

Charlie.

Rose is staring at the Pastor intently, her teeth clenched, her long dark hair wet and hanging like curtains over her pale face. The Pastor cannot move. He is trying but she is preventing him, keeping him at bay with the force of her mind.

'Rose,' says Starling.

Her eyes flicker for a moment and she turns slowly to look in his direction.

Starling feels a tightening in his throat as their eyes meet.

Rose's eyes widen. Her lips begin to move. She tries to speak, but her voice is hoarse. Reading her lips he can see she is saying his name.

'Yes. It's me. Will.'

Her face contorts in pain suddenly and she doubles over. Starling hears a splashing sound as her waters break and pool around her bare feet. At that same moment her hold on the Pastor loosens and his glittering knife sweeps towards her.

'No!' cries Starling. Swinging the pistol, he fires at the Pastor as his knife slices Rose's shoulder. Through the sight of the pistol, Starling sees the Pastor fall as the bullet skims the back of his head, spraying blood over the terrace floor. He stumbles to the ground, trembling.

Starling runs to Rose, whose breathing has become shallow and rapid. His heart pounds with fear and he catches her as she falls. Laying her on the cool tiles, he places his pistol down and wipes her hair from her hot brow.

'Will, is it really you?'

'Yes. I've come for you at last.'

'I don't understand.'

'Don't try to. We have to get you out of here.'

'My baby, Will. Look after it for me.'

Starling shudders. 'Don't talk like that, Rose.' He straightens his back and slips his hands underneath her, preparing to lift her up, but she cries out as a contraction hits her. He lays her down. 'Rose…' But before he finishes he is wrenched back by the hair and a savage punch is launched at his kidney. He gasps and falls to the ground. Looming over him is the pale one-eyed face of the Pastor.

He kicks Starling in the ribs and stamps on his hips. Starling tries to roll away but is weakened by the holy man's brutality. The Pastor crouches down to pick something up. Smiling, he holds up the cut-throat razor. He kneels behind Starling's head and pulls his chin up, exposing his neck. Starling tries to wiggle away but he is weak. He sees the hungry grin and madness in the holy man's one remaining eye.

The blade comes down.

Starling tries to break free but suddenly the Pastor disappears as if sucked away by a vacuum. He hears the crunch of bone and looks back to see the Pastor lying face down by the terrace wall. Rose is standing now and staring with ferocious concentration. She looks towards the statue of the Archangel Michael. Starling watches in awe as the bronze sword arm of the statue turns its blade outwards. Rose looks to the Pastor and he begins to tremble. Within seconds his body flies across the terrace and impales itself on the sword. The Pastor screams as he looks down at the sword sticking out from his chest. Blood fills his mouth and his body goes limp as his cruel and evil life ends.

Rose stumbles forward and Starling rushes to her side.

'Will,' calls Anna.

He looks up to see Anna and Sofia standing at the terrace doorway.

'Help me,' he calls.

'*Bambina!*' shouts Sofia, rushing across the terrace and performing the sign of the cross.

The three of them carry Rose down the steps.

'Ophelia is still here,' says Anna.

'How do you know?'

'I overheard her guards talking. She's sent a search party for Rose and is planning to board her airship in the next fifteen minutes.'

'She'll be leaving from the top of the castle.'

'That's my guess.'

'We have to get Rose out of here.' An idea forms in Starling's head. He turns to the nurse. 'Sofia, is there a way to get Rose out of here without being seen by Ophelia and her guards.'

'*Si*,' she replies, nodding her head.

'Then please take her.'

'*Si, Signore.*'

'Anna, go with them and protect them.'

Anna nods. 'What about you?'

Starling hands the pistol across to Anna. 'I'm not finished here, and someone needs to look after Rose.'

'I understand.'

Rose's body shudders and she cries out again.

'She needs a doctor.'

Anna takes Starling by the arm, leans across and kisses him softly on the lips. She sweeps his hair back and looks at him closely in the eyes. 'I'm sorry,' she says.

'For what?'

She looks away and does not respond, then takes one of Rose's arms, helping her down the stairs.

Starling watches them leave, confused by Anna's parting words. Sorry for what? Clifford Meadows? He doesn't quite understand.

Chapter 49

Carpe Diem

Starling returns to Rose's apartment, picks up the helmet and hurries back down towards the courtyard of the angel. As he reaches the top steps he hears Ophelia's voice and dips out of sight behind a corner wall.

'Keep looking. She can't be far, for heaven's sake!'

He sees her marching up the steps with plumes of blue cigarette smoke following her. Caught within the smoke are Coléridge, two guards and two monks. A shadow appears over the courtyard. Ophelia's airship descends towards the roof terrace. The mouth of the viper is open and the cannon has been released and primed.

As they hurry towards the terrace Starling emerges from the corner, but pulls back when he sees a hooded monk appear from the entrance below the steps of the courtyard. He seems shorter than most other monks and is carrying a shoulder bag and looking up towards the airship. He begins to sprint up the steps running towards the terrace. As he passes, Starling gets a whiff of something familiar, something… exotic. He catches up with the monk and walks alongside him. The monk slows and glances sideways.

'Is it common practice for the Cerastes to spray themselves with Soir de Paris?' asks Starling.

The monk stops and looks at him under the cover of the hood. 'Hello, stranger,' says Madeleine.

'Have you joined the Cerastes?'

She pulls her hood back slightly so that only he can see her face. 'Not quite.' She smiles. 'I am so pleased to see you. I thought you were dead.'

'I'm still here.'

'Did you find your sister?'

'Yes. She's in good hands.'

'I am so happy for you, Will.'

'Are you going where I think you are going?' He nods upwards at the airship.

'Yes,' she says, her smile fading. 'You should leave while you still can.'

'What's in the bag?'

'Gelignite.'

'And the shard?'

Madeleine loosens the buttons on her robe and pulls out the stone, which is wrapped in copper wire attached to a gold chain around her neck.

'Good. Let's go,' he says, hurrying up the steps.

'Wait. You cannot go.'

'Why?'

'Because I expect when I go up I will never come back. This is a suicide mission.'

'I realise that.'

'So go home. Have a nice life.'

'Why don't you give me the explosives and the shard and then you go home and have a nice life? Go help your uncle. He needs you.'

Madeleine exhales quickly. 'He's still alive then?'

'Very much so.'

Madeleine smiles and sighs. 'Thank God. I was so worried.'

'So go home. Help him. The war is not over yet.'

Madeleine shakes her head. 'No. Too many of my friends and family have died because of VIPER. I must finish this.'

'As you know, they have taken almost everything from me. Two heads are better than one. We do this together, Madeleine. If we both die, so be it.'

She meets his gaze and smiles. 'Carpe diem.'

'Carpe diem.'

'For France.'

'For humanity,' says Starling.

'For humanity.' Madeleine pulls up her hood and together they hurry up the steps.

'What's your plan?' asks Starling.

'Not quite sure of that yet.'

'I have something in mind.'

'Good.'

Chapter 50

Countdown

Starling and Madeleine reach the terrace and see the guards and monks hurrying up the airship's ramp behind Coleridge and Ophelia.

Starling quickens his pace, and as he steps on to the ramp he glances back at the limp corpse of the Pastor impaled and bloody on the Archangel Michael's sword. The irony was not lost on him. In the Bible, Michael leads God's army against the forces of evil. If he was a superstitious man he would see the Pastor's death as some sort of sign. But he is not. He carries on and keeps his head down, avoiding the eyes of any that might recognise him.

As he reaches the deck he hears a guard shout, 'Raise the ramp!' The ramp is pulled up, and Starling and Madeleine line up side-by-side with the other guards and monks as Ophelia and Coleridge walk towards the navigation room.

Ophelia is angry. 'I don't care that you have not found her. Radio whoever is down there and have them search every corner and turn over every stone. If Starling has her they won't get far. He will take her to hospital rather than risk the journey out of the city. If the Russians have her, then that's the end of that!'

Coleridge responds but they are already out of earshot.

The guards and monks begin to disperse. Starling shoots a look at Madeleine and signals across the deck at the yellow barrels of gas. Glancing around, he checks no one is watching them with suspicion. Everyone is going about their duties. Starling makes his way across with Madeleine following. Behind the barrels and out of sight, he points at the grey doors with the two sentinel monks.

'That's where we need to get to. The power source is there and beyond it is the navigation room. We just have to get past those two guards.'

'Take one of these,' says Madeleine, handing across a Beretta pistol.

Starling takes it and slides it under his belt in the small of his back. 'Thank you. But I was thinking of something more subtle.'

The grey door opens and a machine operator walks through to the deck. It is the woman in the horn-rimmed spectacles and lab coat. She is carrying four large files with both hands.

'I think we've found our ticket inside. Follow me.' Starling hurries after the machine operator. 'Can I help you with those?'

She looks at him suspiciously, but he smiles sweetly. The woman relaxes, nods her head and hands them across. 'Thank you. They are rather heavy.' She leads him out of the deck and into a corridor with views over the city. 'I must powder my nose. Would you mind?'

'Not at all. I'll wait.'

She disappears into the ladies' room, followed moments later by Madeleine.

The gondola shudders as the airship rises and turns. Starling sees the city below veiled in billowing clouds of black smoke and its people running for shelter from the apocalyptic skies above.

Madeleine appears at the entrance to the ladies' room. Her dark hair is swept back and she is wearing the lab coat and horn-rimmed spectacles. She beckons him across and takes one of the files from him. She removes the printouts from inside and shoves them into a bin by the toilet door, replacing them with six sticks of gelignite.

'Ready?' says Starling.

She nods and they make their way back across the deck towards the grey doors.

An alarm begins to sound and red lights fixed to the ceiling begin to flash. Starling's muscles tighten and Madeleine looks worried. Have they been caught out?

A voice comes over the tannoy. 'Cannon engaged. Five-minute countdown. Ensure you are all at your stations.'

Starling relaxes and follows Madeleine to the grey doors. The sentinels watch them as they approach. Madeleine begins to babble. 'Hurry,' she says to Starling, in a shrill loud voice. 'We only have five minutes and the machine room need these printouts.'

The sentinel on the right steps in front of the door blocking their path. 'I don't recognise you,' he says to Madeleine.

'She's a science officer on loan from another ship,' says Starling.

'And?'

Madeleine interjects, 'Please remove yourself from the doorway. We must deliver these printouts immediately. The machine operators need these codes before the cannon is fired.'

'Show me your papers.'

'We are at war, minutes from firing the cannon without the correct codes and you wish to see my papers?' She pushes her face up to his. 'Ophelia Black personally selected me for this ship. Just consider how angry she will be when the cannon fires with the wrong codes. It may strike one of our own airships. How will you explain that to her?'

The sentinel's brows knit together briefly as he considers his options. After a moment he steps aside to let them through. Madeleine glares at him as he opens the grey doors. Passing through Starling feels the familiar warm blast of steam on his face and hears the mechanical whooshing from two giant fans in the ceiling above them. They make their way across the steel bridge.

'How did you know about the codes?' he asks.

'I made a copy of the microfilm I gave you.'

'Ah yes, the uptight Parisian agent codenamed Marie-Antoinette.'

She regards him with a wry smile. 'Of course. After leaving London I travelled to Lyon where Eoin and I worked hard to interpret the schematic. We were in constant touch with your friend, Edward.'

'Good old Edward.' The mention of Chartres turns his thoughts to his friends. 'Madeleine, my friends Emile and Claudette…' Starling lets the sentence hang. The painful reminder of his dead friends scuppers his train of thought.

'I took them to the local priest. He will see that they get the burial they deserve.'

'Thank you.'

'You do realise we only have one shard and enough explosive to blow *this* ship.'

'Yes, I do. However, I have seen what the shard is capable of. If we do this properly we might just take out more than one.'

'How?'

'I don't know yet.'

Midway across the bridge Starling hears voices, but there seems to be no one in the machine room. Looking down he sees the Tesla cannon surrounded by men in dirty overalls shouting at each other as they prepare the weapon for battle. Turning left, he follows Madeleine across the walkway and up the steps to the bank of machines and the tall pyramidal shaft with its glowing glass sphere on top. A man writing on a clipboard appears from behind it. He frowns. 'Who are you?'

Starling hears the unmistakable *phut* of a silencer pistol. The man topples forward. Madeleine catches him and eases him to the floor. Starling glances around hoping no prying eyes have suddenly appeared. His heart racing, he helps Madeleine drag the man behind the machines and out of sight.

The tannoy crackles. 'Three minutes!' a voice calls. Starling looks down and sees the men under the bridge working faster around the cannon.

'We have to hurry,' he says.

Madeleine slips behind the power source. Starling joins her with the gelignite, watching as she undoes the catches of a panel. She places it on the floor and a blast of scorching heat and blinding green light assaults their faces and eyes. Madeleine takes the explosives and retrieves a Time Pencil from her pocket. She removes the shard from around her neck and ties it with the chain around the explosives. Blue sparks surround her hand. The shard can feel the Tesla power source.

'Three minutes?' she asks, her face pale.

Starling nods his agreement.

Cautiously, she cracks the glass vial, releasing the Time Pencil's acid and inserting it into the soft gelignite. She then places the explosive inside the power source and fixes the panel back on.

'Now what?' she asks.

'This is Ophelia's ship. Arguably the most important. We need it to go rogue.'

'How?'

'We need control of the navigation room first. We do whatever it takes to get that.'

The tannoy crackles once more. 'One minute.'

As they hurry down the steps Starling notices the men are no longer by the cannon. Running over the bridge they slow as the navigation room door slides open and Coleridge walks through. Starling can see Ophelia standing with the captain watching the war in the skies outside.

'Frith!' calls Coleridge. 'What the hell is keeping those figures?'

Starling dips his head as Coleridge approaches.

'Mr Frith!' Coleridge steps onto the bridge and walks down towards the machine room.

Madeleine eases past him. Beneath the bridge the bottom doors of the gondola open. Cool air rushes in. Starling can feel Coleridge's eyes on him.

'One moment,' says Coleridge. His hand reaches across to Starling pushing up his chin. Their eyes meet.

'Starling!' he hisses angrily.

Chapter 51

The Rogue Airship

Starling launches a punch at Coleridge's face but it is deflected, and Coleridge tries to push Starling over the rail. 'Guards!' he calls, his hands clawing at Starling's face.

Starling turns away from the raking fingers and gasps at the long drop to the Vatican City and St Peter's Basilica below. Madeleine is engaged in a gun battle with the captain and his second. Ophelia is nowhere to be seen. Starling pushes harder and, clenching his teeth, he kicks at Coleridge's shins. The older man shifts his leg and Starling is able to slam his knee into his balls. Starling feels his body shuddering. Taking his chance, Starling head butts Coleridge in the nose. It makes a sickening crunch and blood explodes across his face. Coleridge is finished. Starling grabs the lapels of his suit and flips him over the rail. Coleridge's eyes and mouth widen in disbelief as he plunges, arms and legs flailing, towards the ground.

'Hurry, Will,' says Madeleine.

Looking up, Starling sees the captain lying dead and his second nursing a bloody wound in his stomach. Madeleine is thankfully unhurt. The sound of the klaxon reverberates around the bridge forcing them both to cover their ears. They hurry to the navigation room and find Ophelia waiting. She is clutching Starling's Mauser with one trembling hand; in the other is a cigarette, which she sucks at greedily.

Out of the corner of his eye Starling sees Madeleine raise her pistol.

'You are too late,' says Ophelia. 'We are many. We...'

Madeleine squeezes the trigger. The shot blows a hole in the VIPER queen's scrawny throat. Her eyes widen and her jaw begins to moves up and down, as if she is trying to finish her statement. Blood and smoke ooze from the hole and then she collapses, her eyes dead, her twisted life gone forever.

'VA1, this is VA12. What are your orders?' a voice comes over the speaker.

Starling picks up the receiver. 'All ships. Ophelia Black is dead. VA1 is going rogue. Destroy VA1 immediately. Repeat, destroy VA1.'

Starling stares at the large red button on the navigator's control panel. He slams his palm on it. The cannon fires. The beam lashes wildly across the sky and connects with an airship. The ship erupts instantly in a blinding ball of flames.

'What the hell?' shouts a voice over the radio. 'VA1, what is going on?'

'Stand back,' says Starling. Taking out his pistol he fires it at the button, blowing it from the control panel. He looks at Madeleine. 'Time for us to abandon ship.'

'But how? Lifeboats are hardly an option.'

'There's still hope. Come on.' Starling sprints out of the navigation room with Madeleine behind him. Below them, the cannon lashes its fiery green death ray across the skies. They run through the grey doors and past the sentinels. Midway across the deck Starling glances behind him. The sentinels are checking through the doors.

'Quick!' he shouts, heading towards one of the sliding windows that run from floor to ceiling on either side of the deck. He pulls it across and steps out onto the slatted wooden balcony with the angled windows that overlook the world below. At the base of each window is a red roll of material – the ribbons that, together, combine to make the VIPER flag.

From the balcony Starling can see the airship passing over St Peter's Basilica and the dome below. He looks at Madeleine. 'Ready?'

She nods. 'Let's do it.'

Starling opens the window and pushes a red roll outside. It is heavy, the material thick and strong. It tumbles through the air and flutters in the wind below the airship. Madeleine climbs out first, followed by Starling. They scurry down the red ribbon as the airship rises above St Peter's. He sees the dome approaching but the ribbon does not stretch quite far enough.

'Now!' he shouts as the ribbon floats above the immense dome. There is perhaps a ten-foot drop. But the airship continues to rise. 'Drop now!'

Madeleine lets go and falls and Starling swings towards the dome. Terrified, he scrambles to grab on to something as his body slams the surface of the roof and slides over the dome, tumbling to the base where he flips over and manages to grab the ledge. His heart racing, his face damp with perspiration, he clings on hard. Glancing down he sees a further twenty-foot drop to the rooftop below where Madeleine lies – unconscious or dead, he cannot be sure. 'Madeleine!' he calls, but she does not respond.

He sees a column to his right and, holding tight, climbs across like a monkey on a thin branch. Wrapping his legs around the column he shimmies down it and onto a rooftop with statues of saints overlooking St Peter's Square.

He kneels by Madeleine's side and leans close. She is still breathing. Her eyes flicker open and meet his. 'Did we do it?'

He looks up towards the skies. All thirty-six airships are surrounding VA1 whose cannon continues to fire indiscriminately. The sound of half a dozen klaxons fills the air around Rome. And then Starling watches as Ophelia's ship is surrounded by an unearthly blue light. *The shard's power is growing.*

The other ships launch their cannon fire on Ophelia's ship, but somehow the vessel remains undamaged. *The shard is working.*

And then Ophelia's ship blows from the inside with a roaring echoing boom that makes the rooftop quake and the statues around St Peter's square tremble. A bright blue flame swirls out from the remains of the airship and spreads across the skies destroying anything and everything that flies there. Raising his hand to stave off the glare, Starling watches in wonder as Ophelia's fleet, the Red Storm, is reduced to ashes, its deadly gas neutralised by the blue shard.

'We did it,' says Madeleine, pushing herself up with some difficulty.

'How are you feeling?'

'My head is sore. I don't think anything is broken.'

Looking up at the sky Starling can't quite believe what has just happened. VIPER is finished. The Red Storm is now nothing more than ash. He wonders about the shard. Has it been destroyed? The Allied planes are gone too. Some have no doubt been destroyed in the battle; others have escaped, he hopes. The skies are quiet once more as ash falls across the city like black snow.

Chapter 52

Sedova

Starling helps Madeleine up and she dusts herself down and fixes her thick black curls.

'I have to return to Castle St Angelo,' he says.

'Your sister?'

'Yes. Anna is watching over her but who knows what trouble they may run into. A Russian spy called Sedova is searching for her. He is here in Rome.'

'Pyotr Sedova?'

'Yes.'

'Pyotr Sedova is dead. He died in a gulag five years ago.'

Starling frowns at her. 'Are you sure?'

'I am in the business of buying and selling information. I know this stuff.'

'Then who is the Russian spy searching for Rose?'

'We must hurry, Will,' says Madeleine, not meeting his gaze. 'The quickest route will be via Passetto di Borgo,' says Madeleine. 'It is a raised passage above the city designed as a fast escape route for popes whose lives were under threat. It will take us direct from the Vatican City to Castle St Angelo.'

Starling feels that Madeleine knows more that she is letting on but follows her to a weathered door at the base of the dome. It is locked but fortunately also weak. He forces it open and they climb down through narrow passages and then onto a wider staircase, which they sprint down two, three steps at a time. The inside of St Peter's is immense and, in the church itself, some sort of mass seems to be happening. Below he see the congregation: a mixture of priests, nuns, lay people and German and Italian soldiers. God-fearing types driven there by the hellish battle in the heavens above them.

He follows Madeleine across to an exit on the side of the dome that leads them out onto the Vatican wall lined with its pale statues of saints.

'How do you know about this?' says Starling, as they join the narrow walkway that is Passetto di Borgo.

'My parents and I spent a lot of time here when I was young. My father helped restore some of the paintings in the Basilica, including the Sistine Chapel.'

'That's who you get your painting skills from?'

She glances at him with a wry smile but does not say anything.

They sprint across the elevated passage. The passage is less than half a mile in length and they reach the castle within minutes. Inside the rooms are empty and the silence is loud.

'Rose! Anna!' Starling calls, but there is no response. He hurries through the castle shouting their names at the top of his voice. Madeleine does the same. They split up, searching through the rooms in each of the corridors and making their way gradually down each level.

Then, 'Will!' cries Madeleine. 'Hurry!'

Running down the stone steps near the entrance Starling sees the body of the nursemaid lying in a pool of blood. His heart sinks. 'Rose! Anna!' he calls, his throat hoarse and dry. He hears the sound of a vehicle approaching outside. He meets Madeleine's gaze and they both jump up and run down the cobbled stone steps and out through the arched doorways.

-

Agent Sedova had not meant to kill the nursemaid. She had been useful as a midwife enabling safe passage for the child to this godforsaken world. But she'd refused to let the baby leave. Sedova had had no choice.

Now, with the crying child held softly and firmly in one arm, and a pistol in the other, Sedova hurries away from the Red Tower, eyes blinking away the strange black snow, to cross Ponte Sant'Angelo under the watchful gaze of the angels on either side of the bridge. Sedova sees the approaching Russian agents in the stolen baker's van and then stiffens as a voice calls from behind.

It is the last voice Sedova wants to hear.

'Anna!' calls Starling.

Sedova stops and closes her eyes. Shame tears at her soul and she wishes she had time to explain, but he would not understand. She has betrayed him and lied to him. But she has her reasons. Perhaps one day he will understand. He must... she hopes. She hears his footfalls approaching and turns, swinging the pistol in his direction.

He slows; he sees her properly and the colour seeps from his face. 'Anna? What's going on?'

'So you're the Russian spy?' says Madeleine. 'You're the older daughter, I assume. Anastasiya Sedova? A Muscovite. I should have known. That explains your dress sense.'

The Frenchwoman's words mean nothing to Anna. Her eyes never leave Starling's. She can feel the smallest of shakes in her gun hand and fights to steady it.

The van screeches to a stop and she hears the two agents emerge with their rifles clicking.

'Anna, don't do this. Give me the baby.'

'I can't, Will. I'm sorry.'

He shakes his head and she can see his eyes full of disbelief and hurt.

'Anna...'

But she will not be broken. 'Rose is in her apartment. There was no time to get her to a hospital. Go to her. Take her to a doctor.'

Starling glances back at the Red Tower and seems uncertain about what to do.

The two Russian agents are now standing beside her, their rifles trained on Starling and the Frenchwoman.

Sedova retreats to the back of the van and climbs inside to sit among the empty wooden crates, where flour is scattered and the smell of fresh bread lingers. It makes her think of home and she strokes the child's head and tries not to think about Starling. She has turned a corner and there is no going back. Her stomach twists and she feels something die inside her. She has always known this day would come and that it would be hard. She hadn't realised just how hard.

Chapter 53

A Tiny Voice

Starling's hands cup the sides of his head as he watches the baker's van disappear further down the Ponte Sant'Angelo and away from him and Madeleine. He can see Anna and the baby framed in the van's dirty rear window like a murky portrait of the Madonna and child.

'Anna!' he calls at the top of his voice, but the van soon disappears and she is gone. He remembers their last moments together. She had taken Starling by the arm, kissed him softly on the lips, swept back his hair back and said, 'I'm sorry.' He had thought it a delayed and unnecessary apology for Meadows, but it had been something much worse.

She had been lying to him all this time.

He feels hollow inside.

'Will,' says a voice. In his confusion he turns in its direction and sees Madeleine. She takes his hand and squeezes gently. 'Let's go inside. We must find your sister.'

In that moment, despite a creeping desolation, Starling comes to his senses. 'Of course.'

They leave the Ponte Sant'Angelo and run back into the tower. As they hurry inside Starling stops where the body of the nursemaid lies peacefully dead. Despite working for VIPER the woman seemed kind and had doted on Rose. Was Anna responsible for her death? Had she tried to stop Anna taking the child?

'Who was she, Will?' asks Madeleine.

'Someone who cared.'

They run up to the top of the tower and Starling stops outside the apartment when he hears a tiny voice call out. They hurry inside. There is no one in the living room. He dashes to the bedroom and sees Rose lying on the bed, eyes closed, sleeping soundly. The floor to the side of her bed contains bloody blankets and a bucket of bloody water. She is pale but otherwise seems fine.

'Will, look!' says Madeleine.

He follows her gaze to a chest of drawers, which has one protruding drawer at the bottom. Lying inside it, nestled in a blanket is the source of the tiny voice. It is a baby.

'Rose had twins,' he whispers.

'Ooh, poor thing,' says Madeleine crouching down to pick up the child.

'Will?'

Starling turns to see Rose awake and looking up at him. She is drawn and tired.

'I can't believe it's you.' She reaches for him and he bends forward and hugs her tight.

The baby makes a gurgling sound.

'Is that my baby?'

Madeleine carries the child over and lowers her onto the bed. 'Yes, it is.'

Starling watches as Rose smiles lovingly at her child. 'Oh my. Look at you. Aren't you beautiful. And I thought you'd be a boy.'

Despite her poor health, Rose seems happy and Starling does not want to change that. He looks at Madeleine and shakes his head furtively. She nods and he knows she understands that for now Rose must not know about the second child.

Chapter 54

Ana

Ana Sedova cradles the child. Holding it close to her chest, she caresses its cheek and hums an old Russian lullaby, one her beloved father used to sing to her. The journey in the back of the baker's van is bumpy; the wooden crates shake and rattle, yet despite that the child is soon fast asleep. They have driven for over an hour and Ana has been so captivated by the child that she has forgotten about Starling and his sister, the mother of the child she had stolen.

It all comes back to her now, though. Her stomach turns and she closes her eyes. Not only has she betrayed the only man she has ever loved, but she has become someone who robs mothers of their children. Her father would never approve. She was sure of that. But he was gone and she had been left with no choice. She would do it again in a heartbeat… she shakes her head. *No, I couldn't.*

She recalls the birth and how troubled the mother had become. There had been no time to take her to the doctor so they made her comfortable in her apartment despite the war raging in the red skies outside. Ana had fetched water and towels as the labour began. The mother was in pain and had been unable to control her kinetic power. The walls had trembled and cracks had begun to appear in the floor and ceiling. The nursemaid had had no choice but to sedate her and perform the birth herself. The nursemaid pulled out the child and Ana's resolve had wavered. She had decided she could not go through with stealing the baby, despite what it would cost her.

But then, as a thunderous explosion roared outside and an unearthly blue light filled the skies, a second child came.

There were two. This was so unexpected and surely a gift; her mind had raced with possibilities. The mother was still sedated and would be none the wiser. Ana held the second child as the nursemaid placed the first one in a makeshift cot fashioned from the drawer of a dresser. As she cleaned and made the mother comfortable Ana slipped away with the child. But the nursemaid was no fool and pursued her. Regrettably, Ana had had no choice but to kill her. The truth was, the fewer the people who knew about this child, the better. The mother would wake to find her baby safe and well and Ana would be gone with a second child that no one would ever know about.

She almost laughs. That had just been wishful thinking. She leans over and kisses the baby on the nose. The child has somehow brought her an inner peace that she has not felt in a long time. Was this part of its gifts? Was this why people wanted Rose Starling's offspring?

The van drives out of Rome and into remote countryside. Ana looks up through the windscreen and recognises the meeting point.

'Stop here,' she says.

The driver pulls over and Ana gently wraps her arm around the head of the child, protecting its swaddled ears. With the other hand she lifts the pistol and blows a hole in the back of each of the agent's heads. Blood and brains splatter across the windscreen, but she is past caring about such things.

She opens the back door of the van and hurries through the woods, cradling the baby who has not been disturbed by the gunshots at all. She smiles down at it and feels an odd sense of protectiveness, just like she felt with her sister Elena and her mother. She wonders what they are doing now and if they ever think of her.

Twenty minutes into the woods she sees the cabin. There is an ambulance parked outside. She hurries across to it, her eyes darting from side to side.

The cabin door opens and she stops to look at the man standing at the door. Roland Cooper is dressed in his trademark blue pinstripe suit and leans against the doorframe like an old friend welcoming her to his home.

He is anything but a friend.

'Well, well. I never thought you'd actually do it. I must say I am very impressed, Agent Sedova.'

Behind him a small medical team emerges: a doctor and two nurses dressed in whites. One of the nurses tries to take the child, but Ana hesitates.

'Now, now, we had an arrangement, missy.'

Missy.

Ana holds her tongue and fights the urge to plant her fist in his smug face. She hands the baby across, but it begins to cry.

'Wonderful,' says Cooper. 'I will see to it your mother and sister are taken good care of.'

'I want them to go the United States. As we agreed.'

'Yes, Agent Sedova. I plan to send them to Minnesota. It's cold and remote there. They'll love it. A home from home.'

The baby continues to cry loudly.

'Please shut it up,' says Cooper.

The medical team can't seem to calm it down. Ana takes it from them and holds it softly to her bosom. The baby coos and stops crying.

'Seems you have a knack,' says Cooper. 'Perhaps we'll extend your contract for a while longer.' Cooper stands over the child. 'Well, hello young man. And what shall we call you?'

'His name is Peter,' Ana lies, thinking of her father, Pyotr. 'The mother said if it was a boy that's what she would name him.'

Cooper nods his head. 'Then Peter it is.'

Acknowledgements

Thank you to Craig Lye and everyone at Canelo for pulling together the new revised editions of *Sleeper* and *The Red Storm*. A big thank you also to Mark Swan, aka kid-ethic, for the stunning cover design. Finally, thank you David H. Headley, for everything.